THE GREATEST

Dog Stories

EVER

Three Classic Novels

by William H. Armstrong
and Fred Gipson

HARPERCOLLINSPUBLISHERS

CONTENTS

Old Yeller

OLD
YELLER

by

FRED GIPSON

Drawings by Carl Burger

HARPER & ROW, PUBLISHERS, New York
Grand Rapids, Philadelphia, St. Louis, San Francisco
London, Singapore, Sydney, Tokyo, Toronto

99 RRD H   60 59 58 57 56 55 54 53

Library of Congress catalog card number: 56-8780
ISBN 0-060-11545-9
ISBN 0-06-0115-46-7 LIB. BDG.

For my father and mother, Beck and Emma Gipson, whose memorable tales of frontier dogs supplied me with incident and background for this story.

Old Yeller

One

WE called him Old Yeller. The name had a sort of double meaning. One part meant that his short hair was a dingy yellow, a color that we called "yeller" in those days. The other meant that when he opened his head, the sound he let out came closer to being a yell than a bark.

I remember like yesterday how he strayed in out of nowhere to our log cabin on Birdsong Creek. He made me so mad at first that I wanted to kill him. Then, later, when I had to kill him, it was like having to shoot some of my own folks. That's how much I'd come to think of the big yeller dog.

He came in the late 1860's, the best I remember. Anyhow, it was the year that Papa and a bunch of other Salt Licks settlers formed a "pool herd" of their little separate bunches of steers and trailed them to the new cattle market at Abilene, Kansas.

This was to get "cash money," a thing that all Texans were short of in those years right after the Civil War. We lived then in a new country and a good one. As Papa pointed out the day the men talked over making the drive, we had plenty of grass, wood, and water. We had wild game for the killing, fertile ground for growing bread corn, and the Indians had been put onto reservations with the return of U.S. soldiers to the Texas forts.

"In fact," Papa wound up, "all we lack having a tight tail-holt on the world is a little cash money. And we can get that at Abilene."

Well, the idea sounded good, but some of the men still hesitated. Abilene was better than six hundred miles north of the Texas hill country we lived in. It would take months for the men to make the drive and ride back home. And all that time the womenfolks and children of Salt Licks would be left in a wild frontier settlement to make out the best they could.

Still, they needed money, and they realized that whatever a man does, he's bound to take some risks. So they talked it over with each other and with their women and decided it was the thing to do. They told their folks what to do in case the Indians came off the reservation or the coons got to eating the corn or the bears got to killing too many hogs. Then they gathered

[2]

their cattle, burned a trail brand on their hips, and pulled out on the long trail to Kansas.

I remember how it was the day Papa left. I remember his standing in front of the cabin with his horse saddled, his gun in his scabbard, and his bedroll tied on back of the cantle. I remember how tall and straight and handsome he looked, with his high-crowned hat and his black mustaches drooping in cow-horn curves past the corners of his mouth. And I remember how Mama was trying to keep from crying because he was leaving and how Little Arliss, who was only five and didn't know much, wasn't trying to keep from crying at all. In fact, he was howling his head off; not because Papa was leaving, but because he couldn't go, too.

I wasn't about to cry. I was fourteen years old, pretty near a grown man. I stood back and didn't let on for a minute that I wanted to cry.

Papa got through loving up Mama and Little Arliss and mounted his horse. I looked up at him. He motioned for me to come along. So I walked beside his horse down the trail that led under the big liveoaks and past the spring.

When he'd gotten out of hearing of the house, Papa reached down and put a hand on my shoulder.

"Now, Travis," he said, "you're getting to be a big boy; and while I'm gone, you'll be the man of the family. I want you to act like one. You take care of Mama and Little Arliss. You look after the work and

[3]

don't wait around for your mama to point out what needs to be done. Think you can do that?"

"Yessir," I said.

"Now, there's the cows to milk and wood to cut and young pigs to mark and fresh meat to shoot. But mainly there's the corn patch. If you don't work it right or if you let the varmints eat up the roasting ears, we'll be without bread corn for the winter."

"Yessir," I said.

"All right, boy. I'll be seeing you this fall."

I stood there and let him ride on. There wasn't any more to say.

Suddenly I remembered and went running down the trail after him, calling for him to wait.

He pulled up his horse and twisted around in the saddle. "Yeah, boy," he said. "What is it?"

"That horse," I said.

"What horse?" he said, like he'd never heard me mention it before. "You mean you're wanting a horse?"

"Now, Papa," I complained. "You know I've been aching all over for a horse to ride. I've told you time and again."

I looked up to catch him grinning at me and felt foolish that I hadn't realized he was teasing.

"What you're needing worse than a horse is a good dog."

"Yessir," I said, "but a horse is what I'm wanting the worst."

[4]

"All right," he said. "You act a man's part while I'm gone, and I'll see that you get a man's horse to ride when I sell the cattle. I think we can shake on that deal."

He reached out his hand, and we shook. It was the first time I'd ever shaken hands like a man. It made me feel big and solemn and important in a way I'd never felt before. I knew then that I could handle whatever needed to be done while Papa was gone.

I turned and started back up the trail toward the cabin. I guessed maybe Papa was right. I guessed I could use a dog. All the other settlers had dogs. They were big fierce cur dogs that the settlers used for catching hogs and driving cattle and fighting coons out of the cornfields. They kept them as watchdogs against the depredations of loafer wolves, bears, panthers, and raiding Indians. There was no question about it: for the sort of country we lived in, a good dog around the place was sometimes worth more than two or three men. I knew this as well as anybody, because the summer before I'd had a good dog.

His name was Bell. He was nearly as old as I was. We'd had him ever since I could remember. He'd protected me from rattlesnakes and bad hogs while I was little. He'd hunted with me when I was bigger. Once he'd dragged me out of Birdsong Creek when I was about to drown and another time he'd given warning in time to keep some raiding Comanches from stealing and eating our mule, Jumper.

Then he'd had to go act a fool and get himself killed.

It was while Papa and I were cutting wild hay in a little patch of prairie back of the house. A big diamond-back rattler struck at Papa and Papa chopped his head off with one quick lick of his scythe. The head dropped to the ground three or four feet away from the writhing body. It lay there, with the ugly mouth opening and shutting, still trying to bite something.

As smart as Bell was, you'd have thought he'd have better sense than to go up and nuzzle that rattler's head. But he didn't, and a second later, he was falling back, howling and slinging his own head till his ears popped. But it was too late then. That snake mouth had snapped shut on his nose, driving the fangs in so deep that it was a full minute before he could sling the bloody head loose.

He died that night, and I cried for a week. Papa tried to make me feel better by promising to get me another dog right away, but I wouldn't have it. It made me mad just to think about some other dog's trying to take Bell's place.

And I still felt the same about it. All I wanted now was a horse.

The trail I followed led along the bank of Birdsong Creek through some bee myrtle bushes. The bushes were blooming white and smelled sweet. In the top of one a mockingbird was singing. That made me recollect how Birdsong Creek had got its name. Mama had named it when she and Papa came to settle. Mama had told me about it. She said she named it the first day she and Papa got there, with Mama driving the ox cart loaded with our house plunder, and with Papa driving the cows and horses. They'd meant to build closer to the other settlers, over on Salt Branch. But they'd camped there at the spring; and the bee myrtle had been blooming white that day, and seemed like in every bush there was a mockingbird, singing his fool head off. It was all so pretty and smelled so good and the singing birds made such fine music that Mama wouldn't go on.

"We'll build right here," she'd told Papa.

And that's what they'd done. Built themselves a home right here on Birdsong Creek and fought off the Indians and cleared a corn patch and raised me and Little Arliss and lost a little sister who died of a fever.

Now it was my home, too. And while Papa was gone, it was up to me to look after it.

I came to our spring that gushed clear cold water out of a split in a rock ledge. The water poured into a pothole about the size of a wagon bed. In the pothole, up to his ears in the water, stood Little Arliss. Right in our drinking water!

I said: "*Arliss!* You get out of that water."

[7]

Arliss turned and stuck out his tongue at me.

"I'll cut me a sprout!" I warned.

All he did was stick out his tongue at me again and splash water in my direction.

I got my knife out and cut a green mesquite sprout. I trimmed all the leaves and thorns off, then headed for him.

Arliss saw then that I meant business. He came lunging up out of the pool, knocking water all over his clothes lying on the bank. He lit out for the house, running naked and screaming bloody murder. To listen to him, you'd have thought the Comanches were lifting his scalp.

Mama heard him and came rushing out of the cabin. She saw Little Arliss running naked. She saw me following after him with a mesquite sprout in one hand and his clothes in the other. She called out to me.

"Travis," she said, "what on earth have you done to your little brother?"

I said, "Nothing yet. But if he doesn't keep out of our drinking water, I'm going to wear him to a frazzle."

That's what Papa always told Little Arliss when he caught him in the pool. I figured if I had to take Papa's place, I might as well talk like him.

Mama stared at me for a minute. I thought she was fixing to argue that I was getting too big for my britches. Lots of times she'd tell me that. But this time she didn't. She just smiled suddenly and grabbed Little

Arliss by one ear and held on. He went to hollering and jumping up and down and trying to pull away, but she held on till I got there with his clothes. She put them on him and told him: "Look here, young squirrel. You better listen to your big brother Travis if you want to keep out of trouble." Then she made him go sit still awhile in the dog run.

The dog run was an open roofed-over space between the two rooms of our log cabin. It was a good place to eat watermelons in the hot summer or to sleep when the night breezes weren't strong enough to push through the cracks between the cabin logs. Sometimes we hung up fresh-killed meat there to cool out.

Little Arliss sat in the dog run and sulked while I packed water from the spring. I packed the water in a bucket that Papa had made out of the hide of a cow's leg. I poured the water into the ash hopper that stood beside the cabin. That was so the water could trickle down through the wood ashes and become lye water. Later Mama would mix this lye water with hog fat and boil it in an iron pot when she wanted to make soap.

When I went to cut wood for Mama, though, Little Arliss left the dog run to come watch me work. Like always, he stood in exactly the right place for the chips from my axe to fly up and maybe knock his eyeballs out. I said: "You better skin out for that house, you little scamp!" He skinned out, too. Just like I told

[9]

him. Without even sticking out his tongue at me this time.

And he sat right there till Mama called us to dinner.

After dinner, I didn't wait for Mama to tell me that I needed to finish running out the corn middles. I got right up from the table and went out and hooked Jumper to the double shovel. I started in plowing where Papa had left off the day before. I figured that if I got an early start, I could finish the corn patch by sundown.

Jumper was a dun mule with a narrow black stripe running along his backbone between his mane and tail. Papa had named him Jumper because nobody yet had ever built a fence he couldn't jump over. Papa claimed Jumper could clear the moon if he took a notion to see the other side of it.

Jumper was a pretty good mule, though. He was gentle to ride; you could pack in fresh meat on him; and he was willing about pulling a plow. Only, sometimes when I plowed him and he decided quitting time had come, he'd stop work right then. Maybe we'd be out in the middle of the field when Jumper got the notion that it was time to quit for dinner. Right then, he'd swing around and head for the cabin, dragging down corn with the plow and paying no mind whatever to my hauling back on the reins and hollering "Whoa!"

Late that evening, Jumper tried to pull that stunt

on me again; but I was laying for him. With Papa gone, I knew I had to teach Jumper a good lesson. I'd been plowing all afternoon, holding a green cedar club between the plow handles.

I still lacked three or four corn rows being finished when sundown came and Jumper decided it was quitting time. He let out a long bray and started wringing his tail. He left the middle he was traveling in. He struck out through the young corn, headed for the cabin.

I didn't even holler "Whoa!" at him. I just threw the looped reins off my shoulder and ran up beside him. I drew back my green cedar club and whacked him so hard across the jawbone that I nearly dropped him in his tracks.

You never saw a worse surprised mule. He snorted, started to run, then just stood there and stared at me. Like maybe he couldn't believe that I was man enough to club him that hard.

I drew back my club again. "Jumper," I said, "if you don't get back there and finish this plowing job, you're going to get more of the same. You understand?"

I guess he understood, all right. Anyhow, from then on till we were through, he stayed right on the job. The only thing he did different from what he'd have done with Papa was to travel with his head turned sideways, watching me every step of the way.

When finally I got to the house, I found that Mama

had done the milking and she and Little Arliss were waiting supper on me. Just like we generally waited for Papa when he came in late.

I crawled into bed with Little Arliss that night, feeling pretty satisfied with myself. Our bed was a corn-shuck mattress laid over a couple of squared-up cowhides that had been laced together. The cowhides stood about two feet off the dirt floor, stretched tight inside a pole frame Papa had built in one corner of the room. I lay there and listened to the corn shucks squeak when I breathed and to the owls hooting in the timber along Birdsong Creek. I guessed I'd made a good start. I'd done my work without having to be told. I'd taught Little Arliss and Jumper that I wasn't to be trifled with. And Mama could already see that I was man enough to wait supper on.

I guessed that I could handle things while Papa was gone just about as good as he could.

Two

———

IT WAS the next morning when the big yeller dog came.

I found him at daylight when Mama told me to step out to the dog run and cut down a side of middling meat hanging to the pole rafters.

The minute I opened the door and looked up, I saw that the meat was gone. It had been tied to the rafter with bear-grass blades braided together for string. Now nothing was left hanging to the pole but the frazzled ends of the snapped blades.

I looked down then. At the same instant, a dog rose from where he'd been curled up on the ground beside the barrel that held our cornmeal. He was a big ugly slick-haired yeller dog. One short ear had been chewed clear off and his tail had been bobbed so close to his rump that there was hardly stub enough left to wag.

But the most noticeable thing to me about him was how thin and starved looking he was, all but for his belly. His belly was swelled up as tight and round as a pumpkin.

It wasn't hard to tell how come that belly was so full. All I had to do was look at the piece of curled-up rind lying in the dirt beside him, with all the meat gnawed off. That side of meat had been a big one, but now there wasn't enough meat left on the rind to interest a pack rat.

Well, to lose the only meat we had left from last winter's hog butchering was bad enough. But what made me even madder was the way the dog acted. He didn't even have the manners to feel ashamed of what he'd done. He rose to his feet, stretched, yawned, then came romping toward me, wiggling that stub tail and yelling *Yow! Yow! Yow!* Just like he belonged there and I was his best friend.

"Why, you thieving rascal!" I shouted and kicked at him as hard as I could.

He ducked, just in time, so that I missed him by a hair. But nobody could have told I missed, after the way he fell over on the ground and lay there, with his belly up and his four feet in the air, squawling and bellering at the top of his voice. From the racket he made, you'd have thought I had a club and was breaking every bone in his body.

Mama came running to stick her head through the door and say, "What on earth, Travis?"

"Why, this old stray dog has come and eaten our middling meat clear up," I said.

I aimed another kick at him. He was quick and rolled out of reach again, just in time, then fell back to the ground and lay there, yelling louder than ever.

Then out came Little Arliss. He was naked, like he always slept in the summer. He was hollering "A dog! A dog!" He ran past me and fell on the dog and petted him till he quit howling, then turned on me, fighting mad.

"You quit kicking my dog!" he yelled fiercely. "You kick my dog, and I'll wear you to a frazzle!"

The battling stick that Mama used to beat the dirt out of clothes when she washed stood leaning against the wall. Now, Little Arliss grabbed it up in both hands and came at me, swinging.

It was such a surprise move, Little Arliss making fight at me that way, that I just stood there with my mouth open and let him clout me a good one before I thought to move. Then Mama stepped in and took the stick away from him.

Arliss turned on her, ready to fight with his bare fists. Then he decided against it and ran and put his arms around the big dog's neck. He began to yell: "He's my dog. You can't kick him. He's my dog!"

The big dog was back up on his feet now, wagging

[15]

his stub tail again and licking the tears off Arliss's face with his pink tongue.

Mama laughed. "Well, Travis," she said, "it looks like we've got us a dog."

"But Mama," I said. "You don't mean we'd keep an old ugly dog like that. One that will come in and steal meat right out of the house."

"Well, maybe we can't keep him," Mama said. "Maybe he belongs to somebody around here who'll want him back."

"He doesn't belong to anybody in the settlement," I said. "I know every dog at Salt Licks."

"Well, then," Mama said. "If he's a stray, there's no reason why Little Arliss can't claim him. And you'll have to admit he's a smart dog. Mighty few dogs have sense enough to figure out a way to reach a side of meat hanging that high. He must have climbed up on top of that meal barrel and jumped from there."

I went over and looked at the wooden lid on top of the meal barrel. Sure enough, in the thin film of dust that had settled over it were dog tracks.

"Well, all right," I admitted. "He's a smart dog. But I still don't want him."

"Now, Travis," Mama said. "You're not being fair. You had you a dog when you were little, but Arliss has never had one. He's too little for you to play with, and he gets lonely."

I didn't say any more. When Mama got her mind set

a certain way, there was no use in arguing with her. But I didn't want that meat-thieving dog on the place, and I didn't aim to have him. I might have to put up with him for a day or so, but sooner or later, I'd find a way to get rid of him.

Mama must have guessed what was going on in my mind, for she kept handing me sober looks all the time she was getting breakfast.

She fed us cornmeal mush cooked in a pot swung over the fireplace. She sweetened it with wild honey that Papa and I had cut out of a bee tree last fall, and added cream skimmed off last night's milk. It was good eating; but I'd had my appetite whetted for fried middling meat to go with it.

Mama waited till I was done, then said: "Now, Travis, as soon as you've milked the cows, I think you ought to get your gun and try to kill us a fat young doe for meat. And while you're gone, I want you to do some thinking on what I said about Little Arliss and this stray dog."

Three

———

ALL right, I was willing to go make a try for a fat doe. I was generally more than willing to go hunting. And while I was gone, I might do some thinking about Little Arliss and that thieving stray dog. But I didn't much think my thinking would take the turn Mama wanted.

I went and milked the cows and brought the milk in for Mama to strain. I got my rifle and went out to the lot and caught Jumper. I tied a rope around his neck, half-hitched a noose around his nose and pitched the rest of the rope across his back. This was the rope I'd rein him with. Then I got me a second rope and tied it tight around his middle, just back of his withers. This second rope I'd use to tie my deer onto Jumper's back—if I got one.

Papa had shown me how to tie a deer's feet together and pack it home across my shoulder, and I'd done it. But to carry a deer very far like that was a sweat-popping job that I'd rather leave to Jumper. He was bigger and stronger.

I mounted Jumper bareback and rode him along Birdsong Creek and across a rocky hog-back ridge. I thought how fine it would be if I was riding my own horse instead of an old mule. I rode down a long sweeping slope where a scattering of huge, ragged-topped liveoaks stood about in grass so tall that it dragged against the underside of Jumper's belly. I rode to within a quarter of a mile of the Salt Licks, then left Jumper tied in a thicket and went on afoot.

I couldn't take Jumper close to the Licks for a couple of reasons. In the first place, he'd get to swishing his tail and stomping his feet at flies and maybe scare off my game. On top of that, he was gun shy. Fire a gun close to Jumper, and he'd fall to staves. He'd snort and wheel to run and fall back against his tie rope, trying to break loose. He'd bawl and paw the air and take on like he'd been shot. When it came to gunfire Jumper didn't have any more sense than a red ant in a hot skillet.

It was a fine morning for hunting, with the air still and the rising sun shining bright on the tall green grass and the greener leaves of the timber. There wasn't enough breeze blowing for me to tell the wind direc-

[19]

tion, so I licked one finger and held it up. Sure enough, the side next to me cooled first. That meant that what little push there was to the air was away from me, toward the Salt Licks. Which wouldn't do at all. No deer would come to the Licks if he caught wind of me first.

I half circled the Licks till I had the breeze moving across them toward me and took cover under a wild grapevine that hung low out of the top of a gnarled oak. I sat down with my back against the trunk of the tree. I sat with my legs crossed and my rifle cradled on my knees. Then I made myself get as still as the tree.

Papa had taught me that, 'way back when I was little, the same as he'd taught me to hunt downwind from my game. He always said: "It's not your shape that catches a deer's eye. It's your moving. If a deer can't smell you and can't see you move, he won't ever know you're there."

So I sat there, holding as still as a stump, searching the clearing around the Licks.

The Licks was a scattered outcropping of dark rocks with black streaks in them. The black streaks held the salt that Papa said had got mixed up with the rocks a jillion years ago. I don't know how he knew what had happened so far back, but the salt was there, and all the hogs and cattle and wild animals in that part of the country came there to lick it.

One time, Papa said, when he and Mama had first

settled there, they'd run clean out of salt and had to beat up pieces of the rock and boil them in water. Then they'd used the salty water to season their meat and cornbread.

Wild game generally came to lick the rocks in the early mornings or late evenings, and those were the best times to come for meat. The killer animals, like bear and panther and bobcats, knew this and came to the Licks at the same time. Sometimes we'd get a shot at them. I'd killed two bobcats and a wolf there while waiting for deer; and once Papa shot a big panther right after it had leaped on a mule colt and broken its neck with one slap of its heavy forepaw.

I hoped I'd get a shot at a bear or panther this morning. The only thing that showed up, however, was a little band of javelina hogs, and I knew better than to shoot them. Make a bad shot and wound one so that he went to squealing, and you had the whole bunch after you, ready to eat you alive. They were small animals. Their tushes weren't as long as those of the range hogs we had running wild in the woods. They couldn't cut you as deep, but once javelinas got after you, they'd keep after you for a lot longer time.

Once Jed Simpson's boy Rosal shot into a bunch of javelinas and they took after him. They treed him up a mesquite and kept him there from early morning till long after suppertime. The mesquite was a small one, and they nearly chewed the trunk of it in two trying to get to him. After that Rosal was willing to let the javelinas alone.

The javelinas moved away, and I saw some bobwhite quail feed into the opening around the Licks. Then here came three cows with young calves and a roan bull. They stood and licked at the rocks. I watched them awhile, then got to watching a couple of squirrels playing in the top of a tree close to the one I sat under.

The squirrels were running and jumping and chattering and flashing their tails in the sunlight. One would run along a tree branch, then take a flying leap to the next branch. There it would sit, fussing, and wait to see if the second one had the nerve to jump that far. When the second squirrel did, the first one would set up an excited chatter and make a run for a longer leap. Sure enough, after a while, the leader tried to jump a gap that was too wide. He missed his branch, clawed at some leaves, and came tumbling to the ground. The second squirrel went to dancing up and down on his branch then, chattering louder than ever. It was plain that he was getting a big laugh out of how that show-off squirrel had made such a fool of himself.

The sight was so funny that I laughed, myself, and that's where I made my mistake.

Where the doe had come from and how she ever got so close without my seeing her, I don't know. It was like she'd suddenly lit down out of the air like a buzzard or risen right up out of the bare ground around the rocks. Anyhow, there she stood, staring straight at me, sniffing and snorting and stomping her forefeet against the ground.

She couldn't have scented me, and I hadn't moved; but I had laughed out loud a little at those squirrels. And that sound had warned her.

Well, I couldn't lift my gun then, with her staring straight at me. She'd see the motion and take a scare. And while Papa was a good enough shot to down a running deer, I'd never tried it and didn't much think I could. I figured it smarter to wait. Maybe she'd quit staring at me after a while and give me a chance to lift my gun.

But I waited and waited, and still she kept looking at me, trying to figure me out. Finally, she started coming toward me. She'd take one dancing step and then another and bob her head and flap her long ears about, then start moving toward me again.

I didn't know what to do. It made me nervous, the way she kept coming at me. Sooner or later she was bound to make out what I was. Then she'd whirl and be gone before I could draw a bead on her.

She kept doing me that way till finally my heart was flopping around inside my chest like a catfish in a wet sack. I could feel my muscles tightening up all over. I knew then that I couldn't wait any longer. It was either shoot or bust wide open, so I whipped my gun up to my shoulder.

Like I'd figured, she snorted and wheeled, so fast that she was just a brown blur against my gunsights. I pressed the trigger, hoping my aim was good.

After I fired, the black powder charge in my gun threw up such a thick fog of blue smoke that I couldn't see through it. I reloaded, then leaped to my feet and went running through the smoke. What I saw when I came into the clear again made my heart drop down into my shoes.

There went the frightened, snorting cattle, stampeding through the trees with their tails in the air like it was heel-fly time. And right beside them went my doe, running all humped up and with her white, pointed tail clamped tight to her rump.

Which meant that I'd hit her but hadn't made a killing shot.

I didn't like that. I never minded killing for meat. Like Papa had told me, every creature has to kill to live. But to wound an animal was something else. Especially one as pretty and harmless as a deer. It made me sick to think of the doe's escaping, maybe to hurt for days before she finally died.

I swung my gun up, hoping yet to get in a killing shot. But I couldn't fire on account of the cattle. They were too close to the deer. I might kill one of them.

Then suddenly the doe did a surprising thing. 'Way

down in the flat there, nearly out of sight, she ran head on into the trunk of a tree. Like she was stone blind. I saw the flash of her light-colored belly as she went down. I waited. She didn't get up. I tore out, running through the chin-tall grass as fast as I could.

When finally I reached the place, all out of breath, I found her lying dead, with a bullet hole through her middle, right where it had to have shattered the heart.

Suddenly I wasn't sick any more. I felt big and strong and sure of myself. I hadn't made a bad shot. I hadn't caused an animal a lot of suffering. All I'd done was get meat for the family, shooting it on the run, just like Papa did.

I rode toward the cabin, sitting behind the gutted doe, that I'd tied across Jumper's back. I rode, feeling proud of myself as a hunter and a provider for the family. Making a killing shot like that on a moving deer made me feel bigger and more important. Too big and important, I guessed, to fuss with Little Arliss about that old yeller dog. I still didn't think much of the idea of keeping him, but I guessed that when you are nearly a man, you have to learn to put up with a lot of aggravation from little old bitty kids. Let Arliss keep the thieving rascal. I guessed I could provide enough meat for him, too.

That's how I was feeling when I crossed Birdsong Creek and rode up to the spring under the trees below the house. Then suddenly, I felt different. That's when I found Little Arliss in the pool again. And in there with him was the big yeller dog. That dirty stinking rascal, romping around in our drinking water!

"Arliss!" I yelled at Little Arliss. "You get that nasty old dog out of the water!"

They hadn't seen me ride up, and I guess it was my sudden yell that surprised them both so bad. Arliss went tearing out of the pool on one side and the dog on the other. Arliss was screaming his head off, and here came the big dog with his wet fur rising along the ridge of his backbone, baying me like I was a panther.

I didn't give him a chance to get to me. I was too quick about jumping off the mule and grabbing up some rocks.

I was lucky. The first rock I threw caught the big dog right between the eyes, and I was throwing hard. He went down, yelling and pitching and wallowing. And just as he came to his feet again, I caught him in the ribs with another one. That was too much for him. He turned tail then and took out for the house, squawling and bawling.

But I wasn't the only good rock thrower in the family. Arliss was only five years old, but I'd spent a lot of time showing him how to throw a rock. Now I wished I hadn't. Because about then, a rock nearly tore my left ear off. I whirled around just barely in time to duck another that would have caught me square in the left eye.

I yelled, "Arliss, you quit that!" but Arliss wasn't listening. He was too scared and too mad. He bent over to pick up a rock big enough to brain me with if he'd been strong enough to throw it.

Well, when you're fourteen years old, you can't afford to mix in a rock fight with your five-year-old brother. You can't do it, even when you're in the right. You just can't explain a thing like that to your folks. All they'll do is point out how much bigger you are, how unfair it is to your little brother.

All I could do was turn tail like the yeller dog and head for the house, yelling for Mama. And right after me came Little Arliss, naked and running as fast as he could, doing his deal-level best to get close enough tc hit me with the big rock he was packing.

I outran him, of course; and then here came Mama, running so fast that her long skirts were flying, and calling out: "What on earth, boys!"

I hollered, "You better catch that Arliss!" as I ran past her. And she did; but Little Arliss was so mad that I thought for a second he was going to hit her with the rock before she could get it away from him.

Well, it all wound up about like I figured. Mama switched Little Arliss for playing in our drinking water. Then she blessed me out good and proper for being so bossy with him. And the big yeller dog that had caused all the trouble got off scot free.

It didn't seem right and fair to me. How could I be the man of the family if nobody paid any attention to what I thought or said?

I went and led Jumper up to the house. I hung the doe in the liveoak tree that grew beside the house and began skinning it and cutting up the meat. I thought of the fine shot I'd made and knew it was worth bragging about to Mama. But what was the use? She wouldn't pay me any mind—not until I did something she thought I shouldn't have done. Then she'd treat me like I wasn't any older than Little Arliss.

I sulked and felt sorry for myself all the time I worked with the meat. The more I thought about it, the madder I got at the big yeller dog.

I hung the fresh cuts of venison up in the dog run, right where Old Yeller had stolen the hog meat the night he came. I did it for a couple of reasons. To begin with, that was the handiest and coolest place we had for hanging fresh meat. On top of that, I was looking for a good excuse to get rid of that dog. I figured if he stole more of our meat, Mama would have to see that he was too sorry and no account to keep.

But Old Yeller was too smart for that. He gnawed around on some of the deer's leg bones that Mama threw away; but not once did he ever even act like he could smell the meat we'd hung up.

Four

———

A COUPLE of days later, I had another and better reason for wanting to get rid of Old Yeller. That was when the two longhorn range bulls met at the house and pulled off their big fight.

We first heard the bulls while we were eating our dinner of cornbread, roasted venison, and green watercress gathered from below the spring. One bull came from off a high rocky ridge to the south of the cabin. We could hear his angry rumbling as he moved down through the thickets of catclaw and scrub oak.

Then he lifted his voice in a wild brassy blare that set echoes clamoring in the draws and canyons for miles around.

"That old bull's talking fight," I told Mama and Little Arliss. "He's bragging that he's the biggest and toughest and meanest. He's telling all the other bulls that if they've got a lick of sense, they'll take to cover when he's around."

Almost before I'd finished talking, we heard the second bull. He was over about the Salt Licks somewhere. His bellering was just as loud and braggy as the first one's. He was telling the first bull that his fight talk was all bluff. He was saying that *he* was the he bull of the range, that *he* was the biggest and meanest and toughest.

We sat and ate and listened to them. We could tell by their rumblings and bawlings that they were gradually working their way down through the brush toward each other and getting madder by the minute.

I always liked to see a fight between bulls or bears or wild boars or almost any wild animals. Now, I got so excited that I jumped up from the table and went to the door and stood listening. I'd made up my mind that if the bulls met and started a fight, I was going to see it. There was still plenty of careless weeds and crabgrass that needed hoeing out of the corn, but I guessed I could let them go long enough to see a bullfight.

Our cabin stood on a high knoll about a hundred yards above the spring. Years ago, Papa had cleared out all the brush and trees from around it, leaving a couple of liveoaks near the house for shade. That was so he could get a clear shot at any Comanche or Apache coming to scalp us. And while I stood there at the door, the first bull entered the clearing, right where Papa had one time shot a Comanche off his horse.

He was a leggy, mustard-colored bull with black freckles speckling his jaws and the underside of his belly. He had one great horn set for hooking, while the other hung down past his jaw like a tallow candle that had drooped in the heat. He was what the Mexicans called a *chongo* or "droop horn."

He trotted out a little piece into the clearing, then stopped to drop his head low. He went to snorting and shaking his horns and pawing up the dry dirt with his forefeet. He flung the dirt back over his neck and shoulders in great clouds of dust.

I couldn't see the other bull yet, but I could tell by the sound of him that he was close and coming in a trot. I hollered back to Mama and Little Arliss.

"They're fixing to fight right here, where we can all see it."

There was a split-rail fence around our cabin. I ran out and climbed up and took a seat on the top rail. Mama and Little Arliss came and climbed up to sit beside me.

Then, from the other side of the clearing came the second bull. He was the red roan I'd seen at the Salt Licks the day I shot the doe. He wasn't as tall and long-legged as the *chongo* bull, but every bit as heavy and powerful. And while his horns were shorter, they were both curved right for hooking.

Like the first bull, he came blaring out into the clearing, then stopped, to snort and sling his wicked horns and paw up clouds of dust. He made it plain that he wanted to fight just as bad as the first bull.

About that time, from somewhere behind the cabin, came Old Yeller. He charged through the rails, bristled up and roaring almost as loud as the bulls. All their bellering and snorting and dust pawing sounded like a threat to him. He'd come out to run them away from the house.

I hollered at him. "Get back there, you rascal," I shouted. "You're fixing to spoil our show."

That stopped him, but he still wasn't satisfied. He kept baying the bulls till I jumped down and picked up a rock. I didn't have to throw it. All I had to do was draw back like I was going to. That sent him flying back into the yard and around the corner of the cabin, yelling like I'd murdered him.

That also put Little Arliss on the fight.

He started screaming at me. He tried to get down where he could pick up a rock.

But Mama held him. "Hush, now, baby," she said. "Travis isn't going to hurt your dog. He just doesn't want him to scare off the bulls."

Well, it took some talking, but she finally got Little Arliss's mind off hitting me with a rock. I climbed back up on the fence. I told Mama that I was betting on Chongo. She said she was betting her money on Roany because he had two fighting horns. We sat there and watched the bulls get ready to fight and talked and laughed and had ourselves a real good time. We never once thought about being in any danger.

When we learned different, it was nearly too late.

Suddenly, Chongo quit pawing the dirt and flung his tail into the air.

"Look out!" I shouted. "Here it comes."

Sure enough, Chongo charged, pounding the hard-pan with his feet and roaring his mightiest. And here came Roany to meet him, charging with his head low and his tail high in the air.

I let out an excited yell. They met head on, with a loud crash of horns and a jar so solid that it seemed like I could feel it clear up there on the fence. Roany went down. I yelled louder, thinking Chongo was winning.

A second later, though, Roany was back on his feet and charging through the cloud of dust their hoofs had churned up. He caught Chongo broadside. He slammed his sharp horns up to the hilt in the shoulder of the mustard-colored bull. He drove against him so fast and hard that Chongo couldn't wheel away. All he could do was barely keep on his feet by giving ground.

And here they came, straight for our rail fence.

[33]

"Land Sakes!" Mama cried suddenly and leaped from the fence, dragging Little Arliss down after her.

But I was too excited about the fight. I didn't see the danger in time. I was still astride the top rail when the struggling bulls crashed through the fence, splintering the posts and rails, and toppling me to the ground almost under them.

I lunged to my feet, wild with scare, and got knocked flat on my face in the dirt.

I sure thought I was a goner. The roaring of the bulls was right in my ears. The hot, reeking scent of their blood was in my nose. The bone-crushing weight of their hoofs was stomping all around and over me, churning up such a fog of dust that I couldn't see a thing.

Then suddenly Mama had me by the hand and was dragging me out from under, yelling in a scared voice: "Run, Travis, run!"

Well, she didn't have to keep hollering at me. I was running as fast as I ever hoped to run. And with her running faster and dragging me along by the hand, we scooted through the open cabin door just about a quick breath before Roany slammed Chongo against it.

They hit so hard that the whole cabin shook. I saw great big chunks of dried-mud chinking fall from between the logs. There for a second, I thought Chongo was coming through that door, right on top of us. But turned broadside like he was, he was too big to be

shoved through such a small opening. Then a second later, he got off Roany's horns somehow and wheeled on him. Here they went, then, down alongside the cabin wall, roaring and stomping and slamming their heels against the logs.

I looked at Mama and Little Arliss. Mama's face was white as a bed sheet. For once, Little Arliss was so scared that he couldn't scream. Suddenly, I wasn't scared any more. I was just plain mad.

I reached for a braided rawhide whip that hung in a coil on a wooden peg driven between the logs.

That scared Mama still worse. "Oh, no, Travis," she cried. "Don't go out there!"

"They're fixing to tear down the house, Mama," I said.

"But they might run over you," Mama argued.

The bulls crashed into the cabin again. They grunted and strained and roared. Their horns and hoofs clattered against the logs.

I turned and headed for the door. Looked to me like they'd kill us all if they ever broke through those log walls.

Mama came running to grab me by the arm. "Call the dog!" she said. "Put the dog after them!"

Well, that was a real good idea. I was half aggravated with myself because I hadn't thought of it. Here was a chance for that old yeller dog to pay back for all the trouble he'd made around the place.

I stuck my head out the door. The bulls had fought

away from the house. Now they were busy tearing down more of the yard fence.

I ducked out and around the corner. I ran through the dog run toward the back of the house, calling, "Here, Yeller! Here Yeller! Get 'em, boy! Sic em!"

Old Yeller was back there, all right. But he didn't come and he didn't sic 'em. He took one look at me running toward him with that bullwhip in my hand and knew I'd come to kill him. He tucked his tail and lit out in a yelling run for the woods.

If there had been any way I could have done it, right then is when I would have killed him.

But there wasn't time to mess with a fool dog. I had to do something about those bulls. They were wrecking the place, and I had to stop it. Papa had left me to look after things while he was gone, and I wasn't about to let two mad bulls tear up everything we had.

I ran up to the bulls and went to work on them with the whip. It was a heavy sixteen-footer and I'd practiced with it a lot. I could crack that rawhide popper louder than a gunshot. I could cut a branch as thick as my little finger off a green mesquite with it.

But I couldn't stop those bulls from fighting. They were too mad. They were hurting too much already; I might as well have been spitting on them. I yelled and whipped them till I gave clear out. Still they went right on with their roaring bloody battle.

I guess they would have kept on fighting till they

leveled the house to the ground if it hadn't been for a freak accident.

We had a heavy two-wheeled Mexican cart that Papa used for hauling wood and hay. It happened to be standing out in front of the house, right where the ground broke away in a sharp slant toward the spring and creek.

It had just come to me that I could get my gun and shoot the bulls when Chongo crowded Roany up against the cart. He ran that long single horn clear under Roany's belly. Now he gave such a big heave that he lifted Roany's feet clear off the ground and rolled him in the air. A second later, Roany landed flat on his back inside the bed of that dump cart, with all four feet sticking up.

I thought his weight would break the cart to pieces, but I was wrong. The cart was stronger than I'd thought. All the bull's weight did was tilt it so that the wheels started rolling. And away the cart went down the hill, carrying Roany with it.

When that happened, Chongo was suddenly the silliest-looking bull you ever saw. He stood with his tail up and his head high, staring after the runaway cart. He couldn't for the life of him figure out what he'd done with the roan bull.

The rolling cart rattled and banged and careened its way down the slope till it was right beside the spring. There, one wheel struck a big boulder, bouncing that side of the cart so high that it turned over and skidded to a stop. The roan bull spilled right into the spring. Water flew in all directions.

Roany got his feet under him. He scrambled up out of the hole. But I guess that cart ride and sudden wetting had taken all the fight out of him. Anyhow, he headed for the timber, running with his tail tucked. Water streamed down out of his hair, leaving a dark wet trail in the dry dust to show which way he'd gone.

Chongo saw Roany then. He snorted and went after him. But when he got to the cart, he slid to a sudden stop. The cart, lying on its side now, still had that top wheel spinning around and around. Chongo had never seen anything like that. He stood and stared at the spinning wheel. He couldn't understand it. He lifted his nose up close to smell it. Finally he reached out a long tongue to lick and taste it.

That was a bad mistake. I guess the iron tire of the spinning wheel was roughed up pretty badly and maybe had chips of broken rock and gravel stuck to it. Anyhow, from the way Chongo acted, it must have scraped all the hide off his tongue.

Chongo bawled and went running backward. He whirled away so fast that he lost his footing and fell down. He came to his feet and took out in the opposite direction from the roan bull. He ran, slinging his head and flopping his long tongue around, bawling like he'd stuck it into a bear trap. He ran with his tail clamped just as tight as the roan bull's.

It was enough to make you laugh your head off, the way both those bad bulls had gotten the wits scared clear out of them, each one thinking he'd lost the fight.

But they sure had made a wreck of the yard fence.

Five

———

THAT Little Arliss! If he wasn't a mess! From the time
he'd grown up big enough to get out of the cabin, he'd
made a practice of trying to catch and keep every
living thing that ran, flew, jumped, or crawled.

Every night before Mama let him go to bed, she'd
make Arliss empty his pockets of whatever he'd captured during the day. Generally, it would be a tangled-
up mess of grasshoppers and worms and praying bugs
and little rusty tree lizards. One time he brought in a
horned toad that got so mad he swelled out round and
flat as a Mexican *tortilla* and bled at the eyes. Sometimes it was stuff like a young bird that had fallen out
of its nest before it could fly, or a green-speckled spring
frog or a striped water snake. And once he turned out
of his pocket a wadded-up baby copperhead that

nearly threw Mama into spasms. We never did figure out why the snake hadn't bitten him, but Mama took no more chances on snakes. She switched Arliss hard for catching that snake. Then she made me spend better than a week, taking him out and teaching him to throw rocks and kill snakes.

That was all right with Little Arliss. If Mama wanted him to kill his snakes first, he'd kill them. But that still didn't keep him from sticking them in his pockets along with everything else he'd captured that day. The snakes might be stinking by the time Mama called on him to empty his pockets, but they'd be dead.

Then, after the yeller dog came, Little Arliss started catching even bigger game. Like cottontail rabbits and chaparral birds and a baby possum that sulled and lay like dead for the first several hours until he finally decided that Arliss wasn't going to hurt him.

Of course, it was Old Yeller that was doing the catching. He'd run the game down and turn it over to Little Arliss. Then Little Arliss could come in and tell Mama a big fib about how he caught it himself.

I watched them one day when they caught a blue catfish out of Birdsong Creek. The fish had fed out into water so shallow that his top fin was sticking out. About the time I saw it, Old Yeller and Little Arliss did, too. They made a run at it. The fish went scooting away toward deeper water, only Yeller was too fast for him. He pounced on the fish and shut his big mouth down over it and went romping to the bank, where he dropped it down on the grass and let it flop. And here came Little Arliss to fall on it like I guess he'd been doing everything else. The minute he got his hands on it, the fish finned him and he went to crying.

But he wouldn't turn the fish loose. He just grabbed it up and went running and squawling toward the house, where he gave the fish to Mama. His hands were all bloody by then, where the fish had finned him. They swelled up and got mighty sore; not even a mesquite thorn hurts as bad as a sharp fish fin when it's run deep into your hand.

But as soon as Mama had wrapped his hands in a poultice of mashed-up prickly-pear root to draw out the poison, Little Arliss forgot all about his hurt. And that night when we ate the fish for supper, he told the biggest windy I ever heard about how he'd dived 'way down into a deep hole under the rocks and dragged that fish out and nearly got drowned before he could swim to the bank with it.

But when I tried to tell Mama what really happened, she wouldn't let me. "Now, this is Arliss's story," she said. "You let him tell it the way he wants to."

I told Mama then, I said: "Mama, that old yeller dog is going to make the biggest liar in Texas out of Little Arliss."

But Mama just laughed at me, like she always laughed at Little Arliss's big windies after she'd gotten off where he couldn't hear her. She said for me to let Little Arliss alone. She said that if he ever told a bigger whopper than the ones I used to tell, she had yet to hear it.

Well, I hushed then. If Mama wanted Little Arliss to grow up to be the biggest liar in Texas, I guessed it wasn't any of my business.

All of which, I figure, is what led up to Little Arliss's catching the bear. I think Mama had let him tell so many big yarns about his catching live game that he'd begun to believe them himself.

When it happened, I was down the creek a ways, splitting rails to fix up the yard fence where the bulls had torn it down. I'd been down there since dinner, working in a stand of tall slim post oaks. I'd chop down a tree, trim off the branches as far up as I wanted, then cut away the rest of the top. After that's I'd start splitting the log.

I'd split the log by driving steel wedges into the wood. I'd start at the big end and hammer in a wedge with the back side of my axe. This would start a little split running lengthways of the log. Then I'd take a second wedge and drive it into this split. This would split the log further along and, at the same time, loosen the first wedge. I'd then knock the first wedge loose and move it up in front of the second one.

Driving one wedge ahead of the other like that, I

could finally split a log in two halves. Then I'd go to work on the halves, splitting them apart. That way, from each log, I'd come out with four rails.

Swinging that chopping axe was sure hard work. The sweat poured off me. My back muscles ached. The axe got so heavy I could hardly swing it. My breath got harder and harder to breathe.

An hour before sundown, I was worn down to a nub. It seemed like I couldn't hit another lick. Papa could have lasted till past sundown, but I didn't see how I could. I shouldered my axe and started toward the cabin, trying to think up some excuse to tell Mama to keep her from knowing I was played clear out.

That's when I heard Little Arliss scream.

Well, Little Arliss was a screamer by nature. He'd scream when he was happy and scream when he was mad and a lot of times he'd scream just to hear himself make a noise. Generally, we paid no more mind to his screaming that we did to the gobble of a wild turkey.

But this time was different. The second I heard his screaming, I felt my heart flop clear over. This time I knew Little Arliss was in real trouble.

I tore out up the trail leading toward the cabin. A minute before, I'd been so tired out with my rail splitting that I couldn't have struck a trot. But now I raced through the tall trees in that creek bottom, covering ground like a scared wolf.

Little Arliss's second scream, when it came, was louder and shriller and more frantic-sounding than the first. Mixed with it was a whimpering crying sound that I knew didn't come from him. It was a sound I'd heard before and seemed like I ought to know what it was, but right then I couldn't place it.

Then, from way off to one side came a sound that I would have recognized anywhere. It was the coughing roar of a charging bear. I'd just heard it once in my life. That was the time Mama had shot and wounded a hog-killing bear and Papa had had to finish it off with a knife to keep it from getting her.

My heart went to pushing up into my throat, nearly choking off my wind. I strained for every lick of speed I could get out of my running legs. I didn't know what sort of fix Little Arliss had got himself into, but I knew that it had to do with a mad bear, which was enough.

The way the late sun slanted through the trees had the trail all cross-banded with streaks of bright light and dark shade. I ran through these bright and dark patches so fast that the changing light nearly blinded me. Then suddenly, I raced out into the open where I could see ahead. And what I saw sent a chill clear through to the marrow of my bones.

There was Little Arliss, down in that spring hole again. He was lying half in and half out of the water, holding onto the hind leg of a little black bear cub no bigger than a small coon. The bear cub was out on

[47]

the bank, whimpering and crying and clawing the rocks with all three of his other feet, trying to pull away. But Little Arliss was holding on for all he was worth, scared now and screaming his head off. Too scared to let go.

How come the bear cub ever to prowl close enough for Little Arliss to grab him, I don't know. And why he didn't turn on him and bite loose, I couldn't figure out, either. Unless he was like Little Arliss, too scared to think.

But all of that didn't matter now. What mattered was the bear cub's mama. She'd heard the cries of her baby and was coming to save him. She was coming so fast that she had the brush popping and breaking as she crashed through and over it. I could see her black heavy figure piling off down the slant on the far side of Birdsong Creek. She was roaring mad and ready to kill.

And worst of all, I could see that I'd never get there in time!

Mama couldn't either. She'd heard Arliss, too, and here she came from the cabin, running down the slant toward the spring, screaming at Arliss, telling him to turn the bear cub loose. But Little Arliss wouldn't do it. All he'd do was hang with that hind leg and let out one shrill shriek after another as fast as he could suck in a breath.

Now the she bear was charging across the shallows

[*48*]

in the creek. She was knocking sheets of water high in the bright sun, charging with her fur up and her long teeth bared, filling the canyon with that awful coughing roar. And no matter how fast Mama ran or how fast I ran, the she bear was going to get there first!

I think I nearly went blind then, picturing what was going to happen to Little Arliss. I know that I opened my mouth to scream and not any sound came out.

Then, just as the bear went lunging up the creek bank toward Little Arliss and her cub, a flash of yellow came streaking out of the brush.

It was that big yeller dog. He was roaring like a mad bull. He wasn't one-third as big and heavy as the she bear, but when he piled into her from one side, he rolled her clear off her feet. They went down in a wild, roaring tangle of twisting bodies and scrambling feet and slashing fangs.

As I raced past them, I saw the bear lunge up to stand on her hind feet like a man while she clawed at the body of the yeller dog hanging to her throat. I didn't wait to see more. Without ever checking my stride, I ran in and jerked Little Arliss loose from the cub. I grabbed him by the wrist and yanked him up out of that water and slung him toward Mama like he was a half-empty sack of corn. I screamed at Mama. "Grab him, Mama! Grab him and run!" Then I swung my chopping axe high and wheeled, aiming to cave in the she bear's head with the first lick.

But I never did strike. I didn't need to. Old Yeller hadn't let the bear get close enough. He couldn't handle her; she was too big and strong for that. She'd stand there on her hind feet, hunched over, and take a roaring swing at him with one of those big front claws. She'd slap him head over heels. She'd knock him so far that it didn't look like he could possibly get back there before she charged again, but he always did. He'd hit the ground rolling, yelling his head off with the pain of the blow; but somehow he'd always roll to his feet. And here he'd come again, ready to tie into her for another round.

I stood there with my axe raised, watching them for a long moment. Then from up toward the house, I heard Mama calling: "Come away from there, Travis. Hurry, son! Run!"

That spooked me. Up till then, I'd been ready to tie into that bear myself. Now, suddenly, I was scared out of my wits again. I ran toward the cabin.

But like it was, Old Yeller nearly beat me there. I didn't see it, of course; but Mama said that the minute Old Yeller saw we were all in the clear and out of danger, he threw the fight to that she bear and lit out for the house. The bear chased him for a little piece, but at the rate Old Yeller was leaving her behind, Mama said it looked like the bear was backing up.

But if the big yeller dog was scared or hurt in any way when he came dashing into the house, he didn't show it. He sure didn't show it like we all did. Little Arliss had hushed his screaming, but he was trembling all over and clinging to Mama like he'd never let her go. And Mama was sitting in the middle of the floor, holding him up close and crying like she'd never stop. And me, I was close to crying, myself.

Old Yeller, though, all he did was come bounding in to jump on us and lick us in the face and bark so loud that there, inside the cabin, the noise nearly made us deaf.

The way he acted, you might have thought that bear fight hadn't been anything more than a rowdy romp that we'd all taken part in for the fun of it.

Six

———

TILL Little Arliss got us mixed up in that bear fight, I guess I'd been looking on him about like most boys look on their little brothers. I liked him, all right, but I didn't have a lot of use for him. What with his always playing in our drinking water and getting in the way of my chopping axe and howling his head off and chunking me with rocks when he got mad, it didn't seem to me like he was hardly worth the bother of putting up with.

But that day when I saw him in the spring, so helpless against the angry she bear, I learned different. I knew then that I loved him as much as I did Mama and Papa, maybe in some ways even a little bit more.

So it was only natural for me to come to love the dog that saved him.

After that, I couldn't do enough for Old Yeller. What if he was a big ugly meat-stealing rascal? What if he did fall over and yell bloody murder every time I looked crossways at him? What if he had run off when he ought to have helped with the fighting bulls? None of that made a lick of difference now. He'd pitched in and saved Little Arliss when I couldn't possibly have done it, and that was enough for me.

I petted him and made over him till he was wiggling all over to show how happy he was. I felt mean about how I'd treated him and did everything I could to let him know. I searched his feet and pulled out a long mesquite thorn that had become embedded between his toes. I held him down and had Mama hand me a stick with a coal of fire on it, so I could burn off three big bloated ticks that I found inside one of his ears. I washed him with lye soap and water, then rubbed salty bacon grease into his hair all over to rout the fleas. And that night after dark, when he sneaked into bed with me and Little Arliss, I let him sleep there and never said a word about it to Mama.

I took him and Little Arliss squirrel hunting the next day. It was the first time I'd ever taken Little Arliss on any kind of hunt. He was such a noisy pest that I always figured he'd scare off the game.

As it turned out, he was just as noisy and pesky as I'd figured. He'd follow along, keeping quiet like I told him, till he saw maybe a pretty butterfly floating around in the air. Then he'd set up a yell you could have heard a mile off and go chasing after the butterfly. Of course, he couldn't catch it; but he would keep yelling at me to come help him. Then he'd get mad because I wouldn't and yell still louder. Or maybe he'd stop to turn over a flat rock. Then he'd stand yelling at me to come back and look at all the yellow ants and centipedes and crickets and stinging scorpions that went scurrying away, hunting new hiding places.

Once he got hung up in some briars and yelled till I came back to get him out. Another time he fell down and struck his elbow on a rock and didn't say a word about it for several minutes—until he saw blood seeping out of a cut on his arm. Then he stood and screamed like he was being burnt with a hot iron.

With that much racket going on, I knew we'd scare all the game clear out of the country. Which, I guess we did. All but the squirrels. They took to the trees where they could hide from us. But I was lucky enough to see which tree one squirrel went up; so I put some of Little Arliss's racket to use.

I sent him in a circle around the tree, beating on the grass and bushes with a stick, while I stood waiting. Sure enough, the squirrel got to watching Little Arliss and forgot me. He kept turning around the tree limb to keep it between him and Little Arliss, till he was on my side in plain sight. I shot him out of the tree the first shot.

After that, Old Yeller caught onto what game we were after. He went to work then, trailing and treeing the squirrels that Little Arliss was scaring up off the ground. From then on, with Yeller to tree the squirrels and Little Arliss to turn them on the tree limbs, we had pickings. Wasn't but a little bit till I'd shot five, more than enough to make us a good squirrel fry for supper.

A week later, Old Yeller helped me catch a wild gobbler that I'd have lost without him. We had gone up to the corn patch to pick a bait of blackeyed peas. I was packing my gun. Just as we got up to the slabrock fence that Papa had built around the corn patch, I looked over and spotted this gobbler doing our pea-picking for us. The pea pods were still green yet, most of them no further along than snapping size. This made them hard for the gobbler to shell, but he was working away at it, pecking and scratching so hard that he was raising a big dust out in the field.

"Why, that old rascal," Mama said. "He's just clawing those pea vines all to pieces."

"Hush, Mama," I said. "Don't scare him." I lifted my gun and laid the barrel across the top of the rock fence. "I'll have him ready for the pot in just a minute."

It wasn't a long shot, and I had him sighted in, dead to rights. I aimed to stick a bullet right where his wings hinged to his back. I was holding my breath and already squeezing off when Little Arliss, who'd gotten behind, came running up.

"Whatcha shootin' at, Travis?" he yelled at the top of his voice. "Whatcha shootin' at?"

Well, that made me and the gobbler both jump. The gun fired, and I saw the gobbler go down. But a second later, he was up again, streaking through the tall corn, dragging a broken wing.

For a second, I was so mad at Little Arliss I could have wrung his neck like a frying chicken's. I said, "*Arliss!* Why can't you keep your mouth shut? You've made me lose that gobbler!"

Well, little Arliss didn't have sense enough to know what I was mad about. Right away, he puckered up and went to crying and leaking tears all over the place. Some of them splattered clear down on his bare feet, making dark splotches in the dust that covered them. I always did say that when Little Arliss cried he could shed more tears faster than any crier I ever saw.

"Wait a minute!" Mama put in. "I don't think you've lost your gobbler yet. Look yonder!"

She pointed, and I looked, and there was Old Yeller jumping the rock fence and racing toward the pea patch. He ran up to where I'd knocked the gobbler down. He circled the place one time, smelling the ground and wiggling his stub tail. Then he took off through the corn the same way the gobbler went, yelling like I was beating him with a stick.

When he barked treed a couple of minutes later, it was in the woods the other side of the corn patch. We went to him. We found him jumping at the gobbler that had run up a stooping liveoak and was perched there, panting, just waiting for me.

So in spite of the fact that Little Arliss had caused me to make a bad shot, we had us a real sumptuous supper that night. Roast turkey with cornbread dressing and watercress and wild onions that Little Arliss and I found growing down in the creek next to the water.

But when we tried to feed Old Yeller some of the turkey, on account of his saving us from losing it, he wouldn't eat. He'd lick the meat and wiggle his stub tail to show how grateful he was, but he didn't swallow down more than a bite or two.

That puzzled Mama and me because, when we remembered back, we realized that he hadn't been eating anything we'd fed him for the last several days. Yet he was fat and with hair as slick and shiny as a dog eating three square meals a day.

Mama shook her head. "If I didn't know better," she said, "I'd say that dog was sucking eggs. But I've got three hens setting and one with biddy chickens, and I'm getting more eggs from the rest of them than I've gotten since last fall. So he can't be robbing the nests."

Well, we wondered some about what Old Yeller was living on, but didn't worry about it. That is, not until the day Bud Searcy dropped by the cabin to see how we were making out.

Bud Searcy was a red-faced man with a bulging middle who liked to visit around the settlement and sit and talk hard times and spit tobacco juice all over the place and wait for somebody to ask him to dinner.

I never did have a lot of use for him and my folks didn't, either. Mama said he was shiftless. She said that was the reason the rest of the men left him at home to sort of look after the womenfolks and kids while they were gone on the cow drive. She said the men knew that if they took Bud Searcy along, they'd never get to Kansas before the steers were dead with old age. It would take Searcy that long to get through visiting and eating with everybody between Salt Licks and Abilene.

But he did have a little white-haired granddaughter that I sort of liked. She was eleven and different from most girls. She would hang around and watch what boys did, like showing how high they could climb in a tree or how far they could throw a rock or how fast they could swim or how good they could shoot. But she never wanted to mix in or try to take over and boss things. She just went along and watched and didn't say much, and the only thing I had against her was her eyes. They were big solemn brown eyes and right pretty to look at; only when she fixed them on me, it always seemed like they looked clear through me and saw everything I was

[60]

thinking. That always made me sort of jumpy, so that when I could, I never would look right straight at her.

Her name was Lisbeth and she came with her grandpa the day he visited us. They came riding up on an old shad-bellied pony that didn't look like he'd had a fill of corn in a coon's age. She rode behind her grandpa's saddle, holding to his belt in the back, and her white hair was all curly and rippling in the sun. Trotting behind them was a blue-ticked she dog that I always figured was one of Bell's pups.

Old Yeller went out to bay them as they rode up. I noticed right off that he didn't go about it like he really meant business. His yelling bay sounded a lot more like he was just barking because he figured that's what we expected him to do. And the first time I hollered at him, telling him to dry up all that racket, he hushed. Which surprised me, as hard-headed as he generally was.

By the time Mama had come to the door and told Searcy and Lisbeth to get down and come right in, Old Yeller had started a romp with the blue-ticked bitch.

Lisbeth slipped to the ground and stood staring at me with those big solemn eyes while her grandpa dismounted. Searcy told Mama that he believed he wouldn't come in the house. He said that as hot as the day was, he figured he'd like it better sitting in the dog run. So Mama had me bring out our four cowhide bottom chairs. Searcy picked the one I always liked to sit in best. He got out a twist of tobacco and bit off a chew big enough to bulge his cheek and went to chewing and talking and spitting juice right where we'd all be bound to step in it and pack it around on the bottoms of our feet.

First he asked Mama if we were making out all right, and Mama said we were. Then he told her that he'd been left to look after all the families while the men were gone, a mighty heavy responsibility that was nearly working him to death, but that he was glad to do it. He said for Mama to remember that if the least little thing went wrong, she was to get in touch with him right away. And Mama said she would.

Then he leaned his chair back against the cabin wall and went to telling what all was going on around in the settlement. He told about how dry the weather was and how he looked for all the corn crops to fail and the settlement folks to be scraping the bottoms of their meal barrels long before next spring. He told how the cows were going dry and the gardens were failing. He told how Jed Simpson's boy Rosal was sitting at a turkey roost, waiting for a shot, when a fox came right up and tried to jump on him, and Rosal had to club it to death with his gun butt. This sure looked like a case of hydrophobia to Searcy, as anybody knew that no fox in his right mind was going to jump on a hunter.

Which reminded him of an uncle of his that got mad-dog bit down in the piney woods of East Texas. This was 'way back when Searcy was a little boy. As soon as the dog bit him, the man knew he was bound to die; so he went and got a big log chain and tied one end around the bottom of a tree and the other end to one of his legs. And right there he stayed till the sickness got him and he lost his mind. He slobbered at the mouth and moaned and screamed and ran at his wife and children, trying to catch them and bite them. Only, of course, the chain around his leg held him back, which was the reason he'd chained himself to the tree in the first place. And right there, chained to that tree, he finally died and they buried him under the same tree.

Bud Searcy sure hoped that we wouldn't have an outbreak of hydrophobia in Salt Licks and all die before the men got back from Kansas.

Then he talked awhile about a panther that had caught and killed one of Joe Anson's colts and how the Anson boys had put their dogs on the trail. They ran the panther into the cave and Jeff Anson followed in where the dogs had more sense than to go and got pretty badly panther-mauled for his trouble; but he did get the panther.

Searcy talked till dinnertime, said not a word all through dinner, and then went back to talking as quick as he'd swallowed down the last bite.

He told how some strange varmit that wasn't a coyote, possum, skunk, or coon had recently started robbing the settlement blind. Or maybe it was even some*body*. Nobody could tell for sure. All they knew was that they were losing meat out of their smokehouses, eggs out of their hens' nests, and sometimes even whole pans of cornbread that the womenfolks had set out to cool. Ike Fuller had been barbecuing some meat over an open pit and left it for a minute to go get a drink of water and came back to find that a three- or four-pound chunk of beef ribs had disappeared like it had gone up in smoke.

Salt Licks folks were getting pretty riled about it, Searcy said, and guessed it would go hard with whatever or whoever was doing the raiding if they ever learned what it was.

Listening to this, I got an uneasy feeling. The feeling got worse a minute later when Lisbeth motioned me to follow her off down to the spring.

We walked clear down there, with Old Yeller and the blue-tick dog following with us, before she finally looked up at me and said, "It's him."

"What do you mean?" I said.

"I mean it's your big yeller dog," she said. "I saw him."

"Do what?" I asked.

"Steal that bait of ribs," she said. "I saw him get a bunch of eggs, too. From one of our nests."

I stopped then and looked straight at her and she looked straight back at me and I couldn't stand it and had to look down.

"But I'm not going to tell," she said.

[64]

I didn't believe her. "I bet you do," I said.

"No, I won't," she said, shaking her head. "I wouldn't, even before I knew he was your dog."

"Why?"

"Because Miss Prissy is going to have pups."

"Miss Prissy?"

"That's the name of my dog, and she's going to have pups and your dog will be their papa, and I wouldn't want their papa to get shot."

I stared at her again, and again I had to look down. I wanted to thank her, but I didn't know the right words. So I fished around in my pocket and brought out an Indian arrowhead that I'd found the day before and gave that to her.

She took it and stared at it for a little bit, with her eyes shining, then shoved it deep into a long pocket she had sewn to her dress.

"I won't never, never tell," she said, then whirled and tore out for the house, running as fast as she could.

I went down and sat by the spring awhile. It seemed like I liked Bud Searcy a lot better than I ever had before, even if he did talk too much and spit tobacco juice all over the place. But I was still bothered. If Lisbeth had caught Old Yeller stealing stuff at the settlements, then somebody else might, too. And if they did, they were sure liable to shoot him. A family might put up with one of its own dogs stealing from them if he was a good dog. But for a dog that left home to steal from everybody else—well, I didn't see much chance for him if he ever got caught.

After Bud Searcy had eaten a hearty supper and talked awhile longer, he finally rode off home, with Lisbeth riding behind him. I went then and gathered the eggs and held three back. I called Old Yeller off from the house and broke the eggs on a flat rock, right under his nose and tried to get him to eat them. But he wouldn't. He acted like he'd never heard tell that eggs were fit to eat. All he'd do was stand there and wiggle his tail and try to lick me in the face.

It made me mad. "You thievin' rascal," I said. "I ought to get a club and break your back—in fourteen different places."

But I didn't really mean it, and I didn't say it loud and ugly. I knew that if I did, he'd fall over and start yelling like he was dying. And there I'd be—in a fight with Little Arliss again.

"When they shoot you, I'm going to laugh," I told him.

But I knew that I wouldn't.

Seven

———

I DID considerable thinking on what Lisbeth Searcy had told me about Old Yeller and finally went and told Mama.

"Why, that old rogue!" she said. "We'll have to try to figure some way to keep him from prowling. Everybody in the settlement will be mad at us if we don't."

"Somebody'll shoot him," I said.

"Try tying him," she said.

So I tried tying him. But we didn't have any bailing wire in those days, and he could chew through anything else before you could turn your back. I tried him with rope and then with big thick rawhide string that I cut from a cowhide hanging across the top rail of the yard fence. It was the same thing in both cases. By the time we could get off to bed, he'd done chewed them in two and was gone.

[67]

"Let's try the corncrib," Mama said on the third night.

Which was a good idea that might have worked if it hadn't been for Little Arliss.

I took Old Yeller out and put him in the corncrib and the second that he heard the door shut on him, he set up a yelling and a howling that brought Little Arliss on the run. Mama and I both tried to explain to him why we needed to shut the dog up, but Little Arliss was too mad to listen. You can't explain things very well to somebody who is screaming his head off and chunking you with rocks as fast as he can pick them up. So that didn't work, either.

"Well, it looks like we're stumped," Mama said.

I thought for a minute and said, "No, Mama. I believe we've got one other chance. That's to shut him up in the same room with me and Little Arliss every night."

"But he'll sleep in the bed with you boys," Mama said, "and the first thing you know, you'll both be scratching fleas and having mange and breaking out with ringworms."

"No, I'll put him a cowhide on the floor and make him sleep there," I said.

So Mama agreed and I spread a cowhide on the floor beside our bed and we shut Old Yeller in and didn't have a bit more trouble.

Of course, Old Yeller didn't sleep on the cowhide. And once, a good while later, I did break out with a

little ringworm under my left arm. But I rubbed it with turpentine, just like Mama always did, and it soon went away. And after that, when we fed Old Yeller cornmeal mush or fresh meat, he ate it and did well on it and never one time bothered our chicken nests.

About that time, too, the varmints got to pestering us so much that a lot of times Old Yeller and I were kept busy nearly all night long.

It was the coons, mainly. The corn was ripening into roasting ears now, and the coons would come at night and strip the shucks back with their little hands, and gnaw the milky kernels off the cob. Also, the watermelons were beginning to turn red inside and the skunks would come and open up little round holes in the rinds and reach in with their forefeet and drag out the juicy insides to eat. Sometimes the coyotes would come and eat watermelons, too; and now and then a deer would jump into the field and eat corn, melons, and peas.

So Old Yeller and I took to sleeping in the corn patch every night. We slept on the cowhide that Yeller never would sleep on at the house. That is, we did when we got to sleep. Most of the night, we'd be up fighting coons. We slept out in the middle of the patch, where Yeller could scent a coon clear to the fence on every side. We'd lie there on the cowhide and look up at the stars and listen to the warm night breeze rustling the corn blades. Sometimes I'd wonder what the stars were and what kept them hanging up there so high and bright and if Papa, 'way off up yonder in Kansas, could see the same stars I could see.

I was getting mighty lonesome to see Papa. With the help of Old Yeller, I was taking care of things all right; but I was sure beginning to wish that he'd come back home.

Then I'd think awhile about the time when I'd get big enough to go off on a cow drive myself, riding my own horse, and see all the big new country of plains and creeks and rivers and mountains and timber and new towns and Indian camps. Then, finally, just about the time I started drifting off to sleep, I'd hear Old Yeller rise to his feet and go padding off through the corn. A minute later, his yelling bay would lift from some part of the corn patch, and I'd hear the fighting squawl of some coon caught stealing corn. Then I'd jump to my feet and go running through the corn, shouting encouragement to Old Yeller.

"Git him, Yeller," I'd holler. "Tear him up!"

And that's what Old Yeller would be trying to do; but a boar coon isn't an easy thing to tear up. For one thing, he'll fight you from sundown till sunup. He's not big for size, but the longer you fight him, the bigger he seems to get. He fights you with all four feet and every tooth in his head and enough courage for an animal five times his size.

On top of that, he's fighting inside a thick hide that fills a dog's mouth like a wad of loose sacking. The dog has a hard time ever really biting him. He just squirms and twists around inside that hide and won't quit fighting even after the dog's got enough and is ready to throw the fight to him. Plenty of times, Papa and I had seen a boar coon whip Bell, run him off, then turn on us and chase us clear out of a cornfield.

It was easy for me to go running through the dark cornfields, yelling for Old Yeller to tear up a thieving coon, but it wasn't easy for Old Yeller to do it. He'd be yelling and the coon would be squawling and they'd go wallowing and clawing and threshing through the corn, popping the stalks as they broke them off, making such an uproar in the night that it sounded like murder. But, generally, when the fight was all over, the coon went one way and Old Yeller the other, both of them pretty well satisfied to call it quits.

We didn't get much sleep of a night while all this was going on, but we had us a good time and saved the corn from the coons.

The only real bad part of it was the skunks. What with all the racket we made coon fighting, the skunks didn't come often. But when one did come, we were in a mess.

Old Yeller could handle a skunk easy enough. All he had to do was rush in, grab it by the head and give it a good shaking. That would break the skunk's neck, but it wouldn't end the trouble. Because not even a hoot owl can kill a skunk without getting sprayed with his scent. And skunk scent is a smell that won't quit. After every skunk killing, Old Yeller would get so sick that he could hardly stand it. He'd snort and drool and slobber and vomit. He'd roll and wallow in the dirt and go dragging his body through tall weeds, trying to get the scent off; but he couldn't. Then finally, he'd give up and come lie down on the cowhide with me. And of course he'd smell so bad that I couldn't stand him and have to go off and try to sleep somewhere else. Then he'd follow me and get his feelings hurt because I wouldn't let him sleep with me.

Papa always said that breathing skunk scent was the best way in the world to cure a head cold. But this was summertime, when Old Yeller and I didn't have head colds. We would just as soon that the skunks stayed out of the watermelons and let us alone.

Working there, night after night, guarding our precious bread corn from the varmints, I came to see what I would have been up against if I'd had it to do without the help of Old Yeller. By myself, I'd have been run to death and still probably wouldn't have saved the corn. Also, look at all the fun I would have missed if I'd been alone, and how lonesome I would have been. I had to admit Papa had been right when he'd told me how bad I needed a dog.

I saw that even more clearly when the spotted heifer had her first calf.

Our milk cows were all old-time longhorn cattle and didn't give a lot of milk. It was real hard to find one that would give much more than her calf could take. What we generally had to do was milk five or six cows to get enough milk for just the family.

But we had one crumpled-horn cow named Rose that gave a lot of milk, only she was getting old, and Mama kept hoping that each of her heifer calves would turn out to be as good a milker as Rose. Mama had tried two or three, but none of them proved to be any good. And then along came this spotted one that was just raw-boned and ugly enough to make a good milk cow. She had the bag for it, too, and Mama was certain this time that she'd get a milk cow to replace Rose.

The only trouble was, this heifer Spot, as we called her, had been snaky wild from the day she was born. Try to drive her with the other cattle, and she'd run off and hide. Hem her up in a corner and try to get your hands on her, and she'd turn on you and make fight. Mama had been trying all along to get Spot gentled before she had her first calf, but it was no use. Spot didn't want to be friends with anybody. We knew she was going to give us a pile of trouble when we set out to milk her.

I failed to find Spot with the rest of our milk cows one evening, and when I went to drive them up the next day, she was still gone.

"It's time for her to calve," Mama said, "and I'll bet she's got one."

So the next morning I went further back in the hills and searched all over. I finally came across her, holed up in a dense thicket of bee myrtle close to a little seep spring. I got one brief glimpse of a wobbly, long-legged calf before Spot snorted and took after me. She ran me clear to the top of the next high ridge before she turned back.

I made another try. I got to the edge of the thicket and picked me up some rocks. I went to hollering and chunking into the brush, trying to scare her and the calf out. I got her out, all right, but she wasn't scared. She came straight for me with her horns lowered, bawling her threats as she came. I had to turn tail a second time, and again she chased me clear to the top of that ridge.

I tried it one more time, then went back to the house and got Old Yeller. I didn't know if he knew anything about driving cattle or not, but I was willing to bet that he could keep her from chasing me.

And he did. I went up to the edge of the thicket and started hollering and chunking rocks into it. Here came the heifer, madder than ever, it looked like. I yelled at Old Yeller. "Get her, Yeller," I hollered. And Yeller got her. He pulled the neatest trick I ever saw a dog pull on a cow brute.

Only I didn't see it the first time. I was getting away from there too fast. I'd stumbled and fallen to my knees when I turned to run from Spot's charge, and she was too close behind for me to be looking back and watching what Old Yeller was doing. I just heard the scared bawl she let out and the crashing of the brush as Old Yeller rolled her into it.

I ran a piece further, then looked back. The heifer was scrambling to her feet in a cloud of dust and looking like she didn't know any more about what had happened than I did. Then she caught sight of Old Yeller. She snorted, stuck her tail in the air and made for him. Yeller ran like he was scared to death, then cut back around a thicket. A second later, he was coming in behind Spot.

Without making a sound, he ran up beside her, made his leap and set his teeth in her nose.

I guess it was the weight of him that did it. I saw him do it lots of times later, but never did quite understand how. Anyway, he just set his teeth in her nose, doubled himself up in a tight ball, and swung on. That turned the charging heifer a flip. Her heels went straight up in the air over her head. She landed flat of her back with all four feet sticking up. She hit the ground so hard that it sounded like she ought to bust wide open.

I guess she felt that way about it, too. Anyhow, after taking that second fall, she didn't have much fight left in her. She just scrambled to her feet and went trotting back into the thicket, lowing to her calf.

I followed her, with Old Yeller beside me, and we

drove her out and across the hills to the cow lot. Not one time did she turn on us again. She did try to run off a couple of times, but all I had to do was send Old Yeller in to head her. And the second she caught sight of him, she couldn't turn fast enough to get headed back in the right direction.

It was the same when we got her into the cowpen. Her bag was all in a strut with milk that the calf couldn't hold. Mama said we needed to get that milk out. She came with a bucket and I took it, knowing I had me a big kicking fight on my hands if I ever hoped to get any milk.

The kicking fight started. The first time I touched Spot's bag, she reached out with a flying hind foot, aiming to kick my head off and coming close to doing it. Then she wheeled on me and put me on top of the rail fence as quick as a squirrel could have made it.

Mama shook her head. "I was hoping she wouldn't be that way," she said. "I always hate to have to tie up a heifer to break her for milking. But I guess there's no other way with this one."

I thought of all the trouble it would be, having to tie up that Spot heifer, head and feet, twice a day, every day, for maybe a month or more. I looked at Old Yeller, standing just outside the pen.

"Yeller," I said, "you come in here."

Yeller came bounding through the rails.

Mama said: "Why, son, you can't teach a heifer to

stand with a dog in the pen. Especially one with a young calf. She'll be fighting at him all the time, thinking he's a wolf or something trying to get her calf."

I laughed. "Maybe it won't work," I said, "but I bet you one thing. She won't be fighting Old Yeller."

She didn't, either. She lowered her horns and rolled her eyes as I brought Old Yeller up to her.

"Now, Yeller," I said, "you stand here and watch her."

Old Yeller seemed to know just what I wanted. He walked right up to where he could almost touch his nose to hers and stood there, wagging his stub tail. And she didn't charge him or run from him. All she did was stand there and sort of tremble. I went back and milked out her strutted bag and she didn't offer to kick me one time, just flinched and drew up a little when I first touched her.

"Well, that does beat all," Mama marveled. "Why, at that rate, we'll have her broke to milk in a week's time."

Mama was right. Within three days after we started, I could drive Spot into the pen, go right up and milk her, and all she'd do was stand there and stare at Old Yeller. By the end of the second week, she was standing and belching and chewing her cud—the gentlest cow I ever milked.

After all that, I guess you can see why I nearly died when a man rode up one day and claimed Old Yeller.

Eight

———

THE man's name was Burn Sanderson. He was a young
man who rode a good horse and was mighty nice and
polite about taking his hat off to Mama when he dismounted in front of our cabin. He told Mama who he
was. He said he was a newcomer to Salt Licks. He said
that he'd come from down San Antonio way with a little
bunch of cattle that he was grazing over in the Devil's
River country. He said he couldn't afford to hire riders,
so he'd brought along a couple of dogs to help him herd
his cattle. One of these dogs, the best one, had disappeared. He'd inquired around about it at Salt Licks,
and Bud Searcy had told him that we had the dog.

"A big yeller dog?" Mama asked, looking sober and
worried.

"Yessum," the man said, then added with a grin. "And

[*80*]

the worse egg sucker and camp robber you ever laid eyes on. Steal you blind, that old devil will; but there was never a better cow dog born."

Mama turned to me. "Son, call Old Yeller," she said.

I stood frozen in my tracks. I was so full of panic that I couldn't move or think.

"Go on, Son," Mama urged. "I think he and Little Arliss must be playing down about the creek somewhere."

"But Mama!" I gasped. "We can't do without Old Yeller. He's—"

"Travis!"

Mama's voice was too sharp. I knew I was whipped. I turned and went toward the creek, so mad at Bud Searcy that I couldn't see straight. Why couldn't he keep his blabber mouth shut?

"Come on up to the house," I told Little Arliss.

I guess the way I said it let him know that something real bad was happening. He didn't argue or stick out his tongue or anything. He just got out of the water and followed me back to the house and embarrassed Mama and the young man nearly to death because he came packing his clothes in one hand instead of wearing them.

I guess Burn Sanderson had gotten an idea of how much we thought of Old Yeller, or maybe Mama had told some things about the dog while I was gone to the creek. Anyhow, he acted uncomfortable about taking the dog off. "Now, Mrs. Coates," he said to Mama, "your man is gone, and you and the boys don't have much protection here. Bad as I need that old dog, I can make out without him until your man comes."

But Mama shook her head.

"No, Mr. Sanderson," she said. "He's your dog; and the longer we keep him, the harder it'll be for us to give him up. Take him along. I can make the boys understand."

The man tied his rope around Old Yeller's neck and mounted his horse. That's when Little Arliss caught onto what was happening. He threw a wall-eyed fit. He screamed and he hollered. He grabbed up a bunch of rocks and went to throwing them at Burn Sanderson. One hit Sanderson's horse in the flank. The horse bogged his head and went to pitching and bawling and grunting. This excited Old Yeller. He chased after the horse, baying him at the top of his voice. And what with Mama running after Little Arliss, hollering for him to shut up and quit throwing those rocks, it was altogether the biggest and loudest commotion that had taken place around our cabin for a good long while.

When Burn Sanderson finished riding the pitch out of his scared horse, he hollered at Old Yeller. He told him he'd better hush up that racket before he got his brains beat out. Then he rode back toward us, wearing a wide grin.

His grin got wider as he saw how Mama and I were

holding Little Arliss. We each had him by one wrist and were holding him clear off the ground. He couldn't get at any more rocks to throw that way, but it sure didn't keep him from dancing up and down in the air and screaming.

"Turn him loose," Sanderson said with a big laugh. "He's not going to throw any more rocks at me."

He swung down from his saddle. He came and got Little Arliss and loved him up till he hushed screaming. Then he said: "Look, boy, do you really want that thieving old dog?"

He held Little Arliss off and stared him straight in the eyes, waiting for Arliss to answer. Little Arliss stared straight back at him and didn't say a word.

"Well, do you?" he insisted.

Finally, Little Arliss nodded, then tucked his chin and looked away.

"All right," Burn Sanderson said. "We'll make a trade. Just between you and me. I'll let you keep the old rascal, but you've got to do something for me."

He waited till Little Arliss finally got up the nerve to ask what, then went on: "Well, it's like this. I've hung around over there in that cow camp, eating my own cooking till I'm so starved out, I don't hardly throw a shadow. Now, if you could talk your mama into feeding me a real jam-up meal of woman-cooked grub, I think it would be worth at least a one-eared yeller dog. Don't you?"

I didn't wait to hear any more. I ran off. I was so full of relief that I was about to pop. I knew that if I didn't get out of sight in a hurry, this Burn Sanderson was going to catch me crying.

Mama cooked the best dinner that day I ever ate. We had roast venison and fried catfish and stewed squirrel and blackeyed peas and cornbread and flour gravy and butter and wild honey and hog-plum jelly and fresh buttermilk. I ate till it seemed like my eyeballs would pop out of my head, and still didn't make anything like the showing that Burn Sanderson made. He was a slim man, not nearly as big as Papa, and I never could figure out where he was putting all that grub. But long before he finally sighed and shook his head at the last of the squirrel stew, I was certain of one thing: he sure wouldn't have any trouble throwing a shadow on the ground for the rest of that day. A good, black shadow.

After dinner, he sat around for a while, talking to me and Mama and making Little Arliss some toy horses out of dried cornstalks. Then he said his thank-yous to Mama and told me to come with him. I followed with him while he led his horse down to the spring for water. I remembered how Papa had led me away from the house like this the day he left and knew by that that Burn Sanderson had something he wanted to talk to me about.

[84]

At the spring, he slipped the bits out of his horse's mouth to let him drink, then turned to me.

"Now, boy," he said, "I didn't want to tell your mama this. I didn't want to worry her. But there's a plague of hydrophobia making the rounds, and I want you to be on the lookout for it."

I felt a scare run through me. I didn't know much about hydrophobia, but after what Bud Searcy had told about his uncle that died, chained to a tree, I knew it was something bad. I stared at Burn Sanderson and didn't say anything.

"And there's no mistake about it," he said. "I've done shot two wolves, a fox, and one skunk that had it. And over at Salt Licks, a woman had to kill a bunch of house-cats that her younguns had been playing with. She wasn't sure, but she couldn't afford to take any chances. And you can't, either."

"But how will I know what to shoot and what not to?" I wanted to know.

"Well, you can't hardly tell at first," he said. "Not until they have already gone to foaming at the mouth and are reeling with the blind staggers. Any time you see a critter acting that way, you know for sure. But you watch for others that aren't that far along. You take a pet cat. If he takes to spitting and fighting at you for no reason, you shoot him. Same with a dog. He'll get mad at nothing and want to bite you. Take a fox or a wildcat. You know they'll run from you; when they don't run, and try to make fight at you, shoot 'em. Shoot anything that acts unnatural, and don't fool around about it. It's too late after they've already bitten or scratched you."

Talk like that made my heart jump up in my throat till I could hardly get my breath. I looked down at the ground and went to kicking around some rocks.

"You're not scared, are you, boy? I'm only telling you because I know your papa left you in charge of things. I know you can handle whatever comes up. I'm just telling you to watch close and not let anything—*anything*—get to you or your folks with hydrophobia. Think you can do it?"

I swallowed. "I can do it," I told him. "I'm not scared."

The sternness left Burn Sanderson's face. He put a hand on my shoulder, just as Papa had the day he left.

"Good boy," he said. "That's the way a man talks."

Then he gripped my shoulder real tight, mounted his horse and rode off through the brush. And I was so scared and mixed up about the danger of hydrophobia that it was clear into the next day before I even thought about thanking him for giving us Old Yeller.

Nine

———

A BOY, before he really grows up, is pretty much like a wild animal. He can get the wits scared clear out of him today and by tomorrow have forgotten all about it.

At least, that's the way it was with me. I was plenty scared of the hydrophobia plague that Burn Sanderson told me about. I could hardly sleep that night. I kept picturing in my mind mad dogs and mad wolves reeling about with the blind staggers, drooling slobbers and snapping and biting at everything in sight. Maybe biting Mama and Little Arliss, so that they got the sickness and went mad, too. I lay in bed and shuddered and shivered and dreamed all sorts of nightmare happenings.

Then, the next day, I went to rounding up and marking hogs and forgot all about the plague.

Our hogs ran loose on the range in those days, the

same as our cattle. We fenced them out of the fields, but never into a pasture; we had no pastures. We never fed them, unless maybe it was a little corn that we threw to them during a bad spell in the winter. The rest of the time, they rustled for themselves.

They slept out and ate out. In the summertime, they slept in the cool places around the water holes, sometimes in the water. In the winter, they could always tell at least a day ahead of time when a blizzard was on the way; then they'd gang up and pack tons of leaves and dry grass and sticks into some dense thicket or cave. They'd pile all this into a huge bed and sleep on until the cold spell blew over.

They ranged all over the hills and down into the canyons. In season, they fed on acorns, berries, wild plums, prickly-pear apples, grass, weeds, and bulb plants which they rooted out of the ground. They especially liked the wild black persimmons that the Mexicans called *chapotes*.

Sometimes, too, they'd eat a newborn calf if the mama cow couldn't keep them horned away. Or a baby fawn that the doe had left hidden in the tall grass. Once, in a real dry time, Papa and I saw an old sow standing belly deep in a drying up pothole of water, catching and eating perch that were trapped in there and couldn't get away.

Most of these meat eaters were old hogs, however. Starvation, during some bad drought or extra cold winter had forced them to eat anything they could get hold of. Papa said they generally started out by feeding on the carcass of some deer or cow that had died, then going from there to catching and killing live meat. He told a tale about how one old range hog had caught him when he was a baby and his folks got there just barely in time to save him.

It was that sort of thing, I guess, that always made Mama so afraid of wild hogs. The least little old biting shoat could make her take cover. She didn't like it a bit when I started out to catch and mark all the pigs that our sows had raised that year. She knew we had it to do, else we couldn't tell our hogs from those of the neighbors. But she didn't like the idea of my doing it alone.

"But I'm not working hogs alone, Mama," I pointed out. "I've got Old Yeller, and Burn Sanderson says he's a real good hog dog."

"That doesn't mean a thing," Mama said. "All hog dogs are good ones. A good one is the only kind that can work hogs and live. But the best dog in the world won't keep you from getting cut all to pieces if you ever make a slip."

Well, Mama was right. I'd worked with Papa enough to know that any time you messed with a wild hog, you were asking for trouble. Let him alone, and he'll generally snort and run from you on sight, the same as a deer. But once you corner him, he's the most dangerous animal that ever lived in Texas. Catch a squealing pig out of the bunch, and you've got a battle on your hands. All of them will turn on you at one time and here they'll come, roaring and popping their teeth, cutting high and fast with gleaming white tushes that they keep whetted to the sharpness of knife points. And there's no bluff to them, either. They mean business. They'll kill you if they can get to you; and if you're not fast footed and don't keep a close watch, they'll get to you.

They had to be that way to live in a country where the wolves, bobcats, panther, and bear were always after them, trying for a bait of fresh hog meat. And it was because of this that nearly all hog owners usually left four or five old barrows, or "bar' hogs," as we called them, to run with each bunch of sows. The bar' hogs weren't any more vicious than the boars, but they'd hang with the sows and help them protect the pigs and shoats, when generally the boars pulled off to range alone.

I knew all this about range hogs, and plenty more; yet I still wasn't bothered about the job facing me. In fact, I sort of looked forward to it. Working wild hogs was always exciting and generally proved to be a lot of fun.

I guess the main reason I felt this way was because Papa and I had figured out a quick and nearly fool-proof way of doing it. We could catch most of the pigs we needed to mark and castrate without ever getting in reach of the old hogs. It took a good hog dog to pull off the trick; but the way Burn Sanderson talked about Old Yeller, I was willing to bet that he was that good.

He was, too. He caught on right away.

We located our first bunch of hogs at a seep spring at the head of a shallow dry wash that led back toward Birdsong Creek. There were seven sows, two long-tushed old bar' hogs, and fourteen small shoats.

They'd come there to drink and to wallow around in the potholes of soft cool mud.

They caught wind of us about the same time I saw them. The old hogs threw up their snouts and said "Woo-oof!" Then they all tore out for the hills, running through the rocks and brush almost as swiftly and silently as deer.

"Head 'em, Yeller," I hollered. "Go get 'em, boy!"

But it was a waste of words. Old Yeller was done gone.

He streaked down the slant, crossed the draw, and had the tail-end pig caught by the hind leg before the others knew he was after them.

The pig set up a loud squeal. Instantly, all the old hogs wheeled. They came at Old Yeller with their bristles up, roaring and popping their teeth. Yeller held onto his pig until I thought for a second they had him. Then he let go and whirled away, running toward me, but running slow. Slow enough that the old hogs kept chasing him, thinking every second that they were going to catch him the next.

When they finally saw that they couldn't, the old hogs stopped and formed a tight circle. They faced outward around the ring, their rumps to the center, where all the squealing pigs were gathered. That way, they were ready to battle anything that wanted to jump on them. That's the way they were used to fighting bear and panther off from their young, and that's the way they aimed to fight us off.

But we were too smart, Old Yeller and I. We knew better than to try to break into that tight ring of threatening tushes. Anyhow, we didn't need to. All we needed was just to move the hogs along to where we wanted them, and Old Yeller already knew how to do this.

Back he went, right up into their faces, where he pestered them with yelling bays and false rushes till they couldn't stand it. With an angry roar, one of the barrows broke the ring to charge him. Instantly, all the others charged, too.

They were right on Old Yeller again. They were just about to get him. Just let them get a few inches closer, and one of them would slam a four-inch tush into his soft belly.

The thing was, Old Yeller never would let them gain that last few inches on him. They cut and slashed at him from behind and both sides, yet he never was quite there. Always he was just a little bit beyond their reach, yet still so close that they couldn't help thinking that the next try was sure to get him.

It was a blood-chilling game Old Yeller played with the hogs, but one that you could see he enjoyed by the way he went at it. Give him time, and he'd take that bunch of angry hogs clear down out of the hills and into the pens at home if that's where I wanted them— never driving them, just leading them along.

But that's where Papa and I had other hog hunters out-figured. We almost never took our hogs to the pens to work them any more. That took too much time. Also, after we got them penned, there was still the dangerous job of catching the pigs away from the old ones.

I hollered at Old Yeller. "Bring 'em on, Yeller," I said. Then I turned and headed for a big gnarled live-oak tree that stood in a clear patch of ground down the draw apiece.

I'd picked out that tree because it had a huge branch that stuck out to one side. I went and looked the branch over and saw that it was just right. It was low, yet still far enough above the ground to be out of reach of the highest-cutting hog.

I climbed up the tree and squatted on the branch. I unwound my rope from where I'd packed it coiled around my waist and shook out a loop. Then I hollered for Old Yeller to bring the hogs to me.

He did what I told him. He brought the fighting hogs to the tree and rallied them in a ring around it. Then he stood back, holding them there while he cocked his head sideways at me, wanting to know what came next.

I soon showed him. I waited till one of the pigs came trotting under my limb. I dropped my loop around him, gave it a quick yank, and lifted him, squealing and kicking, up out of the shuffling and roaring mass of hogs below. I clamped him between my knees, pulled out my knife, and went to work on him. First I folded his right ear and sliced out a three-cornered gap in the top side, a mark that we called an overbit. Then, from the under side of his left ear, I slashed off a long strip that ran clear to the point. This is what we called an underslope. That had him marked for me. Our mark was overbit the right and underslope the left.

Other settlers had other marks, like crop the right and underbit the left, or two underbits in the right ear, or an overslope in the left and an overbit in the right. Everybody knew the hog mark of everybody else and we all respected them. We never butchered or sold a hog that didn't belong to us or mark a pig following a sow that didn't wear our mark.

Cutting marks in a pig's ear is bloody work, and the scared pig kicks and squeals like he's dying; but he's not really hurt. What hurts him is the castration, and I never did like that part of the job. But it had to be done, and still does if you want to eat hog meat. Let a boar hog get grown without cutting his seeds out, and his meat is too tough and rank smelling to eat.

The squealing of the pig and the scent of his blood made the hogs beneath me go nearly wild with anger. You never heard such roaring and teeth-popping, as they kept circling the tree and rearing up on its trunk, trying to get to me. The noise they made and the hate and anger that showed in their eyes was enough to chill your blood. Only, I was used to the feeling and didn't let it bother me. That is, not much. Sometimes I'd let my mind slip for a minute and get to thinking how they'd slash me to pieces if I happened to fall out of the tree, and I'd feel a sort of cold shudder run all through me. But Papa had told me right from the start that fear was a right and natural feeling for anybody, and nothing to be ashamed of.

"It's a thing of your mind," he said, "and you can train your mind to handle it just like you can train your arm to throw a rock."

Put that way, it made sense to be afraid; so I hadn't bothered about that. I'd put in all my time trying to train my mind not to let fear stampede me. Sometimes it did yet, of course, but not when I was working hogs. I'd had enough experience at working hogs that now I could generally look down and laugh at them.

I finished with the first pig and dropped it to the ground. Then, one after another, I roped the others, dragged them up into the tree, and worked them over.

A couple of times, the old hogs on the ground got so mad that they broke ranks and charged Old Yeller. But right from the start, Old Yeller had caught onto what I wanted. Every time they chased him from the tree, he'd just run off a little way and circle back, then stand off far enough away that they'd rally around my tree again.

In less than an hour, I was done with the job, and the only trouble we had was getting the hogs to leave the tree after I was finished. After going to so much trouble to hold the hogs under the tree, Old Yeller had a hard time understanding that I finally wanted them out of the way. And even after I got him to leave, the hogs were so mad and so suspicious that I had to squat there in the tree for nearly an hour longer before they finally drifted away into the brush, making it safe for me to come down.

Ten

WITH hogs ranging in the woods like that, it was hard to know for certain when you'd found them all. But I kept a piece of ear from every pig I marked. I carried the pieces home in my pockets and stuck them on a sharp-pointed stick which I kept hanging in the corn crib. When the count reached forty-six and I couldn't seem to locate any new bunches of hogs, Mama and I decided that was all the pigs the sows had raised that year. So I had left off hog hunting and started getting ready to gather corn when Bud Searcy paid us another visit. He told me about one bunch of hogs I'd missed.

"They're clear back in that bat cave country, the yonder side of Salt Branch," he said. "Rosal Simpson ran into them a couple of days ago, feeding on pear apples in them prickly-pear flats. Said there was five pigs following three sows wearing your mark. Couple of old bar' hogs ranging with them."

I'd never been that far the other side of Salt Branch before, but Papa told me about the bat cave. I figured I could find the place. So early the next morning, I set out with Old Yeller, glad for the chance to hunt hogs a while longer before starting in on the corn gathering. Also, if I was lucky and found the hogs early, maybe I'd have time left to visit the cave and watch the bats come out.

Papa had told me that was a real sight, the way the bats come out in the late afternoon. I was sure anxious to go see it. I always like to go see the far places and strange sights.

Like one place on Salt Branch that I'd found. There was a high, undercut cliff there and some birds building their nests against the face of it. They were little gray, sharp-winged swallows. They gathered sticky mud out of a hog wallow and carried it up and stuck it to the bare rocks of the cliff, shaping the mud into little bulging nests with a single hole in the center of each one. The young birds hatched out there and stuck their heads out through the holes to get at the worms and bugs the grown birds brought to them. The mud nests were so thick on the face of the cliff that, from a distance, the wall looked like it was covered with honeycomb.

There was another place I liked, too. It was a wild,

lonesome place, down in a deep canyon that was bent in the shape of a horseshoe. Tall trees grew down in the canyon and leaned out over a deep hole of clear water. In the trees nested hundreds of long-shanked herons, blue ones and white ones with black wing tips. The herons built huge ragged nests of sticks and trash and sat around in the trees all day long, fussing and staining the tree branches with their white droppings. And beneath them, down in the clear water, yard-long catfish lay on the sandy bottom, waiting to gobble up any young birds that happened to fall out of the nests.

The bat cave sounded like another of those wild places I liked to see. I sure hoped I could locate the hogs in time to pay it a visit while I was close by.

We located the hogs in plenty of time; but before we were done with them, I didn't want to go see a bat cave or anything else.

Old Yeller struck the hogs' trail at a water hole. He ran the scent out into a regular forest of prickly pear. Bright red apples fringed the edges of the pear pads. In places where the hogs had fed, bits of peel and black seeds and red juice stain lay on the ground.

The sight made me wonder again how a hog could be tough enough to eat prickly-pear apples with their millions of little hairlike spines. I ate them, myself, sometimes; for pear apples are good eating. But even after I'd polished them clean by rubbing them in the sand, I generally wound up with several stickers in my mouth. But the hogs didn't seem to mind the stickers. Neither did the wild turkeys or the pack rats or the little big-eared ringtail cats. All of those creatures came to the pear flats when the apples started turning red.

Old Yeller's yelling bay told me that he'd caught up with the hogs. I heard their rumbling roars and ran through the pear clumps toward the sound. They were the hogs that Rosal Simpson had sent word about. There were five pigs, three sows, and a couple of bar' hogs, all but the pigs wearing our mark. Their faces bristled with long pear spines that they'd got stuck with, reaching for apples. Red juice stain was smeared all over their snouts. They stood, backed up against a big prickly-pear clump. Their anger had their bristles standing in high fierce ridges along their backbones. They roared and popped their teeth and dared me or Old Yeller to try to catch one of the squealing pigs.

I looked around for the closest tree. It stood better than a quarter of a mile off. It was going to be rough on Old Yeller, trying to lead them to it. Having to duck and dodge around in those prickly pear, he was bound to come out bristling with more pear spines than the hogs had in their faces. But I couldn't see any other place to take them. I struck off toward the tree, hollering at Old Yeller to bring them along.

A deep cut-bank draw ran through the pear flats between me and the huge mesquite tree I was heading for, and it was down in the bottom of this draw that the

hogs balked. They'd found a place where the flood waters had undercut one of the dirt banks to form a shallow cave.

They'd backed up under the bank, with the pigs behind them. No amount of barking and pestering by Old Yeller could get them out. Now and then, one of the old bar' hogs would break ranks to make a quick cutting lunge at the dog. But when Yeller leaped away, the hog wouldn't follow up. He'd go right back to fill the gap he'd left in the half circle his mates had formed at the front of the cave. The hogs knew they'd found a natural spot for making a fighting stand, and they didn't aim to leave it.

I went back and stood on the bank above them, looking down, wondering what to do. Then it came to me that all I needed to do was go to work. This dirt bank would serve as well as a tree. There were the hogs right under me. They couldn't get to me from down there, not without first having to go maybe fifty yards down the draw to find a place to get out. And Old Yeller wouldn't let them do that. It wouldn't be easy to reach beneath that undercut bank and rope a pig, but I believed it could be done.

I took my rope from around my waist and shook out a loop. I moved to the lip of the cut bank. The pigs were too far back under me for a good throw. Maybe if I lay down on my stomach, I could reach them.

I did. I reached back under and picked up the first

pig, slick as a whistle. I drew him up and worked him over. I dropped him back and watched the old hogs sniff his bloody wounds. Scent of his blood made them madder, and they roared louder.

I lay there and waited. A second pig moved out from the back part of the cave that I couldn't quite see. He still wasn't quite far enough out. I inched forward and leaned further down, to where I could see better. I could reach him with my loop now.

I made my cast, and that's when it happened. The dirt bank broke beneath my weight. A wagon load of sand caved off and spilled down over the angry hogs. I went with the sand.

I guess I screamed. I don't know. It happened too fast. All I can really remember is the wild heart-stopping scare I knew as I tumbled, head over heels, down among those killer hogs.

The crumbling sand all but buried the hogs. I guess that's what saved me, right at the start. I remember bumping into the back of one old bar' hog, then leaping to my feet in a smothering fog of dry dust. I jumped blindly to one side as far as I could. I broke to run, but I was too late. A slashing tush caught me in the calf of my right leg.

A searing pain shot up into my body. I screamed. I stumbled and went down. I screamed louder then, knowing I could never get to my feet in time to escape the rush of angry hogs roaring down upon me.

[104]

It was Old Yeller who saved me. Just like he'd saved Little Arliss from the she bear. He came in, roaring with rage. He flung himself between me and the killer hogs. Fangs bared, he met them head on, slashing and snarling. He yelled with pain as the savage tushes ripped into him. He took the awful punishment meant for me, but held his ground. He gave me that one-in-a-hundred chance to get free.

I took it. I leaped to my feet. In wild terror, I ran along the bed of that dry wash, cut right up a sloping bank. Then I took out through the forest of prickly pear. I ran till a forked stick tripped me and I fell.

It seemed like that fall, or maybe it was the long prickly-pear spines that stabbed me in the hip, brought me out of my scare. I sat up, still panting for breath and with the blood hammering in my ears. But I was all right in my mind again. I yanked the spines out of my hip, then pulled up my slashed pants to look at my leg. Sight of so much blood nearly threw me into another panic. It was streaming out of the cut and clear down into my shoe.

I sat and stared at it for a moment and shivered. Then I got hold of myself again. I wiped away the blood. The gash was a bad one, clear to the bone, I could tell, and plenty long. But it didn't hurt much; not yet, that is. The main hurting would start later, I guessed, after the bleeding stopped and my leg started to get stiff. I guessed I'd better hurry and tie up the

[105]

place and get home as quick as I could. Once that leg started getting stiff, I might not make it.

I took my knife and cut a strip off the tail of my shirt. I bound my leg as tight as I could. I got up to see if I could walk with the leg wrapped as tight as I had it, and I could.

But when I set out, it wasn't in the direction of home. It was back along the trail through the prickly pear.

I don't quite know what made me do it. I didn't think to myself: "Old Yeller saved my life and I can't go off and leave him. He's bound to be dead, but it would look mighty shabby to go home without finding out for sure. I have to go back, even if my hurt leg gives out on me before I can get home."

I didn't think anything like that. I just started walking in that direction and kept walking till I found him.

He lay in the dry wash, about where I'd left it to go running through the prickly pear. He'd tried to follow me, but was too hurt to keep going. He was holed up under a broad slab of red sandstone rock that had slipped off a high bank and now lay propped up against a round boulder in such a way as to form a sort of cave. He'd taken refuge there from the hogs. The hogs were gone now, but I could see their tracks in the sand around the rocks, where they'd tried to get at him from behind. I'd have missed him, hidden there under that rock slab, if he hadn't whined as I walked past.

[106]

I knelt beside him and coaxed him out from under the rocks. He grunted and groaned as he dragged himself toward me. He sank back to the ground, his blood-smeared body trembling while he wiggled his stub tail and tried to lick my hog-cut leg.

A big lump came up into my throat. Tears stung my eyes, blinding me. Here he was, trying to lick my wound, when he was bleeding from a dozen worse ones. And worst of all was his belly. It was ripped wide open and some of his insides were bulging out through the slit.

It was a horrible sight. It was so horrible that for a second I couldn't look at it. I wanted to run off. I didn't want to stay and look at something that filled me with such a numbing terror.

But I didn't run off. I shut my eyes and made myself run a hand over Old Yeller's head. The stickiness of the blood on it made my flesh crawl, but I made myself do it. Maybe I couldn't do him any good, but I wasn't going to run off and leave him to die, all by himself.

Then it came to me that he wasn't dead yet and maybe he didn't have to die. Maybe there was something that I could do to save him. Maybe if I hurried home, I could get Mama to come back and help me. Mama'd know what to do. Mama always knew what to do when somebody got hurt.

I wiped the tears from my eyes with my shirt sleeves and made myself think what to do. I took off my shirt and tore it into strips. I used a sleeve to wipe the sand

[*107*]

from the belly wound. Carefully, I eased his entrails back into place. Then I pulled the lips of the wound together and wound strips of my shirt around Yeller's body. I wound them tight and tied the strips together so they couldn't work loose.

All the time I worked with him, Old Yeller didn't let out a whimper. But when I shoved him back under the rock where he'd be out of the hot sun, he started whining. I guess he knew that I was fixing to leave him, and he wanted to go, too. He started crawling back out of his hole.

I stood and studied for a while. I needed something to stop up that opening so Yeller couldn't get out. It would have to be something too big and heavy for him to shove aside. I thought of a rock and went looking for one. What I found was even better. It was an uprooted and dead mesquite tree, lying on the bank of the wash.

The stump end of the dead mesquite was big and heavy. It was almost too much for me to drag in the loose sand. I heaved and sweated and started my leg to bleeding again. But I managed to get that tree stump where I wanted it.

I slid Old Yeller back under the rock slab. I scolded him and made him stay there till I could haul the tree stump into place.

Like I'd figured, the stump just about filled the opening. Maybe a strong dog could have squeezed through the narrow opening that was left, but I didn't figure

Old Yeller could. I figured he'd be safe in there till I could get back.

Yeller lay back under the rock slab now, staring at me with a look in his eyes that made that choking lump come into my throat again. It was a begging look, and Old Yeller wasn't the kind to beg.

I reached in and let him lick my hand. "Yeller," I said, "I'll be back. I'm promising that I'll be back."

Then I lit out for home in a limping run. His howl followed me. It was the most mournful howl I ever heard.

Eleven

IT LOOKED like I'd never get back to where I'd left Old
Yeller. To begin with, by the time I got home, I'd
traveled too far and too fast. I was so hot and weak and
played out that I was trembling all over. And that hog-
cut leg was sure acting up. My leg hadn't gotten stiff
like I'd figured. I'd used it too much. But I'd strained
the cut muscle. It was jerking and twitching long before
I got home; and after I got there, it wouldn't stop.

That threw a big scare into Mama. I argued and
fussed, trying to tell her what a bad shape Old Yeller
was in and how we needed to hurry back to him. But
she wouldn't pay me any mind.

She told me: "We're not going anywhere until we've
cleaned up and doctored that leg. I've seen hog cuts
before. Neglect them, and they can be as dangerous as
snakebite. Now, you just hold still till I get through."

I saw that it wasn't any use, so I held still while she got hot water and washed out the cut. But when she poured turpentine into the place, I couldn't hold still. I jumped and hollered and screamed. It was like she'd burnt me with a red-hot iron. It hurt worse than when the hog slashed me. I hollered with hurt till Little Arliss tuned up and went to crying, too. But when the pain finally left my leg, the muscle had quit jerking.

Mama got some clean white rags and bound up the place. Then she said, "Now, you lie down on that bed and rest. I don't want to see you take another step on that leg for a week."

I was so stunned that I couldn't say a word. All I could do was stare at her. Old Yeller, lying 'way off out there in the hills, about to die if he didn't get help, and Mama telling me I couldn't walk.

I got up off the stool I'd been sitting on. I said to her, "Mama, I'm going back after Old Yeller. I promised him I'd come back, and that's what I aim to do." Then I walked through the door and out to the lot.

By the time I got Jumper caught, Mama had her bonnet on. She was ready to go, too. She looked a little flustered, like she didn't know what to do with me, but all she said was, "How'll we bring him back?"

"On Jumper," I said. "I'll ride Jumper and hold Old Yeller in my arms."

"You know better than that," she said. "He's too big and heavy. I might lift him up to you, but you can't

[*111*]

stand to hold him in your arms that long. You'll give out."

"I'll hold him," I said. "If I give out, I'll rest. Then we'll go on again."

Mama stood tapping her foot for a minute while she gazed off across the hills. She said, like she was talking to herself, "We can't use the cart. There aren't any roads, and the country is too rough."

Suddenly she turned to me and smiled. "I know what. Get that cowhide off the fence. I'll go get some pillows."

"Cowhide?"

"Tie it across Jumper's back," she said. "I'll show you later."

I didn't know what she had in mind, but it didn't much matter. She was going with me.

I got the cowhide and slung it across Jumper's back. It rattled and spooked him so that he snorted and jumped from under it.

"You Jumper!" I shouted at him. "You hold still."

He held still the next time. Mama brought the pillows and a long coil of rope. She had me tie the cowhide to Jumper's back and bind the pillows down on top of it. Then she lifted Little Arliss up and set him down on top of the pillows.

"You ride behind him," she said to me. "I'll walk."

We could see the buzzards gathering long before we got there. We could see them wheeling black against the blue sky and dropping lower and lower with each circling. One we saw didn't waste time to circle. He came hurtling down at a long-slanted dive, his ugly head outstretched, his wings all but shut against his body. He shot past, right over our heads, and the *whooshing* sound his body made in splitting the air sent cold chills running all through me. I guessed it was all over for Old Yeller.

Mama was walking ahead of Jumper. She looked back at me. The look in her eyes told me that she figured the same thing. I got so sick that it seemed like I couldn't stand it.

But when we moved down into the prickly-pear flats, my misery eased some. For suddenly, up out of a wash ahead rose a flurry of flapping wings. Something had disturbed those buzzards and I thought I knew what it was.

A second later, I was sure it was Old Yeller. His yelling bark sounded thin and weak, yet just to hear it made me want to holler and run and laugh. He was still alive. He was still able to fight back!

The frightened buzzards had settled back to the ground by the time we got there. When they caught sight of us, though, they got excited and went to trying to get off the ground again. For birds that can sail around in the air all day with hardly more than a movement of their wing tips, they sure were clumsy and awkward about getting started. Some had to keep hopping along the wash for fifty yards, beating the air

[*113*]

with their huge wings, before they could finally take off. And then they were slow to rise. I could have shot a dozen of them before they got away if I'd thought to bring my gun along.

There was a sort of crazy light shining in Old Yeller's eyes when I looked in at him. When I reached to drag the stump away, he snarled and lunged at me with bored fangs.

I jerked my hands away just in time and shouted "Yeller!" at him. Then he knew I wasn't a buzzard. The crazy light went out of his eyes. He sank back into the hole with a loud groan like he'd just had a big load taken off his mind.

Mama helped me drag the stump away. Then we reached in and rolled his hurt body over on its back and slid him out into the light.

Without bothering to examine the blood-caked cuts that she could see all over his head and shoulders, Mama started unwinding the strips of cloth from around his body.

Then Little Arliss came crowding past me, asking in a scared voice what was the matter with Yeller.

Mama stopped. "Arliss," she said, "do you think you could go back down this sandy wash here and catch Mama a pretty green-striped lizard? I thought I saw one down there around that first bend."

Little Arliss was as pleased as I was surprised. Always before, Mama had just sort of put up with his lizard-catching. Now she was wanting him to catch one just for her. A delighted grin spread over his face. He turned and ran down the wash as hard as he could go. Mama smiled up at me, and suddenly I understood. She was just getting Little Arliss out of the way so he wouldn't have to look at the terrible sight of Yeller's slitted belly.

She said to me: "Go jerk a long hair out of Jumper's tail, Son. But stand to one side, so he won't kick you."

I went and stood to one side of Jumper and jerked a long hair out of his tail. Sure enough, he snorted and kicked at me, but he missed. I took the hair back to Mama, wondering as much about it as I had about the green-striped lizard. But when Mama pulled a long sewing needle from her dress front and poked the small end of the tail hair through the eye, I knew then.

"Horse hair is always better than thread for sewing up a wound," she said. She didn't say why, and I never did think to ask her.

Mama asked me if any of Yeller's entrails had been cut and I told her that I didn't think so.

"Well, I won't bother them then," she said. "Anyway, if they are, I don't think I could fix them."

It was a long, slow job, sewing up Old Yeller's belly. And the way his flesh would flinch and quiver when Mama poked the needle through, it must have hurt. But if it did, Old Yeller didn't say anything about it. He just lay there and licked my hands while I held him.

[115]

We were wrapping him up in some clean rags that Mama had brought along when here came Little Arliss. He was running as hard as he'd been when he left. He was grinning and hollering at Mama. And in his right hand he carried a green-striped lizard, too.

How on earth he'd managed to catch anything as fast running as one of those green-striped lizards, I don't know; but he sure had one.

You never saw such a proud look as he wore on his face when he handed the lizard to Mama. And I don't guess I ever saw a more helpless look on Mama's face as she took it. Mama had always been squeamish about lizards and snakes and bugs and things, and you could tell that it just made her flesh crawl to have to touch this one. But she took it and admired it and thanked Arliss. Then she asked him if he'd keep it for her till we got home. Which Little Arliss was glad to do.

"Now, Arliss," she told him, "we're going to play a game. We're playing like Old Yeller is sick and you are taking care of him. We're going to let you both ride on a cowhide, like the sick Indians do sometimes."

It always pleased Little Arliss to play any sort of game, and this was a new one that he'd never heard about before. He was so anxious to get started that we could hardly keep him out from underfoot till Mama could get things ready.

As soon as she took the cowhide off Jumper's back and spread it hair-side down upon the ground, I began to get the idea. She placed the soft pillows on top of the hide, then helped me to ease Old Yeller's hurt body onto the pillows.

"Now, Arliss," Mama said, "you sit there on the pillows with Old Yeller and help hold him on. But remember now, don't play with him or get on top of him. We're playing like he's sick, and when your dog is sick, you have to be real careful with him."

It was a fine game, and Little Arliss fell right in with it. He sat where Mama told him to. He held Old Yeller's head in his lap, waiting for the ride to start.

It didn't take long. I'd already tied a rope around Jumper's neck, leaving the loop big enough that it would pull back against his shoulders. Then, on each side of Jumper, we tied another rope into the one knotted about his shoulders, and carried the ends of them back to the cowhide. I took my knife and cut two slits into the edge of the cowhide, then tied a rope into each one. We measured to get each rope the same length and made sure they were far enough back that the cowhide wouldn't touch Jumper's heels. Like most mules, Jumper was mighty fussy about anything touching his heels.

"Now, Travis, you ride him," Mama said, "and I'll lead him."

"You better let me walk," I argued. "Jumper's liable to throw a fit with that hide rattling along behind him, and you might not can hold him by yourself."

"You ride him," Mama said. "I don't want you walking on that leg any more. If Jumper acts up one time, I'll take a club to him!"

We started off, with Little Arliss crowing at what a fine ride he was getting on the dragging hide. Sure enough, at the first sound of that rattling hide, old Jumper acted up. He snorted and tried to lunge to one side. But Mama yanked down on his bridle and said, "Jumper, you wretch!" I whacked him between the ears with a dead stick. With the two of us coming at him like that, it was more than Jumper wanted. He settled down and went to traveling as quiet as he generally pulled a plow, with just now and then bending his neck around to take a look at what he was dragging. You could tell he didn't like it, but I guess he figured he'd best put up with it.

Little Arliss never had a finer time than he did on that ride home. He enjoyed every long hour of it. And a part of the time, I don't guess it was too rough on Old Yeller. The cowhide dragged smooth and even as long as we stayed in the sandy wash. When we left the wash and took out across the flats, it still didn't look bad. Mama led Jumper in a long roundabout way, keeping as much as she could to the openings where the tall grass grew. The grass would bend down before the hide, making a soft cushion over which the hide slipped easily. But this was a rough country, and try as hard as she could, Mama couldn't always dodge the rocky

[*118*]

places. The hide slid over the rocks, the same as over the grass and sand, but it couldn't do it without jolting the riders pretty much.

Little Arliss would laugh when the hide raked along over the rocks and jolted him till his teeth rattled. He got as much fun out of that as the rest of the ride. But the jolting hurt Old Yeller till sometimes he couldn't hold back his whinings.

When Yeller's whimperings told us he was hurting too bad, we'd have to stop and wait for him to rest up. At other times, we stopped to give him water. Once we got water out of a little spring that trickled down through the rocks. The next time was at Birdsong Creek.

Mama'd pack water to him in my hat. He was too weak to get up and drink; so Mama would hold the water right under his nose and I'd lift him up off the pillows and hold him close enough that he could reach down and lap the water up with his tongue.

Having to travel so far and so slow and with so many halts, it looked like we'd never get him home. But we finally made it just about the time it got dark enough for the stars to show.

By then, my hurt leg was plenty stiff, stiff and numb. It was all swelled up and felt as dead as a chunk of wood. When I slid down off Jumper's back, it wouldn't hold me. I fell clear to the ground and lay in the dirt, too tired and hurt to get up.

Mama made a big to-do about how weak and hurt I was, but I didn't mind. We'd gone and brought Old Yeller home, and he was still alive. There by the starlight, I could see him licking Little Arliss's face.

Little Arliss was sound asleep.

Twelve

———

FOR the next couple of weeks, Old Yeller and I had a rough time of it. I lay on the bed inside the cabin and Yeller lay on the cowhide in the dog run, and we both hurt so bad that we were wallowing and groaning and whimpering all the time. Sometimes I hurt so bad that I didn't quite know what was happening. I'd hear grunts and groans and couldn't tell if they were mine or Yeller's. My leg had swelled up till it was about the size of a butter churn. I had such a wild hot fever that Mama nearly ran herself to death, packing fresh cold water from the spring, which she used to bathe me all over, trying to run my fever down.

When she wasn't packing water, she was out digging prickly-pear roots and hammering them to mush in a sack, then binding the mush to my leg for a poultice.

We had lots of prickly pear growing close to the house, but they were the big tall ones and their roots were no good. The kind that made a good poultice are the smaller size. They don't have much top, but lots of knotty roots, shaped sort of like sweet potatoes. That kind didn't grow close to the house. Along at the last, Mama had to go clear over to the Salt Licks to locate that kind.

When Mama wasn't waiting on me, she was taking care of Old Yeller. She waited on him just like she did me. She was getting up all hours of the night to doctor our wounds, bathe us in cold water, and feed us when she could get us to eat. On top of that, there were the cows to milk, Little Arliss to look after, clothes to wash, wood to cut, and old Jumper to worry with.

The bad drouth that Bud Searcy predicted had come. The green grass all dried up till Jumper was no longer satisfied to eat it. He took to jumping the field fence and eating the corn that I'd never yet gotten around to gathering.

Mama couldn't let that go on; that was our bread corn. Without it, we'd have no bread for the winter. But it looked like for a while that there wasn't any way to save it. Mama would go to the field and run Jumper out; then before she got her back turned good, he'd jump back in and go to eating corn again.

Finally, Mama figured out a way to keep Jumper from jumping. She tied a drag to him. She got a rope and tied one end of it to his right forefoot. To the other end, she tied a big heavy chunk of wood. By pulling hard, Jumper could move his drag along enough to graze and get to water; but any time he tried to rear up for a jump, the drag held him down.

The drag on Jumper's foot saved the corn but it didn't save Mama from a lot of work. Jumper was always getting his chunk of wood hung up behind a bush or rock, so that he couldn't get away. Then he'd have himself a big scare and rear up, fighting the rope and falling down and pitching and bawling. If Mama didn't hear him right away, he'd start braying, and he'd keep it up till she went and loosened the drag.

Altogether, Mama sure had her hands full, and Little Arliss wasn't any help. He was too little to do any work. And with neither of us to play with, he got lonesome. He'd follow Mama around every step she made, getting in the way and feeling hurt because she didn't have time to pay him any mind. When he wasn't pestering her, he was pestering me. A dozen times a day, he'd come in to stare at me and say: "Whatcha doin' in bed, Travis? Why doncha get up? Why doncha get up and come play with me?"

He nearly drove me crazy till the day Bud Searcy and Lisbeth came, bringing the pup.

I didn't know about the pup at first. I didn't even know that Lisbeth had come. I heard Bud Searcy's talk to Mama when they rode up, but I was hurting too bad even to roll over and look out the door. I remember just lying there, being mad at Searcy for coming. I knew what a bother he'd be to Mama. For all his talk of looking after the women and children of Salt Licks while the men were gone, I knew he'd never turn a hand to any real work. You wouldn't catch him offering to chop wood or gather in a corn crop. All he'd do was sit out under the dog run all day, talking and chewing tobacco and spitting juice all over the place. On top of that, he'd expect Mama to cook him up a good dinner and maybe a supper if he took a notion to stay that long. And Mama had ten times too much to do, like it was.

In a little bit, though, I heard a quiet step at the door. I looked up. It was Lisbeth. She stood with her hands behind her back, staring at me with her big solemn eyes.

"You hurting pretty bad?" she asked.

I was hurting a-plenty, but I wasn't admitting it to a girl. "I'm doing all right," I said.

"We didn't know you'd got hog cut, or we'd have come sooner," she said.

I didn't know what to say to that, so I didn't say anything.

"Well, anyhow," she said, "I brung you a surprise."

I was too sick and worn out to care about a surprise right then; but there was such an eager look in her eyes that I knew I had to say "What?" or hurt her feelings, so I said "What?"

"One of Miss Prissy's pups!" she said.

She brought her hands around from behind her back. In the right one, she held a dog pup about as big as a year-old possum. It was a dirty white in color and speckled all over with blue spots about the size of cow ticks. She held it by the slack hide at the back of its neck. It hung there, half asleep, sagging in its own loose hide like it was dead.

"Born in a badger hole," she said. "Seven of them. I brung you the best one!"

I thought: If that puny-looking thing is the best one, Miss Prissy must have had a sorry litter of pups. But I didn't say so. I said: "He sure looks like a dandy."

"He is," Lisbeth said. "See how I've been holding him, all this time, and he hasn't said a word."

I'd heard that one all my life—that if a pup didn't holler when you held him up by the slack hide of his neck, he was sure to turn out to be a gritty one. I didn't think much of that sign. Papa always put more stock in what color was inside a pup's mouth. If the pup's mouth was black inside, Papa said that was the one to choose. And that's the way I felt about it.

But right now I didn't care if the pup's mouth was pea-green on the inside. All I wanted was just to quit hurting.

I said, "I guess Little Arliss will like it," then knew I'd said the wrong thing. I could tell by the look in her eyes that I'd hurt her feelings, after all.

She didn't say anything. She just got real still and

quiet and kept staring at me till I couldn't stand it and had to look away. Then she turned and went out of the cabin and gave the pup to Little Arliss.

It made me mad, her looking at me like that. What did she expect, anyhow? Here I was laid up with a bad hog cut, hurting so bad I could hardly get my breath, and her expecting me to make a big to-do over a little old puny speckled pup.

I had me a dog. Old Yeller was all cut up, worse than I was, but he was getting well. Mama had told me that. So what use did I have for a pup? Be all right for Little Arliss to play with. Keep him occupied and out from underfoot. But when Old Yeller and I got well and took to the woods again, we wouldn't have time to wait around on a fool pup, too little to follow.

I lay there in bed, mad and fretful all day, thinking how silly it was for Lisbeth to expect me to want a pup when I already had me a full-grown dog. I lay there, just waiting for a chance to tell her so, too; only she never did come back to give me a chance. She stayed outside and played with Little Arliss and the pup till her grandpa finally wound up his talking and tobacco spitting and got ready to leave. Then I saw her and Little Arliss come past the door, heading for where I could hear her grandpa saddling his horse. She looked in at me, then looked away, and suddenly I wasn't mad at her any more. I felt sort of mean. I wished now I could think of the right thing to say about the pup, so I could call her back and tell her. I didn't want her to go off home with her feelings still hurt.

But before I could think of anything, I heard her grandpa say to Mama: "Now Mrs. Coates, you all are in a sort of bind here, with your man gone and that boy crippled up. I been setting out here all evening, worrying about it. That's my responsibility, you know, seeing that everybody's taken care of while the men are gone, and I think now I've got a way figured. I'll just leave our girl Lisbeth here to help you all out."

Mama said in a surprised voice: "Why, Mr. Searcy, there's no need for that. It's mighty kind of you and all, but we'll make out all right."

"No, now, Mrs. Coates; you got too big a load to carry, all by yourself. My Lisbeth, she'll be proud to help out."

"But," Mama argued, "she's such a little girl, Mr. Searcy. She's probably never stayed away from home of a night."

"She's little," Bud Searcy said, "but she's stout and willing. She's like me; when folks are in trouble, she'll pitch right in and do her part. You just keep her here now. You'll see what a big help she'll be."

Mama tried to argue some more, but Bud Searcy wouldn't listen. He just told Lisbeth to be a good girl and help Mama out, like she was used to helping out at home. Then he mounted and rode on off.

Thirteen

I was like Mama. I didn't think Lisbeth Searcy would
be any help around the place. She was too little and
too skinny. I figured she'd just be an extra bother for
Mama.

But we were wrong. Just like Bud Searcy said, she
was a big help. She could tote water from the spring.
She could feed the chickens, pack in wood, cook cornbread, wash dishes, wash Little Arliss, and sometimes
even change the prickly-pear poultice on my leg.

She didn't have to be told, either. She was right
there on hand all the time, just looking for something
to do. She was a lot better about that than I ever was.
She wasn't as big and she couldn't do as much as
I could, but she was more willing.

She didn't even back off when Mama hooked Jumper

to the cart and headed for the field to gather in the corn. That was a job I always hated. It was hot work, and the corn shucks made my skin itch and sting till sometimes I'd wake up at night scratching like I'd stumbled into a patch of bull nettles.

But it didn't seem to bother Lisbeth. In fact, it looked like she and Mama and Little Arliss had a real good time gathering corn. I'd see them drive past the cabin, all three of them sitting on top of a cartload of corn. They would be laughing and talking and having such a romping big time, playing with the speckled pup, that before long I half wished I was able to gather corn too.

In a way, it sort of hurt my pride for a little old girl like Lisbeth to come in and take over my jobs. Papa had left me to look after things. But now I was laid up, and here was a girl handling my work about as good as I could. Still, she couldn't get out and mark hogs or kill meat or swing a chopping axe. . . .

Before they were finished gathering corn, however, we were faced with a trouble a whole lot too big for any of us to handle.

The first hint of it came when the Spot heifer failed to show up one evening at milking time. Mama had come in too late from the corn gathering to go look for her before dark, and the next morning she didn't need to. Spot came up, by herself; or rather, she came past the house.

I heard her first. The swelling in my leg was about gone down. I was weak as a rain-chilled chicken, but most of the hurting had stopped. I was able to sit up in bed a lot and take notice of things.

I heard a cow coming toward the house. She was bawling like cows do when they've lost a calf or when their bags are stretched too tight with milk. I recognized Spot's voice.

Spot's calf recognized it, too. It had stood hungry in the pen all night and now it was nearly crazy for a bait of milk. I could hear it blatting and racing around in the cowpen, so starved it could hardly wait.

I called to Mama. "Mama," I said, "you better go let old Spot in to her calf. I hear her coming."

"That pesky Spot," I heard her say impatiently. "I don't know what's got into her, staying out all night like that and letting her calf go hungry."

I heard Mama calling to Spot as she went out to the cowpen. A little later, I heard Spot beller like a fighting bull, then Mama's voice rising high and sharp. Then here came Mama, running into the cabin, calling for Lisbeth to hurry and bring in Little Arliss. There was scare in Mama's voice. I sat up in bed as Lisbeth came running in, dragging Little Arliss after her.

Mama slammed the door shut, then turned to me. "Spot made fight at me," she said. "I can't understand it. It was like I was some varmint that she'd never seen before."

Mama turned and opened the door a crack. She looked out, then threw the door wide open and stood staring toward the cowpen.

"Why, look at her now," she said. "She's not paying one bit of attention to her calf. She's just going on past the cowpen like her calf wasn't there. She's acting as crazy as if she'd got hold of a bait of pea vine."

There was a little pea vine that grew wild all over the hills during wet winters and bloomed pale lavender in the spring. Cattle and horses could eat it, mixed with grass, and get fat on it. But sometimes when they got too big a bait of it alone, it poisoned them. Generally, they'd stumble around with the blind staggers for a while, then gradually get well. Sometimes, though, the pea vine killed them.

I sat there for a moment, listening to Spot. She was bawling again, like when I first heard her. But now she was heading off into the brush again, leaving her calf to starve. I wondered where she'd gotten enough pea vine to hurt her.

"But Mamma," I said, "she couldn't have eaten pea vine. The pea vine is all dead and gone this time of year."

Mama turned and looked at me, then looked away. "I know," she said. "That's what's got me so worried."

I thought of what Burn Sanderson had told me about animals that didn't act right. I said, "Cows don't ever get hydrophobia, do they?"

[*131*]

I saw Lisbeth start at the word. She stared at me with big solemn eyes.

"I don't know," Mama said. "I've seen dogs with it, but I've never heard of a cow brute having it. I just don't know."

In the next few days, while Old Yeller and I healed fast, we all worried and watched.

All day and all night, Spot kept right on doing what she did from the start: she walked and she bawled. She walked mostly in a wide circle that brought her pretty close to the house about twice a day and then carried her so far out into the hills that we could just barely hear her. She walked with her head down. She walked slower and her bawling got weaker as she got weaker; but she never stopped walking and bawling.

When the bull came, he was worse, and a lot more dangerous. He came two or three days later. I was sitting out under the dog run at the time. I'd hobbled out to sit in a chair beside Old Yeller, where I could scratch him under his chewed-off ear. That's where he liked to be scratched best. Mama was in the kitchen, cooking dinner. Lisbeth and Little Arliss had gone off to the creek below the spring to play with the pup and to fish for catfish. I could see them running and laughing along the bank, chasing after grasshoppers for bait.

Then I heard this moaning sound and turned to watch a bull come out of the brush. He was the roan bull, the one that the droopy-horned *chongo* had dumped into the Mexican cart the day of the fight. But he didn't walk like any bull I'd ever seen before. He walked with his head hung low and wobbling. He reeled and staggered like he couldn't see where he was going. He walked head on into a mesquite tree like it wasn't there, and fell to his knees when he hit it. He scrambled to his feet and came on, grunting and staggering and moaning, heading toward the spring.

Right then, for the first time since we'd brought him home, Old Yeller came up off his cowhide bed. He'd been lying there beside me, paying no attention to sight or sound of the bull. Then, I guess the wind must have shifted and brought him the bull's scent; and evidently that scent told him for certain what I was only beginning to suspect.

He rose, with a savage growl. He moved out toward the bull, so trembly weak that he could hardly stand. His loose lips were lifted in an ugly snarl, baring his white fangs. His hackles stood up in a ragged ridge along the back of his neck and shoulders.

Watching him, I felt a prickling at the back of my own neck. I'd seen him act like that before, but only when there was the greatest danger. Never while just facing a bull.

Suddenly, I knew that Mama and I had been fooling ourselves. Up till now, we'd been putting off facing up to facts. We'd kept hoping that the heifer Spot would get over whatever was wrong with her. Mama

[133]

and Lisbeth had kept Spot's calf from starving by letting it suck another cow. They'd had to tie the cow's hind legs together to keep her from kicking the calf off; but they'd kept it alive, hoping Spot would get well and come back to it.

Now, I knew that Spot wouldn't get well, and this bull wouldn't, either. I knew they were both deathly sick with hydrophobia. Old Yeller had scented that sickness in this bull and somehow sensed how fearfully dangerous it was.

I thought of Lisbeth and Little Arliss down past the spring. I came up out of my chair, calling for Mama. "Mama!" I said. "Bring me my gun, Mama!"

Mama came hurrying to the door. "What is it, Travis?" she wanted to know.

"That bull!" I said, pointing. "He's mad with hydrophobia and he's heading straight for Lisbeth and Little Arliss."

Mama took one look, said "Oh, my Lord!" in almost a whisper. She didn't wait to get me my gun or anything else. She just tore out for the creek, hollering for Lisbeth and Little Arliss to run, to climb a tree, to do anything to get away from the bull.

I called after her, telling her to wait, to give me a chance to shoot the bull. I don't guess she ever heard me. But the bull heard her. He tried to turn on her, stumbled and went to his knees. Then he was back on his feet again as Mama went flying past. He charged straight for her. He'd have gotten her, too, only the sickness had his legs too wobbly. This time, when he fell, he rooted his nose into the ground and just lay there, moaning, too weak even to try to get up again.

By this time, Old Yeller was there, baying the bull, keeping out of his reach, but ready to eat him alive if he ever came to his feet again.

I didn't wait to see more. I went and got my gun. I hobbled down to where I couldn't miss and shot the roan bull between the eyes.

Fourteen

WE COULDN'T leave the dead bull to lie there that close
to the cabin. In a few days, the scent of rotting flesh
would drive us out. Also, the carcass lay too close to
the spring. Mama was afraid it would foul up our drinking water.

"We'll have to try to drag it further from the cabin
and burn it," she said.

"Burn it?" I said in surprise. "Why can't we just
leave it for the buzzards and varmints to clean up?"

"Because that might spread the sickness," Mama said.
"If the varmints eat it, they might get the sickness too."

Mama went to put the harness on Jumper. I sent
Lisbeth to bring me a rope. I doubled the rope and tied
it in a loop around the bull's horns. Mama brought
Jumper, who snorted and shied away at the sight of

the dead animal. Jumper had smelled deer blood plenty of times, so I guess it was the size of the bull that scared him. Or maybe like Yeller, Jumper could scent the dead bull's sickness. I had to talk mean and threaten him with a club before we could get him close enough for Mama to hook the singletree over the loop of rope I'd tied around the bull's horns.

Then the weight of the bull was too much for him. Jumper couldn't drag it. He leaned into his collar and dug in with his hoofs. He grunted and strained. He pulled till I saw the big muscles of his haunches flatten and start quivering. But the best he could do was slide the bull carcass along the ground for about a foot before he gave up.

I knew he wasn't throwing off. Jumper was full of a lot of pesky, aggravating mule tricks; but when you called on him to move a load, he'd move it or bust something.

I called on him again. I drove him at a different angle from the load, hoping he'd have better luck. He didn't. He threw everything he had into the collar, and all he did was pop a link out of his right trace chain. The flying link whistled past my ear with the speed of a bullet. It would have killed me just as dead if it had hit me.

Well, that was it. There was no moving the dead bull now. We could patch up that broken trace chain for pulling an ordinary load. But it would never be strong enough to pull this one. Even if Jumper was.

I looked at Mama. She shook her head. "I guess there's nothing we can do but burn it here," she said. "But it's going to take a sight of wood gathering."

It did, too. We'd lived there long enough to use up all the dead wood close to the cabin. Now, Mama and Lisbeth had to go 'way out into the brush for it. I got a piece of rawhide string and patched up the trace chain, and Mama and Lisbeth used Jumper to drag up big dead logs. I helped them pile the logs on top of the bull. We piled them up till we had the carcass completely covered, then set fire to them.

In a little bit, the fire was roaring. Sheets of hot flame shot high into the air. The heat and the stench of burnt hair and scorching hide drove us back.

It was the biggest fire I'd ever seen. I thought there was fire enough there to burn three bulls. But when it began to die down a couple of hours later, the bull carcass wasn't half burnt up. Mama and Lisbeth went back to dragging up more wood.

It took two days and nights to burn up that bull. We worked all day long each day, with Mama and Lisbeth dragging up the wood and me feeding the stinking fire. Then at night, we could hardly sleep. This was because of the howling and snarling and fighting of the wolves lured to the place by the scent of the roasting meat. The wolves didn't get any of it; they were too afraid of the hot fire. But that didn't keep them from gathering for miles around and making the nights hideous with their howlings and snarlings.

And all night long, both nights, Old Yeller crippled back and forth between the fire and the cabin, baying savagely, warning the wolves to keep away.

Both nights, I lay there, watching the eyes of the shifting wolves glow like live mesquite coals in the firelight, and listening to the weak moaning bawl of old Spot still traveling in a circle. I lay there, feeling shivery with a fearful dread that brought up pictures in my mind of Bud Searcy's uncle.

I sure did wish Papa would come home.

As soon as the job of burning the bull was over, Mama told us we had to do the same for the Spot heifer. That was all Mama said about it, but I could tell by the look in her eyes how much she hated to give up. She'd had great hopes for Spot's making us a real milk cow, especially after Old Yeller had gentled her so fast; but that was all gone now.

Mama looked tired, and more worried than I think I'd ever seen her. I guess she couldn't help thinking what I was thinking—that if hydrophobia had sickened one of our cows, it just might get them all.

"I'll do the shooting," I told her. "But I'm going to follow her out a ways from the house to do it. Closer to some wood."

"How about your leg?" Mama asked.

"That leg's getting all right," I told her. "Think it'll do it some good to be walked on."

"Well, try to kill her on bare ground," Mama cautioned. "As dry as it is now, we'll be running a risk of setting the woods afire if there's much old grass around the place."

I waited till Spot circled past the cabin again, then took my gun and followed her, keeping a safe distance behind.

By now, Spot was so sick and starved I could hardly stand to look at her. She didn't look like a cow; she looked more like the skeleton of one. She was just skin and bones. She was so weak that she stumbled as she walked. Half a dozen times she went to her knees and each time I'd think she'd taken her last step. But she'd always get up and go on again—and keep bawling.

I kept waiting for her to cross a bare patch of ground where it would be safe to build a fire. She didn't; and I couldn't drive her, of course. She was too crazy mad to be driven anywhere. I was afraid to mess with her. She might be like the bull. If I ever let her know I was anywhere about, she might go on the fight.

I guess she was a mile from the cabin before I saw that she was about to cross a dry sandy wash, something like the one where Yeller and I had got mixed up with the hogs. That would be a good place, I knew. It was pretty far for us to have to come to burn her, but there was plenty of dry wood around. And if I could drop her out there in that wide sandy wash, there'd be no danger of a fire getting away from us.

I hurried around and got ahead of her. I hid behind a turkey-pear bush on the far side of the wash. But as sick and blind as she was, I think I could have stood out in the broad open without her ever seeing me. I waited till she came stumbling across the sandy bed of the wash, then fired, dropping her in the middle of it.

I'd used up more of my strength than I knew, following Spot so far from the cabin. By the time I got back, I was dead beat. The sweat was pouring off me and I was trembling all over.

Mama took one look at me and told me to get to bed. "We'll go start the burning," she said. "You stay on that leg any longer, and it'll start swelling again."

I didn't argue. I knew I was too weak and tired to take another walk that far without rest. So I told Mama where to find Spot and told her to leave Little Arliss with me, and watched her and Lisbeth head out, both mounted on Jumper. Mama was carrying a panful of live coals to start the fire with.

At the last minute, Yeller got up off his cowhide. He stood watching them a minute, like he was trying to make up his mind about something; then he went trotting after them. He was still thin and rough looking and crippling pretty badly in one leg. But I figured he knew better than I did whether or not he was able to travel. I didn't call him back.

[*141*]

As it turned out, it's a good thing I didn't. Only, afterward, I wished a thousand times that I could have had some way of looking ahead to what was going to happen. Then I would have done everything I could to keep all of them from going.

With Little Arliss to look after, I sure didn't mean to drop off to sleep. But I did and slept till sundown, when suddenly I jerked awake, feeling guilty about leaving him alone so long.

I needn't have worried. Little Arliss was right out there in the yard, playing with the speckled pup. They had themselves a game going. Arliss was racing around the cabin, dragging a short piece of frayed rope. The pup was chasing the rope. Now and then he'd get close enough to pounce on it. Then he'd let out a growl and set teeth into it and try to shake it and hang on at the same time. Generally, he got jerked off his feet and turned a couple of somersets, but that didn't seem to bother him. The next time Arliss came racing past, the pup would tie into the rope again.

I wondered if he wouldn't get some of his baby teeth jerked out at such rough play, but guessed it wouldn't matter. He'd soon be shedding them, anyhow.

I wondered, too, what was keeping Mama and Lisbeth so long. Then I thought how far it was to where the dead cow lay and how long it would take for just the two of them to drag up enough wood and get a fire started, and figured they'd be lucky if they got back before dark.

I went off to the spring after a bucket of fresh water and wondered when Papa would come back. Mama had said a couple of days ago that it was about that time, and I hoped so. For one thing, I could hardly wait to see what sort of horse Papa was going to bring me. But mainly, this hydrophobia plague had me scared. I'd handled things pretty well until that came along. Of course, I'd gotten a pretty bad hog cut, but that could have happened to anybody, even a grown man. And I was about to get well of that. But if the sickness got more of our cattle, I wouldn't know what to do.

Fifteen

It WASN'T until dark came that I really began to get uneasy about Mama and Lisbeth. Then I could hardly stand it because they hadn't come home. I knew in my own mind why they hadn't: it had been late when they'd started out; they'd had a good long piece to go; and even with wood handy, it took considerable time to drag up enough for the size fire they needed.

And I couldn't think of any real danger to them. They weren't far enough away from the cabin to be lost. And if they were, Jumper knew the way home. Also, Jumper was gentle; there wasn't much chance that he'd scare and throw them off. On top of all that, they had Old Yeller along. Old Yeller might be pretty weak and crippled yet, but he'd protect them from just about anything that might come their way.

Still, I was uneasy. I couldn't help having the feeling that something was wrong. I'd have gone to see about them if it hadn't been for Little Arliss. It was past his suppertime; he was getting hungry and sleepy and fussy.

I took him and the speckled pup inside the kitchen and lit a candle. I settled them on the floor and gave them each a bowl of sweet milk into which I'd crumbled cold cornbread. In a little bit, both were eating out of the same bowl. Little Arliss knew better than that and I ought to have paddled him for doing it. But I didn't. I didn't say a word; I was too worried.

I'd just about made up my mind to put Little Arliss and the pup to bed and go look for Mama and Lisbeth when I heard a sound that took me to the door in a hurry. It was the sound of dogs fighting. The sound came from 'way out there in the dark; but the minute I stepped outside, I could tell that the fight was moving toward the cabin. Also, I recognized the voice of Old Yeller.

It was the sort of raging yell he let out when he was in a fight to the finish. It was the same savage roaring and snarling and squawling that he'd done the day he fought the killer hogs off me.

The sound of it chilled my blood. I stood, rooted to the ground, trying to think what it could be, what I ought to do.

Then I heard Jumper snorting keenly and Mama

calling in a frightened voice. "Travis! Travis! Make a light, Son, and get your gun. And hurry!"

I came alive then. I hollered back at her, to let her know that I'd heard. I ran back into the cabin and got my gun. I couldn't think at first what would make the sort of light I needed, then recollected a clump of bear grass that Mama'd recently grubbed out, where she wanted to start a new fall garden. Bear grass has an oily sap that makes it burn bright and fierce for a long time. A pile of it burning would make a big light.

I ran and snatched up four bunches of the half-dried bear grass. The sharp ends of the stiff blades stabbed and stung my arms and chest as I grabbed them up. But I had no time to bother about that. I ran and dumped the bunches in a pile on the bare ground outside the yard fence, then hurried to bring a live coal from the fireplace to start them burning.

I fanned fast with my hat. The bear-grass blades started to smoking, giving off their foul smell. A little flame started, flickered and wavered for a moment, then bloomed suddenly and leaped high with a roar.

I jumped back, gun held ready, and caught my first glimpse of the screaming, howling battle that came wheeling into the circle of light. It was Old Yeller, all right, tangled with some animal as big and savage as he was.

Mama called from outside the light's rim. "Careful,

Son. And take close aim; it's a big loafer wolf, gone mad."

My heart nearly quit on me. There weren't many of the gray loafer wolves in our part of the country, but I knew about them. They were big and savage enough to hamstring a horse or drag down a full-grown cow. And here was Old Yeller, weak and crippled, trying to fight a mad one!

I brought up my gun, then held fire while I hollered at Mama. "Y'all get in the cabin," I yelled. "I'm scared to shoot till I know you're out of the line of fire!"

I heard Mama whacking Jumper with a stick to make him go. I heard Jumper snort and the clatter of his hoofs as he went galloping in a wide circle to come up behind the cabin. But even after Mama called from the door behind me, I still couldn't fire. Not without taking a chance on killing Old Yeller.

I waited, my nerves on edge, while Old Yeller and the big wolf fought there in the firelight, whirling and leaping and snarling and slashing, their bared fangs gleaming white, their eyes burning green in the half light.

Then they went down in a tumbling roll that stopped with the big wolf on top, his huge jaws shut tight on Yeller's throat. That was my chance, and one that I'd better make good. As weak as Old Yeller was, he'd never break that throat hold.

There in the wavering light, I couldn't get a true

bead on the wolf. I couldn't see my sights well enough. All I could do was guess-aim and hope for a hit.

I squeezed the trigger. The gunstock slammed back against my shoulder, and such a long streak of fire spouted from the gun barrel that it blinded me for a second; I couldn't see a thing.

Then I realized that all the growling and snarling had hushed. A second later, I was running toward the two still gray forms lying side by side.

For a second, I just knew that I'd killed Old Yeller, too. Then, about the time I bent over him, he heaved a big sort of sigh and struggled up to start licking my hands and wagging that stub tail.

I was so relieved that it seemed like all the strength went out of me. I slumped to the ground and was sitting there, shivering, when Mama came and sat down beside me.

She put one arm across my shoulders and held it there while she told me what had happened.

Like I'd figured, it had taken her and Lisbeth till dark to get the wood dragged up and the fire to going around the dead cow. Then they'd mounted old Jumper and headed for home. They'd been without water all this time and were thirsty. When they came to the crossing on Birdsong Creek, they'd dismounted to get a drink. And while they were lying down, drinking, the wolf came.

He was right on them before they knew it. Mama

happened to look up and see the dark hulk of him come bounding toward them across a little clearing. He was snarling as he came, and Mama just barely had time to come to her feet and grab up a dead chinaberry pole before he sprang. She whacked him hard across the head, knocking him to the ground. Then Old Yeller was there, tying into him.

Mama and Lisbeth got back on Jumper and tore out for the house. Right after them came the wolf, like he had his mind fixed on catching them, and nothing else. But Old Yeller fought him too hard and too fast. Yeller wasn't big and strong enough to stop him, but he kept him slowed down and fought away from Jumper and Mama and Lisbeth.

"He had to've been mad, son," Mama wound up. "You know that no wolf in his right senses would have acted that way. Not even a big loafer wolf."

"Yessum," I said, "and it's sure a good thing that Old Yeller was along to keep him fought off." I shuddered at the thought of what could have happened without Old Yeller.

Mama waited a little bit, then said in a quiet voice: "It was a good thing for us, son; but it wasn't good for Old Yeller."

The way she said that gave me a cold feeling in the pit of my stomach. I sat up straighter. "What do you mean?" I said. "Old Yeller's all right. He's maybe chewed up some, but he can't be bad hurt. See, he's done trotting off toward the house."

Then it hit me what Mama was getting at. All my insides froze. I couldn't get my breath.

I jumped to my feet, wild with hurt and scare. "But Mama!" I cried out. "Old Yeller's just saved your life! He's saved my life. He's saved Little Arliss's life! We can't—"

Mama got up and put her arms across my shoulder again. "I know, son," she said. "But he's been bitten by a mad wolf."

I started off into the blackness of the night while my mind wheeled and darted this way and that, like a scared rat trying to find its way out of a trap.

"But Mama," I said. "We don't know for certain. We could wait and see. We could tie him or shut him up in the corncrib or some place till we know for sure!"

Mama broke down and went to crying then. She put her head on my shoulder and held me so tight that she nearly choked off my breath.

"We can't take a chance, Son," she sobbed. "It would be you or me or Little Arliss or Lisbeth next. I'll shoot him if you can't, but either way, we've got it to do. We just can't take the chance!"

It came clear to me then that Mama was right. We couldn't take the risk. And from everything I had heard, I knew that there was very little chance of Old Yeller's escaping the sickness. It was going to kill

[152]

something inside me to do it, but I knew then that I had to shoot my big yeller dog.

Once I knew for sure I had it to do, I don't think I really felt anything. I was just numb all over, like a dead man walking.

Quickly, I left Mama and went to stand in the light of the burning bear grass. I reloaded my gun and called Old Yeller back from the house. I stuck the muzzle of the gun against his head and pulled the trigger.

Sixteen

———

DAYS went by, and I couldn't seem to get over it. I couldn't eat. I couldn't sleep. I couldn't cry. I was all empty inside, but hurting. Hurting worse than I'd ever hurt in my life. Hurting with a sickness there didn't seem to be any cure for. Thinking every minute of my big yeller dog, how we'd worked together and romped together, how he'd fought the she bear off Little Arliss, how he'd saved me from the killer hogs, how he'd fought the mad wolf off Mama and Lisbeth. Thinking that after all this, I'd had to shoot him the same as I'd done the roan bull and the Spot heifer.

Mama tried to talk to me about it, and I let her. But while everything she said made sense, it didn't do a thing to that dead feeling I had.

Lisbeth talked to me. She didn't say much; she was

[*154*]

too shy. But she pointed out that I had another dog, the speckled pup.

"He's part Old Yeller," she said. "And he was the best one of the bunch."

But that didn't help any either. The speckled pup might be part Old Yeller, but he wasn't Old Yeller. He hadn't saved all our lives and then been shot down like he was nothing.

Then one night it clouded up and rained till daylight. That seemed to wash away the hydrophobia plague. At least, pretty soon afterward, it died out completely.

But we didn't know that then. What seemed important to us about the rain was that the next morning after it fell, Papa came riding home through the mud.

The long ride to Kansas and back had Papa drawn down till he was as thin and knotty as a fence rail. But he had money in his pockets, a big shouting laugh for everybody, and a saddle horse for me.

The horse was a cat-stepping blue roan with a black mane and tail. Papa put me on him the first thing and made me gallop him in the clearing around the house. The roan had all the pride and fire any grown man would want in his best horse, yet was as gentle as a pet.

"Now, isn't he a dandy?" Papa asked.

I said "Yessir!" and knew that Papa was right and that I ought to be proud and thankful. But I wasn't. I didn't feel one way or another about the horse.

Papa saw something was wrong. I saw him look a

[155]

question at Mama and saw Mama shake her head. Then late that evening, just before supper, he called me off down to the spring, where we sat and he talked.

"Your mama told me about the dog," he said.

I said "Yessir," but didn't add anything.

"That was rough," he said. "That was as rough a thing as I ever heard tell of happening to a boy. And I'm mighty proud to learn how my boy stood up to it. You couldn't ask any more of a grown man."

He stopped for a minute. He picked up some little pebbles and thumped them into the water, scattering a bunch of hairy-legged water bugs. The bugs darted across the water in all directions.

"Now the thing to do," he went on, "is to try to forget it and go on being a man."

"How?" I asked. "How can you forget a thing like that?"

He studied me for a moment, then shook his head. "I guess I don't quite mean that," he said. "It's not a thing you can forget. I don't guess it's a thing that you ought to forget. What I mean is, things like that happen. They may seem mighty cruel and unfair, but that's how life is a part of the time.

"But that isn't the only way life is. A part of the time, it's mighty good. And a man can't afford to waste all the good part, worrying about the bad parts. That makes it all bad. . . . You understand?"

"Yessir," I said. And I did understand. Only, it still

[156]

didn't do me any good. I still felt just as dead and empty.

That went on for a week or better, I guess, before a thing happened that brought me alive again.

It was right at dinnertime. Papa had sent me out to the lot to feed Jumper and the horses. I'd just started back when I heard a commotion in the house. I heard Mama's voice lifted high and sharp. "Why, you thieving little whelp!" she cried out. Then I heard a shrieking yelp, and out the kitchen door came the speckled pup with a big chunk of cornbread clutched in his mouth. He raced around the house, running with his tail clamped. He was yelling and squawling like somebody was beating him to death. But that still didn't keep him from hanging onto that piece of cornbread that he'd stolen from Mama.

Inside the house, I heard Little Arliss. He was fighting and screaming his head off at Mama for hitting his dog. And above it all, I could hear Papa's roaring laughter.

Right then, I began to feel better. Sight of that little old pup, tearing out for the brush with that piece of cornbread seemed to loosen something inside me.

I felt better all day. I went back and rode my horse and enjoyed it. I rode 'way off out in the brush, not going anywhere especially, just riding and looking and beginning to feel proud of owning a real horse of my own.

[*157*]

Then along about sundown, I rode down into Bird-song Creek, headed for the house. Up at the spring, I heard a splashing and hollering. I looked ahead. Sure enough, it was Little Arliss. He was stripped naked and romping in our drinking water again. And right in there, romping with him, was that bread-stealing speckled pup.

I started to holler at them. I started to say: "Arliss! You get that nasty old pup out of our drinking water."

Then I didn't. Instead, I went to laughing. I sat there and laughed till I cried. When all the time I knew that I ought to go beat them to a frazzle for messing up our drinking water.

When finally I couldn't laugh and cry another bit, I rode on up to the lot and turned my horse in. To-morrow, I thought, I'll take Arliss and that pup out for a squirrel hunt. The pup was still mighty little. But the way I figured it, if he was big enough to act like Old Yeller, he was big enough to start learning to earn his keep.

SOUNDER

SOUNDER

BY WILLIAM H. ARMSTRONG

Illustrations by James Barkley

HarperCollins*Publishers*

To Kip, Dave, and Mary

"A man keeps, like his love, his courage dark."
—*Antoine de Saint Exupéry*

Author's Note

FIFTY YEARS AGO I learned to read at a round table in the center of a large, sweet-smelling, steam-softened kitchen. My teacher was a gray-haired black man who taught the one-room Negro school several miles away from where we lived in the Green Hill district of the county. He worked for my father after school and in the summer. There were no radios or television sets, so when our lessons were finished he told us stories. His stories came from Aesop, the Old Testament, Homer, and history.

There was a lasting, magnificent intoxication about the man that has remained after half a century. There was seldom a preacher at the white-washed, clapboard Baptist church in the Green Hill district, so he came often to our white man's church and sat alone in the balcony. Sometimes the minister would call on this eloquent, humble man to lead the congregation in prayer. He would move quietly to the foot of the balcony steps, pray with the simplicity of the Carpenter of Nazareth, and then return to where he sat alone, for no other black people ever came to join him.

He had come to our community from farther south, already old when he came. He talked little, or not at all, about his past. But one night at the great center table after he had told the story of Argus, the faithful dog of Odysseus, he told the story of Sounder, a coon dog.

It is the black man's story, not mine. It was not from Aesop, the Old Testament, or Homer. It was history—*his* history.

That world of long ago has almost totally changed. The church balcony is gone. The table is gone from the kitchen. But the story remains.

W. H. ARMSTRONG

SOUNDER

THE TALL MAN stood at the edge of the porch. The I
roof sagged from the two rough posts which held
it, almost closing the gap between his head and
the rafters. The dim light from the cabin window
cast long equal shadows from man and posts. A
boy stood nearby shivering in the cold October
wind. He ran his fingers back and forth over the
broad crown of the head of a coon dog named
Sounder.

"Where did you first get Sounder?" the boy asked.

"I never got him. He came to me along the road when he wasn't more'n a pup."

The father turned to the cabin door. It was ajar. Three small children, none as high as the level of the latch, were peering out into the dark. "We just want to pet Sounder," the three all said at once.

"It's too cold. Shut the door."

"Sounder and me must be about the same age," the boy said, tugging gently at one of the coon dog's ears, and then the other. He felt the importance of the years—as a child measures age— which separated him from the younger children. He was old enough to stand out in the cold and run his fingers over Sounder's head.

No dim lights from other cabins punctuated the night. The white man who owned the vast endless fields had scattered the cabins of his Negro sharecroppers far apart, like flyspecks on a whitewashed ceiling. Sometimes on Sundays the boy walked with his parents to set awhile at one of the distant cabins. Sometimes they went to the meetin' house. And there was school too. But it was far away at the edge of town. Its term began after harvest and ended before planting time.

2

Two successive Octobers the boy had started, walking the eight miles morning and evening. But after a few weeks when cold winds and winter sickness came, his mother had said, "Give it up, child. It's too long and too cold." And the boy, remembering how he was always laughed at for getting to school so late, had agreed. Besides, he thought, next year he would be bigger and could walk faster and get to school before it started and wouldn't be laughed at. And when he wasn't dead-tired from walking home from school, his father would let him hunt with Sounder. Having both school and Sounder would be mighty good, but if he couldn't have school, he could always have Sounder.

"There ain't no dog like Sounder," the boy said. But his father did not take up the conversation. The boy wished he would. His father stood silent and motionless. He was looking past the rim of half-light that came from the cabin window and pushed back the darkness in a circle that lost itself around the ends of the cabin. The man seemed to be listening. But no sounds came to the boy.

Sounder was well named. When he treed a coon or possum in a persimmon tree or on a wild-grape vine, his voice would roll across the flatlands. It wavered through the foothills, louder than any other dog's in the whole countryside.

What the boy saw in Sounder would have been totally missed by an outsider. The dog was not much to look at—a mixture of Georgia redbone hound and bulldog. His ears, nose, and color were those of a redbone. The great square jaws and head, his muscular neck and broad chest showed his bulldog blood. When a possum or coon was shaken from a tree, like a flash Sounder would clamp and set his jaw-vise just behind the animal's head. Then he would spread his front paws, lock his shoulder joints, and let the bulging neck muscles fly from left to right. And that was all. The limp body, with not a torn spot or a tooth puncture in the skin, would be laid at his master's feet. His master's calloused hand would rub the great neck, and he'd say "Good Sounder, good Sounder." In the winter when there were no crops and no pay, fifty cents for a possum and two dollars for a coonhide bought flour and overall jackets with blanket linings.

But there was no price that could be put on Sounder's voice. It came out of the great chest cavity and broad jaws as though it had bounced off the walls of a cave. It mellowed into half-echo before it touched the air. The mists of the flatlands strained out whatever coarseness was left

4

over from his bulldog heritage, and only flutelike redbone mellowness came to the listener. But it was louder and clearer than any purebred redbone. The trail barks seemed to be spaced with the precision of a juggler. Each bark bounced from slope to slope in the foothills like a rubber ball. But it was not an ordinary bark. It filled up the night and made music as though the branches of all the trees were being pulled across silver strings.

While Sounder trailed the path the hunted had taken in search of food, the high excited voice was quiet. The warmer the trail grew, the longer the silences, for, by nature, the coon dog would try to surprise his quarry and catch him on the ground, if possible. But the great voice box of Sounder would have burst if he had tried to trail too long in silence. After a last, long-sustained stillness which allowed the great dog to close in on his quarry, the voice would burst forth so fast it overflowed itself and became a melody.

A stranger hearing Sounder's treed bark suddenly fill the night might have thought there were six dogs at the foot of one tree. But all over the countryside, neighbors, leaning against slanting porch posts or standing in open cabin doorways and listening, knew that it was Sounder.

"If the wind does not rise, I'll let you go hunting with me tonight." The father spoke quietly as he glanced down at boy and dog. "Animals don't like to move much when it's windy."

"Why?" the boy asked.

"There are too many noises, and they can't hear a killer slipping up on them. So they stay in their dens, especially possums, because they can't smell much."

The father left the porch and went to the woodpile at the edge of the rim of light. The boy followed, and each gathered a chunk-stick for the cabin stove. At the door, the father took down a lantern that hung on the wall beside a possum sack and shook it. "There's plenty of coal oil," he said.

The boy closed the door quickly. He had heard leaves rattling across the frozen ground. He hoped his father didn't hear it. But he knew the door wouldn't shut it out. His father could sense the rising wind, and besides, it would shake the loose windowpanes.

Inside the cabin, the boy's mother was cutting wedge-shaped pieces of corn mush from an iron pot that stood on the back of the stove. She browned them in a skillet and put them on the tin-topped table in the middle of the room. The boy and the three younger children ate their sup-

6

per in silence. The father and mother talked a little about ordinary things, talk the boy had heard so many times he no longer listened. "The crop will be better next year. There'll be more day work. The hunting was better last year."

This winter the hunting was getting worse and worse. The wind came stronger and colder than last year. Sometimes Sounder and his master hunted in the wind. But night after night they came home with an empty brown sack. Coons were scarcely seen at all. People said they had moved south to the big water. There were few scraps and bones for Sounder. Inside the cabin, they were hungry for solid food too. Corn mush had to take the place of stewed possum, dumplings, and potatoes.

Not long after supper, Sounder's master went out of the cabin and stood listening, as he always did, to see if he could hear the cold winter wind beginning to rise in the hills. When he came back into the cabin, he took off his blanket-lined overall jacket and sat behind the stove for a long time. Sounder whined at the door as if he were asking if someone had forgotten to light the lantern and start across the fields of dead stalks to the lowlands or past the cottonwoods and jack oaks to the hills. The boy took Sounder some table scraps in a tin pan. As Sounder licked the bottom of the pan it rattled against a loose board in the porch as if somebody were walking across the floor.

Later, when it was time for the smaller children in the cabin to go to bed, Sounder's master got up, put on his overall jacket, and went outside. He did not take the lantern or Sounder or the boy with him. The stern order to the coon hound to go back under the porch came in through the cabin door, and Sounder's whining continued long after the footsteps on the frozen path had died out.

Inside the cabin, the boy's mother sat by the stove, picking kernels of walnuts with a bent hairpin. The woman watched each year for the walnuts to fall after the first hard frost. Each day she went with the children and gathered all that had fallen. The brownish-green husks, oozing their dark purple stain, were beaten off on a flat rock outside the cabin. On the same rock, the nuts were cracked after they had dried for several weeks in a tin box under the stove. When kernel-picking time came, before it was dark each day, the boy or the father took a hammer with a homemade handle, went to the flat rock, and cracked as many as could be kerneled in a night.

8

The troubled whimper of a child came through the little door that led to the shed-room where the children slept.

"You must go to bed soon," the mother said. "Your little brother gets addled in his sleep when you ain't in bed with him."

The boy reached into his mother's lap, where the golden half-kernels lay in the folds of her apron. She slapped his hand away. "You eat the crumbs from the bottom of the hull basket," she said. "I try to pick two pounds a night. That's thirty cents' worth. Fifteen cents a pound at the store if they're mostly half-kernels and dry. The man won't pay if they're all in crumbs."

Sometimes the woman told the boy stories she had heard at the meetin' house. "The Lord do powerful things" she would say. The boy liked it when she told her stories. They took away night loneliness. Night loneliness was always bad when the younger children had gone to bed, or when the father was not in the cabin. "Night loneliness is part fearing," the boy's mother had once said to him. But the boy was never afraid when his father was near.

Perhaps she too felt the loneliness that came with the wind as it passed the cabin outside, and the closeness of a world whose farthest border in

9

the night was the place where the lamp light ended, at the edge of the cabin walls. So she told the boy a story of a mighty flood which the Lord had sent to wash away all the evil in the world. When the story was over, she sent the boy to bed and continued picking out kernels and adding them to the neat mound in the folds of her apron.

The boy pressed his head deep into his straw pillow. The pillow was cold, but it felt smooth, and it smelled fresh. He had the same feeling he got when he rubbed his face against the sheets that hung on the clothesline every Monday. His mother washed his pillowcase and sheet every week, just like she did for the people who lived in the big house down the road. He buried himself deep in his side of the straw tick; he felt where the wooden slats of the bed crossed under his body. He rolled close to his little brother and tucked the edge of the coverlet under his body to keep out the cold that seeped up through the straw ticking. His little brother's body warmed him.

He heard Sounder whimpering under the porch. But Sounder was warm because the boy's father had put two burlap sacks under the porch for the time when the hard frosts came. The boy thought there must be two pounds of nuts in the pile on his mother's lap. His mother always said "Two pounds is a good night's work if you can start early and there ain't a sick child to rock."

He wondered where his father had gone without Sounder; they always went together at night. He heard the thump, thump, thump of Sounder's paw hitting the underneath side of the porch floor as he scratched at a flea in his short tan hair.

The boy dreamed of the stalk land covered by the Lord's mighty flood. He wondered where the animals would go if the water rose over the foothills. "Cabins built on posts would just float like boats, porch and all," he assured himself in a whisper. If they floated from the far ends of the land and all came together, that would be a town, and he wouldn't be lonely anymore . . .

*   *   *

When the boy awoke in the morning, he went to the window. He remembered his dream of the flood covering the stalk land. He called the younger children. His breath steamed up the windowpane. He wiped the steam away with the bottom of his fist. His dream had not come true. There was no floodwater rising in the bottomland. Except for frost on the ground, everything looked just the same as it had yesterday. The younger children looked, saw nothing, and asked, "What is it?"

The big blue-enameled possum kettle was boiling on top of the chunk stove. It had two lids and doubled for cooking and heating. The boy felt the brown paper bag of walnut kernels on the shelf behind the stove. "Yes," he said to his mother, "I think there are two pounds."

He stood close to the warm stovepipe, turning one cheek and then the other to its glowing warmth. He circled his arms in a wide embrace around the pipe and rubbed his hands together. The warmth ran up his sleeves and down over his ribs inside his shirt and soaked inward through his whole body. He pulled in deep breaths from above the stove to catch the steam escaping from under the kettle's lid as it bounced up and down, breaking the rhythm of the bubbles that went *lob, lob, lob* on the surface of the fast-boiling pot.

In a skillet on the second stove lid there were pork sausages! He sniffed the thin lines of smoke curling up from under the edges of each of them. Pork sausage was for Christmas. But he knew it wasn't Christmas yet. His mother put a pan of cold biscuits on the lid of the possum kettle to

12

warm. She was humming to herself. The lid stopped jumping up and down, and the steam began to whistle softly as it squeezed from under the lid.

The smell that came from under the lid wasn't possum. It was ham bone. The boy had only smelled it twice in his life, once before in his own cabin, and once when he was walking past the big house down the road. The sausage and ham-bone smells filled up the cabin and leaked out through the cracks in the floor and around the door. They excited Sounder, and now he was scratching at the door.

Sounder hadn't had much to eat yesterday. Besides a few scraps, he had had one cold biscuit. When flour was scarce, the boy's mother would wrap the leftover biscuits in a clean flour sack and put them away for the next meal. Then they would be put in a pan, sprinkled with a little water to keep them soft, and warmed over. The boy called to Sounder to stop and go away. His mother stopped her humming and said, "Shush, child, you'll wake your father."

Then she went back to her humming. His mother always hummed when she was worried. When she held a well child on her lap and rocked back and forth, she sang. But when she held a

13

sick child close in her arms and the rocker moved just enough to squeak a little, she would hum. Sometimes she hummed so softly that the child heard the deep concerned breathing of terror above the sound of the humming. The boy always thought her lips looked as though they were glued together when she hummed. They seemed to be rolled inward and drawn long and thin. Once when she kissed him good night when he was sick, they were cold, he remembered. But when she sang or told stories, her lips were rolled out, big and warm and soft.

Outside, the wind still blew, the sun was weak, and the earth was gray. Several times the boy went out to bring wood for his mother. He ate sausage and biscuits at the tin-topped table with the other children.

When his father got up, he chopped some wood and sat by the fire. The top of the possum kettle bounced up and down again because the biscuit pan had been moved. The father lifted the lid now and then. With the big wire fork that had a wooden handle, he pulled the ham half out of the water and turned it over. The boy felt warm and proud inside when he saw his father's great hand take hold of the handle of the hot lid without using a pot rag the way his mother always did. Finally his father took from the shelf a flat

14

oak slab, bigger than any of the pans or dishes, and put it on the table.

The boy liked to smell the oak slab. It smelled like the Mercy Seat meetin'-house picnic held every summer. He also liked to rub his fingers on the edge of the slab, for it was soft and smooth where the grease had soaked it. His father had hollowed it out during long winter evenings as he sat by the stove. The boy had cleaned up the shavings and slipped them under the door of the stove when the draft was open. They burned with a bright flame, and they made a great mystery for the boy: The curled ones straightened out as they burned, but the straight ones curled up.

The boy remembered when the oak slab had had ham on it before. One year his father had won a pig in a shooting match and raised it to a hog. They had eaten one ham and traded one for beans and flour at the store. That year they had spareribs and chitlins and pan scrapple. Sometimes when the boy's father helped butcher hogs down at the big house, he would bring home spareribs and sowbelly—lots of sowbelly, but not much spareribs.

The boy's father took the ham from the kettle and put it on the oak slab. "Save the ham-boilin' for Sounder," he reminded the boy's mother.

"Sounder will eat good now," the boy said.

The father sharpened the butcher knife with the whetstone he used to whet his scythe and his goose-necked brier hook in the summer when he cut brambles and young sumac in the fencerows. He cut big pieces of ham, and they stuck out from under the brown tops of the biscuits. It was like a Christmas bigger than a pork-sausage Christmas. The boy slipped a piece of the fat rind into a biscuit and took it out to Sounder. When the ham-boiling had cooled, he filled Sounder's pan and ran his fingers up and down the great dog's back as he lapped it up.

The windows of the cabin stayed steamed up almost all day, the kettle had boiled so long. The cold wind continued to blow outside. Nothing moved except what the wind moved—dead leaves under the cabin, brown blades and stalks from the fields which were dead and ready to be blown away, bare branches of poplars, and the spires of tall pines. Toward evening the father wiped the steam away from the glass and looked out a couple of times. The dry cottonwood chunks burned like gunpowder in the stove. In one or two spots the side of the stove gave off a red glow.

With the flavor of ham and biscuit still in his mouth, the boy felt good. He watched his mother as she patched his father's overalls with a piece of ticking. The combination of faded blue overall cloth and gray-and-white-striped ticking looked odd. One time at the meetin'-house picnic, boys with patches the same color as their overalls had laughed at him and pointed to the checkered gingham on the knees of his overalls. He had felt mad and hurt. But his mother had said, "Pay no mind, child," and had led him away. He hoped no one would laugh at his father. His father wouldn't be hurt. He didn't get hurt. He would get mad and fight back, and the boy was always afraid when his father got mad.

When the woman had patched the torn place, she got the walnut basket, folded her apron in her lap, and began to pick out the golden-brown kernels. The boy thought she would sing, but the rocker only moved enough to squeak. She hummed softly, and her lips looked glued together. "Look down, look down that lonesome road." The boy wished she would stop humming and tell a story about the Lord or King David, but she kept humming *That Lonesome Road.*

The boy decided it was lonesomer in bed in the dark than it was staying up. He was glad he could set a long time after the young children had gone to bed. Once he had been gathering weeds which his father had cut at the edge of a lawn. On the

17

lawn a lady sat under a tree reading a story aloud to some children. He wished his mother or father could read. And if they had a book, he would hold the lamp by the chair so they could see the words and never get tired. "One day I will learn to read," he said to himself. He would have a book with stories in it, then he wouldn't be lonesome even if his mother didn't sing.

THE ROAD WHICH passed the cabin lay like a thread
dropped on a patchwork quilt. Stalk land, fallow
fields, and brushland, all appeared to be sewn together by wide fencerow stitches of trees. Their
bare branches spread out to join together the separate patches of land. Weeds grew on either side
of the road in summer, and a thin strip of green
clung to life between the dusty tracks. In summer
a horse and wagon made almost no noise in the

II

19

soft earth. In winter when the ground was frozen, the rattle of wheels and each distinct hoofbeat punctuated the winter quiet. When the wind blew, little clouds of dust would rise in the road and follow the wind tracks across the fields.

The boy was allowed to go as far as he wanted to on the road. But the younger children couldn't go past the pine clump toward the big house and the town, or the bramble patch where they picked blackberries in summer in the other direction. Almost no one passed on the road in winter except to buy flour at the store far down the road or to go to the town of a Saturday. Even in summer a speck on the horizon was a curiosity. People sitting on cabin porches would wonder whether the speck would take the form of man, woman, or child.

The third day after the boy had awakened to the smell of ham bone and pork sausage, it was still cold and the wind still blew. But the cabin still smelled good, and there was plenty to eat. Just as dark was gathering, the boy started to go to the woodpile to bring in wood for the night. The dim light of the lamp ran past the boy as he stood motionless in the open cabin door.

"Shut the door," the boy's father called from where he sat near the stove. But the boy did not move.

Just past the edge of the porch three white men stood in the dim light. Their heavy boots rattled the porch floor, and the boy backed quickly into the cabin as they pushed their way in.

"There are two things I can smell a mile," the first man said in a loud voice. "One's a ham cookin' and the other's a thievin' nigger."

"Get up," the second man ordered. The warm, but frozen circle of man, woman, and three small children around the stove jumped to their feet. A stool on which a child had been sitting fell backward and made a loud noise. One of the men kicked it across the room. The boy did not move from his place just inside the door.

"Here's the evidence," said the first man. He jerked at the grease-spotted cloth on the tin-topped table. The oak slab and the half-eaten ham fell to the floor with a great thud and slid against the wall.

"You know who I am," said the first man as he unbuttoned his heavy brown coat and pulled it back to show a shiny metal star pinned to his vest. "These are my deputies." The stranger nearest the door kicked it shut and swore about the cold.

"Stick out your hands, boy," ordered the second man. The boy started to raise his hands, but the man was already reaching over the stove, snap-

21

ping handcuffs on the outstretched wrists of his father.

The click of the handcuffs was like the click of a gate latch at the big house where the boy had once gone with his father to work. He had swung on the gate and played with the latch until someone had called out from the house, "If you want to swing on a gate, boy, swing on the one behind the house. Get away from the front."

The third stranger, who had not spoken, turned toward the door. "I'll bring up the wagon." But he did not open the door.

Suddenly the voice of the great dog shattered the heavy, seemingly endless silence that came between the gruff words of the sheriff and those of his men. Sounder was racing toward the cabin from the fields. He had grown restless from waiting to go hunting with his master and had wandered away to hunt alone. That's why he hadn't warned them. He always barked and sometimes, even in daytime, he would start from under the porch, the hair on his back straightening before anyone had sighted a moving speck at the far end of the road. "Somebody's comin' or a creature's movin'" the boy's mother would say.

Now he was growling and scratching at the door. The noise seemed to undo the fearful shock

that had held the smaller children ashen and motionless. The youngest child began to cry and hid
behind his mother. He tugged at her apron, but
the woman did not move.

The men were speaking roughly to Sounder's
master. "That tear in your overalls where the
striped ticking is—that's where you tore them on
the door hook of the smokehouse. We found
threads of torn cloth in the hook. You gonna wear
nothing but stripes pretty soon. Big, wide black
and white stripes. Easy to hit with a shotgun."

The deputy who had started out to bring up
the wagon kicked the closed door and swore at
the dog on the other side.

"Go out and hold that mongrel if you don't
want him shot." He held the door ajar the width
of the boy's body and thrust him out. The boy fell
on the back of the dog, whose snarling jaws had
pushed into the light between the boy's legs. A
heavy boot half pushed, half kicked the entangled
feet of the sprawled boy and the nose of the dog
and slammed the door. "Get that dog out of the
way and hold him if you don't want him dead."

The boy, regaining his balance, dragged Sounder off the porch and to the corner of the cabin.
Then the deputy, hearing the barking move back
from the door, opened it and came out. He walked

out of the circle of light but returned soon leading a horse hitched to a spring wagon. A saddled horse followed behind the wagon.

The appearance of the horses and the added confusion of people coming from the cabin roused Sounder to new fury. The boy felt his knees give. His arms ached, and his grip on the dog's collar was beginning to feel clammy and wet. But he held on.

"Chain him up," said the sheriff.

The boy thought they were telling him to chain up Sounder, but then he saw that one of the men had snapped a long chain on the handcuffs on his father's wrists. As the men pushed his father into the back of the wagon his overalls caught on the end of the tail-gate bolt, and he tore a long hole in his overalls. The bolt took one side of the ticking patch with it. The man holding the chain jerked it, and the boy's father fell backward into the wagon. The man swung the loose end of the chain, and it struck the boy's father across the face. One of the deputies pulled the chain tight and tied it to the wagon seat. The two deputies climbed on the wagon seat; the sheriff mounted the saddled horse. The cabin door was open; the boy's mother was standing in the doorway. He did not see his brother and sisters.

24

Sounder was making an awful noise, a half-strangled mixture of growl and bark. The boy spoke to him, but the great paws only dug harder to grip the frozen earth. Inch by inch the boy was losing his footing. Numbness was beginning to creep up his arms and legs, and he was being dragged away from the corner of the house.

The wagon started, and the sheriff rode behind it on his horse. Sounder made a great lunge forward, and the boy fell against the corner of the porch. Sounder raced after the wagon. No one yelled after him. The mother stood still in the doorway. The deputy who wasn't holding the reins turned on the seat, aimed his shotgun at the dog jumping at the side of the wagon, and fired. Sounder fell in the road, and the sheriff rode around him. Sounder's master was still on his back in the wagon, but he did not raise his head to look back.

The boy struggled to his feet. His head hurt where he had hit it against the corner of the porch. Now his mother spoke for the first time since he had opened the door to bring in wood. "Come in, child, and bring some wood."

Sounder lay still in the road. The boy wanted to cry; he wanted to run to Sounder. His stomach felt sick; he didn't want to see Sounder. He sank to his knees at the woodpile. His foot hurt where

the door had been slammed on it. He thought he
would carry in two chunk-sticks. Maybe his
mother would drag Sounder out of the road. Maybe she would drag him across the fields and bury
him. Maybe if she laid him on the porch and put
some soft rags under him tonight, he might rise
from the dead, like Lazarus did in a meetin'-house
story. Maybe his father didn't know Sounder was
dead. Maybe his father was dead in the back of
the sheriff's wagon now. Maybe his father had
said it hurt to bounce over the rough road on his
back, and the deputy had turned around on the
seat and shot him.

The second chunk-stick was too big. It slipped
out of the boy's arms. Two of his fingers were
bruised under the falling wood.

Suddenly a sharp yelp came from the road. Just
like when a bee stung Sounder under the porch
or a brier caught his ear in the bramble, the boy
thought. In an instant the boy was on his feet.
Bruised foot and fingers, throbbing head were
forgotten. He raced into the dark. Sounder tried
to rise but fell again. There was another yelp, this
one constrained and plaintive. The boy, trained in
night-sight when the lantern was dimmed so as
not to alert the wood's creatures, picked out a
blurred shape in the dark.

Sounder was running, falling, floundering, rising. The hind part of his body stayed up and moved from side to side, trying to lift the front part from the earth. He twisted, fell, and heaved his great shoulders. His hind paws dug into the earth. He pushed himself up. He staggered forward, sideways, then fell again. One front leg did not touch the ground. A trail of blood, smeared and blotted, followed him. There was a large spot of mingled blood, hair, and naked flesh on one shoulder. His head swung from side to side. He fell again and pushed his body along with his hind legs. One side of his head was a mass of blood. The blast had torn off the whole side of his head and shoulder.

The boy was crying and calling Sounder's name. He ran backward in front of Sounder. He held out his hand. Sounder did not make a sign to stop. The boy followed the coon dog under the porch, but he went far back under the cabin. The boy was on his knees, crying and calling, "Sounder, Sounder, Sound . . ." His voice trailed off into a pleading whisper.

The cabin door opened, and the boy's mother stood in the door. The pale light of the lamp inside ran past the woman, over the edge of the porch, and picked out the figure of the boy on his hands and knees. "Come in, child," the woman said. "He is only dying."

28

Inside the cabin the younger children sat huddled together near the stove. The boy rubbed his hands together near the stovepipe to warm them. His bruised fingers began to throb again. His foot and his head hurt, and he felt a lump rising on the side of his head. If Sounder would whimper or yelp, I would know, the boy thought. But there was no sound, no thump, thump, thump of a paw scratching fleas and hitting the floor underneath.

"Creatures like to die alone," the mother said after a long time. "They like to crawl away where nobody can find them dead, especially dogs. He didn't want to be shot down like a dog in the road. Some creatures are like people."

The road, the boy thought. What would it be like? Did the shotgun blast a hole in the road?

"I ain't got the wood," the boy said at last. "I'll light the lantern and get it."

"You know where the wood is. You won't need the lantern," the woman said.

The boy paused in the doorway. Then he took the lantern from the nail where it hung beside the possum sack. He took the lantern to the stove, lit a splinter of kindling through the open door-draft, and held it to the lantern wick the way his father always did. His mother said nothing to him. She spoke to the younger children instead. "I ain't fed you yet."

When he got outside, the boy did not go to the woodpile. He followed the trail of blood in its zigzag path along the road. At the end of it there was a great wide spot, dark on the frozen ground. Little clumps of Sounder's hair lay in the blood. There was no hole where the shotgun had blasted. At the edge of the dark stain, the boy touched his finger to something. It was more than half of Sounder's long thin ear. The boy shivered and moved his finger away. He had seen dead lizards and possums and raccoons, but he'd never seen a human animal, like Sounder, dead.

It wouldn't work, he thought. But people always said to put things under your pillow when you go to bed, and if you make a wish, it will come true. He touched Sounder's ear again. It was cold. He picked it up. One edge of it was bloody, and jagged like the edge of a broken windowpane. He followed the zigzag trail back along the road, but he could scarcely see it now. He was crying again. At the corner of the porch he took the possum sack from the nail where it hung and wiped the ear. It gave him the shivers. He jumped down quickly, and holding the lantern near the ground, tried to see under the porch. He called Sounder. There was no sound. He went back to wiping the ear. His throat hurt. He put the ear in the pocket of his overall jacket. He was going to put it under his pillow and wish that Sounder wasn't dead.

The wind had stopped blowing. This would have been a good hunting night, he thought. Far away, a single lantern was moving into the foothills. The boy was still crying. He had not forgotten the wood. Now he put out the lantern and hung it against the wall. He went to the woodpile, picked up two chunk-sticks, and went into the cabin.

The loneliness that was always in the cabin, except when his mother was singing or telling a story about the Lord, was heavier than ever now. It made the boy's tongue heavy. It pressed against his eyes, and they burned. It rolled against his ears. His head seemed to be squeezed inward, and it hurt. He noticed grease spots on the floor where the oak slab and the ham had fallen. He knew his mother had picked them up. His father would be cold, he thought, with that great rip in his overalls.

His mother sat by the stove. "You must eat," the woman said. The boy had been outside a long time. His mother had fed the other children, and they were already in bed. She did not take down her walnut basket to begin the slow filling of her apron with fat kernels. She did not sing or even hum. "Child . . . child" she would say with long spaces between. Sometimes she would murmur to herself with her eyes closed. His little brother would murmur and be addled in his sleep tonight, the boy thought. He would set as long as his mother would let him. Maybe his mother would let him set and listen all night.

The boy listened for a yelp, a whine, a thump, thump, thump under the floor. There was no sound. His mother's rocker did not even move enough to squeak. One chunk-stick burning atop another in the stove rolled against the stove door with a slight thump. The boy started toward the cabin door.

"You know it was the stove," the mother said as she reached for the poker to push the wood back from the door.

"It sounded outside," the boy said as he pulled the door closed after him.

Soon he returned carrying the lantern. "I want to look more," he said. "I keep hearin' things." He lit the lantern from the stove as he had done before. His mother said nothing. He had thought she might say "Hang it back, child" as she often did when he wanted to go along the fencerows and hunt with Sounder after dark.

Outside, he murmured to himself, "That was

32

the stove, I reckon." He put the lantern on the ground and tried to see under the cabin. Nothing moved in the dim light. He wished the light would shine in Sounder's eyes and he would see them in the dark, but it didn't. Backing from under the porch on his hands and knees, he touched the lantern and tipped it over. He grabbed it by the wire rim that held the top of the globe and burned his hand. "Don't let it fall over; it'll explode" his father had said to him so many times when they hunted together. He sucked his burned fingers to draw out the fire. Sounder's pan was on the ground, and someone had stepped on it. The mean man who had kicked him with his big boot, the boy thought. He straightened it as best he could with his hurt fingers and put it on the porch.

He blew out the lantern and hung it by the possum sack. He stood on the porch and listened to the faraway. The lantern he had seen going into the foothills had disappeared. There were gravestones behind the meetin' house. Some were almost hidden in the brambles. If the deputy sheriff had turned around on the seat of the wagon and shot his father, the visiting preacher and somebody would bring him back and bury him behind the meetin' house, the boy thought. And if Sounder dies, I won't drag him over the hard earth. I'll carry him. I know I can carry him if I try hard enough, and I will bury him across the field, near the fencerow, under the big jack oak tree.

The boy picked up Sounder's bent tin pan and carried it into the cabin. The woman pushed back in her chair for a brief second in surprise and half opened her mouth. But, seeing the boy's face in the lamplight, she closed her mouth, and the rocker came slowly back to its standing position— her head tilted forward again, her eyes fixed on the boy's uneaten supper, still warming on the back of the stove.

In the corner of the room next to the dish cupboard, the boy filled Sounder's tin with cold ham-boiling from the possum kettle. "What's that for, child?" asked the mother slowly, as though she were sorry she had asked and would like to take it back.

"For if he comes out."

"You're hungry, child. Feed yourself."

The boy put Sounder's tin under the porch, closed the door, pushed the night latch, sat down behind the stove, and began to eat his supper.

IN THE MORNING the boy's mother did not cook any pork sausage for breakfast. The ham was on the tin-topped table, but she did not uncover it. Everybody had biscuits and milk gravy. There was still a faint smell of ham, but the boy missed the scent of sausage coming up to him as he stood warming himself. He had hurried out and called Sounder and looked under the house before he had finished buttoning his shirt, but his mother

III

35

had made him come in. She knew he would be crawling under the cabin, so she made him put on last year's worn-out overalls and a ragged jacket of his father's that came down to his knees. It wouldn't keep out much cold because it was full of holes.

The boy's mother put what was left of the pork sausage and the ham in a meal sack. When she had wrapped her walnut kernels in brown paper and tied them with string, she tied a scarf around her head and put on a heavy brown sweater that had pink flannel-outing patches on the elbows. She put the brown package in the basket she always carried when she went to the store. She put the meal sack over her shoulder.

"I'm taking the kernels to the store to sell them," she said to the boy. She did not say where she was going with the meal sack she had swung over her shoulder.

"Watch the fire, child," she said. "Don't go out of hollerin' distance and leave the young ones. Don't let them out in the cold.

"Warm some mush in the skillet for you all to eat at dinnertime. I'll be home before suppertime.

"Whatever you do, child, don't leave the children with a roaring fire and go lookin' for Sounder.

You ain't gonna find him this day. If a stranger comes, don't say nothin'."

The boy had nodded each time she spoke. He thought he would say "Yes" or "Don't worry, I will," but he didn't. He pushed the younger children back out of the cold and closed the door.

As his mother stepped off the porch and started for the road she began to hum softly to herself. It was a song the boy had heard her sing many nights in the cabin:

> *You gotta walk that lonesome valley,*
> *You gotta walk it by yourself,*
> *Ain't nobody else gonna walk it for you.*

The boy wanted to run after her. He watched as she became smaller and smaller, until the meal sack over her shoulder was just a white speck. The rest of her became a part of the brown road and the gray earth. When the white speck had faded into the earth, the boy looked up at the sky.

"No sun to thaw things out today," he said aloud to himself. His father always spoke aloud to the wind and the sky, and sometimes to the sun when he stood on the porch in the morning, especially when it rose out of the far lowland cottonwoods and pines like a great ball of fire. "Warmin' the cold bones" his father would say. And

37

preparing for a hunt, his father would caution a full moon, hanging over the foothills, "Don't shine too bright, you'll make the creatures skittish." And Sounder too, settin' on his haunches, would speak to the moon in ghost-stirrin' tones of lonesome dog-talk.

People would be very mean to his mother today, the boy thought. He wondered if she would tell them that the ham had slid across the floor. If she told them, they might just throw it out and feed it to their dogs. They might let his mother keep it and bring it home again. They wouldn't let her keep the pork sausage, for it was wrapped in clean white paper and not cooked. They might push and pull his mother and put her in the back of a spring wagon and take her away too. She would spill the walnut kernels, and then she wouldn't be able to sell them to buy sowbelly and potatoes.

The boy had hoped the sun would shine. It would soften the frozen crust of earth and make it easier for him to dig a grave for Sounder—if he found Sounder. If Sounder was dead, he hoped no one would come along and see him carrying the grub hoe and shovel across the field to the big jack oak. They would ask what he was doing. If anybody passed while he was digging the grave,

he would hide in the fencerow. If they saw him,
they might run him off the land.

He felt like crying, but he didn't. Crying would
only bother him. He would have his hands full of
tools or be carrying Sounder's body. His nose
would start dripping and be powerful troublesome because he wouldn't have a free hand to
wipe it.

He took in an armload of wood and punched
up the fire. "Don't open the stove door," he cautioned the younger children. "I have to go out
some more." He went to his bed and took
Sounder's ear from under the pillow. He would
bury it with Sounder. He smelled his pillow. It
still smelled clean and fresh. He put the ear in his
pocket so the children wouldn't ask questions as
he passed them on the way out. He smoothed his
pillow. He was glad his mother washed his sheet
and pillowcase every week, just like she did for
the people who lived in the big houses with curtains on the windows. About twice a year his
mother washed a lot of curtains. The clothesline
was filled with them, and they were thin and
light and ruffled and fluffy. It was more fun to rub
your face against the curtains than on the clean
sheets every Monday. The curtains, moving in
the breeze, were like the sea's foam. The boy had

never seen sea foam, but his mother had told him that when the Lord calmed the mighty Jordan for people to cross over, the water moved in little ripples like curtains in a breeze, and soft white foam made ruffles on top of the water.

The boy had never looked out of a window that had curtains on it. Whenever he passed houses with curtains on the windows, he remembered that if he put his face close against the curtains on the washline he could see through them. He thought there were always eyes, close against the curtains, looking out at him. He watched the windows out of the corner of his eye; he always felt scared until he had passed. Passing a cabin was different. In a cabin window there were just faces with real eyes looking out.

He could go out now, he thought. The wood in the stove had burned down some, and it would be safe. Besides, he would be close by for a while. Getting the body of Sounder from under the cabin wouldn't be easy. The younger children would bother him; they would ask a lot of questions like "Why is Sounder dead?" and "Will he stay dead?" and many more that he would not want to answer.

"When I'm out, don't be yellin' for me. I'll be through in a while," he said to the smallest child, who was looking out of the window, his chin barely high enough to rest on the sill.

There's no hurry, the boy thought. I have all day, and it's still early. And he looked out of the window too. "If you're inside you look out, and if you're outside you look in, but what looks both ways? That's a riddle; what's the answer?" He directed it to no child in particular. And no one answered. "What's the answer?" the boy repeated, and then he answered his own riddle. "The window is the answer; it looks both ways." None of the children paid any attention.

"I must go now," said the boy to his brother and sisters, "before it gets colder. The wind is starting up, so keep the door shut."

Sounder had not died in his favorite spot right behind the porch steps where he had a hole dug out and where the boy's father had put two coffee sacks for a pallet. His mother had said, "Sounder will crawl to the darkest, farthest part of the cabin." That's why she had made the boy put on his ragged clothes.

The boy could not see all the way under the cabin. At one time rats had lived there, and they had pushed up the earth in some places so that it almost touched the beams. They did this so they could gnaw through the floor from below.

He hurt his head and shoulders on nails sticking down from above as he crawled. He hurt his knees and elbows on broken glass, rusty sardine cans, and broken pieces of crockery and dishes. The dry dust got in his mouth and tasted like lime and grease. Under the cabin it smelled stale and dead, like old carcasses and snakes. The boy was glad it was winter because in summer there might have been dry-land moccasins and copperheads under the cabin. He crawled from front to back, looking along the spaces between the beams.

Sounder was not to be seen. The boy would have to go back and forth. Maybe Sounder had pushed with his hind feet and dug a hole into which he had settled. The threadbare knees of last year's overalls opened up, and his bare knees scraped the soil. His father's long jacket caught under his knees as he crawled and jerked his face down into the dust. Cobwebs drooped over his face and mouth. His mouth was so dry with dust that he could not spit them out.

He crawled over every spot under the cabin, but Sounder's body was not there. The boy felt in his pocket. He had lost Sounder's ear under the cabin. It made no difference. It could be buried there.

But where was Sounder's body? he wondered.

Perhaps the injuries in the side of his head and shoulder were only skin wounds. They looked so terrible, but maybe they were not bad after all. Perhaps Sounder had limped down the road, the way the wagon had taken his master, and died. Perhaps he had only been knocked senseless and that was why he zigzagged so crazily, running for the cabin.

No wild creature could have carried the dead body away. Foxes could carry off dead squirrels and possums. But no animal was big enough to drag Sounder's body away. Maybe the boy, looking under the cabin with the lantern, had caused Sounder to crawl out the other side and die in the brown stalk land.

The boy was crying now. Not that there was any new or sudden sorrow. There just seemed to be nothing else to fill up the vast lostness of the moment. His nose began to run and itch. The tears ran down through the cobwebs and dust that covered his face, making little rivulets. The boy rubbed his eyes with his dirty hands and mixed dust with tears. His eyes began to smart.

He followed the road the way the wagon had taken his father as far as he dared leave the fire and the children in the cabin, still in hollering distance. There was no sign of Sounder's body.

He spiraled the brown stalk land in ever-widening circles, searching the fencerows as he went. Under the jack oaks and the cottonwoods there was nothing. In the matted Scotch-broom tangle he visualized the great tan body as he carefully picked each step. But the dog was not there.

IV   AFTER THE BOY had fed the children and eaten something himself, he sat down by the warm stove and looked out of the window. There was nothing else to do. Now and then a cloud would cross the sun that had finally burned its way out of the gray. The boy watched the cloud shadows roll over the fields and pass over the cabin. They darkened the window as they passed.

He carried in wood for the night before the sun

began to weaken. Then he looked out of the window again to where his mother would appear. Finally he saw a speck moving on the road. He watched it grow.

"She's coming," he said to the younger children, and they crowded around him and pushed their faces against the window. "She's been gone long enough to walk to town and more," he added.

"What will she bring?" one of the children asked.

"She'll bring nothin', but maybe things to eat. She won't bring no stick candy. Don't ask her for none. Don't ask her nothin'."

Several times during the day the boy had said to himself, "Maybe they'll let him come home if she takes back the stuff. Some people might, but some won't." But his father was not with her.

"I gave the stuff back," she said when she got to the cabin.

The boy's throat hurt with a great lump, and when he swallowed, it would hurt more. If his father had come, it would have been easy. Together they could have found Sounder's body and buried him.

When the boy's mother heard that he had not found Sounder under the cabin, she stood in the doorway and thought for a long time. If one of the children had stood in the door that long, she would have said "Go in or out, child."

"Creatures like to die under somethin'," she said at last, "and there ain't nothin' else close to crawl under. He wasn't hit in his vitals, I reckon. He's got a flesh wound. He's gone into the woods to draw out the poison with oak-leaf acid."

Now she shut the door and put her basket on the tin-topped table. "Poke up the fire," she said to the boy. "Oak leaves has strong acid that toughens the skin, just like the oak bark that they use to tan leather in the tannery. The creature beds down with the wound against a heap of oak leaves. The leaves make a poultice that draws out the poison and heals the wound with a hard brown scab. That's why creatures head for the swampland around the big water when the mange hits. Wet leaves heals better."

"Sounder's blood would wettin the leaves," the boy said after he had stood a long time with the poker in his hand. His eyes were fixed on the open stove door, watching the yellow flame change shape and turn to blue and red.

"Sounder was jumping at the wagon and hard to hit," the boy's mother said. "I think maybe he was hit a glancing shot that tore off the hide on his head and shoulder. If he was, he's gone to the jack-oak woods to heal himself. The Lord shows

48

His creatures how to do. If he ain't dead now, he'll come limpin' home, powerful hungry, in time."

"Tomorrow or the day after?" the boy asked.

"Longer, maybe four days, or more like seven. But don't be all hope, child. If he had deep head wounds, he might be addled crazy and not know where he wandered off to die."

The boy's mother had brought home the empty meal sack. In her basket she had some fat meat, potatoes, and a small bottle of vanilla flavoring, which she had bought with the money she got for her walnut kernels. From the bottom of the basket she took the folded brown paper bag into which she poured each night's pickin's and put it on the shelf. She also brought home an empty cardboard box which the storekeeper had given her. She didn't say where she had been, besides the store, or what had happened. The boy could see that her eyes were filled with hurt and said nothing. The younger children remembered not to ask any-thing except, looking in the empty box, one said, "Nothin' in here?"

"I'm gonna use it to put a cake in," the mother said.

"Better go out and crack nuts for the night's pickin' before dark," she said to the boy.

The boy scooped up a tin pail of nuts from the

49

big box under the stove and went out to the flat cracking stone. With his knees still sore from crawling under the cabin, he hesitated a long time before he knelt on the frozen earth. Standing, he looked one way and then another, tracing the fencerows that had more oaks than other trees, the far lowland woods and the foothills. "I'll go there first tomorrow," he said to himself as he faced the foothills. "There's big patches of oak trees there. And whenever Sounder was given his head, he picked the hills for huntin'."

When night came, his mother hummed and picked kernels. She did not tell a story. The boy wanted to ask who carried in wood to keep the people in jail warm. He knew they had big stoves in big jails. Once his mother had told him a story about three people named Shadrach, Meshach, and Abed-nego who were in jail. Some mean governor or sheriff got mad and had them thrown right into the jail stove, big as a furnace, but the Lord blew out the fire and cooled the big stove in a second. And when the jail keeper opened the stove door, there stood Shadrach, Meshach, and Abed-nego singing:

Cool water, cool water;
The Lord's got green pastures and cool water.

"Tell me about Joseph in the jail and the stone

quarry in Egypt and chiselin' out rocks to make ole Pharaoh's gravestone," the boy asked. But his mother went on humming, and the boy went back to his thinking.

No stove could be that big, he thought. He watched the red coals through the open draft in the stove door brighten each time the wind blew loud enough to make a low whistling noise in the stovepipe. A burning chunk-stick fell against the inside of the stove, but the boy did not try to convince himself that it might be the thump of Sounder scratching fleas underneath the floor. He was thinking of tomorrow.

Tomorrow he would go into the woods and look for Sounder. "The wind whistlin' in the pipe is bothersome," he said. He hated the cold wind. It blew through his clothes and chilled his body inside and made him shiver. He hoped the wind would not be blowing in the woods tomorrow. The wind made the woods noisy. The boy liked the woods when they were quiet. He understood quiet. He could hear things in the quiet. But quiet was better in the woods than it was in the cabin. He didn't hear things in cabin quiet. Cabin quiet was long and sad.

"Turn the pipe-damper a little and the whistlin' will stop," his mother said at last.

The next day he walked the great woodlands,

51

calling Sounder's name. The wind blew through his clothes and chilled him inside. When he got home after dark, his clothes were torn. His throat hurt with a great lump choking him. His mother fed him and said, "Child, child, you must not go into the woods again. Sounder might come home again. But you must learn to lose, child. The Lord teaches the old to lose. The young don't know how to learn it. Some people is born to keep. Some is born to lose. We was born to lose, I reckon. But Sounder might come back."

But weeks went by, and Sounder did not come back.

*   *   *

One night the boy learned why his mother had brought home the bottle of vanilla flavoring. Now it was Christmas and she was making a cake. When the four layers were spread out on the tin-topped table and she began to ice them, the boy noticed that she put three together in a large cake and made a small one of the leftover layer.

"Why we having two cakes?" the boy asked. But she was humming to herself and did not answer him. When she had finished, she put the

52

small cake on the top shelf of the dish cupboard. The big one she put in the cardboard box she had brought from the store.

The sweet smell of baking and vanilla had drawn the smaller children from the stove to the edge of the table. The woman reached over or walked around them as she worked. "I'm done," she finally said. "You can lick the pans."

The boy had not moved from his chair by the stove. Today he had searched the oak clumps along the far fencerows for Sounder. He never got the sweet pan till last, anyway. It always went from youngest to oldest, and there was never much left when his turn came.

"You're tired and worried poorly," his mother said. And she handed him the icing pan.

In the morning the woman told the boy that she wanted him to walk to town, to the jail behind the courthouse, and take the cake to his father. "It's a troublesome trip," she said. "But they won't let women in the jail. So you must go." She tied a string around the cardboard box and said, "Carry it flat if your hands don't get too cold. Then it'll look mighty pretty when you fetch it to him." She stood at the edge of the porch until he was far enough away not to be able to look back and see her crying, then called to him,

"Whatever you do, child, act perkish and don't grieve your father."

On the road, the boy felt afraid. He had been to the town at Christmastime before. Not on Christmas Day, but a few days before, to help his father carry mistletoe and bunches of bittersweet berries that his father sold by the wall in front of the courthouse or on the corner by the bank. And sometimes, when it was getting late and they still had trimmings to sell, his father would go to the back door of houses along the street and say "Ma'am, would you need some trimmin's?" and hold up the biggest sprig of mistletoe left in his grain sack. They usually sold most of the mistletoe, the boy remembered, but bunches of bittersweet that the boy had carried all day were always left over to be thrown in a fence corner on the way home. "Ain't no good for nothin' now" his father would say.

From early fall until gathering time, the father and boy kept their eyes peered for the golden-green clumps with white berries that grew high up in the forks of water elm and sycamore trees. Bittersweet was easy. "Pull down one vine and trim it, and you've got as much as a man can carry" his father always said. "But it takes a heap of fearful climbin' for mistletoe." They had al-

54

ready started gathering, and half a grain sack of mistletoe was still hanging against the side of the cabin. "If she hadn't had such a big load, she might have taken it," the boy said to himself.

The boy's fearful feeling increased as he got nearer town. There were big houses and behind the curtained windows there were eyes looking out at him. There would be more people now, and somebody might say "What you got in that box, boy?" or "Where you goin', boy?"

Church bells were ringing in the town. It was Christmas, and some people went to church on Christmas. In town the people he saw were laughing and talking. No one noticed him and he was glad. He looked at the store windows out of the corner of his eye. They were silvery and gold and green and red and sparkling. They were filled with toys and beautiful things. With the Christmas money from peddling, his father had bought what toys he could for the boy and his little brother and sisters. They had worn-out toys too. People in the big houses where his mother worked had given them to her to bring home.

He always wished they would give his mother an old book. He was sure he could learn to read if he had a book. He could read some of the town signs and the store signs. He could read price figures. He wanted to stop and stand and look straight at the windows, but he was afraid. A policeman would come after him. Perhaps the people had offered his mother old books, but she had said "No use, nobody can read in our cabin." Perhaps the people knew she couldn't read and thought her feelings would be hurt if they offered her the books their children had used up and worn out. The boy had heard once that some people had so many books they only read each book once. But the boy was sure there were not that many books in the world.

It was cold, but there were a few people standing or sitting along the wall in front of the courthouse. Winter or summer, there were always people there. The boy wondered if they knew it was Christmas. They didn't look happy like some of the people he had seen. He knew they were looking at him, so he hurried quickly past and around the corner to the back of the courthouse. The front of the courthouse was red brick with great white marble steps going up to a wide door. But the back was gray cement and three floors high, with iron bars over all the windows.

The only door that led into the jail had a small square of glass at about the height of a man, and there were iron bars over the glass. The boy was not tall enough to see through the glass. He

clutched the box close to him. He felt that something was about to burst through the door. In the middle of the door there was a great iron knocker. The boy knew he had to knock at the door; he wished he could be back in the great woods. He could hear voices inside the windows with the iron bars. Somewhere a voice was singing "God's gonna trouble the water." From one of the windows there came the sound of laughter. Now and then a door slammed with the deep clash of iron on iron. There was a rattle of tin pans. The boy felt very lonely. The town was as lonely as the cabin, he thought.

A large red-faced man opened the door and said, "You'll have to wait. It ain't visitin' hours yet. Who do you want to see? You'll have to wait." And he slammed the door before the boy could speak.

It was cold on the gray side of the building, so the boy went to the corner near the wall where the people and visitors stood or sat. The sun was shining there. The boy had forgotten it was still Christmas, the waiting seemed so long. A drunk man staggered along the street in front of the courthouse wall, saying "Merry Christmas" to everyone. He said "Merry Christmas" to the boy, and he smiled at the boy too.

Finally the great clock on the roof of the courthouse struck twelve. It frightened the boy because it seemed to shake the town. Now the red-faced man opened the door and let several people in. Inside, the man lined everybody up and felt their clothes and pockets. He jerked the cardboard box from the boy and tore off the top. The boy could hear iron doors opening and closing. Long hall-ways, with iron bars from floor to ceiling, ran from the door into the dim center of the building. The man with the red face squeezed the cake in his hands and broke it into four pieces. "This could have a steel file or hacksaw blade in it," he said. Then he swore and threw the pieces back in the box. The boy had been very hungry. Now he was not hungry. He was afraid. The man shoved the box into the boy's hands and swore again. Part of the cake fell to the floor; it was only a box of crumbs now. The man swore again and made the boy pick up the crumbs from the floor.

The boy hated the man with the red face with the same total but helpless hatred he had felt when he saw his father chained, when he saw Sounder shot. He had thought how he would like to chain the deputy sheriff behind his own wagon and then scare the horse so that it would run faster than the cruel man could. The deputy would fall and bounce and drag on the frozen road. His fine leather jacket would be torn more than he had torn his father's overalls. He would yell and curse, and that would make the horse go faster. And the boy would just watch, not trying to stop the wagon. . . .

The boy would like to see the big red-faced man crumpled on the floor with the crumbs. Besides the red face, the boy had noticed the fat, bulging neck that folded down over the man's collar and pushed up in wrinkled circles under his chin. The bull neck of the man reminded the boy of the bull he had seen die in the cattle chute at the big house where his father worked. The horse doctor had been trying to vaccinate the bull in the neck, but the rope through the ring in the bull's nose didn't keep the bull from tossing his head from side to side, knocking the horse doctor against the side of the chute. Then the horse doctor had gotten mad and said, "Get a chain. I'll make him stand still."

When the chain was snapped around the bull's neck, the farm hands pulled it over the crossbar of the chute posts and hooked it. But when the horse doctor stuck the bull in the neck, he lunged backward, set his front feet with his whole weight against the chain, and choked himself to death before one of the farm hands could jab him with a pitchfork and make him slacken the chain. The legs of the bull folded under him and the chain buried itself in the fat of his neck. When the farm hands finally got the chain unhooked from the crossbar, the bull's head fell in the dirt, and blood oozed out of its mouth and nostrils. . . .

The bull-necked man would sag to his knees, the boy thought, and crumple into a heap on the floor. Just the way the bull did, the boy thought, and blood would ooze out of his mouth and nose.

"Get up," the red-faced man said, "you wanta take all day?" The boy stood up. He felt weak and his knees shook, but there were no more tears in his eyes.

The red-faced man took a big iron key on a ring as big around as the boy's head and unlocked one of the iron gates. He pushed the boy in and said, "Fourth door down." Passing the three doors, the boy could feel eyes following him. He saw men, some sitting on cots, some standing behind the iron gates with their hands on the bars, looking at him. Each step echoed against the iron ceiling and made him sound like a giant walking. Far down the long iron-grated corridor a sad voice was singing:

> *Far away on Judah's plains*
> *The shepherds watched their sheep.*

The boy's father stood with his hands on the bars. He did not have his hands and feet chained together. Seeing the hands that could handle a hot pot lid without a pot rag, open the stove door without using a poker, or skin a possum by holding the hind legs of the carcass with one hand and the hide with the other and just pulling, the boy knew his father could have choked the cruel man with the bull neck.

The father looked at the boy and said, "Child." On the way, the boy had thought about what he would say to his father. He had practiced talking about his mother selling kernels at the store and buying the cake makings, his little brother and sisters being all right, no strangers coming past, not finding Sounder's body. And he was going to ask his father where Sounder came to him along the road when he wasn't more'n a pup. He practiced saying them all over and over to get the quiver and the quiet spells out of his voice because his mother had said, "Whatever you do, child, act perkish and don't grieve your father."

But the boy was full of mixed hate and pity now, and it addled him. There was an opening in the bars with a flat, iron shelf attached on the inside. The boy had left the lid of the box on the floor. Now he pushed the box through the opening and said, "This was a cake, before—" But he couldn't finish. An awful quiet spell destroyed all his practice.

"Sounder might not be dead," the boy said. He knew his father was grieved, for he swallowed hard and the quiet spells came to him too.

"I'll be back 'fore long," said his father.

From somewhere down the corridor there came a loud belly laugh, and a loud voice called out, "Listen to the man talk."

"Tell her not to grieve." His father was almost whispering now.

"Sounder didn't die under the cabin." But the boy couldn't keep the quivering out of his voice.

"Tell her not to send you no more." The quiet spells were getting longer. The man stopped looking through the bars at the boy and looked down at the cake.

"If he wasn't shot in his vitals," the boy said, "he might get healed in the woods." Then there was a long quiet spell that was split in the middle by the loud clank of an iron door banging shut.

"Tell her I'll send word with the visitin' preacher."

The big red-faced man with the bull neck opened the corridor door and yelled, "Visitin' over." The boy felt numb and cold, like he had felt standing outside the jail door. He choked up. He had grieved his father. He hated the red-faced man, so he wouldn't cry until he got outside.

"Come on, boy," the man yelled, swinging the big key ring.

"Go, child," the father said. "Hurry, child."

The boy was the last person through the big iron door. The bull-necked man pushed him and said, "Git, boy, or next time you won't get in."

THE BOY MOVED quickly around the corner and V
out of sight of the iron door and the gray cement
walls of the jail. At the wall in front of the courthouse he stood for a while and looked back. When
he had come, he was afraid, but he felt good in
one way because he would see his father. He was
bringing him a cake for Christmas. And he wasn't
going to let his father know he was grieved. So
his father *wouldn't* be grieved.

Now the sun had lost its strength. There were only a few people loafing around the courthouse wall, so the boy sat for a spell. He felt numb and tired. What would he say to his mother? He would tell her that the jailer was mean to visitors but didn't say nothing to the people in jail. He wouldn't tell her about the cake. When he told her his father had said she shouldn't send him again, that he would send word by the visiting preacher, she would say "You grieved him, child. I told you to be perk so you wouldn't grieve him."

Nobody came near where the boy sat or passed on the street in front of the wall. He had forgotten the most important thing, he thought. He hadn't asked his father where Sounder had come to him on the road when he wasn't more'n a pup. That didn't make any difference.

But along the road on the way to the jail, before the bull-necked man had ruined everything, the boy had thought his father would begin to think and say "If a stray ever follard you and it wasn't near a house, likely somebody's dropped it. So you could fetch it home and keep it for a dog."

"Wouldn't do no good now," the boy murmured to himself. Even if he found a stray on the way home, his mother would say "I'm afraid, child.

Don't bring it in the cabin. If it's still here when mornin' comes, you take it down the road and scold it and run so it won't foller you no more. If somebody come lookin', you'd be in awful trouble."

A great part of the way home the boy walked in darkness. In the big houses he saw beautiful lights and candles in the windows. Several times dogs rushed to the front gates and barked as he passed. But no stray pup came to him along the lonely, empty stretches of road. In the dark he thought of the bull-necked man crumpled on the floor in the cake crumbs, like the strangled bull in the cattle chute, and he walked faster. At one big house the mailbox by the road had a lighted lantern hanging on it. The boy walked on the far side of the road so he wouldn't show in the light. "People hangs 'em out when company is comin' at night," the boy's father had once told him.

When court was over, they would take his father to a road camp or a quarry or a state farm. Would his father send word with the visiting preacher where he had gone? Would they take his father away to the chain gang for a year or two years before he could tell the visiting preacher? How would the boy find him then? If he lived closer to the town, he could watch each day, and when they took his father away in the wagons where convicts were penned up in huge wooden crates, he could follow.

The younger children were already in bed when the boy got home. He was glad, for they would have asked a lot of questions that might make his mother feel bad, questions like "Is everybody chained up in jail? How long do people stay in jail at one time?"

The boy's mother did not ask hurtful questions. She asked if the boy got in all right and if it was warm in the jail. The boy told her that the jailer was mean to visitors but that he didn't say nothing to the people in jail. He told her he heard some people singing in the jail.

"Sounder ain't come home?" the boy said to his mother after he had talked about the jail. He had looked under the porch and called before he came into the cabin.

Now he went out, calling and looking around the whole cabin. He started to light the lantern to look more, but his mother said, "Hang it back, child. Ain't no use to fret yourself. Eat your supper, you must be famished."

"He said not to come no more," the boy finally said to his mother when he had finished his supper. "He said he'll send word by the visitin' preacher." He poked up the fire and waited for his mother to ask him if he had been perk and didn't grieve his father, but she didn't. He warmed himself and watched a patch of red glow the size of his hand at the bottom of the stove. He could see the red-faced man lying on the jail floor with blood oozing out of the corners of his mouth. After a long quiet spell the rocker began to squeak, and it made the boy jump, but his mother didn't notice. She began to rock as she picked out walnut kernels. She hummed for a while, and then she began to sing like she was almost whispering for no one to hear but herself:

You've gotta walk that lonesome valley,
You've gotta walk it by yourself,
Ain't nobody else gonna walk it for you . . .

In bed, the pressure of the bed slats through the straw tick felt good against the boy's body. His pillow smelled fresh, and it was smooth and soft. He was tired, but he lay awake for a long time. He thought of the store windows full of so many things. He thought of the beautiful candles in windows. He dreamed his father's hands were chained against the prison bars and he was still standing there with his head down. He dreamed that a wonderful man had come up to him as he was trying to read the store signs aloud and had said, "Child, you want to learn, don't you?"

In the morning the boy lay listening to his

mother as she opened and closed the stove door. He heard the damper squeak in the stovepipe as she adjusted it. She was singing softly to herself. Then the boy thought he heard another familiar sound, a faint whine on the cabin porch. He listened. No, it couldn't be. Sounder always scratched before he whined, and the scratching was always louder than the whine. Besides, it was now almost two months later, and the boy's mother had said he might be back in a week. No, he was not dreaming. He heard it again. He had been sleeping in his shirt to keep warm, so he only had to pull on his overalls as he went. His mother had stopped singing and was listening.

There on the cabin porch, on three legs, stood the living skeleton of what had been a mighty coon hound. The tail began to wag, and the hide made little ripples back and forth over the ribs. One side of the head and shoulders was reddish brown and hairless; the acid of the oak leaves had tanned the surface of the wound the color of leather. One front foot dangled above the floor. The stub of an ear stuck out on one side, and there was no eye on that side, only a dark socket with a splinter of bone showing above it. The dog raised his good ear and whined. His one eye looked up at the lantern and the possum sack where they hung against the wall. The eye looked past the boy and his mother. Where was his master? "Poor creature. Poor creature," said the mother and turned away to get him food. The boy felt sick and wanted to cry, but he touched Sounder on the good side of his head. The tail wagged faster, and he licked the boy's hand.

The shattered shoulder never grew together enough to carry weight, so the great hunter with the single eye, his head held to one side so he could see, never hopped much farther from the cabin than the spot in the road where he had tried to jump on the wagon with his master. Whether he lay in the sun on the cabin porch or by the side of the road, the one eye was always turned in the direction his master had gone.

The boy got used to the way the great dog looked. The stub of ear didn't bother him, and the one eye that looked up at him was warm and questioning. But why couldn't he bark? "He wasn't hit in the neck" the boy would say to his mother. "He eats all right, his throat ain't scarred." But day after day when the boy snapped his fingers and said "Sounder, good Sounder," no excited bark burst from the great throat. When something moved at night, the whine was louder, but it was still just a whine.

71

Before Sounder was shot, the boy's mother always said "Get the pan, child" or "Feed your dog, child." Now she sometimes got the pan herself and took food out to Sounder. The boy noticed that sometimes his mother would stop singing when she put the food pan down at the edge of the porch. Sometimes she would stand and look at the hunting lantern and possum sack where they hung, unused, against the cabin wall. . . .

*   *   *

The town and the jail seemed to become more remote and the distance greater as each day passed. If his father hadn't said "Don't come again," it wouldn't seem so far, the boy thought. Uncertainty made the days of waiting longer too.

The boy waited for the visiting preacher to come and bring word of his father. He thought the people for whom his mother washed the soft curtains could certainly write and would write a letter for his mother. But would someone in the jail read it for his father? Perhaps none of the people in jail could read, and the big man with the red face would just tear it up and swear. The visiting preacher might write a letter for the boy's father. But how would it get to the cabin since no mailman passed and there was no mailbox like the boy had seen on the wider road nearer the town?

The boy wanted to go to the town to find out what had happened to his father. His mother always said "Wait, child, wait." When his mother returned laundry to the big houses, she asked the people to read her the court news from their newspapers. One night she came home with word of the boy's father; it had been read to her from the court news. When the younger children had gone to bed, she said to the boy, "Court's over." And then there was one of those long quiet spells that always made the boy feel numb and weak.

"You won't have to fret for a while about seein' him in jail. He's gone to hard labor."

"For how long?" the boy asked.

"It won't be as long as it might. Folks has always said he could do two men's work in a day. He'll get time off for hard work and good behavior. The court news had about good behavior in it. The judge said it."

"Where's he gonna be at?" the boy asked after he had swallowed the great lump that filled up his throat and choked him.

"Didn't say. The people that has the paper says

it don't ever say wher' they gonna be at. But it's the county or the state. Ain't never outside the state, the people says."

"He'll send word," the boy said.

VI NOW THE CABIN was even quieter than it had been before loneliness put its stamp on everything. Sounder rolled his one eye in lonely dreaming. The boy's mother had longer periods of just humming without drifting into soft singing. The boy helped her stretch longer clotheslines from the cabin to the cottonwood trees at the edge of the fields. In the spring the boy went to the fields to work. He was younger than the other workers.

He was afraid and lonely. He heard them talking quietly about his father. He went to do yard work at the big houses where he had gathered weeds behind his father. "How old are you?" a man asked once when he was paying the boy his wages. "You're a hard worker for your age."

The boy did not remember his age. He knew he had lived a long, long time.

And the long days and months and seasons built a powerful restlessness into the boy. "Don't fret" his mother would say when he first began to talk of going to find his father. "Time's passin'. Won't be much longer now."

To the end of the county might be a far journey, and out of the county would be a far, far journey, but I'll go, the boy thought.

"Why are you so feared for me to go?" he would ask, for now he was old enough to argue with his mother. "In Bible stories everybody's always goin' on a long journey. Abraham goes on a long journey. Jacob goes into a strange land where his uncle lives, and he don't know where he lives, but he finds him easy. Joseph goes on the longest journey of all and has more troubles, but the Lord watches over him. And in Bible-story journeys, ain't no journey hopeless. Everybody finds what they suppose to find."

The state had many road camps which moved from place to place. There were also prison farms and stone quarries. Usually the boy would go searching in autumn when work in the fields was finished. One year he heard "Yes, the man you speak of was here, but I heard he was moved to the quarry in Gilmer County." One year it had been "Yes, he was in the quarry, but he was sick in the winter and was moved to the bean farm in Bartow County." More often a guard would chase him away from the gate or from standing near the high fence with the barbed wire along the top of it. And the guard would laugh and say "I don't know no names; I only know numbers. Besides, you can't visit here, you can only visit in jail." Another would sneer "You wouldn't know your old man if you saw him, he's been gone so long. You sure you know who your pa is, kid?"

The men in striped convict suits, riding in the mule-drawn wagons with big wooden frames resembling large pig crates, yelled as they rode past the watching boy, "Hey, boy, looking for your big brother? What you doing, kid, seeing how you gonna like it when you grow up?" And still the boy would look through the slats of the crate for a familiar face. He would watch men walking in line, dragging chains on their feet, to see if he

78

could recognize his father's step as he had known it along the road, coming from the fields to the cabin. Once he listened outside the gate on a Sunday afternoon and heard a preacher telling about the Lord loosening the chains of Peter when he had been thrown into prison. Once he stood at the guardhouse door of a quarry, and some ladies dressed in warm heavy coats and boots came and sang Christmas songs.

In his wandering the boy learned that the words men use most are "Get!" "Get out!" and "Keep moving!" Sometimes he followed the roads from one town to another, but if he could, he would follow railroad tracks. On the roads there were people, and they frightened the boy. The railroads usually ran through the flat silent countryside where the boy could walk alone with his terrifying thoughts. He learned that railroad stations, post offices, courthouses, and churches were places to escape from the cold for a few hours in the late night.

His journeys in search of his father accomplished one wonderful thing. In the towns he found that people threw newspapers and magazines into trash barrels, so he could always find something with which to practice his reading. When he was tired, or when he waited at some

80

high wire gate, hoping his father would pass in the line, he would read the big-lettered words first and then practice the small-lettered words.

In his lonely journeying, the boy had learned to tell himself the stories his mother had told him at night in the cabin. He liked the way they always ended with the right thing happening. And people in stories were never feared of anything. Sometimes he tried to put together things he had read in the newspapers he found and make new stories. But the ends never came out right, and they made him more afraid. The people he tried to put in stories from the papers always seemed like strangers. Some story people he wouldn't be afraid of if he met them on the road. He thought he liked the David and Joseph stories best of all. "Why you want 'em told over'n over?" his mother had asked so many times. Now, alone on a bed of pine needles, he remembered that he could never answer his mother. He would just wait, and if his mother wasn't sad, with her lips stretched thin, she would stop humming and tell about David the boy, or King David. If she felt good and started long enough before bedtime, he would hear about Joseph the slave-boy, Joseph in prison, Joseph the dreamer, and Joseph the Big Man in Egypt. And when she had finished all about Joseph, she would say "Ain't no earthly power can make a story end as pretty as Joseph's; 'twas the Lord."

The boy listened to the wind passing through the tops of the tall pines; he thought they moved like giant brooms sweeping the sky. The moonlight raced down through the broken spaces of swaying trees and sent bright shafts of light along the ground and over him. The voice of the wind in the pines reminded him of one of the stories his mother had told him about King David. The Lord had said to David that when he heard the wind moving in the tops of the cedar trees, he would know that the Lord was fighting on his side and he would win. When David moved his army around into the hills to attack his enemy, he heard the mighty roar of the wind moving in the tops of the trees, and he cried out to his men that the Lord was moving above them into battle.

The boy listened to the wind. He could hear the mighty roaring. He thought he heard the voice of David and the tramping of many feet. He wasn't afraid with David near. He thought he saw a lantern moving far off in the woods, and as he fell asleep he thought he heard the deep, ringing voice of Sounder rising out of his great throat, riding the mist of the lowlands.

WHEN THE BOY came home after each long trip in search of his father, the crippled coon hound would hobble far down the road to meet him, wag his tail, stand on his hind legs, and paw the boy with his good front paw. But never a sound beyond a deep whine came from him. The bits of news he might bring home his mother received in silence. Someone had heard that his father was moved. Someone had been in the same work gang

VII

with his father for four months last summer on the Walker county road. When she had heard all he had heard, she would say "There's patience, child, and waitin' that's got to be."

Word drifted back that there had been a terrible dynamite blast in one of the quarries that had killed twelve convicts and wounded several others. His mother had had the people read her the story from their newspapers when she carried the laundry. None of the prisoners killed was the boy's father.

The months and seasons of searching dragged into years. The boy helped his mother carry more and more baskets of laundry to and from the big houses; the clotheslines grew longer and longer. The other children, except for the littlest, could fetch and tote too, but they didn't like to go by themselves.

"Time is passing" the woman would say. "I wish you wouldn't go lookin', child." But when one of the field hands had heard something or when somebody said that a road camp was moving, she would wrap a piece of bread and meat for the boy to eat on the way and say nothing. Looking back from far down the road, the boy would see her watching at the edge of the porch. She seemed to understand the compulsion that started him on each long, fruitless journey with new hope.

Once the boy waited outside the tall wire fence of a road camp. Some convicts were whitewashing stones along the edge of a pathway that came toward the gate near where he stood. One might be his father, he thought. He could not tell until they got closer, for they crawled on their hands and knees as they bent over the stones. He leaned against the fence and hooked his fingers through the wire. If none of them was his father, they might know something anyway, he thought. He wished they would stand up and walk from one stone to the next. Then he would know his father easily by his walk. He could still remember the sound of his footsteps approaching the cabin after dark, the easy roll of the never-hurrying step that was the same when he went to work in the morning and when he came home from the long day in the fields. The boy had even been able to tell his father's walk by the swing of the lantern at his side. But none of the men whitewashing the round rocks that lined the path stood up and walked. They crawled the few feet from stone to stone, and crawling, they all looked the same.

Suddenly something crashed against the fence in front of the boy's face. A jagged piece of iron tore open the skin and crushed the fingers of one of his hands against the fence. Lost in thought and watching the convicts, the boy had not seen the guard, who had been sitting under a tree with a shotgun across his knees, get up and come to a toolbox filled with picks and crowbars which stood near the fence.

The piece of iron lay on the inside of the fence at the boy's feet. Drops of blood from his fingers dripped down the fence from wire to wire and fell on the ground. The boy pulled his fingers away from the wire mesh and began to suck on them to stop the throbbing. Tears ran down over his face and mixed with the blood on his hand. Little rivulets of blood and water ran down his arm and dropped off the end of his elbow.

The guard was swaying back and forth with laughter. His gun lay on the lid of the open toolbox. His arms swung in apelike gyrations of glee, and he held another piece of iron in one hand and his cap in the other. A white strip of forehead, where his uniform cap kept off the sun, shone between his brown hair and his sunburned face. His laughter had burst the button from his tieless shirt collar, and a white strip outlined his gaunt neck. For a second he reminded the boy of a garden scarecrow blowing in the wind, body and head of brown burlap stuffed with straw, the head tied on with a white rag just like the white band around the guard's neck, the head tilting from side to side, inviting a well-placed stone to send it bouncing along a bean row.

The men whitewashing the rocks made no sounds. No one among them suddenly raised himself to the height of a man almost as tall as a cabin porch post.

"He ain't there," the boy murmured to himself. If he was, the boy knew, by now he would be holding the scarecrow of a man in the air with one hand clamped all the way around the white strip on the skinny neck, the way he had seen Sounder clamp his great jaws on a weasel once, with the head stuck out one side of the jaws and the body the other. And the man would wheeze and squirm like the weasel had. His legs would paw the air in circles like his hands, then he would go limp, and the boy's father would loosen his grip, and the man in the brown uniform would fall in a heap, like when somebody untied the white rag that held the scarecrow to the stake. And the heap would roll down the slope and lodge against the fence, like the scarecrow rolled along a bean row until it caught in the brambles at the edge of the garden.

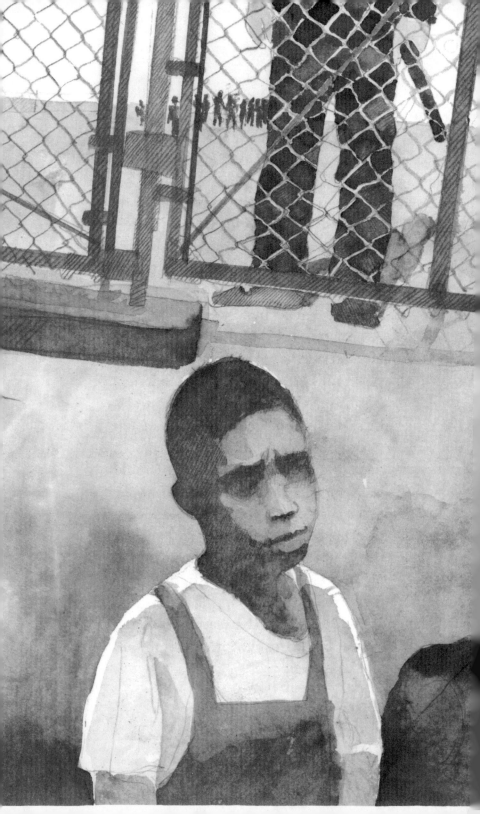

Feeling defeat in the midst of his glee because the boy had not run but stood still and defiant, sucking the blood from his bruised fingers, the guard stopped laughing and yelled at him, "That'll show you, boy! Git! And git fast!" The boy turned and, without looking back, began to walk slowly away. The guard began to laugh again and threw the scrap of iron over the fence. It landed a few feet from the boy. He looked at the iron and he looked at the man. The white spot between his hair and his eyes was the spot. The iron would split it open with a wide gash, and blood would darken the white spot and make it the color of the man's sunburned face. And the stone that David slung struck Goliath on his forehead; the stone sank into his forehead, and he fell on his face on the ground, the boy thought. But he left the iron on the ground.

Still sucking his fingers, the boy looked once more at the men whitewashing the stones. They were almost at the gate. He didn't need to wait and ask. His father was not crawling among them.

*　　　*　　　*

Later that day, passing along a street in a strange and lonely town, he saw a man dump a

89

box of trash into a barrel. He noticed that a large brown-backed book went in with the trash. He waited until the man went back into the building and then took the book from the barrel. It was a book of stories about what people think. There were titles such as Cruelty, Excellent Men, Education, Cripples, Justice, and many others. The boy sat down, leaned back against the barrel, and began to read from the story called Cruelty.

> I have often heard it said that cowardice is the mother of cruelty, and I have found by experience that malicious and inhuman animosity and fierceness are usually accompanied by weakness. Wolves and filthy bears, and all the baser beasts, fall upon the dying.

The boy was trying to read aloud, for he could understand better if he heard the words. But now he stopped. He did not understand what it said; the words were too new and strange. He was sad. He thought books would have words like the ones he had learned to read in the store signs, words like his mother used when she told him stories of the Lord and Joseph and David. All his life he had wanted a book. Now he held one in his hands, and it was only making his bruised fingers hurt more. He would carry it with him anyway.

90

He passed a large brick schoolhouse with big windows and children climbing on little ladders and swinging on swings. No one jeered at him or noticed him because he had crossed the street and was walking close up against the hedge on the other side. Soon the painted houses ran out, and he was walking past unpainted cabins. He always felt better on his travels when he came to the part of town where the unpainted cabins were. Sometimes people came out on the porch when he passed and talked to him. Sometimes they gave him a piece to eat on the way. Now he thought they might laugh and say "What you carryin', child? A book?" So he held it close up against him.

"That's a school too," the boy said to himself as he stood facing a small unpainted building with its door at the end instead of the side, the way cabin doors were. Besides, he could always tell a school because it had more windows than a cabin.

At the side of the building two children were sloshing water out of a tin pail near a hand pump. One threw a dipper of water on a dog that came from underneath to bark at the boy. The school was built on posts, and a stovepipe came through the wall and stuck up above the rafters. A rusty tin pipe ran from the corner of the roof down to the cistern where the children were playing.

The dog had gone back under the building, so the boy entered the yard and moved toward the children. If one of them would work the pump handle, he could wash the dried blood off his hand. Just when he reached the cistern, a wild commotion of barking burst from under the floor of the school. Half a dozen dogs, which followed children to school and waited patiently for lunchtime scraps and for school to be over, burst from under the building in pursuit of a pig that had wandered onto the lot. In the wild chase around the building the biggest dog struck the tin drainpipe, and it clattered down the wall and bounced on the cement top of the cistern. With a pig under the building and the dogs barking and racing in and out, the school day ended.

Two dozen or more children raced out the door, few of them touching the three steps that led from the stoop to the ground. Some were calling the names of dogs and looking under the building. The boy found himself surrounded by strange inquiring eyes. Questions came too fast to answer. "You new here?" "Where you moved to?" "That your book?" "You comin' here to school?" "Kin you read that big a book?" The boy had put his bruised hand into his pocket so no one could see it. Some of the children carried books too, but none were as big as the one he held close against his side.

Just when the commotion was quieting down, a man appeared at the schoolhouse door. The children scattered across the lot in four directions. "Tell your pa that he must keep his pig in the pen," he called to one child.

Then it was quiet. The boy looked at the man in the doorway. They were alone now. The dogs had followed the children. And the pig, hearing a familiar call from the corner of the lot, had come grunting from his sanctuary and gone in the direction of the call.

In his many journeyings among strangers the boy had learned to sniff out danger and spot orneriness quickly. Now, for the first time in his life away from home, he wasn't feared. The lean elderly man with snow-white hair, wearing Sunday clothes, came down the steps. "This pipe is always falling," he said as he picked it up and put it back in place. "I need to wire it up."

"I just wanted to wash my hand. It's got dried blood on it where I hurt my fingers."

"You should have run home."

"I don't live in these parts."

"Here, I'll hold your book, and I'll pump for you." And the mellow eyes of the man began to search the boy for answers, answers that could be found without asking questions.

"We need warm soapy water," the teacher said. "I live right close. Wait 'til I get my papers and lock the door, and I'll take you home and fix it."

The boy wanted to follow the man into the schoolhouse and see what it was like inside, but by the time he got to the steps the man was back again, locking the door. "I usually put the school in order after the children leave," he said, "but I'll do it in the morning before they get here."

At the edge of the school lot the man took the road that led away from the town. They walked without much talk, and the boy began to wish the man would ask him a lot of questions. When they had passed several cabins, each farther from the other as they went, the man turned off the road and said, "We're home. I live here alone. Have lived alone for a long time." Fingering the small wire hook on the neatly whitewashed gate which led into a yard that was green, the teacher stopped talking.

A cabin with a gate and green grass in the yard is almost a big house, the boy thought as he followed the man.

Inside the gate the man went along the fence,

94

studying some plants tied up to stakes. He began to talk again, not to the boy, but to a plant that was smaller than the others. "You'll make it, little one, but it'll take time to get your roots set again."

The boy looked at the white-haired old man leaning over like he was listening for the plant to answer him. "He's conjured," the boy whispered to himself. "Lots of old folks is conjured or addled." He moved backward to the gate, thinking he'd better run away. "Conjured folks can conjure you," the boy's mother always said, "if you get yourself plain carried off by their soft spell-talk."

But before the boy could trouble his mind anymore, the man straightened up and began talking to him. "Some animal dug under the roots and tore them loose from the earth. It was wilted badly and might have died. But I reset it, and I water it every day. It's hard to reset a plant if it's wilted too much; the life has gone out of it. But this one will be all right. I see new leaves startin'."

"What grows on it?" the boy asked, thinking it must be something good to eat if somebody cared that much about a plant.

"It's only a flower," the man said. "I'll water it when the earth has cooled a little. If you water a plant when the earth is too warm, it shocks the roots."

Inside the cabin the man started a fire in the cookstove and heated water. As he washed the boy's hand with a soft white rag he said, "You musta slammed these fingers in a awful heavy door or gate." Before the boy could answer, the teacher began to talk about the plant he must remember to water.

He don't wanta know nothin' about me, the boy thought.

"When I saw your book, I thought you were coming to enroll for school. But you don't live in these parts, you say."

"I found the book in a trash barrel. It has words like I ain't used to readin'. I can read store-sign words and some newspaper words."

"This is a wonderful book," said the teacher. "It was written by a man named Montaigne, who was a soldier. But he grew tired of being a soldier and spent his time studying and writing. He also liked to walk on country roads."

The teacher lit two lamps. The boy had never seen two lamps burning in the same room. They made the room as bright as daylight.

"People should read his writings," the man continued. "But few do. He is all but forgotten." But the boy did not hear. He was thinking of a cabin that had two lamps, both lit at the same time, and

96

two stoves, one to cook on and one to warm by. The man sat in a chair between two tables that held the lamps. There were books on the tables too, and there were shelves filled not with pans and dishes, but with books. The mellow eyes of the man followed the boy's puzzled glances as they studied the strange warm world in which he had suddenly found himself.

"I will read you a little story from your book." The boy watched as the fingers of the man turned the pages one way and then the other until he found what he wanted to read.

"This is a very short story about a king named Cyrus, who wanted to buy the prize horse that belonged to one of his soldiers. Cyrus asked him how much he would sell the horse for, or whether he would exchange him for a kingdom. The soldier said he would not sell his prize horse and he would not exchange him for a kingdom, but that he would willingly give up his horse to gain a friend. . . . But now I have told you the whole story so there's no use for me to read it."

"You've been a powerful good friend to take me in like this," the boy said at last. "My fingers don't hurt no more."

"I am your friend," said the man. "So while I heat some water to soak your hand and make your cot for the night, you tell me all about yourself."

"I had a father and a dog named Sounder," the boy began. . . .

"WHO'S BEEN KINDLY to your hurts?" the boy's mother asked as she looked down at the clean white rags that bandaged the boy's fingers. Rocking on the porch, she had seen the white dot swinging back and forth in the sun when the boy wasn't much more than a moving spot far down the road. "For a while I wasn't sure it was you," she said. "Why you walkin' fast? You done found him? Is your hand hurt bad? Is that a Bible some-

VIII

99

body's done mistreated?" The woman's eyes had come to rest on the book the boy held in his good hand.

"No. It's a book. I found it in a trash can."

"Be careful what you carry off, child," his mother said. "It can cause a heap o' trouble."

"I got somethin' to tell," the boy said as he sat down on the edge of the porch and ran his bandaged fingers over the head of the great coon dog who had stopped his jumping and whining and lay at the boy's feet with his head cocked to the side, looking up with his one eye. The younger children sat in a line beside the boy, waiting to hear.

"Is he poorly?" the woman asked slowly. "Is he far?"

"It's about somethin' else," the boy said after a long spell of quiet. "I ain't found him yet."

The boy told his mother and the children about his night in the teacher's cabin. The teacher wanted him to come back and go to school. He had been asked to live in the teacher's cabin and do his chores. The children's eyes widened when they heard the cabin had two lamps, two stoves, and grass growing in a yard with a fence and a gate. He told how the teacher could read and that there were lots of books on shelves in the cabin.

100

"Maybe he will write letters to the road camps for you," the mother said, " 'cause you'll be so busy with schoolin' and cleanin' the schoolhouse for him that you can't go searchin' no more."

"Maybe I'd have time," the boy said. "But he says like you, 'Better not to go. Just be patient and time will pass.' "

"It's all powerful puzzlin' and aggravatin', but it's the Lord's will." The boy noticed that his mother had stopped rocking; the loose boards did not rattle as the chair moved on them.

"The teacher said he'd walk all the way and reason about it if you didn't want me to come to him. You don't want me to go, but I'll come home often as I can. And sometime I might bring word."

"It's a sign; I believes in signs." The rocker began to move back and forth, rattling the loose boards in the porch floor. "Go child. The Lord has come to you."

*   *   *

When he returned to the cabin with books on the shelves and the kind man with the white hair and the gentle voice, all the boy carried was his book with one cover missing—the book that he couldn't understand. In the summers he came home to take his father's place in the fields, for cabin rent had to be paid with field work. In the winter he seldom came because it took "more'n a day's walkin' and sleepin' on the ground."

"Ain't worth it" his mother would say.

Each year, after he had been gone for a whole winter and returned, the faithful Sounder would come hobbling on three legs far down the road to meet him. The great dog would wag his tail and whine. He never barked. The boy sang at his work in the fields, and his mother rocked in her chair and sang on the porch of the cabin. Sometimes when Sounder scratched fleas under the porch, she would look at the hunting lantern and the empty possum sack hanging against the wall. Six crops of persimmons and wild grapes had ripened. The possums and raccoons had gathered them unmolested. The lantern and possum sack hung untouched. "No use to nobody no more," the woman said.

The boy read to his brother and sisters when he had finished his day in the fields. He read the story of Joseph over and over and never wearied of it. "In all the books in the teacher's cabin, there's no story as good as Joseph's story" he would say to them.

The woman, listening and rocking, would say "The Lord has come to you, child. The Lord has certainly come to you."

Late one August afternoon the boy and his mother sat on the shaded corner of the porch. The heat and drought of dog days had parched the earth, and the crops had been laid by. The boy had come home early because there was nothing to do in the fields.

"Dog days is a terrible time," the woman said. "It's when the heat is so bad the dogs go mad." The boy would not tell her that the teacher had told him that dog days got their name from the Dog Star because it rose and set with the sun during that period. She had her own feeling for the earth, he thought, and he would not confuse it.

"It sure is hot," he said instead. "Lucky to come from the fields early." He watched the heat waves as they made the earth look like it was moving in little ripples.

Sounder came around the corner of the cabin from somewhere, hobbled back and forth as far as the road several times, and then went to his cool spot under the porch. "That's what I say about dog days," the woman said. "Poor creature's been addled with the heat for three days. Can't find no place to quiet down. Been down the road

103

nearly out o' sight a second time today, and now he musta come from the fencerows. Whines all the time. A mad dog is a fearful sight. Slobberin' at the mouth and runnin' every which way 'cause they're blind. Have to shoot 'em 'fore they bite some child. It's awful hard."

"Sounder won't go mad," the boy said. "He's lookin' for a cooler spot, I reckon."

A lone figure came on the landscape as a speck and slowly grew into a ripply form through the heat waves. "Scorchin' to be walkin' and totin' far today," she said as she pointed to the figure on the road.

A catbird fussed in the wilted lilac at the corner of the cabin. "Why's that bird fussin' when no cat's prowlin? Old folks has a sayin' that if a catbird fusses 'bout nothin', somethin' bad is comin'. It's a bad sign."

"Sounder, I reckon," the boy said. "He just passed her bush when he came around the cabin."

In the tall locust at the edge of the fence, its top leaves yellowed from lack of water, a mockingbird mimicked the catbird with half a dozen notes, decided it was too hot to sing, and disappeared. The great coon dog, whose rhythmic panting came through the porch floor, came from under the house and began to whine.

104

As the figure on the road drew near, it took shape and grew indistinct again in the wavering heat. Sometimes it seemed to be a person dragging something, for little puffs of red dust rose in sulfurous clouds at every other step. Once or twice they thought it might be a brown cow or mule, dragging its hooves in the sand and raising and lowering its weary head.

Sounder panted faster, wagged his tail, whined, moved from the dooryard to the porch and back to the dooryard.

The figure came closer. Now it appeared to be a child carrying something on its back and limping.

"The children still at the creek?" she asked.

"Yes, but it's about dry."

Suddenly the voice of the great coon hound broke the sultry August deadness. The dog dashed along the road, leaving three-pointed clouds of red dust to settle back to earth behind him. The mighty voice rolled out upon the valley, each flutelike bark echoing from slope to slope.

"Lord's mercy! Dog days done made him mad." And the rocker was still.

Sounder was a young dog again. His voice was the same mellow sound that had ridden the November breeze from the lowlands to the hills. The boy and his mother looked at each other. The cat-

106

bird stopped her fussing in the wilted lilac bush. On three legs, the dog moved with the same lightning speed that had carried him to the throat of a grounded raccoon.

Sounder's master had come home. Taking what might have been measured as a halting half step and then pulling a stiff, dead leg forward, dragging a foot turned sideways in the dust, the man limped into the yard. Sounder seemed to understand that to jump up and put his paw against his master's breast would topple him into the dust, so the great dog smelled and whined and wagged his tail and licked the limp hand dangling at his master's side. He hopped wildly around his master in a circle that almost brought head and tail together.

The head of the man was pulled to the side where a limp arm dangled and where the foot pointed outward as it was dragged through the dust. What had been a shoulder was now pushed up and back to make a one-sided hump so high that the leaning head seemed to rest upon it. The mouth was askew too, and the voice came out of the part farthest away from the withered, wrinkled, lifeless side.

The woman in the still rocker said, "Lord, Lord," and sat suffocated in shock.

"Sounder knew it was you just like you was comin' home from work," the boy said in a clear voice.

Half the voice of the man was gone too, so in slow, measured, stuttering he told how he had been caught in a dynamite blast in the prison quarry, how the dead side had been crushed under an avalanche of limestone, and how he had been missed for a whole night in the search for dead and wounded. He told how the pain of the crushing stone had stopped in the night, how doctors had pushed and pulled and encased the numb side of his body in a cast, how they had spoken kindly to him and told him he would die. But he resolved he would not die, even with a half-dead body, because he wanted to come home again.

"For being hurt, they let me have time off my sentence," the man said, "and since I couldn't work, I guess they was glad to."

"The Lord has brought you home," the woman said.

The boy heard faint laughter somewhere behind the cabin. The children were coming home from the creek. He went around the cabin slowly, then hurried to meet them.

"Pa's home," he said and grabbed his sister,

108

who had started to run toward the cabin. "Wait. He's mighty crippled up, so behave like nothin' has happened."

"Can he walk?" the youngest child asked.

"Yes! And don't you ask no questions."

"You been mighty natural and considerate," the mother said to the younger children later when she went to the woodpile and called them to pick dry kindling for a quick fire. When she came back to the porch she said, "We was gonna just have a cold piece 'cause it's so sultry, but now I think I'll cook."

Everything don't change much, the boy thought. There's eatin' and sleepin' and talkin' and settin' that goes on. One day might be different from another, but there ain't much difference when they're put together.

Sometimes there were long quiet spells. Once or twice the boy's mother said to the boy, "He's powerful proud of your learnin'. Read somethin' from the Scriptures." But mostly they just talked about heat and cold, and wind and clouds, and what's gonna be done, and time passing.

As the days of August passed and September brought signs of autumn, the crippled man sat on the porch step and leaned the paralyzed, deformed side of his body against a porch post. This

109

was the only comfortable sitting position he could find. The old coon dog would lie facing his master, with his one eye fixed and his one ear raised. Sometimes he would tap his tail against the earth. Sometimes the ear would droop and the eye would close. Then the great muscles would flex in dreams of the hunt, and the mighty chest would give off the muffled whisper of a bark. Sometimes the two limped together to the edge of the fields, or wandered off into the pine woods. They never went along the road. Perhaps they knew how strange a picture they made when they walked together.

About the middle of September the boy left to go back to his teacher. "It's the most important thing," his mother said.

And the crippled man said, "We're fine. We won't need nothin'."

"I'll come for a few days before it's cold to help gather wood and walnuts."

The broken body of the old man withered more and more, but when the smell of harvest and the hunt came with October, his spirit seemed to quicken his dragging step. One day he cleaned the dusty lantern globe, and the old dog, remembering, bounced on his three legs and wagged his tail as if to say "I'm ready."

The boy had come home. To gather the felled trees and chop the standing dead ones was part of

110

the field pay too. He had been cutting and dragging timber all day.

Sometimes he had looked longingly at the lantern and possum sack, but something inside him had said "Wait. Wait and go together." But the boy did not want to go hunting anymore. And without his saying anything, his father had said, "You're too tired, child. We ain't goin' far, no way."

In the early darkness the halting, hesitant swing of the lantern marked the slow path from fields to pine woods toward the lowlands. The boy stood on the porch, watching until the light was lost behind pine branches. Then he went and sat by the stove. His mother rocked as the mound of kernels grew in the fold of her apron. "He been mighty peart," she said. "I hope he don't fall in the dark. Maybe he'll be happy now he can go hunting again." And she took up her singing where she had left off.

> *Ain't nobody else gonna walk it for you,*
> *You gotta walk it by yourself.*

*   *   *

Sounder's scratching at the door awakened the boy. It was still night, but the first red glow of dawn was rising in a faint crescent over the pine woods.

"Sounder just couldn't poke slow enough for your father," the mother said to the boy as they stood in the doorway, straining and sifting the dark for some movement.

"Lantern wouldn't burn out in this time," the boy said. "No sign of light. He must have fallen or got tired. Sounder will show me."

Sounder was already across the road into the stalk land, whining, moving his head from one side to the other, looking back to be sure that the boy was following.

Across the stalk land, into the pine woods, into the climbing, brightening glow of the dawn, the boy followed the dog, whose anxious pace slowed from age as they went. "By a dog's age, Sounder is past dying time," the boy said half aloud. Fear had always prompted him to talk to himself.

Deep in the pine woods, along a deserted logging road, the boy and dog came to a small open space where there had once been a log ramp. The sun was just beginning to drive its first splinters of light through the pines, bouncing against tree trunks and earth. At the foot of one of the trees the boy's father sat, the lantern still burning by his side.

112

"So tuckered out he fell asleep," the boy said to himself.

But the figure did not move when Sounder licked his hand. The boy put his hand on his father's good shoulder and shook ever so gently. The chin did not lift itself; no eyes turned up to meet the boy. "Tired, so tired."

When the boy returned to the cabin and told his mother, her lips grew long and thin and pale. But when she finally spoke, they were warm and soft as when she sang. "When life is so tiresome, there ain't no peace like the greatest peace—the peace of the Lord's hand holding you. And he'll have a store-bought box for burial 'cause all these years I paid close attention to his burial insurance."

They buried the boy's father in the unfenced lot behind the meetin' house. The preacher stood amid the sumac and running briars before the mound of fresh red earth and read:

> The Lord is my shepherd; I shall not want,
> He maketh me to lie .down in green
> pastures.

* * *

"There's plenty of wood, and I must go back to school," the boy told his mother several days after

113

they had buried his father. "Sounder ain't got no spirit left for living. He hasn't gone with me to the woods to chop since Pa died. He doesn't even whine anymore. He just lies on his coffee sacks under the cabin steps. I've dug a grave for him under the big jack oak tree in the stalk land by the fencerow. It'll be ready if the ground freezes. You can carry him on his coffee sacks and bury him. He'll be gone before I come home again."

And the boy was right. Two weeks before he came home for Christmas, Sounder crawled under the cabin and died. The boy's mother told him all there was to tell.

"He just crawled up under the house and died," she said.

The boy was glad. He had learned to read his book with the torn cover better now. He had read in it: "Only the unwise think that what has changed is dead." He had asked the teacher what it meant, and the teacher had said that if a flower blooms once, it goes on blooming somewhere forever. It blooms on for whoever has seen it blooming. It was not quite clear to the boy then, but it was now.

Years later, walking the earth as a man, it would all sweep back over him, again and again, like an echo on the wind.

114

The pine trees would look down forever on a lantern burning out of oil but not going out. A harvest moon would cast shadows forever of a man walking upright, his dog bouncing after him. And the quiet of the night would fill and echo again with the deep voice of Sounder, the great coon dog.

Savage Sam

SAVAGE SAM

by

FRED GIPSON

Decorations by Carl Burger

1817

HARPER & ROW, PUBLISHERS
New York, Hagerstown, San Francisco, London

This book I dedicate to some mighty loyal and faithful companions—every hogdog, cowdog, trailhound and flea-infested kitchen-robbing potlicker mongrel who helped to make a Big Adventure of my childhood.

Fred Gipson
Mason, Texas

Savage Sam

Sam

One

THIS is a tale about a dog we called Savage Sam. It's
partly about me, too, and about Papa and Little Arliss
and a girl named Lisbeth Searcy and some others. But it's
mainly about Sam, on account of without him, there
wouldn't have been much of a tale to tell or anybody left
to tell it.

Sam's papa was Old Yeller, known as the best catch dog
and the worst camp robber in all our part of the Texas
hill country. His mama was a blue-tick trail hound be-

longing to Lisbeth's grandpa, Bud Searcy, a blowhard neighbor of ours who lived over in the Salt Licks settlement.

Sam was born in a badger hole and given to us by Lisbeth.

Papa was the one who named him Savage Sam. He did it as a joke. This was back when Sam was still just an old clumsy, big-footed, rump-sprung pup, sort of liver-speckled, with flop-hound ears, a stub tail and a pot belly that was all appetite.

I remember when Papa did it. Mama had set a panful of table scraps out in the yard for Sam. Greedy as always, Sam was gulping those scraps down like he couldn't wait. Papa stood watching him. Finally, his eyes started twinkling and he went to pulling at one horn of his long black mustache.

"It appears to me," he said, speaking extra sober, "that when it comes to tackling a wheat-flour biscuit or a chunk of roast venison, we own about the most savage dog in the State of Texas!"

This set us all to laughing; and after that, we started calling Sam "Savage Sam."

As it turned out, the name wasn't a bad fit. For Sam would fight. Even as a pup, he'd fight. He had that much of Old Yeller in him.

You couldn't count all the battles he used to pull off with the passel of house cats that always followed Little Arliss to the cowpen at milking time.

Little Arliss was my brother. He was about six then, and just learning to milk. He wasn't doing a bad job of it, either, except that he got so little milk in the bucket. Most of it he squirted into the open mouths of the mewing cats. It tickled him to angle the milk streams so high above their heads that the cats had to rear up on their hind legs and prance around, trying to reach it.

Then here would come Sam, wanting his share of the milk. This always made the cats mad. They'd jump on him, clawing and squawling. And while Sam couldn't whip them yet, still, he had the grit to stand his ground and make a fight of it.

I'd hear the commotion and come running, yelling at Arliss to quit fooling with them cats and get the milking done. Arliss, he'd yell back, telling me to shut my mouth and let him alone. And when I didn't, he was just as liable as not to pitch his milk bucket into the cowpen dirt and grab up a rock to throw at me.

Being about fifteen at the time and considered too big to fight back, I'd have to skin out for the house, hollering for help. Then here would come Mama, calling for Arliss to behave himself before she took a mesquite sprout to him. Behind her would come Papa, ready to back up her threat, if need be, but always laughing his head off at the general all-round hullabaloo.

Well, anyhow, Sam still wasn't much more than a big overgrown pup, maybe eighteen months old, when this bad trouble hit us.

It was in the first days of September in 1870 or '71; I disremember which.

I do recollect that me and Papa had just finished grubbing brush off a patch of new ground we planned to break and sow to winter wheat. It was nearly dinnertime. We shouldered our grubbing tools and packed them off to the cabin.

We were hot and thirsty and tired. We drank half the water in the brassbound cedar bucket hanging by a chain from a pole rafter in the dog run. We sat down in cowhide-bottomed chairs and leaned back against the walls. We let the south breeze blow against our sweaty clothes, drying them out and cooling us off. We yanked out the spines of prickly pear and tasajillo cactus that had our britches pinned to our legs.

Mama came out to sit with us while she churned a batch of sour cream, hoping to get fresh butter by the time the cornbread browned for dinner.

We'd all just got good settled when we heard a sound that jerked us to our feet. It was the clatter of horse hoofs coming at a dead run along the trail that led beside Birdsong Creek.

We stepped out into the clear. We shaded our eyes with our hands to break the blinding glare of the sunlight, and looked down the slope toward the spring where we got our drinking water.

Giant live oaks, cottonwoods, and bur oaks grew beside the spring. Mustang-grape vines drooped from their branches. Trees and vines laid down such a black shade that it was hard to see anything under them. Then I caught a flash of movement and Papa said, "Why, it's old Blowhard Bud, himself! Wonder what sort of bur he's got under his tail this time."

We stood and waited till Bud Searcy came galloping

out of the shade, spurring his crowbait horse into a final sprint up the slant toward our cabin. Riding behind him, holding to the cantle of the saddle, was Lisbeth.

The second they rode into the sunlight, I knew something was wrong. I could tell by the long-barreled shotgun Searcy packed across his saddle bow. I could tell by the six-shooter and bowie knife that hung from a leather belt he wore around his fat belly. Mostly, I could tell by the way Searcy rode, with his head held high and jerking from one side to the other like an old steer scenting blood.

Then he was sliding his jaded horse to a stop at our front-yard gate and fixing us all with a wild, fierce stare.

"*Injuns!*" he shouted. "Raiding all over the country!"

Mama gasped. I felt a little cold snake of fear go wiggling along my backbone and noticed how Papa suddenly stiffened.

"Indians?" Papa said. "Where? At Salt Licks?"

"No," Searcy said. "At Loyal Valley. Run off a bunch of horses there last night!" He turned to Lisbeth and said in a calmer voice, "Slip down, honey. This old pony, he's a mite winded."

The pony was worse than winded. He'd been run clear off his feet. He stood now with his head down and his forefeet spraddled. He sucked for air in great gasps. His flanks quivered. Sweat ran in little rivers down the insides of his hind legs, wetting the red sand.

"Who saw them?" Papa asked.

Lisbeth slid from the horse's rump to the ground. She straightened and smoothed down the skirt of her dress. She was maybe thirteen, with long blond hair and big solemn

[5]

brown eyes that looked at you in a way that always made you feel bashful and awkward.

She looked at me now. I squirmed and looked away toward Mama. I took notice of how white-faced and anxious Mama looked, how she kept wiping her hands on her cooking apron, when they weren't even wet.

"Why, nobody, I reckon," Searcy answered. He pressed forked fingers against his lips and spat tobacco juice into the sand. "Best I could learn, the horses turned up missing at daylight this morning. Fourteen head, belonging to a feller named Buschwaldt." He heaved himself down out of the saddle.

Papa said, "Missing horses don't have to mean Indians. Horses can stray."

"Not them horses," Searcy said. "Buschwaldt said Injuns got 'em. Told Tom McDougal they did. Tom, he said it sounded like Injuns to him. And you know Tom ain't a man to lie—lessen maybe they's a little money involved."

He turned and handed his bridle reins to Lisbeth.

"Here, honey," he said. "Better go water this old pony. Might shuck him out a few ears of corn, too, while you're at it. Build back his strength to pack us home."

Lisbeth turned to lead the horse off to water. I felt a great relief. Searcy's Indian story didn't sound like much to me. I figured I knew now what he was up to. Searcy made a practice of riding around, peddling tall-tale news. And the price you paid for hearing it was generally a big hearty meal for him and a feed for his horse.

I guess Papa was thinking the same thing, for he looked relieved, too. But Mama didn't.

[6]

"Where's Little Arliss?" she said in a tight voice.

"Off in the hills somewhere," I told her. "Him and Sam. Heard Sam on the trail of a varmint not thirty minutes ago."

"Go get him," she said sharply.

I looked into her anxious eyes, then toward Papa. Papa seemed dubious, but nodded his head. "Might be better you did, son," he said. "Till we can get the straight of this."

I turned and headed for the corral to saddle a horse. I was too worn out from brush grubbing to trample all over the hills in the hot sun, hunting Arliss afoot. Behind me, I heard the hurt and anger in Searcy's voice as he flared up at Papa.

"Git the straight of it!" he said hotly. "Well, I'll just tell you a thing, Jim Coates. If you've got a defenseless youngun foot-loose in the hills, the chances are, them murdering hostiles has done ketched and sculped him!"

I wished he'd shut up. That sort of scare talk was sure to upset Mama; and I was willing to bet there wasn't a lick of truth in it. But hushing up Bud Searcy was like trying to stop dry leaves from rattling in a high wind. The way he kept his tongue wagging, you'd think it was hinged in the middle and loose at both ends. What talking time he'd lose from now till Mama called us to dinner would be just enough to spit tobacco juice all over the white creek sand we kept spread in the dog run between the two rooms of our cabin. And once at the table, he'd eat and talk till the last scrap of food was gone. After that, he'd go back to talking and spitting more tobacco juice till

[7]

along in the cool of the evening, when maybe he'd finally saddle up and ride off home, acting like he'd done a big favor by paying us a visit.

My roan horse, Blue, nickered a welcome as I pushed open the corral gate. Our plow mule, Jumper, though, he wheeled and raced to the far side of the corral. There he stood, snorting and stomping the ground with his forefeet, eying me like I was a colt-eating Mexican lion. Jumper was seventeen or eighteen years old, but he did his best to act like he was still the wildest bronc mule that ever jumped from under a set of harness.

In some ways, Jumper had a lot in common with old man Searcy.

I caught Blue and pitched a saddle on him. I was just cinching up the girth when Lisbeth led her grandpa's sweat-lathered pony into the corral.

"Could I go with you, Travis?" she asked.

"Not on that run-down pony," I said. "He's still shaking with the weak trembles."

"I know," Lisbeth said. "But—"

She broke off there without finishing. She stood waiting while I jerked loose the cinch and dragged the saddle from the back of her grandpa's pony. I stripped the bridle over his ears and the bits out of his mouth. Then I turned to the log crib to shuck out some corn for him.

"And that blue roan of mine," I added over my shoulder. "I'm not right sure he's safe to ride double."

Actually, Blue would pack double without turning a hair. But I didn't mind having Lisbeth think the horse I rode was about half dangerous.

She didn't say anything. I looked up from my corn-shucking, and the disappointment in her eyes was plain.

I recollected how I'd hurt Lisbeth's feelings the time she'd brought the six-weeks-old Sam to me as a present. That was when me and Old Yeller had got cut up so bad by a bunch of range hogs. And what with still having a grown dog at the time, I'd told Lisbeth I was too sick to be pestered with a pup right then. So she'd given Sam to Little Arliss and gone off and had herself a good cry about it.

Mama, she learned what I'd done and hopped all over me, fussy as a wet hen, telling me I ought to be ashamed, telling me what a nice, sweet-natured little girl Lisbeth was and how she just worshiped the very ground I walked on. And while I wasn't interested in having anybody worship the ground I walked on, I did, after thinking on it a spell, come to see that Mama was right. When you got down to scratch, you had to admit that—for a girl—Lisbeth was just about as fine a person as you could expect to come across in a week's ride.

Now, looking at her, all of a sudden I wanted to take her along.

"Look," I said. "Old Jumper, he won't let your pony eat without trying to rob him. Why don't I just saddle him for you to ride?"

Her eyes lit up. "That'll be fine," she said. "Only, don't bother with a saddle. I'm used to riding bareback."

So I went and tied a catch rope around Jumper's neck. I held down a hand for Lisbeth to step into and boosted her up astride Jumper. I looped a noose of the rope around

Jumper's nose, handed the slack end up to her for a guide rein, and she was all fixed. I fed Searcy's pony in a hollow log Papa had split open and made into a feed trough. Then I mounted Blue and we rode out into the hills to search for Little Arliss.

Our part of Texas was a rough country of brushy hogback ridges and rock-bench slopes, with wide mesquite flats and deep-cut canyons and tight little valleys studded with great gnarled live oaks. Willows, pecans, elms, and cottonwoods lined the watercourses.

It was also a country where the weather was generally too hot or too cold, too wet or too dry. But this year had been one of the rare good ones, when the summer rains came heavy and regular, so that now the bluestem grass covered the ground like the shaggy pelt of some huge animal. It stood tall and green as a wheat field, clear to the tops of the highest ridges. The hot sunlight put a glimmer and sheen on the blades as they bowed before the running wind waves.

Ripe prickly-pear apples shone red through the tossing grass. Cenizo bloomed lavendar. And snow-white against the green of the grass drooped long, top-heavy sprays of flowering bee myrtle, filling the air with their sharp, clean fragrance.

Wild bees hummed about the flowers, and I was just recollecting the last bee tree me and Papa had cut when Lisbeth goosed Jumper up beside me.

"Travis," she asked, "you think Grandpa is right? About the Indians, I mean?"

Knowing what a windbag her grandpa was, it would have crowded me to believe there was an Indian in the country if I'd caught one chasing him. Still, I couldn't hardly say that to Lisbeth. So I said, "I don't much think so. Been a long time since Indians raided in these parts. Eight or nine years, best I remember."

Her eyes widened. "You can remember?" she asked.

I could remember, all right. It stuck in my mind like a bad dream you sometimes get after eating a bait of fried hog liver for supper.

. . . Me, lying belly-flat on the puncheon floor under the bed where Papa had shoved me . . . Listening to the thundering reports of the rifles inside and outside the cabin . . . to the hysterical baying of our watchdogs . . . to the scared bawling of the milk cows and their calves . . . to the snorting and whistling of the horses in the corral . . . to the unearthly screeches of the attacking Comanches . . . to the splintering crash of wood, as arrows and rifle balls slammed into the thick logs of our cabin walls . . . to that terrible, lonesome cry of spent bullets wailing off into the brush . . . to the quick footsteps of Papa and old man Mercer and his harelipped boy Dude as they hurried from the porthole windows to hand Mama their empty guns and grab up the ones she'd just reloaded.

Me, lying there, hearing it all and seeing nothing . . . Till, finally, the harelipped boy staggered backward, circled, stumbled against the bed, and went down . . . where I watched his heels drum against the floor boards as he died.

[11]

It was no trouble to remember. None at all. But the telling wasn't so easy; and I don't guess I made much of a job of it, because when I got through, all Lisbeth could think of to say was, "Wasn't you scared?"

I told her that I guessed I was—some—but I was quick to point out that I was about the size of Little Arliss at the time, and added that I didn't reckon I'd be so scared now.

"Well, I'd a-been scared," Lisbeth said. "Just pure-dee scared to death!"

Lisbeth's grandpa held the reputation of being the biggest liar in the country. On the other hand, Lisbeth was so open and honest about everything that sometimes she put you to shame.

We rode quiet up a long slant, topped out a high rise, and Lisbeth pulled Jumper to a stop.

"Listen!" she said. "I believe I hear Sam."

I stopped and listened. Sure enough, from across the next rise, I caught the ringing trail cry of Savage Sam. From the sound of it, Sam was driving hard, telling the whole wide world that he had some varmint on the run and was taking it yonder.

This was the main difference between Sam and his papa. Old Yeller had been the worst thief, the biggest glutton, the fiercest fighter, and the greatest old fraud you ever saw. To some extent, Sam had inherited all these traits; but from his mama, he had come up with one thing extra. From his eyes on out to the tip end of his muzzle, Sam was every inch a trail hound. He had a nose on him that wouldn't quit. At the age of seven months, he was done treeing squirrels for Little Arliss, who had to knock them out with rocks because Papa wouldn't let him pack a gun.

By the time Sam was a year old, he'd pick up the trail of a fox or coon and hang it for a two- and three-hour stretch. And always behind him chased Little Arliss, yelling encouragement, just as eager as Sam to bring the varmint to bay, where he'd join in the rowdy battle that was sure to follow.

"Just listen to him," Lisbeth said. "Hasn't he got the prettiest sounding voice? Prettier even than his mama."

Sam had that, all right. Let him open on a trail, and you couldn't keep from listening. High-pitched and far-reaching, his voice held some special quality that left the bell pure notes ringing strong in your ears long after you knew Sam had to be clear out of hearing distance.

Time and again, I'd caught myself stopping whatever work I was doing, just to stand and listen to the sweet wild call of that old pup's trail cry. If Papa happened to be working with me, I noticed that he always stopped to listen, too. Then, pretty soon, he'd grin and shake his head and say, "Savage Sam and Little Arliss! Now, ain't that a pair for you? Wilder than a couple of thicket-raised shoats!"

Then we'd go back to work, maybe hoeing careless weeds out of the young corn. And the hot sun would burn down on my back and the sweat would drip from under my hatbrim, stinging my eyes with salt, and I'd get tired and feel the hoe handle raising a blister inside my hand and get to wishing that Sam would lose his trail and shut up, so I wouldn't have to listen to him and be reminded of how much fun him and Little Arliss were having while I was stuck there in the field, practically working myself to death.

And never once did it enter my head that a time would come when I'd be listening for that wild trail cry of Sam's, clinging to it like it was the last shred of hope left in a world of complete despair.

Travis

Two

WE rode toward Sam's voice. We crossed a wide draw where the grass grew so tall I could touch it with my hand from where I sat in the saddle.

We jumped a little bunch of deer and watched them go racing through the grass with their white tails flared. One was a buck with a spread of antlers the size of a rocking chair—and I hadn't thought to pack along a gun.

We reached the top of the next rise overlooking a deep-cut canyon and pulled up to listen. For a second, we

[15]

thought we heard Sam's voice. We hunted a break in the wall till we found where a cow trail twisted down through the brush. We followed the trail. It got steeper and rougher the further we went. The brush dragged and rattled against our legs. And what with Blue and Jumper slipping and having to rump-slide down the steepest places, kicking up loose rocks that came clattering down the trail after us, we stirred up a considerable racket and some dust.

Down at the bottom, we stopped to let Blue and Jumper sip seep water out of a pothole in the rocks. For a minute, everything was quiet, and that's when we heard Arliss and Sam again.

The best I could tell, they were no longer trailing a varmint. Sounded more like they had it treed. Only, the sounds were muffled, as if coming up out of a deep well. I wasn't even certain what direction they came from.

Then Blue lifted his head, to chomp his bridle bits and spatter water down on the flat rocks. And when he'd finished, he caught the sound, too, and bent his ears up the canyon. So we rode off in that direction; and sure enough, when we rounded a shoulder of broken rocks, we located Sam and Arliss.

That is, we located the hole they were in.

The mouth of the hole opened under a ledge at the base of a high cliff. The hole was about the size of a barrel, and ran far back into the rocks. Out of the hole came Sam's steady barking and Arliss's excited voice.

"Git him, Sam!" Arliss was urging. "Grab him, boy! Chew him up!"

I stepped down out of my saddle. Behind me, I heard the gravel crunch as Lisbeth's feet hit the ground. I went and stuck my head into the hole and caught the smell of stale dust and the rank scent of some wild animal. It was too dark in there to see anything.

I hollered into the hole. I said, "Arliss! What have y'all got back in there?"

"A bobcat!" Arliss said, all excited.

"A bobcat?" I said. I didn't much believe him.

"You bet!" Arliss said. "A big old tom. I'm poking him with a stick."

He must have poked him again, for I heard the angry snarling of a cat.

"Arliss!" I hollered. "You come back out of that hole!"

"Not till we git this old bobcat," Arliss said.

"You let that bobcat alone!" I said. "You hear me? You get him riled, he's liable to come out of there and eat you alive!"

"He can't come out," Arliss said. "Me 'n' old Sam, we're in here so tight, we got his hole stoppered up!"

That pesky Arliss. Trying to reason with him was like butting your head against a stooping post oak.

"Looks like I'll have to go in there after him," I told Lisbeth, and went crawling back into the hole.

I could hear Arliss and Sam and the bobcat scratching and scrambling around. I could hear them hollering and barking and growling. They were stirring up enough dust to choke a gray mule and making such a racket you couldn't hear yourself think.

The further in I crawled, the smaller the hole got.

[17]

Finally, I was lying flat on my belly, squeezed in so tight that I shut out all the light. I couldn't go any further; all I could do was feel around in the dark till I located one of Arliss's rusty bare feet. I took a good tight grip on his ankle and went to backing out.

Arliss threw a conniption fit. "You turn me a-loose, Travis Coates!" he railed at me. "You don't turn me a-loose, I'll bust you with a rock!"

He'd have done it, too, if there'd been room enough. Any time Arliss threatened you with a rock, you'd better duck. Like it was, though, the best he could do was kick me in the mouth a couple of times with his free foot before he set it against the wall of the cave, bracing himself against my pull. Then I couldn't budge him.

Well, I'd pulled enough armadillos out of holes to beat him at that game.

You take an armadillo. You ever let him get set in a hole with all four feet braced against the sides, it'd take a yoke of oxen to yank him out. On the other hand, you can set back on his horny tail with a steady pull—not straining, but just keeping a steady pressure on him—and after a while, you'll feel his legs give a little. Then you know you've got him.

That's how I got Arliss. I just let him scream and threaten me with murder while I kept a steady pull on his one leg. When finally I felt the other leg start quivering, I gave a hard yank and slid him back out of that hole like he'd been greased with tallow.

He came out fighting, and the first glimpse I got of his dirty, tear-streaked face made me wish I'd dragged out the bobcat instead. I barely ducked in time to keep him from busting my head open with a fist-sized rock.

I grabbed and held Arliss's rock hand and yelled at him to behave himself, while he screamed at me to turn him loose. And we were still down on our hands and knees, scrambling around, when Sam and the big bobcat came waltzing out into the open, all wrapped up in each other's arms.

They landed right on top of me and Little Arliss, roaring and snarling, clawing and biting. I flung myself one way and Arliss went the other. But as fast and furious as Sam and that bobcat fought, they were all over both of us two or three times while we were still trying to get from under.

Once, they caught me flat of my back with my mouth open, and Sam shoved a hind foot down my throat clear up to the hock, it seemed like, before he jerked it back out.

I was yelling and Arliss was yelling and Lisbeth was screaming and Blue and Jumper were shying around, whistling and snorting and popping the rocks with their ironshod hoofs, so that altogether it was a right noisy and exciting fight.

When finally I got to my feet, I saw right off what Sam was learning gradually: he had overmatched himself. That big bobcat was ripping him to pieces.

Well, Sam was nobody's fool. He'd been in enough scraps to know when he was licked. The first chance he got to cut loose from the cat, he took it. He tucked his tail and came running toward me and Arliss, bawling for help.

That should have ended the fight. But by now, this old bobcat was so fuzzed-up mad, he wasn't satisfied to call it quits. He charged after Sam with his teeth bared, his yellow eyes glaring, and his ears flattened to his head. He was still out for blood, and it didn't· seem to matter whose blood it was. The instant Sam swept around to get behind me, I was the next handiest thing in reach; so the cat sprang at me.

All I had time to do was give him a good hard kick. This shook him, but not enough. He caught my leg and clung to it and began clawing and biting as fiercely as he'd worked on Sam.

I went stumbling backward and sat down with a jolt that rattled my teeth. I went to yelling again and kicking at the bobcat with my other foot. I wasn't doing much good, though, and I guess the bobcat would have soon had me chewed up worse than Sam if it hadn't been for Arliss moving in, swinging the big rock he'd meant to bust me with.

Arliss was little for his age; but put a throwing rock in his hand, and he got bigger in a hurry. Now, he cut down on this bobcat with all he had. He laid that rock up against the rascal's head so hard that it addled him. You never saw such wallowing and pitching and squawling and leaping as that bobcat did. It was worse than the fits a game rooster will pull off after you've wrung his neck.

I came to my feet. Blue snorted loud. Sam came charging past me with his hackles raised, barking furiously. I looked around and felt my heart stop cold.

Indians!

[20]

They were all around us.

Some were mounted. Others were leaping from their horses and racing toward us, brandishing rifles and long lances.

All this I saw in one quick flash, just as a loop of hair rope came swishing through the air and dropped down around me.

The loop was jerked shut with a force that pinned my arms to my sides and yanked me off my feet. I hit the ground hard. I heard Lisbeth scream, then Little Arliss. A second later, I screamed, too, as I felt myself being dragged across the canyon bed at a speed that had me bouncing over the rocks.

The rocks cut and banged me and scraped the hide off in chunks. Then my head slammed against one and everything went black except for a great shower of pin-wheeling stars.

When I came to, I was nearly as addled as the bobcat had been. The ground rocked and heaved. The high canyon wall leaned out over me, then swayed back in the other direction. But gradually my head cleared and I was able to take note of what was going on.

I found myself astride a big rawboned bay horse. My shirt and hat were gone. My hands were tied behind me. A big tall Indian with long ropes of hair down his back was lashing my feet against the bay's ribs with a strip of rawhide pulled up tight under the horse's belly. The bay was snorting and lunging sideways, but couldn't do much, on account of a squat Indian swinging to his head. This

Indian had a leg and one arm hooked over the bay's neck. He held a tight-handed grip on the bay's underjaw, and had his teeth clamped shut over one ear. Most of his weight swung from that ear.

I tried to kick free, but the tall Indian's grip on my foot was too tight. A second later, he had my feet bound. He grunted to the squat Indian, who released his grip on the horse and dropped free. The bay snorted, ran backward a few steps, then bogged his head and went to bawling and pitching.

Well, I'd tried my hand a few times at riding pitching horses. But I'd never done it scared to death, like now, with my hands tied behind me and my feet pulled so tight against a horse's ribs that there was no give anywhere. The first jump whipped my head back, and the jolt I got when he hit the ground shot a stab of pain up my spine. I couldn't seem to stiffen my neck, and after that, just had to ride limp, with my head snapping back and forth like the popper on a bullwhip.

If the bay had kept pitching, he would have broken my neck. But he was more scared than mean. He didn't make more than half a dozen jumps before he went piling into a band of some fifty other horses held against a crook in the canyon wall by a couple of mounted Indians. There, he threw up his head and quit pitching. He shied around till he stood with the others, all stomping their feet and whistling wild.

For the first time, then, I got to see what was happening to Lisbeth and Little Arliss.

Both had been caught. Lisbeth was already mounted

in front of an Indian with a broken nose. He held her
tight against him with a hand clamped over her mouth.
All I could see of her face was her big scared eyes.

With Arliss, though, things were different. A short-
coupled Indian had hold of him. He'd caught up a fistful
of Arliss's shaggy hair and had the strength to swing
Arliss's heels clear of the ground. But he still lacked some
having Arliss captured.

This was because every time he yanked the screaming
Arliss up close enough, Arliss either kicked him or hammered him with a big rock he'd somehow got his hands on.

Also, there was Sam.

I'd never seen Sam so savage before. I'd never seen him
attack with such deadly fury. It was plain that he didn't
look on this fight as a big romp, like he and Arliss had just
pulled off with the bobcat. This wasn't the sort of scrap
that Sam would turn tail to any time the going got too
rough.

Sam saw this for what it was: a kill-or-be-killed proposi-
tion. And no naked wild man was going to sling Sam's
running partner around by the hair of the head so long as
Sam could do anything about it. Sam tore into the Indian
with his eyes glazed and his hackles standing in a ragged
ridge along his backbone. His fangs cut bloody grooves in
the Indian's neck and shoulders.

So, with Sam and Arliss teaming up on him like that, the
squat Indian was kept right busy—and with nobody to
help him out.

Because not one of the others offered to take a hand in
the fight. Instead, they stood off and watched and yelped

[23]

with laughter. From the tone of their voices, they made hoorawing remarks and waited to see how it would all come out. Like the whole thing was a great big joke.

There for a little bit, it looked like Sam and Arliss might win. For Sam made another leap, sank his teeth into the Indian's neck, and took him to the ground. But the fall broke Sam's grip. The Indian rolled instantly to his feet. Pitching Arliss aside, he snatched a tomahawk from his belt. Sam wheeled and charged again—and the Indian chopped him down.

The stone blade caught Sam in the back. It sent him screeching, leaving a trail of blood as he wallowed down a rocky slant in a frenzy of pain. He disappeared behind some great shards of rock. And before he was out of sight, the Indian had whirled and caught Arliss again. He bent and grabbed him by a leg this time. Holding him upside down and out away from him, he strode quickly toward his horse.

All the other Indians now turned toward their mounts. Some of the horses they mounted wore bridles and forked-stick saddles covered over with buffalo hides. Others were barebacked and had only single strips of rawhide half-hitched around their underjaws to serve as guide reins.

As scared and stunned as I was, I couldn't help taking notice of how easily those naked savages mounted up. No matter how a boogered horse might lunge or shy around, the Indian that meant to ride him would just make a quick running jump and land astride before the horse could get from under.

The only one to miss was the big tall Indian who had captured me. He'd just made a leap at his horse when I heard him grunt. I saw him whirl in mid-air and tumble to the ground as if slapped down by a heavy blow. Then I heard the crashing report of a rifle coming from far back up on the ridge.

Instantly, the tall Indian bounded to his feet, clutching at a blood-spurting hole inside his right leg. All the others took wild looks around, then went to whooping and screeching, lashing their mounts, circling to get behind the whistling band of loose horses and scare them into a run.

The rifle spoke again. The bullet glanced off a rock and went screaming away. I twisted around, trying to see who was doing the shooting, and nearly got my head snapped off again as the big bay made a sudden leap and went tearing off down the canyon bed, running wild with the rest of the loose horses.

I never did hear the third shot. There was too much whooping and yelling, too much hoof-popping clatter, too many echoes slamming back and forth between the canyon walls. All I saw was a running horse stumble and go down. His rider leaped from his back and ran beside him as the fallen horse slid forward with his outstretched nose rooting a furrow in a sand bed. Then a loose horse came by and the Indian leaped astride and went to drumming his heels against this horse's ribs, urging him to greater speed.

We rode at a stampede run down the rocky bed of the

[25]

twisting canyon. I looked around for Lisbeth and Arliss. I didn't see Lisbeth, but the glimpse I caught of Arliss made me sick.

To the left and a little behind me rode the squat Indian. He still held Arliss by one heel. Every stitch of clothes had been torn from Arliss's body. He swung, head down, beside the running horse, with the thorny brush raking his naked hide.

I thought to myself: *His head ever strikes a tree or a boulder, it'll kill him.*

We went crashing through a grove of Spanish oak. An outspread branch slapped the side of my head. I bent forward and laid my cheek against the bay's neck so I could shed the brush better. But I couldn't see any more of what was happening to Little Arliss or Lisbeth.

Apache

Three

WE raced north, following the crooks and turns of the canyon. We traveled at a dead run; and in some places, the bed of the watercourse was so rough and jumbled with boulders, I didn't see how the horses kept on their feet.

Finally, the canyon walls began to fan out, spreading wider and wider, till at last there were only sweeping slopes slanting away from the creek. Here, the Indians swung the racing herd up the slope to the west, still driving at the same killing pace.

There were no trees on this slope, except for a few gnarled mesquite and now and then a round-topped live oak. The rest was just brush—catclaw, chapote, bluethorn, tasajillo cactus, prickly pear, and bee myrtle. None of it was more than horse high. It tore at my legs, but there was no danger of its knocking me from my horse. I raised my head and took another look around.

Off to one side, I saw Little Arliss again, still held by one foot, but now lying head down across the lap of the Indian who had caught him. He lay limp and jostling, like he was dead. But I guessed he must still be alive. Why else would the Apache keep packing him?

Lisbeth was still being held upright in her captor's saddle. He wasn't holding his hand over her mouth any more, but her face was dead white, and the terrible fear I saw in her eyes kindled in me a fire of hate that flared hotter and fiercer with every mile of ground we covered. She looked toward me once, and I saw her mouth move, but I couldn't hear her voice.

I was helpless now. They had me bound hand and foot. If they were smart, that's the way they'd keep me, too. Because, if I ever got loose and got my hands on the red devils who held Lisbeth and Arliss, I'd claw their eyes out. I'd choke them to death. I'd hammer their heads in with a rock or rip their bellies open with my pocketknife. And if one of them finally chopped me down, like that one had done Savage Sam, that would be all right, too—just so I got some of them first!

We went tearing on through the brush, but the slant was

long and tiring to the running horses. Some began to lag. I saw Jumper running at the outside of the herd. He still wore the frazzled leavings of his rope, but he'd trampled most of it to pieces under his feet. I could see him edging further and further off. I knew in a minute what he was up to, and I hoped he got away.

But one of the Indians saw him, too, and went charging past and stabbed him in the rump with a lance. This put more life into Jumper than I'd seen him show for a long time. He spurted forward, wringing his tail and braying, slinging his high-held head from side to side, traveling at a pace that soon had him leading the bunch.

He put on such a silly show that he set all the Indians to pointing and laughing as they dashed back and forth through the brush, prodding the stragglers into a faster run.

Out of the tail of my eye, I caught a glimpse of the big tall Indian who'd been shot. He rode my horse, Blue. He stood off in the left stirrup, trying to favor the bullet wound inside his right leg. He held a hand clamped over the wound to keep it from rubbing against the saddle. Blood seeped from between his fingers, staining his buckskin leggings and spreading down over the saddle skirts. From the way he rode, he must have been suffering a lot from that wound.

I thought to myself: *Maybe he'll bleed to death.* That would cheer me some.

He looked up and caught my eye on him. I don't guess he could read what I was thinking, but something about my look seemed to give him an idea.

[29]

He spanked Blue across the rump with his lance, crowding him up beside me. He looped the bridle reins around the saddle horn so they couldn't drop to the ground and maybe trip and throw Blue. Then he leaped from the saddle, grabbed me by the foot, and went running beside me.

We had topped out the rise by this time. Now, headed downhill, the horses—even the stragglers—picked up speed, so that again we went charging along at a pace that made a blur of the brush and the ground beneath me.

How that tall Indian could hold to my foot and keep pace with the rawboned bay I rode, I'll never know. But he did it, crashing through or ducking under the taller brush, leaping lightly over the clumps of prickly pear and tasajillo, never once faltering, never once dragging at my foot, never once really breaking his stride, which was as long-reaching and smooth-flowing as that of a running cat.

I could ride there beside him and hate him. I could tell myself that I hoped he bled to death before sundown. But watching him run like he did, I couldn't help marveling. He might be a cruel, merciless savage, but he was all man.

Watching him, I took note of the fact that he was different from the others. As I've said, he was taller and better built than his heavyset companions. On top of that, where all the others wore streaks of white paint from ear to ear across the bridges of their noses, this one had his whole face covered with slanted stripes of black and red. Where they were naked from breechclouts down to peak-toed moccasins except for wrap-around leggings reaching nearly to their knees, this one wore fringed buckskin breeches that

[30]

covered him from feet to waist, except for holes in the seat
that left bare the rounded cheek muscles of his rump. Also,
he wore fringed and beaded moccasins of tanned snake-
skin—rattlesnake, from the brown diamond pattern marks—
with the tails of ground squirrels attached to the heels.

The main difference, however, was the way he wore his
hair. The others had their hair parted in the middle and
chopped off to shoulder length. Some wore colored head-
bands of twisted cloth to hold their hair in place, and some
wore their hair braided into tight little pigtails that flipped
around behind their ears.

My big Indian, though, had two parts in his hair, with
a streak of yellow marking each part. The parts ran from
each side of his forehead back to the crown, leaving a
V-shaped forelock into which he'd stuck a long yellow
feather. From there on, his hair hung in two long cowtail
twists, wrapped at intervals with yellow string, till finally
they were left to flare in six-inch tassels that all but brushed
the ground. As he ran, these cowtails flopped and whipped
about like scared snakes in tall grass.

Something about those ropes of hair fascinated me. I
kept watching them. I kept telling myself that no man,
even a wild Indian, could grow hair that long. And finally,
I saw that I was right. Only about a foot and a half of it
was his. The rest was horsetail hair that he'd braided into
his own to make the tails longer.

From what I'd heard Papa and others tell of Plains Indians, I judged this big one to be Comanche. He was tall
for a Comanche, but he wore Comanche garb. The peak-
toed moccasins marked the others as Apache. How come a

[31]

lone Comanche raiding with a bunch of Apaches, I didn't know; but it wasn't a question to bother with now. My worry was how to get me and Lisbeth and Little Arliss away from the painted-faced devils.

That job would fall to me, and I knew it. Arliss—if he was still alive—was too little; and Lisbeth—well, she was just a girl.

But how to go about it? That's what had me plagued. How could a sixteen-year-old boy whip or outsmart fifteen wild Indians? And him tied hand and foot?

Then I thought about the man who'd shot from the top of the ridge. Whoever he was, he'd get the word out. He'd hurry to Salt Licks and round up Papa and some of the settlers, and they'd be on our trail in no time.

That lifted my hopes. There were some crack rifle shots and experienced Indian hunters at Salt Licks.

One of them went by the name of Burn Sanderson. Sanderson was a good friend of ours. He'd been the one to let us have Old Yeller when Papa was gone and we'd been in such desperate need of a watchdog. Old Yeller had been Sanderson's best cow dog, yet he'd swapped him off to Little Arliss for a horned toad and a good home-cooked meal that Mama fixed up for him.

Sanderson had ridden for the Texas Rangers and was a real Indian tracker. Papa claimed Sanderson could track wild bees in a blizzard, that he would hang an Indian trail like a bloodhound.

Thinking of Papa and Sanderson taking our trail sent a warm feeling through me, yet I wondered if even Sanderson could work out our trail fast enough to overhaul us.

We raced on through the hills. The wild things scattered and fled before us. Cottontails streaked for the nearest brush cover. So did the deer. Jack rabbits took to the open places, depending on speed for safety. Once, the running horses shied at a big covey of bob-white quail that exploded under their noses. Another time, the band split and streamed past on both sides of a black she bear, who rose to stand on her hind legs. She roared a warning at them to keep away from the pair of whimpering cubs at her heels. We jumped a couple of long-bearded wild gobblers. They saddle-trotted ahead of us for a little way, then took to the air with heavy wing beats.

Where the ground was bare and rocky, the thudding hoofbeats of the horses was like thunder in my ears. When we struck a wide mesquite flat, the sound of our passing faded, the hoofbeats muffled by the thick, matted turf of the tall-waving grass. But no matter what sort of country we crossed, we kept traveling at the same horse-killing pace.

The horse I rode became lathered with sweat. The sweat soaked through my pants, stinging and galling the flesh of my legs, which were already rubbed raw from being bound so tight to the bay's back. My head throbbed from the blows it had taken among the rocks. The hot sun burned down on my naked shoulders till I knew I'd be on fire with sunburn before night.

I thought of Little Arliss, stripped naked. I wondered if he'd sunburn, too, but guessed he wouldn't. His skin was tougher. He was used to running around naked in hot weather and having Mama fuss at him for not being decent.

[33]

I guessed Mama wouldn't fuss at him now. I guessed that by now, she was clear out of her mind with worry for us all, praying to get us back, even if she knew Arliss would run naked as a summer-hatched chicken for the rest of his life.

I looked toward Arliss. He still lay limp across the saddle. But now he was watching his captor out of the corners of his eyes.

I'd seen that look before. Arliss was studying up some sort of devilment.

It was good to know he was that much alive. But it scared me, too. I hoped he'd hold off starting a ruckus till I could get free to help him out.

We rode till the sun sank behind the ridges, its last rays setting fire to the underbelly of a thunderhead that threatened rain. We topped out a high, rocky, cedar-covered ridge and went plunging down a long slant toward the Llano River. In the fading light the water looked like gold running between red rock banks. When we got closer, the gold grayed to silver.

We hit the river where the banks were high and the water looked deep. Downstream, I could see the ripple of shoal water flowing over a shallow bottom where the crossing would have been easy; but if the Indians saw the shallow water, they paid it no mind. They kept driving straight ahead.

At the bank, some of the horses tried to shy away from a ten-foot jump-off. But the Indians came racing up on either side. With whoops and lashes, they sent the horses plunging over the bank into water so deep that the bay I rode sank clear under.

I thought I was a goner, for sure, when the water closed over my head. But in a little bit, the bay rose to the surface and struck out for the far bank, swimming like he was used to it.

I missed the grip of the big Indian's hand on my foot. I looked around, half blinded by the water streaming down out of my hair. I hoped the big devil had got knocked down by a scared horse and trampled to death.

But luck was against me. There he was, alive as ever, hanging to the tail of the swimming bay with one hand, holding onto his lance with the other.

I noticed him looking downriver and grinning. It came to me then that all the other Indians were hollering and laughing. I looked across the backs of a lot of swimming horses and saw a sight that set my heart to flopping around like a catfish in a wet sack.

It was Arliss. On the fight again!

Like I'd suspected a good ways back, he'd been playing possum, waiting to get a break. Now, something must have happened to give him that break. For there he was, all balled up on that Indian's head like a boar coon fighting a trail hound.

He had a bare foot planted firm on each of the Indian's shoulders. He had a tight grip with both hands on the Indian's hair. But what counted most was the fact that he had a mouthful of the rascal's left ear between his teeth and

[35]

was setting back on it, shaking and tugging for all he was worth, doing his dead-level best to tear that ear out by the roots.

The howling Apache fought back. He hammered the side of Arliss's head with his fist. He slapped his face. He pulled his hair. He grabbed him by one foot and tried to yank him loose. But nothing did any good. The way Arliss kept his teeth set in that ear put me in mind of what I'd always heard tell about a snapper turtle—that once he shuts his jaws down on your finger, he won't turn loose till it thunders. Anyhow, all the yanking and tugging the Apache did only helped Arliss to pull that much harder on his ear.

With all this, the Apache was having trouble with his horse. The horse was scared. The way he kept lunging up to paw at the surface with his forefeet, it was plain that he'd never been in swimming water. Then there was all this racket and commotion on his back. And worst of all, with Arliss riding clear up on the Apache's head, the load was topheavy and kept pulling the horse off balance.

So, while the Apache fought Arliss on top of his head, he was kept just as busy shifting his weight, trying to keep his horse right side up in the water.

Altogether, it was too much for the horse. I saw that he was never going to make it.

"Turn him loose, Arliss!" I yelled.

If Arliss heard, he paid me no more mind than he generally did. The horse rolled over and went under. Arliss and the Apache sank with him, with the Apache still fighting at Arliss and Arliss still clinging grimly to his ear hold.

[36]

Relieved of his load, the horse rose to the surface almost at once. He got footing where the water shallowed, and went lunging and scrambling over the rock bottom toward the bank.

Arliss and the Apache stayed under longer, so long that it scared me. Then the Apache came up without Arliss. Also without his ear. All he had left of that ear was a ragged stump that spewed blood down the side of his neck and reddened the water about his shoulders.

He held there where he came up, treading water and looking around in fury, searching for Arliss.

The other Indians hooted at him. They pulled at their ears to show that they still had theirs and kept pointing to the Apache's bloody stump.

It was plain that none of this pleased the wounded Apache, and I sure hoped that when Arliss came to the top —if he ever did—he'd be out of reach of that Indian.

And he was. I'd heard Papa declare that when it came to swimming, all Arliss lacked being a fish was a couple of gill slits and a forked tail. When his head finally popped out of the water, he was close to the far bank, swimming among the lead horses.

The Apache saw him at once and struck out after him, swimming fast. But Arliss beat him to the bank and went out into the flat-rock ledge among the slipping, scrambling horses.

Then my bay struck bottom and went buck-jumping up a slick rock slant toward dry ground, and for a second there, I lost sight of Arliss. When next I saw him, he was

clear of the plunging horses and racing toward me along
the rock ledge, yelling at the top of his voice, "Don't let
him git me, Travis! Don't let him git me!"

I sure didn't blame him for being scared; for hard after
him came the furious Indian. He had his tomahawk raised,
and there was a murderous glare in his black eyes.

I was frantic to save Arliss, but couldn't think up any
way to do it. All I could do was yell at him, "*Run, Arliss,
run!*" Which was silly, because Arliss was running faster
than I'd ever seen him run in his life.

But it wasn't fast enough. The Apache was gaining on
him with every step he took, and I heard Lisbeth scream.

From behind the bay stepped the tall Comanche. He
grabbed Arliss by the hair and slung him up astride the bay
horse behind me. He turned, grinning, to poke his lance
out toward the charging Apache. The murdering devil all
but ran himself through on the point of the lance before
he could get stopped.

He backed up with an angry shout. From the way he
flung up his tomahawk, I could see he aimed to go to war
with the Comanche. But he changed his mind pretty quick
when the Comanche moved toward him, drawing back his
lance for a throw.

From there on, they aired their lungs with jabber talk
that got louder and hotter by the second. The other Indians came to crowd around and take the Comanche's side
of the argument. They jeered at the one-eared Apache till
finally he wheeled away, his mouth twisted with rage. He
stalked off toward his horse and with a running jump
landed astride the animal. He lashed him cruelly across

the rump and sent him scrambling up the rock-bench slope toward higher ground.

The others then rounded up the scattered horses, and we were on the move again, but no longer at such break-neck speed. We jogged along in the afterglow of the sunset. And, while the Comanche's grip on my foot was as iron tight as ever, it felt good to have Little Arliss behind me with his arms around my waist.

After a while, he said in a worried whisper, "Travis, you reckon I'll be part Injun now?"

"Whatta you mean?" I said.

"That rascal's ear," he said. "I et it."

I started, twisted around to look back at him. "You *what?*"

"Well, I didn't aim to!" he defended. "But I stayed under too long and had to suck for air. And when I did, I got a bellyful of water—and I swallered that ear whole."

It must have been nerves that did it. This sure wasn't any time or place for laughing. But I couldn't help myself. I laughed right out loud and kept on laughing till the tears came and the Indians began moving in close to watch me, curious and puzzled.

If, like Papa was always saying, a big laugh is better for your health than a strong dose of medicine, I was lucky to get in such a good one when I did. As it turned out, I had a long way to go before I was to get another one.

Comanche

Four

We crossed a sharp ridge and clattered down into a tight
little valley. More than half the valley was encircled by
walls of red sandstone. At one place, huge live oaks and
elms grew at the base of the cliff and leaned their branches
out over a small pool of water. A bunch of wild longhorn
cattle, mostly cows and calves, were gathered at the pool.
One or two were still on their feet, drinking; the rest lay
on the grassy bank, chewing their cuds, done bedded
down for the night.

Our appearance startled the cattle. They scrambled to their feet. The old cows gave loud sniffs, tossed widespread horns, and quit the water hole in a rattle-hocked run. The calves fled after them, holding their tails curled high over their backs.

Instantly, all the Indians except my Comanche and Lisbeth's Apache went chasing after the cattle. They fitted feathered arrows into their bows as they rode.

One chunky mustard-colored calf wasn't as fast as the others. The lead Apache raced up beside it and let fly. His arrow drove clear through the calf's rib cage, the bloody point sticking out three inches on the other side. The calf blatted, and its heels flew high as it tumbled to the ground.

One cow—the calf's mama, I guess—heard the calf and wheeled about. She headed straight for the lead Apache, whose horse hadn't slowed yet. She charged to meet the horse, with her tail crooked and wicked horns lowered. She bawled her wrath.

The Apache was one who rode with a single guide rein. Now, he all but yanked his horse's underjaw out of socket, trying to haul him around. The horse reared, squealing, spun on his hind feet, but lost his balance. Down he came, all in a doubled-up heap.

This would have caught most riders under him, but the Apache was too nimble. He was clear of his fallen horse and running almost before his feet touched the ground. Which was sure lucky for him. Because this old mama cow wasn't bluffing. The horse was up on his forefeet, lifting his rump from the ground, when she hit him. She drove long, sharp horns hard into his shoulders, knocking

[41]

him back to the ground. The horse screamed and rolled, and the cow hit him again, sinking her horns to the hilt in his soft belly. There she held him, pawing and bawling, trying to drive the horns deeper.

The other Apaches charged up to fill her with arrows and to drive their long lances into her sides and back. But the old cow died slow and hard and not before she'd gored to death the horse she evidently thought was responsible for the death of her calf.

Most of this, me and Arliss watched from the back of the bay horse as he stood in the water hole, drinking in great gulps. Like the others, he'd been kept going at a hard run for most of a long, hot day, with never a chance for a drink, even when we crossed the river. So, when the mounted Apaches pulled off to go shoot the calf, the loose horses had kept going till they reached the water hole. There they had plunged in belly-deep, drinking like they couldn't get enough.

Out on the bank, the Comanche and the Apache who held Lisbeth stood watching the others. Now, one of the Apaches dropped the loop of his rope over the hind leg of the dead calf and came riding toward us, dragging the calf through the tall grass at a fast run. The others followed, leaving the dead cow and the horse where they lay.

At the water's edge, the hunters slid from their horses and came to drink, too.

Well, the water hadn't been much to begin with—just a seep hole, with patches of green scum and slimy frog eggs floating on top and all sorts of tadpoles and bugs and wriggling water worms underneath. And, what with the way the horses had plunged in, trampling around and pawing up the bottom ooze, the water sure didn't look fit to drink.

But none of this bothered the Indians. They tore up fistfuls of grass, wadded it, and laid it on the surface of the water. They lay flat and drank through these grass strainers till they got their fill, then got up and went to butcher the calf.

The way they ripped into that calf's belly with their knives and the parts of it they ate raw was a sight to gag a snake.

Even Arliss, who would generally eat anything he could get his hands on, sneered at them.

"Nasty as buzzards, ain't they?" he said.

The Apache with the broken nose dragged Lisbeth over and tried to make her eat some of the entrails, but she turned sick-white in the face and tried to throw up.

This made the Apache mad. He slapped her flat of her back. He bent and grabbed her by one arm and dragged her over to the water hole. There, he shoved her face under. When she lifted it, strangling and coughing, he shoved it under again.

I thought he was going to drown her. I shouted at him, near to crying with helpless rage.

"You let her alone!"

Little Arliss jumped down off the horse. He ran splashing through the dirty water toward the bank. He grabbed up a rock and drew it back for a throw, threatening the Apache in a shrill voice.

"You quit that!" he demanded. "You don't quit that, I'll bust you with this here rock!"

That stopped the ugly Apache from mistreating Lisbeth.

It wasn't the threat of Little Arliss's rock, of course. In fact, the Apache didn't pay as much attention to that rock as he might ought to have. What stopped him was the sight of Arliss standing there, stark naked, with that big rock in his hand and looking so little and so fierce.

The sight seemed to tickle the Apache. His round face split in a wide grin. He turned Lisbeth loose and started backing off, making such a big show of how scared of Little Arliss he was that he set all the other Indians to laughing.

By now, most of the horses had drunk their fill. They started wading out of the water, headed for graze. The bay I rode started to follow. He was met at the bank by the Comanche, who reached out with a bloody knife and cut the rawhide thong that bound my feet.

I felt the sting of the keen blade as it also sliced on through into my leg. But the cut was shallow, and by now I was hurting in so many places, one little extra pain made no difference.

The Comanche motioned me to dismount, and I lifted a sore leg over the bay's neck and slid down off his shoulder. After so many hours of riding bound, my legs were numb. They buckled under me, and I pitched to the ground.

The Comanche yanked me to my feet. Lisbeth came to hold me steady till the blood got to circulating again. I told her I wanted water. She helped me to get down and stretch out where I could reach it and got a wad of grass for me to drink through.

I'll never forget that drink. Dirty and scummy as the water was, when it hit my parched throat, it seemed like the freshest, sweetest-tasting stuff I'd ever swallowed.

After I'd drunk, Lisbeth and Arliss helped me to my feet. The Comanche had walked off and left us. A few steps away, a big boulder stuck up out of the grass not far from a couple of cottonwood trees. I staggered toward it, dragging the long strip of rawhide still tied to my left foot. I sat down in the shade and leaned against the flat, slanting side of the boulder, making myself as comfortable as I could. Lisbeth and Arliss came to sit, silent and scared, beside me.

It crossed my mind that it was shameful for Little Arliss to go around naked in front of Lisbeth; but I guessed Lisbeth realized that in our fix, clothes didn't amount to a heap.

The Indians paid us no mind. The gloom of the coming night was fast filling the tiny valley. The savages wound up their first filthy feast, then got busy doing the things that needed to be done before full dark shut in.

A couple started skinning out the calf and chunking up the meat, piling it onto the spread-out hide. Two more went to catch up and hobble the saddled horses. They didn't bother to remove the saddles. One dragged up a long crooked branch of dead mesquite. He broke this into short lengths by beating the pole across a boulder. He gathered up the shattered pieces and carried them to a little sand bed beside the water. There he laid them out fan-shaped, like the spokes of a wagon wheel. Another Indian came and set the flared skirt of a dead bear-grass clump in the center, where the hub of the wheel would have been. In his other hand, he carried a long bear-grass bloom stalk, which was also dead.

While I sat there watching, my mind seemed to split and go off in two directions.

One part was hard at work figuring out a plan of escape. When full dark came, I'd get Lisbeth to untie my hands. We'd watch till the Indians all went to sleep. Then we'd sneak out among the grazing horses. We'd pick the three fastest ones: my horse, Blue; the bay I'd been tied to; and a big rangy glass-eyed paint that one of the Apaches rode. They'd be easy to catch, on account of how tired they had to be. We'd mount up, start yelling to stampede the rest of the horses—and be a long time gone!

The other half of my mind centered on how the savages aimed to get a fire started. Lisbeth's grandpa, who claimed to know all about Indians, along with everything else, had once told me and Arliss how Indians built their fires. He said they half-hitched a tight bowstring around a pointed stick. By moving the bow back and forth, they could twirl the stick so fast that the point of it, pressed down into spunk wood, would set the wood on fire.

Me and Arliss had to try it, but by the time we got our fire-making outfit rigged up, old man Searcy had eaten and gone; so we tried it alone. All we ever raised, though, was a big sweat, some blisters on our hands, and not even one little wisp of smoke.

As it turned out, these Indians didn't bother with a

[46]

bowstring. Instead, the one with the dead bear-grass stalk took his knife and cut the stalk into a couple of sticks about two feet long. He whittled slanted notches near the ends of each stick, then spilled a fistful of dry sand into the notches. He squatted down on his hunkers and went to rubbing the notched ends together.

He rubbed fast, stopping now and then to spill more sand into the notches. Finally, the ends of the sticks went to smoking, and he shoved them under the bladed skirt of the bear-grass clump. He continued to rub, and smoke curled up faster. The second Apache got down on his hands and knees and blew on the place till it glowed. When he blew again, the glow got brighter, and sparks flew. On the third try, the whole clump burst into flame. The yellow smoke boiled high, and I scented the foul stench that burning bear grass gives off, on account of the oil in the blades.

I watched the Apaches pile small sticks and pieces of shattered bark on the fire to keep it going. I guessed now I could tell old man Searcy a thing or two about Indian fire-making.

Lisbeth whispered, "You want I should untie your hands?"

"Not yet," I said. "Wait till dark."

"I wish we was back to home!" Arliss said.

The whimper and longing in his voice didn't sound like the Arliss who'd fought like a wildcat when captured, who'd eaten one Apache's ear and stood off another with a rock. But I knew how he felt. No matter how wide a boy likes to range in the daytime, when night comes on, he

[47]

wants to be home, where he can sleep in his own bed and feel safe with his own folks. Especially if he's a little boy. As big as I was, I still had the same feeling a lot of the time. Right now, I had it plenty strong.

"You wait," I told him. "We'll get back home!"

"How?" he wanted to know.

"I got plans," I said.

There wasn't a doubt in my mind but what my plans would work.

The bear-grass clump burned down till its stench was gone. The Apaches brought up their hide-load of meat for cooking. Some of the chunks they laid on flat rocks which they shoved up close to the fire. Most of the meat, however, they just pitched right onto the glowing coals, where it started sizzling and frying.

Watching the fire-making, I'd forgotten the Comanche. Now, I saw him come in out of the gathering darkness. In one hand, he packed a wad of some sort of green weeds. In the other, he carried a small brass pot. He filled the pot with water and set it near the fire. He rolled the weeds between his hands, crushing and bruising them. The weeds filled the air with a rank, sharp scent that reminded me of crushed bull nettles. Then he dropped the weeds into the pot of water.

The Comanche sat down facing the fire and spread his knees wide apart. He bent over to examine the gunshot wound inside his leg. He slipped his knife from his belt and cut a foot-long slit in his buckskin breeches and spread the slit. In the firelight, I could see the bloody

[48]

hole in his flesh. A few inches away, a bluish lump stood up under the skin. The Comanche pressed the sides of this lump between thumb and forefinger, making it stand higher, then sliced across the lump. The blood spurted. The Comanche laid aside his knife. He dug a finger into the gaping wound and gouged out the rifle ball lodged there. He wiped it clean on his breeches leg and held it up to examine it by the firelight.

The other Indians crowded around, wanting a look at the ball. The Comanche handed it to one. They all took turns examining it, while the Comanche lifted his weeds out of the brass pot and held them pressed against the wounds in his leg. I guessed they were some sort of medicine weed.

After a while, the Apaches lost interest in the rifle ball. One of them tossed it to the Comanche, who put it away in a little doeskin pouch at his belt.

The Indians lifted the sizzling meat from the fire on the blades of their knives and blew on it to cool it off. When they ate, they didn't cut off slices and put them into their mouths. Instead, they bit into the whole chunk, then sliced the meat off even with their teeth.

We watched them eat and smelled the cooking meat; and when you're hungry, I don't guess there's a better smell on earth than that of beef roasting over a mesquite-wood fire. Arliss got up and started toward them.

"I'm gonna git us some of that," he said.

"You better not tamper with them devils," I warned.

He didn't even look back. "I'm hongry," he said, and kept going.

[49]

He circled wide around the Apache whose ear he'd eaten and went to squat beside the Comanche.

"Gimme the loan of your knife," he said.

All he got was a blank stare, the Comanche not understanding. Arliss frowned with impatience. He pointed toward the roasting meat, then reached for the Comanche's knife. He lifted his voice, as if shouting would help the Comanche to understand.

"All I want is some meat," he explained.

For a wonder, the Comanche gave him the knife. Arliss stabbed the point of it into the biggest chunk of meat on the fire.

Instantly, the Comanche slapped the knife out of Arliss's hand, while all about him the squatted Apaches jerked to their feet, barking out sharp words of alarm. They glared down at Arliss, their eyes hot with anger.

Arliss glared back at them. "What's the matter?" he demanded. "Dang it! We're just as hongry as y'all are!"

The Comanche reached down and picked up the knife. The chunk of meat still hung to the blade. He held the meat out away from his body, staring at it like maybe it was poisoned. With a quick jerk of his wrist, he slung the meat off the blade of his knife, flinging it far out into the grass.

Arliss scowled. He stood looking hurt and mad while the Comanche wiped his knife blade across the leg of his breeches.

With the blade clean, the Comanche turned his back on the fire and lifted both hands—one holding the knife—high above his head. He looked up at the sky. He started talking in a singsong chant that reminded me of a brush-arbor preacher calling on the Almighty to save the souls of all us black-hearted sinners.

The chant went on for a good long spell. Listening to it gave me the creeps. But when it was finally over, the Indians all seemed to feel better and went back to eating.

That is, all but the Comanche. He handed the knife back to Arliss, then held Arliss's hand and showed him how to run the blade under a piece of meat instead of through it.

"I don't see what difference it makes," Arliss said.

I didn't, either. I didn't know then that no Comanche or Apache ever spears cooking meat. For some reason, that's considered an insult to their gods and is liable to bring down a mess of trouble on the tribe.

Arliss started toward us, careful to keep the meat balanced across the blade of the knife. With a grunt, the one-eared Apache rose suddenly to his feet. He stepped in front of Arliss and reached for the knife. Arliss pulled it back out of reach.

The Comanche barked at the Apache. The Apache turned on him, jabbering loud and hostile. It was plain that he didn't trust Arliss with a knife; and I guess he had some reason not to.

The Comanche heard him out, but didn't answer. He came and took the knifeload of hot meat from Arliss and brought it to us. He laid the meat on top of the boulder beside me and let Arliss use the knife to cut it into bite-sized pieces. Then he took the knife back and squatted down to make a careful study of us while we ate.

With my hands still tied, I couldn't feed myself, so Lisbeth did it for me. The meat was scorched on the outside, and half raw on the inside. It was all messed up with ashes and sand that gritted between my teeth. But it tasted good and was filling, and I began to feel almost grateful to the Comanche.

It bothered me, though, the way he kept studying us, watching our every move like we were some sort of curious varmints he'd never seen before. It made me mad, too.

I glared at him. "You needn't look at us like that," I said. "You're the wild one. Not us!"

He didn't answer. He just moved up closer, where I got a full load of his scent. It was rank and wild smelling, a strong mixture of armpit sweat and wood smoke and rancid grease and other odors I couldn't name.

He bent forward and stared straight into my eyes, looking long and hard, like a man trying to see through a smoky window glass to what's on the other side.

I stared back at him for as long as I could, then looked away.

My glance fell on the rawhide shield he wore on his left arm. It was round and dished, made of fire-hardened buffalo hide, with the hair on the inside. It was ornamented with a ring of grisly dried scalps dangling from its rim.

It wasn't the scalps that caught my interest, though. They just reminded me of all the people he'd murdered, and made me shudder. What took my eye was the strange designs painted on the face of the shield. It happened to be tilted at just the right angle for the firelight to show up a moon, some stars, snakes, turtles, and other figures, all laid out in such exact positions that they made a pattern I seemed to recognize.

An idea popped into my head. I looked up at the sky. It spread over us like a great blue star-studded bowl turned upside down. I studied the positions of the bigger stars for a moment, then looked back at the shield.

I'd been right. That thick-hided shield hadn't been made just to turn arrows and rifle balls. It mapped the sky in detail. I wondered if the Comanche could use it some way as a guide.

It shook me, coming to learn that a wild Indian was that smart. I couldn't have figured out and made a sky-map like that to save my skin; and I'd already learned enough to read three or four books all the way through. It gave me a new respect for the Comanche.

But this respect turned to hot resentment a few minutes later. We'd just finished up the last scrap of meat when suddenly, quick as a cat, the Comanche leaped on me and grabbed my feet. He had them tied together before I could even think to fight back.

I guess the surprise was just as big for Lisbeth and Arliss. Neither of them tried to run. They stood popeyed with scare till the Comanche had tied them up with extra strings that he carried in his belt.

When he finished, he just sort of heaped us up in a pile and went on back to the fire, where he dug out more meat and went to eating again.

I lay there, thinking hard. I couldn't figure out that Comanche. He didn't make sense. How come he'd treat us good one minute, then the next turn on us like a biting dog? I studied on it a good while, but I didn't come up with any answer that satisfied.

As the Indians got their fill of meat, they backed off from the fire. They squatted on their heels and smoked cigarettes of strong-scented tobacco rolled in clipped corn shucks. A couple loosened bowstrings that had evidently gotten wet when we crossed the river. They pushed the ends of the bows into the sand and let them stand with limp strings dangling near the fire, giving them a chance to dry out. They talked awhile, then, one by one, threw their cigarette butts into the fire and sprawled in the grass. They didn't bother to put a guard out, like white men would have done.

The fire died down. Things began to get quiet except for the usual night sounds—the call of the whippoorwills, the piping of the frogs around the water, the twittering of birds in the trees, the munching noises the horses made grazing on the grass.

Up on the hog-back ridge we had crossed, a wolf howled long and mournfully. Another one pitched in and helped out. They'd caught the scent of fresh meat, but I guessed sight of the fire had them stood off.

They tuned in on another big howl and beside me I felt a shiver run through Lisbeth. I felt sorry for her. I could remember when the howling of wolves used to make me shiver with scare.

Lisbeth said in a shaky whisper, "What're we going to do, Travis?"

I glanced toward the Indians. They all lay quiet. Maybe

they weren't asleep yet, but best I could tell, they all had their eyes shut.

I whispered to Lisbeth, "Ease over close and get my knife out of my pocket. But take your time and be quiet about it."

I felt her shift around, slow and careful. Then her hand was in my pocket, fishing for my knife.

She got it, but couldn't thumb open the blade. I told her to hold it up to my mouth, and I bit the blade open. She cut the rawhide string binding my hands. Then I took the knife and cut us all free.

"Now, keep quiet," I warned. "Till we're dead certain they're all asleep."

We lay still and waited. I held the pocketknife open in my hand. When the time came, I wanted to be all set to cut the horse hobbles in a hurry.

The edge of a full moon began to inch up over the ridges. A "Comanche moon" was what the settlers called it, because it was during the time of a September full moon when the Comanches did most of their raiding. I guessed now it might get to be called an "Apache moon."

The fire died to a weak glow among the ashes. The wolves hushed their howling. A little later, I heard them snarling and growling at each other over the carcasses of the dead horse and the old longhorn cow who'd killed him. From the lower end of the valley came the booming hoot of a great horned owl. It was a ghostly sound and lonesome.

Listening to the owl set my mind to drifting. It slid way back in time to when I was just a knothead youngun,

[55]

three or four years old, and pestering Mama every night to tell me what the owls were saying. And Mama came and stood right over me, her face all lighted up with fun, and I heard her say, like always, "Why, can't you tell? They're saying 'Who's cooking for yoo-oo? Who's cooking for *yoo*-all?'" So I laughed and snuggled down deeper into my corn-shuck bed, feeling warm and safe, knowing all along who was cooking for us.

Little Arliss

Five

I GUESS in times of danger, a body's got senses working for him that he doesn't even know about. I didn't hear anything. I don't remember smelling or feeling anything. And, dozed off like I was, I sure couldn't have seen that Apache already crouched over and reaching for Lisbeth. Yet suddenly the warning shot through me, so strong and chilling that I lunged to my feet and had the blade of my pocketknife buried in the back of the ugly devil almost before my eyes popped open.

[57]

He went down under my knife blow with a howl of pain. He landed on hands and knees, then pitched sideways across Lisbeth, who screamed as she fought to get out from under him. I went after him. I tripped over Little Arliss as he started up with a cry of fear. I fell hard. But I was done reaching for the black twisting shadow of the Apache, and I had my knife into him a second time when I hit the ground.

Then I was on him and all over him, kill-crazy with fear and rage.

Behind me, I could hear the rest of the camp come shouting to life, and while I struggled and stabbed and slashed, I thought: *They'll get you. They'll kill you for this!* But then I told myself: *Not before I get this one, they won't!*

I was wrong on both counts.

I didn't get this one, because, during our desperate fight there in the moonlight, he was lucky enough to grab my knife hand and, in spite of how I'd cut him up, he still had the strength to sling me head over heels through the air.

I landed in the sand and got a mouthful of it, and that's where the others caught me and took over. The reason, I guess, that they didn't kill me for trying to kill him was that they could think up worse things to do.

They slapped me to the ground, where they kicked me. They yanked my boots from my feet and tore my pants off. They built up the fire and burnt my pants and boots, and then they jabbed glowing firebrands against my naked hide.

I'd lost my knife when I landed in the sand, but it wouldn't have done me any good now. They were too many for me. The grip of their hands on me was too tight. No matter how I bucked and pitched, I couldn't escape those firebrands. All I could do was grit my teeth against the horrible pain till I could smell the stench of my own flesh scorching. Then I'd lose control and scream and get to listen to the devils yelp with laughter every time I did.

How long this lasted, I don't know. Not long, I guess, else they'd have killed me. After a while, I blacked out, and when I came to, they were stringing me up to a drooping branch of one of the cottonwoods.

I hung face down, with my feet and hands tied together behind my back, with my weight all but pulling my arms out of socket at the shoulders. I hung so near the ground that my chest almost touched it. To add to my torment, one of the Apaches brought a big flat rock and laid it across my head, so that it kept my face pressed into the sand.

There I hung for the rest of the night, suffering more agony than it seems like a body could stand, suffering till I couldn't even think to wonder what had happened to Lisbeth and Little Arliss.

I suffered so much that every now and then I'd hear somebody groan, then come to realize that it was me. And every time I groaned, one of the Apaches would come and twist my ears or beat me with a stick or kick me again. I tried hard to stop groaning and couldn't. But after a while, I stopped anyhow, without trying—maybe because I was too far gone.

Out in the wild places, there are sounds to tell you when day is breaking, even if you're shut off from seeing the first faint light. In our country, the first sound is ordinarily the singing of the coyotes. Then comes the chatter and quarreling of the scissortail flycatchers. After that, it may be the fussing of the redbirds or the sharp clear call of a bob-white rooster quail in a hurry to get the day started. Or, if you happen to be in the right place, you can hear the heavy wing blows of wild turkeys threshing the tree branches as they quit their roosts, generally hitting the ground scattered, so that they've got to do a lot of yelping and stalking around to find each other again.

Such sounds are bound to have been all around me the next morning at daybreak. Yet, wrapped tight as I was in a black smothering coat of pain, I heard none of them.

Only one sound managed to get through to the part that was still me, and it had to have been the faintest, most faraway sound of them all. It was a clear, sweet, high-ringing bell note, as familiar a sound as I'd ever heard, yet one that in my tortured state I couldn't seem to place. It came through to me, over and over, almost as regular as my heartbeat, ringing out high, then fading, only to ring out again.

It fretted me, not being able to recognize that sound. I worried about it, certain that it was a thing within reach of my knowing, if only I could grab a hold on it. But my mind was like a red ant in a doodle-bug hole, clawing its way up the slant to the very edge of the trap, only to have the loose dry sand give way underfoot and let it slide back to the bottom. If only there was some way I could climb out of this trap of pain, I'd know in a second what that sound was.

Then, close beside me, I heard Little Arliss come alive, his voice shrill with excitement. "Listen! That's Savage Sam! He's a-trailin' us up!"

I came to my senses with a jolt. That was it. That's what my mind had been reaching for. The voice of Savage Sam!

Again, his faint, far-carrying trail cry came riding in on the still morning air. The sound of it raised a lump in my throat and put the sting of tears in my eyes.

There was a quick rush of footsteps toward me. The flat rock was shoved off my head. I twisted my stiff neck enough to recognize the figure of the tall Comanche as he cut me down from the cottonwood branch and dragged me over to the slanted boulder. He propped me against it, then left out in a run.

For a couple of seconds, the relief from hanging was so great that I almost fainted. Then the blood began to circulate in my legs and arms once more, and the pain of it made me dizzy and sick.

When my head cleared a little, I took a blurred look around. In the half-light of the coming day, I could see the Indians hustling about in a big hurry of excitement. One was bringing the horse herd in on the run, the hobbled horses goat-jumping awkwardly to keep up. Several Apaches ran out to meet the herd, where they were quick to free the hobbled horses. Others were busy picking up what loose gear they'd left lying around. Two scattered the ashes and charred wood left from last night's campfire, while another came running up with a dead bee-myrtle bush to sweep the place clean. Now, three came toward us, leading horses at a sweeping trot. One of them was the Comanche. He led the big bay I'd ridden the day before.

On reaching me, he jerked loose the knots in the string binding my feet. He yanked me to my feet, motioning for me to mount up.

How he expected me to climb astride that tall bay after what I'd been through the night before, I don't know. I couldn't even stand. I felt myself going down and twisted sideways so that I landed on my shoulder instead of my face. With a growl of anger, the Comanche grabbed me by the hair and one leg and flung me astride the horse. The bay's hair stung the galled places inside my bare legs.

While the Comanche bound me to the bay, I looked across to where two Apaches were tying Lisbeth and Little Arliss, each to a separate horse.

The sight of Arliss was enough to make me take a second look. He'd been painted all over, the same red as the skin of the Indians. Tied on his head was the tanned skin from a buffalo skull, with the curved black horns still attached. A foot of neck hide hung down over Arliss's back and shoulders like a black woolly cape.

A closer look at the Apache binding Lisbeth to her horse made my gorge rise. It was the broken-nosed one that I'd worked over with my pocketknife the night before. I'd laid his flesh open with enough deep cuts and slashes to have killed an ordinary man and it made me furious that he hadn't died. But I could take some satisfaction in seeing how his wounds still seeped blood and how he crippled around. He was bad hurt, all right. I guessed he'd think twice before he laid a hand on Lisbeth again if I was anywhere in reach.

I wished I hadn't lost my pocketknife, though.

I said to Lisbeth and Arliss, "Why didn't y'all run last night? While I had my knife in that rascal?"

Lisbeth looked at me, then quickly away. "Wasn't nowhere to run to," she said.

"Anywhere would have done," I said. "Anywhere to get away from these red devils!"

Lisbeth didn't answer. She didn't look at me, either. She just sat there and kept her head turned away.

Then it came to me why she wouldn't look at me. I glanced down at myself and felt goose pimples of shame break out all over. I'd known it all along, of course, but the agony I'd suffered during the night had put it out of my mind. Now I saw that not only had I been painted as red as Little Arliss—I'd also been stripped just as naked!

Arliss said, "You wait till old Sam catches up! Then we'll git away!"

Mention of Sam took my mind off my nakedness. It was hard to believe that Sam was alive. I'd seen him chopped down by that tomahawk. I'd heard his screech of pain and seen the trail of blood he'd left as he'd gone wallowing and pitching down the slant of rocks.

Yet there was no doubt about it. He was not only still alive, he was on our trail. Or, anyhow, on the trail of Little Arliss. I'd heard him trailing Arliss often enough to recognize the pitch of his voice, which was different from when he was trailing a varmint. He was three or four miles behind, and not driving too fast, but coming on, sure and steady.

It was the constant ringing of Sam's voice that had the Indians disturbed. I could tell that by the way every now and then one of them would halt whatever he was doing to cock an ear in the direction of our back trail. I could tell by the quick uneasy glances they kept flinging over their shoulders, by the sharp questioning bark of their voices.

Maybe they didn't know what it was. Maybe they'd never heard the singing voice of a trail hound before. Or maybe they knew exactly what it was and figured a band of armed white men was following that dog.

There was no way of knowing what they thought or didn't think, but one thing I could tell for certain: they knew *something* was on their trail, and they didn't like it and were bent on quitting that part of the country in a hurry.

Still looking away from me, Lisbeth spoke up, her voice desperate with hope. "You think anybody'll be with Sam?"

"Could be," I said, knowing the odds were all against it.

"Sure they is!" Arliss put in. "Betcha Sam's bringing Papa and a dozen others. First thing you know, there'll be dead Injuns scattered all over creation!"

The Apaches mounted up, the wounded Comanche grabbed me by the foot, and we were on the move again, traveling fast.

I rode with the brush scratching and clawing at my

bare legs, wishing I could feel as confident as Little Arliss. I wished I could believe that the man who'd shot the Comanche had also seen Sam get cut down and had gone to him and carried him home and got Papa and all the other settlers they could round up and taken Sam back and put him on our trail and followed him all the rest of the day and on through the night. But I knew that was asking for a lot of luck.

Still, just knowing that Sam was on our trail gave me a lift. It was foolish, of course. Against the Indians, Sam would last about as long as it would take a whirlwind to suck up a dry corn shuck. Yet, for some reason, hope rode high inside me as we left the little half-moon valley, traveling north, climbing a rocky rise, where the fast hoofbeats of the horses rang out sharp and loud in the still morning air.

At the top of the rise, two of the Apaches split off from the main bunch and swung right. Then my hopes withered.

It was plain those two meant to quarter in on our back trail and take a look at whatever was following us. They rode in the direction I figured would take them to the river at about where we'd crossed it the evening before. There, I guessed, they'd wait till Sam entered the water and started swimming across. Then they'd cut down on him with bows and arrows. And if they missed the first shots, they'd have plenty of time for seconds and thirds, what with Sam being out there in the open.

Thinking of Sam's getting killed with no chance to fight back made me heartsick. But since I couldn't help him,

I tried to put my mind to problems I might could handle.

One of the main ones was how to keep from getting my head knocked off my shoulders. For by now, we had hit the bottom of the other side of the ridge, and here the country changed suddenly from sandstone to granite gravel and from short brush to thick stands of scrub blackjack and post oak. A heavy crop of acorns had the oak branches sagging. They hung at just the right height for the smaller ones to whip you blind or for the bigger ones to knock you clean off your horse if you weren't tied on.

I laid my head low against the bay's neck, then thought of Lisbeth and Little Arliss. They were mounted on loose horses now, and maybe wouldn't know how to protect themselves.

I lifted my head, searching. I spotted Lisbeth and Arliss riding close together. Their hands weren't tied, and both rode with a fistful of mane to help hold themselves on. That was good. But while Arliss had caught on to ride with his head down, like me and the Indians, Lisbeth hadn't. She was still trying to sit up straight, and having to duck and dodge every whichaway and still getting whipped over the head every time her horse ran under a tree. Any second now, she was liable to get slammed by a heavy tree branch that'd knock her off balance.

It gave me the cold chills to think what would happen if she ever slipped down to hang under her running horse. His hammering hind feet would crush her skull in a minute.

I yelled at her. "Lisbeth! Lay down on him. Like Little Arliss!"

She flung me a scared glance, then laid her head down beside her horse's neck. There, the drooping branches could still claw at her long hair and rake and tear at her dress. But hugged down close to her mount, she wasn't so likely to get knocked loose.

We rode a long time this way, then swept down into a broad open flat, where the timber thinned out, giving way to big granite boulders that stood high above the tall grass. The boulders were pink and orange, grayed over with age and weather. They looked old and solemn and quiet, like tombstones in a graveyard. One, nearly as big and a lot taller than our cabin, looked exactly like a monstrous Indian. He was squatted, with arms folded, wrapped to his chin in a blanket of pink-flowering morning-glory vine, and gazing out upon the rising sun.

I wasn't the only one to take notice of that rock. Before we'd reached it, the Comanche running beside me called out and pointed. The others looked and came suddenly alert. They swung their running horses wide around the Indian rock and kept glancing fearfully back over their shoulders long after we'd passed it.

I guess they were superstitious and looked on that big rock as some sort of heathen god. I know the sight of it prickled my scalp.

We rode past a little lake. Heavy live-oak timber stood back a way from it. Between the timber and the water's edge bloomed the bluest flowers I ever saw, and the blue of them was reflected in the water.

[67]

We skirted the timber and went racing through the blue flowers, crushing them, and on through a tall stand of cattail grass, out of which red-wing blackbirds rose in clouds, screaming at us for disturbing them.

We left the lake and crossed a slight knoll. We went plunging down through a tall stand of yellow blooming sunflowers whose stalks and leaves dragged fuzzy-rough and stinging against my bare skin. We crashed through a stand of willows that lined a wide sandy creek bed. A trickle of shallow water wound back and forth across the sand.

At one place, the sand was quick and sucked at the horses' feet, so that the animals had to pitch and lunge to fight free of bogging clear up to their bellies. Then we went out through more willows, entering an open, grassy flood plain that led alongside the creek.

We followed this creek for miles. Now and then the oak and pecan timber would squeeze in too close to the willows. When this happened, nearly always we could see open ground on the opposite side of the creek; so we'd cross over and keep going.

We rode till the sun got high and hot and set fire to my skin, some of which had already blistered from exposure the day before. We rode till flecks of white foam flew back from the horse's mouth to sting my eyes. We rode till the bay was in a lather of sweat, and the salt of that sweat stung my galled crotch.

I hoped Lisbeth and Little Arliss weren't suffering like I was. Lisbeth, of course, still had on her dress; and torn and tattered as it was by now, I figured it still had to be some protection. Arliss, he was used to the sun and wasn't likely to blister. Yet, riding naked and tied down hard to a sweat-lathered horse, he was bound to be rubbed raw, the same as me.

But if Arliss suffered, he wasn't letting out one whimper. He rode quiet, gripping a handful of horse mane, and glared black murder at the savages.

That was one thing I could tell for certain about Little Arliss—they hadn't taken the fight out of him yet!

I felt real proud of him.

My last drink of water had been the night before, and now thirst began to add to my misery. I kept hoping that at one of our many crossings of the sandy creek the Indians would stop for water, but they didn't. They never let up and finally swung away from the creek, heading northwest across more rocky, brush-covered hills.

We came to the San Saba River, with its clear, sparkling waters purling over and around the rocks. It seemed like I just *had* to have a drink of that water; but I didn't get one, and neither did many of the horses. Some of the leaders got a few sips before the Indians came whooping up from behind, to send them splashing across the shallow stream with their ironshod hoofs popping loud against the flat rocks.

Then it was more hills, more brush, more rocky, deep-cut draws and canyons, with my suffering mounting steadily, so that after a time I rode in a daze of agony and hardly noticed when the ground began to smooth out and become open, rolling grassland.

Gradually, however, I did become aware of a moun-

[69]

tain that stood alone, some distance away from the hills.

We rode toward it, and I noticed that one side was a gentle, brush-covered slope that rose higher and higher till suddenly it chopped square off, leaving a bare-rock cliff with different shades of coloring. We approached the sloping side.

We had reached the foot of the mountain, where the grass began to thin out and the brush to take over, when I heard the frightened wail of a rabbit.

An Apache riding just ahead of me heard it, too. He slid his running horse to a squat and waved his lance aloft. All the others swung their mounts toward him, leaving the loose horses to run on ahead. The Indians cut in front of me so quickly that my bay was forced to stop.

I heard the rabbit cry out again, then saw a cottontail dart from under a tickle-tongue bush and race off into the brush. At the same time, I saw the branches of the bush shake, then caught a glimpse of a snake slithering his way to the top. It was a prairie racer and in its mouth was a struggling half-grown cottontail.

The snake climbed quickly to the top of the bush. There it lay, with its whip body crooked around the thorny branches. If it heard or saw the horses and Indians gathering around, it paid them no mind, but went right to work swallowing its catch.

The cottontail was four times bigger around than the biggest part of the snake. But the snake seemed to know what it was doing. It had its mouth clamped shut over the nose of the cottontail, and I could see the widespread jaws spreading wider as the snake's neck muscles flattened and swelled, flattened and swelled, somehow always shoving those jaws forward to take in a bit more of the rabbit's nose.

I guess a snake's got the same right to eat as anybody else. I'd killed and eaten plenty of cottontails and never thought much about it. But, like most people, I always did hate snakes, and it was an ugly thing to sit and watch this one swallow down a helpless baby rabbit.

To me, it was strange, the way the Indians gathered round to watch, silent and intent, some even dismounting to come bend over the bush for a closer look.

I got to watching the Indians more than the snake. All yesterday and most of this morning, they'd kept on the run like they'd expected to be caught any minute. Then, at the cry of a captured animal, they'd stopped to waste all this time watching the rabbit get swallowed by a snake —as curious about it as Little Arliss might have been. It didn't make sense.

But then, what about an Indian did make sense? Why would they raid for horses, then run them so hard and long that half of them would end up wind-broken and worthless? Why capture us, then mistreat us till we were liable to die on their hands before they ever got to wherever they meant to take us?

There was no answer to that one. So I just sat there on the bay horse, dizzy with thirst and the pain of the sun blazing down on my fire burns, which were now beginning to fester and seep clear water.

I looked up the brushy slope, searching for Lisbeth and Little Arliss. The horses had scattered. Some were grazing, but most of them stood spraddle-legged with their heads down, trying to get back their wind. I saw Lisbeth not too far away, and Little Arliss a couple of hundred yards off, both still tied to their horses and looking toward us, both wondering, I guess, at what was going on.

We waited there for twenty, maybe thirty minutes, watching the snake stretch himself wider and wider and squeezing the rabbit down smaller and smaller as he swallowed it. Finally, the hind feet of the rabbit disappeared. The snake's muscles quit working for a moment and the snake lay still.

That's when several of the watching Indians straightened and grunted, sounding like they were satisfied with the show. Then, grinning, the one-eared Apache drew his tomahawk from his belt. With a quick flashing stroke, he chopped the snake's head clean off; and they all whooped with laughter as the rest of snake's body whipped high into the air, then spilled down out of the bush onto the ground. The headless snake was still writhing and twisting and slinging spurts of blood around when the Indians turned to mount up and ride toward the top of the mountain.

Apache

Six

THE highest part of the mountain was at the brink of the cliff, and that's where we stopped. Here the riders rounded up the loose horses and held them, bunched tight against the edge, while they all gazed out across the country beyond. It was a vast expanse of rolling grassland, broken in only a few places by dark, straggling lines of timber which marked the watercourses. It stretched on and on toward the west, farther than a body could believe, reaching so far out that it finally faded to nothing in the misty blue haze of distance.

This, I knew, was the edge of the South Plains, a lower section of *El Llano Estacado,* as the Spanish called that great wilderness of grass that some said reached north from the Rio Grande clear into Canada. I'd heard tell of it, but never seen it before; and in spite of how dazed I was with hurts and doubts and fears, my first glimpse of all that wide spread of emptiness struck me a solid jolt.

Once Papa had tried to tell me and Little Arliss what the ocean looked like, but this was the first time I ever got a clear picture of what he was talking about.

I'd been told that white men had crossed this country, but only the Indians knew it; and now I wondered how even they could know it all. It was just so big!

I looked to see what they searched for. A mile out, I located a band of antelope. Some were grazing and some were lying down. All seemed contented and willing to take things easy, except for four sentinels that stood away from the herd a piece, each guarding a different side. The sentinels stood stock-still and high-headed, alert to give warning of any danger.

Farther out, so far that the rising heat waves made everything wavery, I saw lumps of black against the green of the grass. I took these to be buffalo, but couldn't know for sure.

And overhead, high against a few cotton-white puff-balls of clouds, a couple of eagles wheeled slowly on widespread wings, screaming at regular intervals.

Those were the only living creatures I could see. They

must have been all the Indians could see, too, for finally one of them grunted, and they all turned to search our back trail.

They looked it over just as closely, but not for so long. Then one reached into a buckskin bag hanging to his belt and drew out a little square mirror of polished steel. He squinted up at the sun. He swung his horse around to face a different direction, then held up the mirror. With quick twists of his wrists, he flicked the face of the mirror back and forth.

Where I sat my horse, watching, I was almost facing the mirror; and once, a blaze of reflected sunlight caught me full in the eyes, nearly blinding me.

After that, I turned and looked along our back trail, like the Indians; and before long, I saw a quick wink of light from some high place far back in the wooded hills. Then another and another.

There were some sharp, barking words among the Indians. It came to me then what was going on. This bunch was swapping signals with other Indians, probably the two who had gone to ambush Sam.

Evidently, the Indians were satisfied with what they'd learned. They all relaxed. The herders opened up and let the loose horses move away from the edge of the cliff. They got behind them and drove them back down the side of the mountain. At the bottom, we swung west, then north past the face of the cliff, traveling at a walk, which gave the horses time to nip at the grass clumps as we moved along.

An hour later, the two Apaches who had left at daylight overtook us. They came galloping up on lathered mounts, driving six more horses ahead of them. All stopped then to hold a big jabbering powwow.

I looked the new horses over. It was a relief to note that they all wore the same brand, a Circle Seven on the right hip. That meant that they had been stolen from Charlie Severs, who raised horses along the Llano. They hadn't been taken from Papa or any of the other Salt Licks settlers who might be on our trail now.

The newcomers acted braggy about something. They talked big and waved their lances and rifles about in the air. When the others didn't appear too happy about what they had to say, one of the newcomers got mad. He stabbed his lance into the ground. He glared around at the others, daring anybody to pick up the quarrel.

Nobody did, but I noticed that the main bunch seemed uneasy about something; and when we moved on, it was at a fast pace again. It wasn't a dead run, like before, but it was at a pretty smart clip.

I rode with the trotting Comanche holding to my foot. I numbed myself the best I could against the burning pain of my outside body and the fearful dread that lay cold and heavy on my inside.

I kept asking myself, *Did they get Sam?* I didn't see how they could have missed if they'd gone back after him. And what with the way they'd all got so excited when they heard his voice, that's bound to have been what they went for.

Still, there were those extra horses they'd brought in. Could they have run onto the horses and forgotten Sam?

Or did they kill Sam first and then pick up the horses? I could tell myself that whether they'd killed Sam or not wasn't likely to make much difference in what happened to us. Yet, it seemed like I just had to know, and my mind kept gnawing at it like a dog worrying an old bone.

A gentle breeze started pulling in from the south, cooling my sunburned back and setting the tall grass to nodding and whispering. The breeze grew stronger. It lifted and set streaming the manes and tails of the horses. It raced across the grass in great shimmering waves, and the whispering of the grass grew louder. By noon, the wind drove with a force that all but flattened the grass to the ground and had it booming like far-off thunder.

I looked to the north, expecting to see the makings of a big rainstorm. All I could see, though, was the glint and sparkle of the hot sunlight on the tossing grass. If there was a rain cloud building up, it had to be clear off the rim of the earth.

We didn't see any buffalo for a while, but their trails were everywhere. Some trails were worn so deep and narrow that I could see where the grass-swelled bellies of the huge animals had scraped both sides of the trail, dragging loose little wads of hair that still stuck to the dirt walls. Mostly, we followed one buffalo trail or another; but if we happened to be crossing them and came to a deep one, the horses all had to jump it.

I guess it was the whoop and roar of the wind that made our meeting with the two white men such a big surprise for both parties.

We came jog-trotting down off the high prairie into a cut-bank draw. The draw led into a wide-open flat that I could see just beyond. The high dirt banks shut off the wind for a moment, and I remember feeling the touch of relief you always notice when you first take cover from a high wind. Then we were out in the open again and there, gathered around a water hole, was a band of some thirty mares with colts, along with a couple of stud horses.

The studs were fighting. They were reared up and squealing, chopping at each other with their forefeet, trying to grab neck holds with their bared teeth.

Just beyond, in the shade of a cottonwood, squatted a couple of white men. They sat on their spurs, holding the bridle reins of their saddled mounts while they watched the studs fight. One was an old man dressed in buckskins and wearing his hair long under a wide-brimmed black hat. The other was maybe twenty-five or -six, and wore the usual cowhand garb.

Suddenly the white men saw us. They came to their feet with shouts of alarm, while the mounted Apaches cut loose with whoops and screeches. All this racket stampeded the mares and colts, so that they wheeled away from the water, snorting and lunging. They scattered and got in the way of the Indians and gave the white men time to mount up.

"Cut for the dugout!" I heard the old man yell.

Then all of us—white men, mounted Indians, our horses, and the whole band of mares, colts, and studs—took out down the draw in a wild run.

The two white men had six-shooters and knew how to

use them, judging by the number of horses they shot from under the Apaches.

But hitting an Apache was something else. All the white men had to shoot at was a part of one leg hooked across the back of a horse and a shield clamped against the horse's neck. The rest hung out of sight on the off side.

At first, I couldn't see how those red devils could cling to a running horse like that. Then I noted that they had tied loops in their horses' manes and had their shield arms run through the loops. Hanging there, using their mounts' bodies for protection, they shot from under the necks of the horses. Some used bows and arrows. Most of them fired repeater rifles. One or two made short throws with their feathered lances.

The only real chance the white men ever had was when they knocked a rider's horse down. Then all they'd get was one quick running shot before the Indian had bounded to the back of another horse and slipped down off its side, where the horse's body would protect him.

The Apaches got the young man first. I saw him throw up his hands and slip from the saddle. He hit the ground, and the frightened horses snorted and lunged aside, trying to keep from stepping on him; but they were too hard pressed from behind. Some trampled on him, anyhow.

Then we were past, and I looked ahead in time to see the old man's horse stumble and start going down. But the old man was nimble as any Indian; he quit his saddle and hit the ground running and he ran with a speed that had his long gray hair streaming backward from under his hat.

I saw then the place he was making for: the dark hole of a dugout set in the side of a sharp slope near some live oak trees. Feathered arrows stabbed the ground around his racing feet and rifle balls kicked up spurts of dust beyond. But nothing touched him; and for a second, I thought he was going to make it.

Then a ball took him in the back, seeming to lift him clear off his feet before tumbling him to the ground. Instantly, he rolled over, got to his hands and knees, and shot a horse from under another Apache.

He was still snapping an empty six-shooter in their faces when the yelping pack leaped from their horses to swarm over him.

My Comanche bounded ahead to clutch the running bay by one ear and his underjaw, dragging him to a stop beside the close-packed Indians. The group parted, and I saw the old man now lying flat on his back, with a lance thrust through his side, pinning him to the ground.

Arliss's one-eared Apache held the lance. A moon-faced, bandy-legged Indian had a grip on the old man's long hair. Both held drawn knives and argued furiously. Others joined in the argument.

Finally, Gotch Ear snatched his lance from the old man's body. He grabbed up the black hat that lay on the ground close by and clapped it on his head. He shoved his way roughly through the group and walked off, his face a thundercloud of anger. It was plain he'd lost the argument over the old man's scalp.

I'd sat watching, petrified with horror, and got a bigger shock when I saw the old man's eyelids flutter open. He looked straight up at me. He gasped. His body jerked, then slowly flattened and lay quiet. His eyes were still open and still staring up at me; but the light had gone out of them. He wasn't seeing me any more.

Bandy Legs scalped him then and waved the scalp aloft, yelping his pleasure.

The Indians were real proud of what they'd done. They strutted and they boasted and they bragged. They robbed the dead men of their knives, six-shooters, and rifles and argued over who was to get which. They held an even hotter argument over who the scalp of the young man belonged to. They rounded up the scattered mares and colts, pointing out special animals to admire. They circled the milling band of horses and gloated at the big haul they'd made.

I'd heard tell that Plains Indians prized stolen horses above anything else, and it was easy to see that when this bunch finally reached camp—wherever that was—they figured to make a real showing.

All their boasting and bragging sickened me. I looked away from it toward the skimpy camp of the white men. Their shelter they'd made by digging a hole back into a dirt bank. They'd roofed the hole over with logs, then piled dirt on top of the logs. They'd raised a garden there on that dirt roof, packing water to it, I guess, from the creek below. Some okra and tomato plants were still alive. I could see the red of several ripe tomatoes among the green of the sprawling vines.

Near the dugout door was the ash pile of a still smouldering campfire. It was ringed with flat rocks and on the rocks sat a fire-blackened coffee pot and a big Dutch oven.

The sign was easy to read. The old man and the young one had come to raise horses on free grass. They'd brought along a bunch of mares and a couple of studs. They'd aimed to rough it out here in the wilds, gambling on staying alive till they could build up a horse herd worth trailing to New Orleans or maybe to California—just wherever they figured on horses bringing the best price. It was a way of raising a good stake of cash money for whatever they hoped to do later on down the line.

A lot of young men took that gamble in those days. Once me and Papa had talked some about giving it a whirl. But Mama, she'd put her foot down, hard; and for every man we could mention who had cleaned up a pot of money that way, she could name three who'd lost both their horses and their hair.

At the time, I'd been mighty disappointed and had looked on Mama's arguments as the same brand of scare talk you could generally expect of womenfolks. Now, I could see Mama'd had some room to argue.

In the excitement, I hadn't missed my Comanche. Suddenly, he appeared in the doorway of the dugout, packing a roll of blankets and a couple of hackamores of braided horsehair. This loot he carried to my horse, Blue. He hung the hackamores over the saddle horn and tied the blankets on back of the cantle. Then he came toward me, wearing a puzzled frown on his paint-streaked face as he studied a small object in his hand.

I didn't pay him much mind. I was too sick with hurt

[82]

and shock to care what he had found. But when he held it up to me, I looked.

It was a tintype picture of a young woman. She was about twenty years old. She wore the stiff, scared smile that most people wear when they're getting their pictures struck. But she was a pretty woman, with long blond hair like Lisbeth's. She didn't look like Lisbeth, yet there was something about her eyes and the curve of her lips that gave you the same warm feeling. You could tell at a glance that she was the sort a young man would love—wanting her bad enough to take most any sort of gamble to provide her with a nice home and the pretty things a woman generally hopes for.

The Comanche withdrew the picture and peered up at me like he wanted the answer to some question on his mind. I didn't know what the question was, but I boiled with plenty of hot answers.

"You stinking, murdering devils!" I railed at him. "You kill her man, then expect me to tell you who she is and where she is and how you can get your filthy hands on her!"

I was all wound up to tell him more, but got stopped by a loud commotion.

It was Gotch Ear, black hat and all, mounted on one of the stud horses. The stud was reared high, pawing the air with his forefeet. At the same time, he was running backward on his hind feet and squealing his rage.

Maybe I was wrong, but the thought hit me that in mounting that stud, Gotch Ear was making a strong bid for glory. He'd been jeered at for losing an ear to Little

[83]

Arliss. The Comanche had stood him off with a lance when he tried to get revenge. Then he'd laid claim to the long-haired scalp of the old man, but the others had let Bandy Legs have it. Now, he aimed to wipe out the shame of all this with a show-off ride on a bad horse.

Well, it was a ride to watch and remember. The stud was reared so high it looked like he was bound to topple over. Then he dropped back to the ground and started whirling in a tight circle. He whirled with a speed hard to believe. He had his neck bowed, his ears laid back, and his teeth bared. He was doing his savage best to bite that Apache's leg clear in two. But Gotch Ear rode with his leg always just a little out of reach.

The stud was big and stout and a mean fighter. He had plenty of other tricks in his bag. Quick as lightning, he whipped his head around for a bite at the other leg. This time, he came so close that he left tooth marks on Gotch Ear's leg, which set all the watching Apaches to yelping.

Missing out on that bite, the stud reared again. When he came down this time, it was to tuck his tail and bog his head and take out across the draw, pitching and bawling the wildest I ever saw.

That Gotch Ear was a rider. All he had to hold onto was a fistful of mane and a sense of balance. All he rode was a little patch of that stud's back no bigger than the palm of your hand. His legs and one free arm, they were loose as rags. They flew out in all directions. Just now and then one of them swung back to touch the stud's neck or shoulder or maybe his ribs before flinging out into the air again.

And all the time, the bawling stud was putting everything he had into unloading that Indian. He pitched forward, sideways, and in circles. He crawfished. He rolled
his belly up to the sun. And every time he landed, it was
with all four legs as stiff as crowbars and all four feet
planted close together—hitting the ground so hard, you
could have stood a quarter of a mile off and heard the
whoomp of the air in his belly.

Yet not once did I see daylight between Gotch Ear's
rump and that little patch of back hide it seemed glued to.
Gotch Ear had that stud horse rode. He had him rode right
down to a whisper—if it hadn't been for his black hat.

I guess he'd never worn a hat before. He didn't seem to
know the importance of pulling one down to a tight set
before mounting a bad horse.

Now the hat loosened and with every leap the stud made,
it inched forward a little, till finally it was clear down on
Gotch Ear's nose, shutting off his vision.

That's when Gotch Ear made his big mistake. He
reached to straighten his hat and lost his balance.

The stud threw him so high I saw him swap ends in the
air above the highest branches of a stooping mesquite that
stood between us.

He landed on his feet, running, but he was still lucky
that mesquite stood so close by. For the stud had wheeled
and was after him with a fire in his eyes that said he aimed
to kill an Indian.

I hoped he caught him.

He nearly did, too. His breath was warming the seat of

Gotch Ear's breechclout when that Apache leaped half-way up the trunk of the stooping mesquite and went scrambling toward a higher perch.

There he squatted, barely out of reach of the screaming stud, who reared high, chopping loose great chunks of bark from the tree trunk with flailing hoofs, biting off smaller branches in his savage attempt to get at the man who'd tried to ride him. There Gotch Ear squatted, forced to listen to the delighted yelps and jeers of his companions, who took their time and hoorawed him to their hearts' content. And in both cases, he was helpless to do more than glare around with hate and defiance.

Satisfied at last with the fun they'd had, the others moved in on the stud. They whipped him and goaded him with lance points until they finally drove him away.

Even after they'd done so, Gotch Ear squatted there in the mesquite a good long while before he climbed down. He wasn't scared. He was just mad—and pouting.

Here he'd gone and made a try to prove himself as much a man as any of the others, and what had come of it? He'd lost everything—his pride, his dignity, the respect he'd hoped to win.

All he had left was his big black hat.

Apache

Seven

LIKE before, when we got around to leaving out, it was in a high run. We swept up out of the draw onto higher ground and went charging across the open prairie like there wasn't a minute to lose.

We jumped a small band of antelope. They went racing off at an angle, their white-tail flags lifted high, traveling at a far greater speed than ours. We skirted a mile-wide prairie-dog town, where thousands of the plump little gray-yellow dogs sat over their holes and barked at us in squeaky voices, quick to drop back into the ground when we came too close.

Living among the dogs were tiny brown owls with big heads and great white circles around their eyes. Alarmed by our passing, they skipped and hopped from one hole to another.

We stampeded several small bunches of buffalo, then one great herd that numbered in the thousands. The pounding hoofs of the shaggy beasts shook the earth as they lumbered across the prairie, leaving in their wake a boil of dust and trash that the whooping wind whipped back into our faces.

An hour of this sort of travel, and the horse herd began to string out, the tougher and faster animals taking the lead.

Among the stragglers was old Jumper; and this time, I could tell, he wasn't throwing off. The Indians shouted at him. They lashed him cruelly. They jabbed his rump with their lances till the blood came and Jumper brayed with the pain of it. Still, he kept falling further behind.

All mules are born tough, and Jumper was one of the toughest. Yet, a mule's not built for speed; and Jumper was old—too old to stand up to the relentless pace set by the Indians. He'd just about gone his limit, and no amount of mistreatment was going to make him keep up much longer.

The Apaches kept after him, though, and got four or five more miles out of him before we dropped down into a wide flat draw that wound in from the west.

There was runoff water here, left from the last rains. It

stood in a number of potholes strung out along the draw. White-flowering cacanilla and scattered bunches of quick-growth mesquite stood among the tall sunflowers.

Thirsty horses plunged into the potholes, taking us captives with them. The horses drank and churned up the water with pawing hoofs, drank some more, then straggled out, looking for graze.

But Jumper didn't drink. Goaded by the Indians, he'd managed to stumble along until he was within sight of the water. But the second they let up on him, he'd stopped and stood there among the trampled sunflowers, with his head down and his shoulders hunched, shivering all over.

The Indians came and bellied down for a drink, again sucking up the water through wadded-grass strainers.

Gotch Ear was the first to rise. He hadn't had the sense to shove his black hat to the back of his head while he drank. Now, water spilled down from its brim and the wind blew it into his face. All he did about it, though, was to give his head a quick shake, like a wet dog, slinging water in all directions as he walked away.

I paid him no more mind, for now the Comanche rose from the water and came toward me. I hoped desperately that he aimed to turn me loose for a drink. I hadn't had water since the night before. All morning, I'd been spitting cotton, till finally I'd gotten too dry for even that. Now, my throat was on fire, and it seemed like if I didn't get water soon, I'd go crazy.

The Comanche came on and had just started working the knots loose at my feet when I heard Little Arliss scream. I looked toward where he sat tied to his drinking horse and saw him staring in horror at some sight I hadn't yet seen.

"They've kilt him!" he cried out. "Travis! They've went and kilt old Jumper!"

I looked around. Jumper still stood, head down and trembling, the same as before; only, now, his life's blood gushed out through a slit across his gullet. Beside him, Gotch Ear wiped a bloody knife blade clean across the old mule's rump.

Jumper tried to bray, but all that came out was a strangled cough and a big gout of blood. The cough shook him. His legs buckled and he went down.

Arliss was suddenly wild with rage. He cut loose with a stream of words so foul you wouldn't believe a boy his age could know them. He screamed at Gotch Ear, and while he swore, he hammered frantically at his horse's back with balled-up fists, scaring the horse into lunging up out of the water hole. The animal shied around, snorting and whistling.

"Arliss!" I shouted at him. "You hush that cussing! You hear me?"

I was scared of the anger I could see mounting in Gotch Ear's face as he listened to Little Arliss's ranting and raving. Gotch Ear didn't have to understand the words to know he was being insulted. Now, he jabbed his knife into his belt and went striding through the sunflowers toward Little Arliss. His black eyes glittered with such evil intent that I panicked.

"Arliss!" I screamed. "You listen to me, now. You hush up that cussing!"

For once, Arliss listened. Or, more likely, he'd just reached a breaking point. Anyhow, he hushed suddenly; his face crumpled, and he tucked his chin and burst into tears, crying so hard that he didn't even fight back when Gotch Ear came and jerked loose the knots binding him to the horse.

Gotch Ear yanked him off the horse by one leg and slung him fifteen feet through the air. Arliss landed in one of the shallow potholes with a splash.

Gotch Ear stood back, grinning like he'd done something special.

The Comanche hauled me down off the bay and got mad all over again because I couldn't stand. He grabbed me by the hair. He dragged me to the water and dropped me face down in it. Now I could drink, all right, but I might have drowned afterward, trying to back uphill with my hands tied behind me, if the weeping Arliss hadn't waded out in time to give me a hand.

Arliss clung to me, shaking with sobs. He kept saying over and over, "They went and kilt old Jumper, Travis! They went and kilt old Jumper!"

Like he thought I could do something about it.

"Well, crying won't help," I told him.

I'd never seen Arliss like this before. I'd seen him cry plenty of times—mostly when he was fighting mad about something. But I'd never seen him break down and sob his heart out, like he was doing now. And it was the first time I could ever remember his calling on me for comfort.

That shook me almost worse than seeing old Jumper killed.

With my burning thirst dulled a little, I looked around for shade. I saw a small dark patch under a bunch-topped mesquite. I staggered to my feet and had a dizzy spell. My ears roared; the ground rocked under me. I waited till the spell passed, then went stumbling toward the mesquite, with the weeping Arliss still clinging to me.

I flopped down in the shade. Lisbeth came toward us with tears running down her cheeks. She squatted beside Arliss and put her arms around him. She loved him up and tried to comfort him like Mama would have done. She tore a rag from her petticoat and went and soaked it in the water and came back and washed Arliss's face.

As she turned to wash me, she glanced toward the Indians. She gasped and looked quickly away. She said in a horrified voice, "Don't look now, Travis!"

So, naturally, I looked—and saw the Indians cutting chunks of meat from Jumper's rump.

My rage against the Indians rose to a pitch that nearly drove me wild.

I thought back over all the years we'd had Jumper. I remembered the many times he'd made me so mad that I'd wanted to kill him myself—for wheeling and kicking; for balking when he thought a load was too heavy; for always hunting something to take a scare at, so he'd have an excuse for running away and tearing up a cart or plow or a set of harness; for deciding for himself when it was time to quit work, sometimes taking out right in the middle of the field and heading for the cabin.

Yet, for all the years we'd had him, old Jumper had

done the heavy work around our place. He'd pulled our plows. He'd hauled in our crops. He'd dragged up building logs. He'd packed in the wild meat we shot. When we cleared new ground or gathered slab rocks for fence building, it had been old Jumper's strength and sweat that had gone into moving those drag-sled loads of rock.

On top of all that, Jumper was *our* mule, which, I guess, was the main thing. Generally speaking, whatever thing belongs to you, whether it happens to be good or bad, seems to become a part of you. So that when you see it destroyed—especially in the cruel way we saw old Jumper destroyed—well, it's just natural for the hurt to go deeper.

There for a little bit, I was right on the edge of throwing in with Arliss and crying my eyes out—all on account of a cantankerous, butt-head mule.

The Indians gathered dead wood and built a fire around the trunk of a squat green mesquite. They brought long strips of backstrap and rump meat, cut from Jumper's carcass. They hung the strips in the forks of the mesquite and across the lower branches, where the heat of the fire could roast them.

They gutted the old mule and cut off a four- or five-foot section of the main gut. They tied up one end of it, making it into a sack. They filled this sack with water, then tied up the other end. They carried it to one of the saddled horses and hung it across the saddle and tied it down, so it wouldn't slip off. Then they went back and squatted around the fire and started eating the ends off the meat strips which hung closer to the fire and cooked faster than the rest.

They'd take their knives and lift the ends of the strips out away from the fire and blow on them till they could bite into the meat. Then they'd slice off the bite and let the rest of the strip swing back to hang over the fire and cook a while longer.

When a strip of meat had cooked enough to suit them, they'd lift it from the fire-blackened branch it hung on and hang it higher. When four or five of these strips had hung away from the fire long enough to cool, they'd tie them into a bundle and go catch a saddled horse and tie the bundle to the saddle.

After a while, the Comanche brought a strip of meat and handed it to Lisbeth and gave her his knife to cut it with. Then he squatted down on his hunkers to make another careful examination of us. I couldn't tell if he was the only one who cared whether we got anything to eat, or if he was just curious and looking for an excuse to study us some more.

Arliss had nearly stopped crying, but sight of that meat broke him down again.

"I can't eat none of old Jumper," he wailed.

"Eat it," I told him. "The way it's been, no telling when you'll eat again."

"But I can't," he sobbed. "What'd old Jumper think? Us eatin' him?"

"Jumper won't care," Lisbeth said. "He knows you got to eat." She cut him off a chunk. "Anybody can eat an Indian's ear can eat mule meat!"

Arliss held the meat and stared down at it and dripped tears all over it. Then he looked up at me.

"You think old Jumper won't mind?" he asked.

"He won't mind," I said.

So Arliss bit into the meat, and once started, ate it all and a couple more pieces. Which was better than I did. I couldn't hardly choke it down to save my life, and I noticed Lisbeth didn't have much better luck.

After all our wild rush to get to where we were, the Indians now lazed around camp like they had all the time in the world. Some kept right on eating, stopping now and then to go for a drink of water or to slice fresh strips of meat from old Jumper's carcass. Some sprawled for a snooze in the skimpy shade of the mesquites. Some just sat around smoking and talking.

This gave the horses a chance to graze and rest up. It give Little Arliss time to cry himself to sleep. And it gave Lisbeth a chance to help me down to water for another drink.

After that, I lay still and let her wash the dirt and stinging salt sweat from my fire- and sunburned body. Then she went to the fire and lifted down a cooled strip of meat. None of the Indians raised any fuss, and she brought it and began rubbing it gently into my burns.

"There's not much grease in it," she said, "but it was the fattest piece I could find."

"It'll help," I said. "Old Jumper wasn't the sort of mule to put on much fat."

That was about all that was said between us the whole

time we were there; after all, what else was there to say?

Along in the shank of the evening, after the sun had sunk past the point of being so scorching hot, the Indians came and tied us back on our horses.

The Comanche flung me astride the bay; and it took all I had to keep from screaming when my raw skin touched the prickly, sweat-salted hairs of the horse's back. It was like being set astraddle of a coal of fire.

Lisbeth, I could tell, was plenty miserable, too, but she didn't cry out. Arliss, tougher than either of us, didn't seem to mind at all. My big worry about him was that he didn't fight back. He just sat on his horse with his head bent and his eyes shut, like he was asleep.

"Arliss," I called to him. "You keep awake and hold on. You slip down under the belly of that horse, and he'll scatter your brains all over the ground!"

Arliss paid me no mind.

Lisbeth touched heels to her horse and moved him up beside Little Arliss.

"Wake up, Arliss," she said.

Arliss paid her no mind, either.

Lisbeth reached out and got hold of one horn of Arliss's buffalo headdress. She used it to shake his head.

Arliss came alive then. He grabbed her wrist and held it.

"Whatta you shaking me around for?" he complained. "I ain't done nothing."

"Just trying to keep you awake," Lisbeth said.

"Well, I ain't sleeping," he said. "I'm just setting here,

thinking. About how they went and kilt old Jumper. I'm aiming to make somebody pay for that!"

The Indians had spread out and rounded up the grazing horses, and now we headed west in a jog trot. We followed the winding watercourse, now and then cutting across some of its widest crooks.

The wild and worrisome wind that had tugged at us for so long had settled down to a gentle, cooling breeze. And what with my thirst gone and a little meat inside me, I was able to take my mind off my hurting and put it back to figuring out a plan of escape. There *had* to be some way of getting us out of the fix we were in.

I thought hard, but couldn't seem to come up with anything better than the plan I'd worked out the night before. I still felt that if Broken Nose hadn't come for Lisbeth when he did, that plan might have worked. It still looked like our best bet, if we could ever catch the Indians off guard.

The big trouble now was the loss of my knife. Without it, we'd have to steal horses that weren't hobbled, and that wouldn't be easy. I was a pretty high jumper when I put myself to it. With luck, I just might manage to sneak up on a horse and leap astride, like the Indians did. But that wouldn't work for Lisbeth and Little Arliss.

I tried to think up ways to steal a knife that Lisbeth might keep hidden inside her dress. Just then, one of the Apaches cut loose with a shout, and I felt the Comanche's grip tighten on my leg. I started up out of my thinking and took a quick look around.

At first, all I saw was mounted Indians racing back and

forth behind the herd, whooping and lashing the horses, goading them into a run. The Comanche spanked my bay and he leaped forward to join the others. Then I looked further out and saw a sight that kicked my heart up into my throat.

It was *soldiers!*

There were fifteen or twenty of them. They were still half a mile off, but it was easy to tell they were United States cavalrymen by the blue of their uniforms, by the way they rode in double-rank file.

I heard the brassy blare of a bugle. I saw the glint of sunlight on the officer's saber blade, lifted high for the signal to charge.

I rode with the blood pounding in my eardrums. I rode with my hopes in as wild a stampede as the spooked horses racing along beside me. I watched the soldiers come charging down upon us, gaining fast, dead certain in my own mind that our freedom was just a few minutes off.

Once those troopers hit us, I guessed these bloodthirsty devils would learn what real fighting was all about. United States soldiers were *trained* to kill Indians. They'd cut this bunch to pieces in no time.

Maybe that's what my Comanche thought, too. Or maybe, like some of the horses, he'd traveled too fast for too long and was beginning to wear down. Anyhow, I felt his grip leave my foot and looked around to see him leap high. He landed back of me astride the bay and went to whacking his lance across the big horse's rump, trying to get more speed out of him.

By now, the stolen horses were stretched out, thundering over the turf at a pace that the colts and weaker horses couldn't hold. One by one, these began to fall behind, and the screeching Indians let them. They had no time now for whipping up the stragglers. The soldiers, evidently mounted on fresh horses, were gaining too fast.

The bay I rode was a big rangy horse with plenty of bottom. Even with a rider, he could have held his own with most horses in the bunch. But under the double load he packed now—better than three hundred pounds—he didn't stand a chance. In spite of the beating the Comanche gave him, he began to fall behind.

The guns of the troopers opened on us. Ahead of me a horse turned a somersault; but his rider didn't turn with him. He hit the ground, still on his feet. A moment later, he had leaped out onto the back of a passing horse.

We tore into another stand of mesquite and tall sunflowers. The mesquites were scrubby, just high enough for their thorny branches to whip my face. I bent low to the left and felt the Comanche lean down on the right. A second later, I learned that it wasn't just to shed the brush that he'd bent down. It was to cut my right foot free of its bindings. Suddenly, he straightened and gave me a hard shove.

I hit the ground rolling, so that it was no real hurt that made me lie there in the sunflowers dead still for a long moment. It was just shock and surprise at being free.

Then I leaped to my feet, aware of the pound of horses' hoofs charging past, knowing it was the soldiers by the clank and rattle of their gear. I went racing toward them

[99]

through the mesquites and sunflowers, screaming at the top of my voice, "Kill 'em! Kill 'em!"

I broke out into the clear, still screaming, as the tail end of the column swept past.

Then I jerked up short. Barely in time, I realized that the last trooper had swung his rifle around and was taking aim at me!

I yelled and flung myself to the ground. The rifle crashed. A spindly mesquite sprout toppled and fell across me. The stub that was left stood just back of where I'd stood an instant before.

I lunged to my feet, scared and mad. I ran out to where I could see the troops tearing along after the Indians. I spotted the one who had fired at me.

"You crazy fool!" I shouted after him. "Can't you see I'm white?"

The words had barely left my mouth when it came to me that I was the fool, not him. How could he know I wasn't an Indian? Me, stark naked and painted up like one.

All of a sudden, I went chasing after the soldiers and the fleeing Indians. I went racing through the tall grass, dragging a strip of rawhide still tied to one ankle. It was hard to run, with my hands tied behind me, but I put on more speed than I'd have thought possible.

I paid no mind to the viney nettles that stung my ankles. I hardly felt the goat-head burs stabbing the soles of my bare feet. I didn't bother about getting mistaken for an Indian and shot at again. All I had on my mind was seeing the kill.

I didn't expect to catch up and get in on it; but maybe if I ran fast enough, I'd get to *see* it.

I ran fast enough, and I saw it. I topped out a little high knoll; and there, strung out before me not more than half a mile off, was the battle, with Indians screeching, soldiers yelling, guns booming, and arrows flying. It was a running fight and a real slaughter.

But it was all going the wrong way. What was getting slaughtered was horses and soldiers!

It was a repeat, on a bigger scale, of what had taken place when the Indians had jumped the two horse raisers. The soldiers killed the horses, while the Indians killed the soldiers.

All my life I'd been told that Indians couldn't shoot for shucks, but here I learned better. I saw the soldiers spill from their saddles, one after another. Time and again, I saw an Indian's horse shot from under him; but always the Indian hit running, and only seconds later was mounted again and hanging down the off side of the horse, where the soldier's bullets couldn't reach him.

The sight was so sickening that I quit watching it. I didn't have to see the soldiers falling or a gap widening between them and the fleeing Indians to know how the fight would wind up.

I looked ahead, searching through the white puffs of gunsmoke. I caught a glimpse of Lisbeth's blond hair glinting in the sun. For just a moment, the curved black horns of Little Arliss's buffalo headdress stood out sharp against the skyline. Then both swept out of sight, swallowed up by distance and the tall waving grass.

I hadn't cried when the Indians captured us. I hadn't cried when they tormented me or when they slaughtered old Jumper. Up to this time, I'd fought back when I could and endured when I couldn't.

But to see Lisbeth and Little Arliss disappear into that vast, wild, unknown land, to realize how little and defenseless they were against the cruel savages they rode with— that was too much. I dropped to the ground and cried like a baby—while over and around me, the grass went right on nodding and whispering, like the tearing hurt inside me had no meaning at all.

Just when I left the knoll and wandered back down to water, I don't know. I was in too much of a daze. All I remember is going back to one of the potholes and drinking, then crawling out into waist-deep water, where I lay with my head on a grass bank, watching some black, yellow-legged mud daubers digging up little balls of mud at the water's edge, listening to the swelling scream of cicadas singing in the mesquites, knowing the kind of despair that goes beyond all resentment and rage.

I'd lost Lisbeth and Little Arliss. I'd been all the protection they'd had against what lay in store for them, yet I'd failed. Now Lisbeth—quiet, shy little Lisbeth—would become the squaw of that stinking Broken Nose, if she was that lucky. And Arliss? Give them time, and they'd not only make him Indian, they'd have him *thinking* Indian. Long before he was grown, he'd be raiding and killing and lifting scalps with the best of their warriors.

I was done. I was whipped. I could think on such things

and not even feel the urge to cry any more. One way or another, I could manage to get back home, but I felt no desire to do so. With Lisbeth and Little Arliss lost, I didn't care if I never saw home again—or even if I lived.

Sam

Eight

I WAS so far gone, I might have let Sam get past without ever knowing he was there except for a piece of pure luck. After passing up a dozen good drinking places, Sam left the trail long enough to come and lap water out of the very pothole I lay in.

It wasn't till I *saw* him that I realized how long I'd been hearing his coming.

I lunged to my feet. "Sam!" I yelled at the top of my voice. "*Sam!*"

It startled Sam. I guess it was surprise enough to have startled anything, the way I jumped up and yelled, then started running toward him, knocking water in every direction.

Sam backed off. His hackles rose. He bared his teeth and growled a warning for me to keep my distance.

I stopped, as startled now as Sam had been. I couldn't believe it, him backing off and growling, like I was some sort of dangerous varmint.

"Sam!" I shouted at him. "What's the matter with you?"

I started toward him again. Sam backed a step further, then crouched low to the ground. His eyes took on a glassy shine and there was an even bigger threat in his growl this time.

I stopped, ready to cry.

"*Sam!*" I wailed. "Don't you know me? I'm Travis!"

But Sam didn't know me and wasn't about to let me come any closer. I stood where I was, staring at him, till finally I understood what the trouble was.

A dog's faith in his eyesight is mighty frail. His belief in what he hears isn't a whole lot stronger. What he mainly depends on is his nose; and what he can't scent, he's not going to put much trust in. Especially, out in wild country like this, with danger on every hand.

How could I expect Sam to recognize me? Me, lunging up out of the water, naked as a skinned rabbit, running toward him, hollering my head off—and the wind in the wrong direction for him to catch my scent. It's a wonder he hadn't already jumped me!

I turned and went wading downstream, half circling

[105]

Sam, talking to him as I went, so full of new hope that it seemed like I'd pop wide open.

"All right, Sam," I told him. "Stay where you are. Hold what you got. Keep trying to bluff me off. Just wait till I get downwind from you. Then I'm coming out of here; and if you're butt-headed enough to jump me, I'll pick me up a club and knock some sense into your fool head."

That was sure a big threat to carry out, with my hands still tied, but it was just blowhard talk. It didn't mean a thing, except that I was so happy to see that old flop-eared, big-jointed dog that I didn't have good sense.

Sam watched me with a wary eye as I waded down-stream; but I could tell before I ever got to where I wanted that he was beginning to suspect who I was. His hackles flattened along his backbone. His curled-back lips sagged, hiding his bared fangs. Gradually, he rose from his crouch and stood there, beginning to prick up his ears with interest.

I waded to where the wind ripples ran across the water straight from me to Sam. I stood there long enough for him to get a full load of my scent and give it consideration. Then I called to him.

"All right, Sam," I said. "Here I come!"

He knew me then. He let out a little whimpering whine. He wrung his stub tail so hard he twisted his whole rump end. He cut loose with a loud bawl; and here he came, plunging in high leaps through water too deep for good wading and too shallow for swimming. Wild with joy, he leaped at me, slamming into my chest with the force of a runaway horse. He knocked the wind out of me and tumbled me flat of my back. Then he was all over me, whimpering and yelling and pawing, shoving me under, then slapping me in the face with his big old slobbery tongue every time I got my head up. He was so happy about our meeting, it looked for a minute like he was going to drown me.

Then I got my head up and my wind back and shouted at him, "Sam, you big old ox! Get off of me!"

Sam got off, giving me a chance to get up and wade toward the bank. Only, he still couldn't keep from play-nipping at my heels and reaching out to hook a forefoot around one of my ankles, all but tripping me every step I took.

"Cut it out, Sam!" I ordered and kicked him away.

So he let me alone till I reached the bank. Then he played the same old trick he always played on me and Arliss after we'd been swimming and got out and put our clothes on. He sneaked up real close and shook himself, popping his ears, and showering me all over with a fine spray of water.

But this time the joke was on him. He couldn't dirty my clothes. I didn't have any on!

He backed off, getting set to look pitiful and put-upon. He knew he had a scolding coming. When it didn't come, he seemed puzzled and about half disappointed.

I called him over and told him to stand still. I examined the wound in his back. The tomahawk had made a bad gash that looked deep enough to have crippled him, but hadn't. The wound was well clotted over and I couldn't see any blowfly sign.

Before I'd quite finished, Sam did a thing that most dogs can't do. He turned around and looked me square in the eye, and his gaze didn't waver. There was a question in his eyes, the same question that was already beginning to drive me crazy. It was: *When do we get going?*

Well, I was ready to go now. But how was I to go anywhere or do anything with my hands tied behind me?

Sam didn't give me much time to figure out that problem. After handing me that one straight, questioning look, he got restless. He whined. He circled me a couple of times. Then he struck out through the sunflowers and scrub mesquite. A minute later, I heard him open with that high-singing trail cry.

I jumped to my feet in sudden panic.

"Wait, Sam!" I called after him. "Come back here, Sam!"

All the answer I got was that high-singing voice as he opened a second time.

Then I knew Sam wasn't coming back and he wasn't waiting. Not for me or anybody else. He'd gone back and picked up the trail of Little Arliss, and he aimed to hang with that trail as long as there was a trace of scent to follow.

The thought of being left behind, of being alone again, filled me with terror. I went running after Sam, straining frantically at the rawhide binding that held my hands together.

The way my hands came loose might have seemed like a miracle if I hadn't felt so silly about it. Anybody in his right mind would have known how much rawhide would

[108]

stretch after all the soaking I'd given it back there in the water.

I freed my hands. I stooped and untied the long strip of rawhide I'd been dragging from my left foot. Then I went racing after Sam, calling encouragement to him.

"Go get 'em, Sam," I urged. "Hang with that trail, boy!"

With hands and feet free, I felt light as a feather. I felt strong enough to keep up with Sam, no matter how fast and far he traveled. I felt like I could run from now on.

I ran, so elated that when I came upon the first dead soldier, lying sprawled in the grass, I passed him by with hardly a glance. Just as I came in sight of the second one, however, I stubbed my toe against a hidden rock, and the pain of it knocked some sense back into my head.

I didn't like what I had to do, but I knew I had to do it.

It didn't bother me much, pulling off the trooper's boots and pants. What gave me the creeps was getting his shirt. It was pinned to him, front and back, with a three-foot arrow sticking clear through. But with Sam's trail cry drawing further and further away, I had no time to be squeamish. I grabbed the bloodied arrowhead and broke it off. I rolled the soldier over on his back. I caught hold of the feathered shaft and yanked it clear and flung it aside. Then I unbuttoned the shirt, stripped it off, and put it on.

The shirt was too long, the hat too small, the pants too big in the waist and too short in the legs. But the boots were nearly a perfect fit. Which was the main thing. That,

[109]

and the six-shooter that hung at my belt and the rifle I carried in my hand.

The six-shooter was a Colt .45, the rifle a single-shot breech-loading .45–70 Springfield. There was plenty of ammunition for both.

I wondered if what troopers were left alive would return for their dead or if the Indians might backtrack to lift some scalps, but nobody came and I never knew why.

I'd worked fast as I could, but the sun was already down and Sam's trail cry was coming in mighty faint when I struck out after him again. I couldn't run so fast now. I was packing too big a load. But I didn't mind. I had clothes to protect me, weapons to fight with, and Sam to lead me to wherever the Indians were taking Lisbeth and Little Arliss.

I kept an eye out for a loose horse as I ran. With a horse under me—a good stout, grain-fed cavalry horse, or even one of the weaker horses the Indians had let fall behind— I'd be a lot better off than afoot.

I didn't see any horses, though, except dead ones and a few lost and whinnying colts. One of the colts was sucking a dead mare, and it made me sad, knowing that was the last time he'd ever get a bait of milk from his mama.

The blue-green of the grass changed to purple as night came on, then gradually became silver under the light of the rising moon. I ran through the shining grass, following wherever the rise and fall of Sam's trail voice led me. I set a stiff pace. Sam wasn't a fast trailer, just steady, and I looked to overhaul him before long.

But I didn't.

I could gain on him at times. Every now and then, the pitch and rhythm of his voice would change, telling me that the scent he followed had got mixed up or wiped out. Then he'd be quiet for a while; and I'd throw on a new batch of speed, certain I'd catch him while he circled to pick up the lost trail.

But always, before I got there, he'd open, and off he'd go again, driving sure and steady.

This went on for hours. The sweat poured; it wet my clothes and stung my wounds. The stiff trooper boots wore blisters on my heels. The rifle, the six-shooter, and the canvas belts of ammunition got heavier and heavier. Once, I stumbled and fell flat of my face in the grass. Another time, while crossing a rocky little ravine, I sensed danger in time to leap high and far out off a low ledge. The big rattler's strike missed me by a bare inch and I felt his heavy body slide down off my leg as he drew back, buzzing angrily, coiling for another strike.

I didn't stop to kill him; I couldn't afford the time. I had to catch Sam.

I used that thought like a whiplash to keep me going. I'd keep saying to myself: *I got to catch Sam. I got to catch Sam.*

When the sting went out of that thought, I'd prod myself with another. I'd think: *If that streak-faced Comanche can run all day, I can run all night!* Or, *If I lose Sam, I've lost Lisbeth and Little Arliss!*

I ran till my lungs were on fire and ready to burst. I ran till my legs lost all feeling and became dead stumps jolting the rest of my pain-racked body. I ran till I forgot to goad myself, till I even forgot why I was running. From then on, all that kept me on my feet and still going was that wild, sweet-ringing call of Sam's trail cry.

It was like I was tied to that call, and the pull of it never let up, so that I was led on and on, long after the last of my strength had run out.

I finally caught Sam—but only because he stopped again for water. And if water had been plentiful, I wouldn't have caught him then. I was too far behind.

I got my first sight of him as he stood out in the middle of a broad flat wash that wound through the grass. The bed of the wash was filled with deep sand. In the moonlight, the sand looked smooth, clean-swept and golden, except for a wide, dark streak where the trampling hoofs of hard-driven horses had pitted and rumpled it.

There was no surface water in the sand; all of the flow was underneath. But in one place, the water was so near the top that it seeped into one of the deeper horse tracks. It was out of this track that Sam was trying to drink.

Some dogs would have known to dig deeper; but Sam had never before needed to dig for water. What I found him doing, when I came staggering toward him, was lapping up what little water he could get, then backing off and waiting for the track to fill again.

He whined and wagged his stump tail as I dropped down beside him, gasping for breath. He was glad enough to see me, but what pleased him even more, it looked like, was for me to use my hands to claw out a foot-deep hole in the sand.

The underground water seeped in faster. Sam shoved in to get the first drink. While he was at it, I slipped the leather belt out of my sagging soldier pants and looped it around his neck. The other end I snapped into the buckle of my six-shooter belt.

"Now, you rascal," I panted. "You're not getting away from me again."

I crowded in beside him. We both drank from the same water hole. Then I rolled over and lay flat of my back in the sand, and couldn't have found more comfort in a bed with a goose-feather mattress.

From far out in the wilderness of shining grass lifted the howl of a great gray loafer wolf. Instantly, Sam rose with a snarl.

I reached out and pulled him toward me. "Hush up and lay down," I told him.

He hushed up, but he didn't lie down. Instead, he started nosing over my body, searching out my wounds. I lay with my sweat-soaked shirt unbuttoned and open, and he could get at some of the worst ones. He started a gentle licking of the wounds, and I didn't stop him. His wet tongue felt soft and soothing, and I knew from past experience how healing the lick of a dog's tongue can be.

The wolf howled again. Sam paid him no mind. And me —well, I fell asleep so fast that I never even heard the last of the howl.

A clawing pain brought me awake. My eyes popped open. I found Sam standing over me, whimpering and whining, pawing my sore body with a forefoot.

I shoved him aside. I sat up and looked around. The sun stood better than an hour high. The morning breeze had already started up and set the grass to whispering.

I was thirsty again. I rolled over and drank from the hole in the sand. Then I tried to get to my feet and almost didn't make it, I was that stiff all over. Also, my soldier clothes were stuck tight to several festering sores that Sam hadn't been able to reach. It all but took my breath to pull my clothes loose.

But these were outside pains, and I'd had them long enough to be used to them. *Inside,* I felt fine. Inside, I felt ready to take up the trail that Sam was so anxious to follow again.

But first, I needed to put Sam on a leash. I'd learned a lesson. Maybe I could run as fast as Sam could trail, but I sure couldn't run for as long at a time. Last night, I'd caught him out of sheer luck. Let him get that big a lead on me again, and my luck might not hold.

Sam kept whining and tugging at my belt, restless to get gone.

"Be still," I scolded.

He hushed and stood waiting while I thought. The belt wouldn't do; it was too short. Anyhow, without it to hold up my oversized pants, they'd be down around my ankles before I'd taken a dozen steps. I considered the cartridge belts, but they were too short.

I looked around, thinking hard. My eye lit on a clump of bear grass growing at the edge of the sandy wash. That's what I needed! Those long green spiny blades were nearly as stout as rawhide. Back home, we always used them for binding bundles of corn-top fodder. Tie a bunch of them together, and they'd make as fine a leash as a body could want.

I headed for the bear grass. Out of pure habit, I reached into my pocket for a knife to cut the blades—and found one! It would sure make the job easier. I went to cutting the blades and knotting them together. Each blade was better than a foot long. Twelve to fifteen would be a-plenty.

I was done with making the leash when I heard a rustling in the grass. I stiffened. I reached for my rifle lying beside me, then noticed Sam. He'd heard the sound, too. He stood with his muzzle lifted, his ears pricked up. But he didn't raise a hackle, and he didn't growl. I knew then that whatever made the rustling sound was no threat to us. Just some varmint, I guessed.

I tied the leash around Sam's neck. I worked the belt through the loops in my pants, drew up the slack, and buckled it. Then I led Sam through the grass to see what was making those odd clicking and clacking sounds—like pieces of dry wood being slapped together.

I made a cautious approach, holding my rifle ready.

What I found was a couple of dry-land terrapins. They were big ones, with shells the size of dinner plates. And they were fighting—I guess. I'd never seen terrapins fight; and if this was a fight, it was the most peculiar one I ever watched.

Best I could tell, all either terrapin had in mind was to flop the other one over on his back. It was a real curiosity to watch them. I wondered how a terrapin could know that once he was turned upside down, he'd be helpless.

Suddenly, my interest in the terrapins took a different turn. I remembered a long-winded yarn old man Searcy had once told about eating roasted terrapins with some friendly Kiowas. I hadn't eaten since I'd choked down a few bites of old Jumper the day before and I was hungry.

With a rifle, I could kill game; but let me start shooting around, and the Indians were sure to hear the shots and send somebody back to get me.

It seemed shameful to kill something as helpless as these old terrapins. But I crushed their shells with my rifle butt. I gutted them with my pocketknife. I sliced the good meat away from the broken shells and divided it with Sam.

We ate it raw. We didn't have time for cooking, even if I could have built a fire with sticks, like the Indians, which I doubted.

The meat smelled pretty rank and was tough to chew; but I ate it, and my stomach held it, and I felt confident that it would give me strength to keep going.

Getting Sam back on the trail was no problem. The horse tracks were plain in the sandy wash; and it didn't take him but a minute to nose out the scent he wanted.

He wrung his stub tail. He threw up his head and opened with his bell-ringing voice. Then he took a sudden spurt ahead, and that's when the trouble started.

Sam had never before run a trail while on a leash; and when he hit the end of that string and got jerked up short, he threw a wall-eyed fit.

He was worse than Little Arliss when he got mad. He

wheeled around, snapping and snarling at the string. He reared up and threw his weight against it, trying to break loose. He hit the ground, wallowing and screeching. He leaped high into the air and turned a somersault. He ran circles around me, yelping and pitching and bawling. The capers he cut, you'd have thought he was a bull calf that had been roped for the first time.

I kept hanging to the leash and shouting at him, telling him to cut out that foolishness and behave himself. For all the good it did, I could have been hollering straight into a big wind.

I don't know how I'd ever have got him stopped if he hadn't taken a second wallowing fit and wrapped himself up in that string so tight he couldn't move.

Then when I got my hands on him, I didn't know what to do. If I turned him loose, he'd get away from me. If he kept fighting that leash, we sure couldn't get anywhere. And to keep messing with him like this, I ran the risk of getting him so aggravated he'd quit the trail for good.

I sat and studied on it a good long while.

So far, all I'd done was fuss at him. What if I took time off and explained the situation, telling him what had to be done and why?

It seemed worth a try. Sam was a butt head and always would be. If he hadn't been, he'd never have hung with the trail this far. On the other hand, he'd never been a dang fool, either.

I led him back to water. We both drank again out of the same hole. I spoke soft to him and hugged him up and scratched his ears and stroked his back and bragged on him. And, being as greedy for praise as anybody else, Sam lapped it all up like it was a bowl of sweet cream. In no time, I had him so proud of himself, he was wriggling all over and slapping me in the face with a wet tongue to show that we were in complete agreement on what a fine dog he was.

That's when I pushed him away and laid it on the line.

"Now, look, Sam," I said. "We're both after the same thing. We stick together, maybe we can do it. We get split up, we don't have a chance. Them Indians, they'll shoot you and lose me, and that'll be the last anybody'll ever see of Lisbeth and Little Arliss. You understand?"

I don't guess a dog understands many words, but I think he can listen and tell more than a lot of people believe about the feeling back of the words. And right then, I was so desperate to make Sam understand that I'll always believe some of my feelings got through to him.

Anyhow, he stood quiet and heard me out, then whined and came to lay his head on my knee and look up at me, like he was *trying* to understand. So I got up and led him back to the trail and hissed him out, and he took it.

This time I was all set for him. When he opened and spurted forward, I was quick to go with him, giving him plenty of slack line, so he wouldn't get jerked up short again.

And it worked. He opened a second time; and we took off across that great rolling sea of grass, running together, with Sam's bell-clear voice rising and falling with a regularity and sureness that put strength in my muscles and lifted my hopes clear out of all reason.

The sun was high and hot and I was beginning to tire when we came upon a little cluster of cone-shaped hills. Prickly pear grew on their slopes and the green pads of the pear were studded with ripe red apples. At the base of one hill stood a lone mott of scrub live oaks, and the trail we followed led straight toward it.

I was thinking that under those oaks would be a good place for us to shade up till I caught my breath, when Sam's trail cry broke in the middle. He came to a sudden halt, stood stiff-legged, with his hackles rising. He growled.

Indians, I thought, and dropped out of sight into the grass.

"Down, Sam!" I said in a low voice. "Get down and keep quiet!"

Sam crouched beside me, still growling.

I felt my body tighten with scare, but there was no panic. If a couple of Apaches had heard Sam and dropped back to make a kill, I'd come for the same thing. Only, I aimed to kill first.

I tried to think what best to do. As things stood now, I couldn't see them, but they had to have spotted the place where I'd dropped into the grass. Pulling Sam along, I started crawling off to one side. I crawled fast, depending on the wind-tossed grass to hide my motion and muffle any sound.

Fifty yards away, I changed course and began a slower, more careful crawl toward the oaks. I planned to carry the fight to the savages from this direction while they watched for me in another.

I was closer to the oaks than I really wanted to be before

an opening in the grass allowed me to peer through. But I couldn't see anything; the shade under the trees was too dense.

Then I stiffened. A shadowy form had shifted. Another one moved, and I heard a low grunt. Beside me, Sam uttered another low rumbling growl.

"Sh-h-h-h!" I shushed him and he hushed, but it was plain he didn't like the setup.

I eased my rifle to my shoulder and waited. I wanted that first shot to count. After that, if they rushed me, I'd have to depend on the six-shooter and I wasn't too sure of myself with it.

A figure moved again, taking shape against a patch of sunlight on the far side of the mott. Best I could tell, one of the savages had lifted his head for a look around. I thought I saw a feather sticking up out of his hair.

I drew a fine bead on that head and squeezed off. The gun barked. The butt slammed against my shoulder. Black-powder gunsmoke fogged the air and through the fog came what sounded like the squeal of a stuck pig. Then the thicket exploded, and here they came—not Indians at all, but a band of javelina hogs!

I lunged up, bug-eyed with surprise, as they rushed me, coughing and roaring, popping gleaming white teeth. Then the mass of them cut my feet from under me, trampling me with their little hard hoofs, slashing at me with razor-sharp tusks. Their rank musky scent all but choked off my breath before I could scramble back to my feet and start clubbing them off with my rifle butt.

It was Sam who saved me, partly by dealing out more

punishment, mostly by making more noise. His loud roars and savage snarls as he battled the hogs seemed to attract the fierce little animals away from me to him.

The pack around me thinned. I saw a chance to run and took it. I tore out around the slope of that hill, yelling as I ran, "Run, Sam! Run!"

When I looked back, I saw that Sam had thrown the fight to the javelinas and was high-tailing it through the grass, with the pigs chasing after him. Sam was leading them away from me. Maybe he knew he could outrun those nasty little fighters and I couldn't.

I quit running and sat down on a little rock ledge to catch my breath. I felt a stinging pain across my left foot and glanced down to find a long slash in the leather across the instep of my boot. I pulled the boot off and examined my foot. There was a bleeding groove in the flesh, but the cut wasn't deep. I examined myself for more wounds, but all I found was my six-shooter belt cut nearly in two.

I'd come out lucky. Javelinas on the prod can be nearly as dangerous as razorback range hogs.

While I waited for Sam to come back, I thought what a fool stunt I'd pulled. Letting my imagination get the upper hand of me so that I'd mistaken javelinas for Indians. Alone in a wild country like this, a body couldn't afford such mistakes. Any one could be his last.

I told myself that, from now on, I'd watch closer and think quicker. I'd be sharp-eyed and wary, dangerous as any wild animal. I wouldn't let myself get caught short a second time.

And while I sat there, telling myself these things, I was making the worst mistake yet.

It wasn't till the faint sound of Sam's trail cry came floating back to me from far out on the prairie that I realized what I'd done.

I started up in panic. "Sam!" I called. "Sam!"

I went plunging down the slope, sick with knowing what a fool I'd been. I set a pace that I couldn't possibly hold, yet I knew I had to hold it if I hoped to keep in hearing distance of Sam.

For Sam was back on the trail of Little Arliss and had no time to lose.

I lasted for maybe an hour before the ground began to rock and heave under me, making me stumble. I slowed then, hoping for the dizzy spell to pass. Instead, the ground rose up and slammed me in the face, and I went spinning far out into some great dark and empty place where not even the call of Sam's trail cry could reach me any more.

Papa

Nine

A HAND touched my face. I started up in terror. Crouched over me, black against the blinding sunlight, was a man figure.

Like a trapped animal, I lunged up and clutched his throat, choking off his shout of alarm.

He threw himself backward, dragging me with him. He clawed desperately at my hands, and other hands joined his, all seeking to break the strangle hold I held.

But I was too strong. All of me—all the rage and pain

and fear and loneliness and awful despair I'd known—was in my hands, and no force on earth had the strength to break their grip.

Then, through the shouts and confusion and my blind rage to kill, Papa's voice reached me.

"Travis!" he was shouting. "Turn him loose, boy. Turn him loose, I say!"

That broke the spell. It took away my strength. Big Burn Sanderson was now able to break my grasp on Herb Haley's throat, and I looked on in stunned surprise as Haley flung himself aside and lay in the grass, sucking for air in great raspy gasps.

Sanderson was squatted on his heels beside me. He still held my hands, but his blue eyes were as warm and friendly as ever. He glanced over my head and said in a joking voice, "Be dog, Jim, I hope this boy don't never take a sudden dislike to me!"

Then I knew whose strong arms held me from behind.

"Papa!" I cried.

I whirled, jerking free of Sanderson, getting a glimpse of several Salt Licks settlers before looking up into Papa's familiar face. Then the tears came, blurring everything, and the shivers got me, so that I just lay back in Papa's arms, crying and shaking all over.

Papa held me close. "It's all right, boy," he comforted. "Just take it easy for a minute and you'll be all right."

"Give him some water," somebody said, and I recognized Ben Todd's voice.

I heard the slosh of water inside a canteen and the squeal of a metal cap being unscrewed. I dragged my

[124]

shirt sleeve across my eyes, wiping away the tears, and reached a shaky hand for the canteen. I lifted it and let the water, with its stale, tinny taste, go rattling down my parched throat.

Old man Searcy hawked and spat, like he always did before spinning some long-winded yarn.

"Puts me in mind of a time I'm on a cow hunt in the cedar brakes west of Hornsby's Bend," he began. "Dry as a powderhouse, the country is, and—"

"Not now, Mr. Searcy," Papa interrupted.

Searcy said in a complaining voice, "Well, all I aimed to tell was how them dogs of our'n—"

"It'll keep, Mr. Searcy," Sanderson cut in.

Mention of dogs made me jerk the canteen from my mouth. I came to my feet.

"Sam!" I cried out. "We got to catch Sam!"

Sanderson came to his feet with me. He asked, "How big a lead you think he's got?"

I glanced up at the sun. "It's hard to tell," I said. "An hour—maybe two. Don't know for certain when I blacked out."

Lester White moved in to peer at me with a questioning look in his black eyes. White was a newcomer to Salt Licks. He was from Virginia, in search of grassland on which to raise fine horses. He was young and handsome and rode better horses and wore finer clothes than anybody else. He talked different from us, too. Some settlers looked on him as being a dandy, with too much book learning to have any sense.

Now he said, "Apparently, young man, you are saying

[125]

that a dog has been on this trail for more than forty-eight hours."

"Yes, sir," I said. "Sam's been trailing Little Arliss from the start."

White backed off, looking thoughtful. "That's hard to believe," he said.

Papa looked to Sanderson. "You think we can catch him before night?" he asked.

"If we hump it," Sanderson said. "But we'll be whipping over and under if that old pot-hound pup's got more than a two-hour lead."

A sudden thought hit Papa. He felt of my forehead. He pulled aside one half of my unbuttoned shirt. He stared at my skin, now fiery with sunburn. He saw, the swollen, festering sores made by the Indians' firebrands. He got gray in the face.

"This boy's not able to ride," he said to Sanderson. "Feel of him. Look at this!"

" 'Course I can ride!" I protested.

His eyes grave with concern, Sanderson pulled open the other side of my shirt. The men all crowded in close, staring at my wounds in fearful awe.

Lester White's black eyes flashed me a quick look of sympathy. Uncle Pack Underwood, a lean old wolf of a man, turned away to stare out across the prairie, his lined face bleak with a dark and brooding bitterness. Bud Searcy went all to pieces. Tears spilled down his bearded cheeks and his lips started quivering.

"My grandbaby!" he cried out. "My pore little grand-girl! Have they abused her?"

"Not yet," I said. "I got a knife into the one that tried it. He won't try again—for a while! But Little Arliss—they got him stripped naked. And he keeps fighting back!"

Sanderson dropped my shirt and shook his head. "He's bad hurt, all right," he said to Papa.

" 'Course I'm hurt!" I flared. "I been hurt since night before last. But it hasn't stopped me, has it?"

"The boy's got guts," Ben Todd said. Todd was a shy, heavyset man who said little and spent most of his time wild-bee hunting.

"No question," Lester White agreed.

Any other time, I'd have felt proud of such a compliment, but right now it didn't matter what anybody thought.

"I tell you, we've got to catch Sam!" I said. "He's hot on the trail of Little Arliss!"

Sanderson nodded and turned to Papa. "He's right," he said. "We sure need to overhaul that dog."

Herb Haley got to his feet, rubbing his throat and still eying me warily. I felt bad about trying to choke him, but it seemed like he ought to make allowance for the shape I was in.

Uncle Pack said, "We could grease the boy. That'd help some."

Papa looked doubtful—and desperate. He said to me, "You think you could make it, son? If we greased you good, all over?"

"He's *got* to make it!" Searcy said wildly. "I tell you, if them heathen abuse my little grandgirl—"

He broke down without finishing and went to crying.

I said to Papa, "Forget the greasing. We got no time."

"We'll take time," Sanderson said. He turned to Herb Haley. "Herb, will you slice the rind off that side of bacon in my saddlebag?"

Herb Haley was still keeping an eye on me, like he expected me to jump him again.

"Allow me!" Lester White said. He went for the bacon rind.

Papa and Sanderson started stripping me.

Wiley Crup, a squint-eyed man with a squirrel mouth and the figure of a sand-hill crane, came to stand over us. Across his shoulder, muzzle forward, he packed a rifle about the size and weight of a crowbar. It was a .50 caliber Sharps, used for buffalo hunting.

Now, he set the butt of his rifle to the ground and laid a forearm across the muzzle. He leaned his weight on the gun while he stared at Sanderson.

"Was I ramroding this hunt," he said, "which I ain't—not even being considered for election—I might point out a little matter what's being overlooked."

Sanderson glanced at him. "Speak your piece, Wiley," he invited. "We ain't above listening."

"Well, here's the thing," Wiley drawled. "We start out on this siwash hunt with eight men on eight horses. We pick up this boy—who aims to ride double?"

All were silent a moment, considering, before Ben Todd said, "Couldn't we swap about?"

"Not the way Sanderson threatens to travel," Crup declared. "We ride at that pace, a double load'll have ever' horse in this outfit dragging out his tracks by sundown."

I never had liked Wiley Crup. He was always too con-
tentious and suspicious of everything and everybody. And
after he'd taken up hide hunting a couple of years back,
you'd have thought he was the only man ever to shoot a
buffalo or see an Indian.

I said, hot with resentment, "I'll take it afoot. I'll run,
holding to somebody's stirrup. Like the Comanche."

"Comanch!" Crup exclaimed. He whirled on Sanderson. "You said they was Pache!" he charged. "Said you
could tell by the sign!"

Sanderson shot me a puzzled look.

"They *are* Apaches," I said. "All but one. He's Comanche. Somebody shot him, back there where they caught
us. It hurt him to ride, so he—"

Sanderson cut in. "Thought that one looked Comanche,
when I fired on him."

Crup snorted his disbelief. "How come a Comanch
raidin' with a bunch of Paches? Everybody knows they're
mortal enemies."

Sanderson shrugged. "*Quién sabe?*" he said. "A loner,
most likely. Hubbed trouble with his own tribe, maybe,
and threw in with the Apaches."

"Yeah, maybe!" Crup sneered. "And maybe you don't
know sic 'em about the sign you read."

Sanderson paid no more mind to Crup's insult than he
would to a worrisome gnat, but Uncle Pack spoke up in a
raspy voice.

"Wiley," he said, "you ain't to blame for being born a
fool. That weren't yore doing. But it wouldn't hurt you
none if you tried to overcome the handicap."

Crup's face darkened with resentment.

"The main question is," Sanderson said, "can we overhaul that dog before dark. With Sam, we can trail all night. Without him, we'll have to wait around for daylight."

Papa started rubbing the bacon rind gently over my body. The curing salt stung my wounds, but I knew that it and the grease would help to heal them.

"As for Travis," Sanderson went on, "he's young, and tough as an old boot heel. Feed and water him, and he'll make it. Won't you, boy?"

He grinned and winked at me.

It was just a little thing; yet sometimes, just a little is all a body needs to pull himself back together. Burn Sanderson was my friend. He had confidence in me. That alone was enough to lift my spirits and help me to throw off the shakes.

Also, there was a big belly-filling bait of grub they fed me. Fried salt-cured bacon. Corn-meal hoecakes cooked in the grease after the bacon was done. It was cold leftovers from the last meal they'd eaten. It was salty. It was greasy. It had a little sand and some ashes in it. It was hard-scrabble, pore folks' grub that, back home, nobody ate except at the tail end of winter when game was scarce and the range cattle were thin.

Yet I gobbled it down like it was a Christmas dinner with all the fixings. It was exactly what I needed, especially the salt. You keep pouring out sweat like I'd done for the last couple of days and nights, and pretty soon your body gets to craving salt almost worse than a good meal.

While I ate, the men hammered at me with questions. I answered between bites. When I came to the part about the Indian and soldier fight, Sanderson shook his head.

"Injuns all armed with modern rifles, I guess?"

"Yes, sir," I said. "Mostly Henry .44's."

"That's the army for you," he said. "Sending troops out with single-shot Springfields to face sixteen-shot repeaters. Poor devils didn't have a chance."

Wiley Crup snorted with contempt. "Far as I'm consarned," he said, patting the scarred stock of his monster rifle, "all them fancy, new-fangled guns can be throwed in the creek. Me, I'm sticking to this old Christian Sharps britch-loading Big Fifty."

"But gosh dog, Wiley," Herb Haley exclaimed. "Packing that much artillery, it's enough to make your horse swaybacked."

"Maybe," Crup said smugly. "But she can accommodate a paper cartridge, a linen one, or just plain loose powder and lead. It's all the same to her. She'll still pack a ball a thousand yards. I've kilt buffler at better'n five hunderd."

Papa wanted to know more about the Comanche. Finally, he said to Sanderson: "Burn, if that Indian can run like that, we can. And it'd sure save on horseflesh."

"I'm ready to take my turn," Lester White said. "I'm as fit as any man alive."

Sanderson sized up White's trim figure. "You look it, Mr. White," he said. "But dealing with Injuns, a man can turn up some real surprises."

"We can sure give it a try," Papa persisted.

Sanderson nodded and got to his feet. "And if we hope to catch that dog before dark," he said, "it's time we got on the move."

Every man in the outfit was well mounted, even to Bud Searcy, who'd borrowed a big old apron-faced sorrel from Papa, a horse that wasn't much to look at, but one with plenty of staying power. Compared, however, to the proud-stepping, catfooted bay that Lester White rode, all our horses looked scrubby as Indian ponies. White called the bay a "hunter," whatever that meant, and one glance at the long clean lines of him told you that here was a horse to take you there and bring you back, and do it in a hurry.

Sanderson mounted me on his horse and hung his spurs and gun gear to the saddle horn. Papa tried to argue with him, claiming Sanderson ought to stay mounted all the time, him being the only real tracker in the outfit.

But Sanderson wouldn't listen. "I'm young and fast afoot," he said. "And a one-eyed candy peddler could trail that many horses running through green grass. Anyhow, I been elected boss of this outfit, and I ain't yet had a chance to throw my weight around."

He grinned up at Papa, spanked the rump of his horse, and said, "Let's go!"

So we took off, riding hard, with Papa in the lead, with Sanderson holding to my stirrup, with me gritting my teeth against the pain of the saddle.

In spite of the pain, I felt a lot better. I wasn't alone any more; and I no longer had to carry the full load of responsibility for Lisbeth and Little Arliss.

[132]

Sanderson ran for better than an hour before he gave under the strain. He didn't say anything, but I began to feel the pull of him on my stirrup. I called ahead to Papa, and Sanderson didn't argue when Papa reined up and Lester White insisted on taking Sanderson's place.

Sanderson wiped the streaming sweat from his face with his shirt sleeve and shook his head.

"I got to admit," he panted, "I ain't the man that Comanche is."

"I expect none of us are," Papa said. "Not on foot, anyhow."

White said nothing, but looked determined to show himself the equal of any man, red or white. He ran, holding to Sanderson's stirrup, for maybe fifteen minutes longer than Sanderson had. Then he, too, had to give it up.

When he could get back his breath, he asked, "How long at a time did this Comanche run?"

"Half a day," I told him.

He stared at me in astonishment. "At a pace this swift?"

"Not always," I said. "Most of the time, though."

"And packing a rifle ball in one leg," Sanderson pointed out with a wry grin.

That knocked some of the little-rooster strut out of Lester White. But he was man enough to take it without making excuses. He mounted up, looking thoughtful and a bit shaken, and offered a stirrup to Ben Todd.

Todd surprised us all. To look at the chunky bee hunter, nobody would have figured him for a runner. Yet, with short legs flying, he held the stiff pace we'd set for mile after mile without any evidence of strain, so that I began to think he could equal the Comanche.

But after better than a couple of hours, he, too, had to call it quits and let Herb Haley take over.

Following Haley, the others took turns, even to Bud Searcy, who was outraged when Papa and Sanderson tried to tell him he was too old.

"I didn't come along to be a drag on this chase," he declared.

So we kept driving, nine men and eight horses, pushing to the limit of endurance, traveling across a rolling sea of grass so vast that it seemed to have no beginning and no end, moving under a spread of sky that stretched out beyond any distance a body could bring himself to believe. And still the trail led on.

The sun sank lower. Men and horses began to lag. Papa's face, grim and determined up to now, began to take on a bleak, anxious look. I fought a losing fight with the dread mounting inside me.

For, with the coming of sunset, the cross wind that had blown all day shut down, leaving hardly a ripple on the grass. Now, I could no longer tell myself that the wind was carrying Sam's voice away from us. Now, I had to face up to the fact that night would soon set in, blotting out the trail, and we still hadn't come within hearing distance of Sam.

Then Sanderson shouted and pointed. I looked ahead. Far out against the sinking sun, I saw a swirl of buzzards. They were dipping and diving, only to rise again on great flapping wings. They circled low above the grass, evidently wanting to settle down, but kept scared off by a danger we couldn't see.

I snatched at a new hope. That could be Sam out yonder! He could have stopped to feed on the carcass of some animals the Indians had shot for meat. It might be him, keeping the buzzards fought off.

It turned out to be Sam, all right. And there was plenty of meat for him to feed on. Scattered about in the little swag where we found him lay the skinned carcasses of eighteen buffalo.

But Sam wasn't feeding on any of the meat. He was too busy fighting off a snarling pack of gray loafer wolves.

The minute we rode in sight, it was easy to read the setup. The wolves had been feeding on the dead buffalo. Sam, intent on following the trail of Little Arliss, had come charging down upon them before he knew they were there. The wolves had jumped him, and they'd been too many for him. Sam had fought his way to the fallen trunk of a dead willow that lay at the edge of a buffalo wallow. There, backed up against the log, where the gnarled, upthrust roots protected his rump, he'd made his stand.

With rump and one side protected, he fought with his head extended, with his forefeet drawn far back under his body, making his legs hard to get at. He met each charge with a roar and a frenzy of cutting and slashing that sent wolf after wolf reeling back, screeching with pain. Yet, with his other side wide open, so that two or three wolves could rush him at once, it was still just a matter of time

[135]

before one of them locked jaws with him and dragged him out to where the others could hamstring and cut him to pieces.

It was the uproar of Sam's battle with the wolves that had the buzzards disturbed. Now, the big ugly birds circled higher as we went rushing in, and the black shadows of their wings glided across the grass.

Travis

Ten

I LED the charge toward the fight and drew my six-shooter, aiming to kill me some wolves. Others did the same. But Sanderson called out, telling us to hold our fire.

"Whip 'em off with your catch ropes," he yelled.

We holstered our guns and reached down ropes of braided rawhide. We shook out loops and swung them high. And the snarling pack, bent on killing Sam, paid us no mind until we were among them.

Our loops whistled as they cut through the air. Surprised wolves yelped and fell away from the sting of our lashings. They wallowed and pitched and screeched. Men shouted. Excited horses squealed and lunged and lashed out with their heels.

It was over and done with, almost before it started. The routed pack scattered and slunk to cover.

Wiley Crup complained in a sour voice, "With guns, we could a-kilt 'em."

"And brung down a whole passel of redskins on our necks," Uncle Pack pointed out. "Was any in hearing range."

I looked down at Sam. He was still crouched half under the log, staring at us. He looked worse surprised than the time, back home, when he started to shake an old mama possum to death and slung a whole shower of baby possums loose from her pouch.

His look was so comical that even Papa grinned a little as the two of us dismounted and walked toward him.

"Sam!" Papa called to him in a warm voice. "Come here, you big old ugly devil!"

Such familiar talk broke Sam's trance. Here he came, charging us like a lumbering bull. He bawled a welcome, which likely had as much to do with his relief at being saved from the wolves as it did with his joy in seeing us.

But if Sam's pleasure in the meeting was partly selfish, so was ours. In fact, I felt almost grateful to the wolves. They'd held Sam up long enough for us to overtake him. Now, I figured, our chances for catching up with the Indians were at least double what they'd been.

So me and Papa squatted on our heels and let Sam lick

and maul us around and spatter blood all over us—like we were the greatest people on earth.

Finally, I caught and held him so we could look him over. He had a deep gash across the bridge of his nose, and one ear had been cut to ribbons. Both wounds leaked considerable blood, but neither was crippling.

Lester White came up and looked Sam over, making a careful study of him from every angle. At last, he asked, "What are his blood lines, Mr. Coates?"

Sanderson, walking past, answered for Papa. "That Sam," he said, "is a Genuine Amalgamated Pot-Hound." Without cracking a smile, he moved on, leaving White looking doubtful.

"I don't believe I'm familiar with the breed," he said uncertainly.

Papa rose to his feet. For the moment, his face was relaxed, and I saw the old familiar twinkle in his eyes.

"It's not an uncommon one," he said, "here in Texas."

He left and walked out through the grass, as if searching for something.

It was good to see Papa smile again. Even for just that little bit. It was proof that our catching up with Sam had lifted his hopes.

A moment later, he was back, packing an old sun-dried buffalo chip. He broke it into pieces. He crushed and rolled the pieces between his hands till they became trashy dust. He started spilling the dust down over Sam's wounds.

White watched in puzzled silence. When the dust clotted and checked the flow of blood, he exclaimed, "Amazing! Truly amazing."

While all this went on, Sanderson was giving orders for pitching camp.

"We'll eat and rest our horses," he said, "then pull out along about moonrise."

He sent Herb Haley and Ben Todd riding out to scout the higher ground and told the others to slip the bridle bits from the mouths of their horses so they could drink and get some graze.

"And you better tie up that old pup," he called to me and Papa. "We don't want him taking off on that trail again till we're ready to go with him."

All that was left of the bear-grass leash I'd made for Sam was the part tied around his neck. So Papa brought a rope, and we tied Sam to the willow log.

"Now, you stay with him," Papa ordered, "and make sure he don't gnaw that rope in two." He peered at me closer. "You hurting much?"

"Some," I said. "Mostly, I'm just tired and hungry."

Sanderson and old man Searcy came up.

Sanderson said, "Might better strip him and let him lay in that water till we get supper. Water's mighty healing for the sort of wounds he's got."

"That's sure a fact," Searcy declared. "Don't know how many old winter sores I've cured, once spring come and the water warmed up enough I could run a trotline for catfish. I'm fixing to give my old beat-up feet a good soaking right now."

Searcy sat down with a grunt and began pulling off his boots. White looked at the brackish, green-scum water and then back at Sanderson.

"Do you mean to say," he asked, "that water as filthy as this possesses curative powers?"

Sanderson nodded. "Sometimes," he said, "it looks like the nastier it is, the better it heals."

"It ought to cool his fever, anyhow," Papa said.

So they helped me out of my sweaty soldier clothes and spread them out on the log to dry.

Some buffalo had wallowed a pothole in the mud beside the log. Black water had seeped back into the hole, filling it. I waded out and lay down. The water was sun-warmed and stank of rot. The bottom ooze was soft and slimy.

I thought to myself, *If filthy water is healing, this ought to cure me.* But I had to admit that as it closed over my sore body, it sure *felt* healing.

Old man Searcy sat on the log and soaked his feet in the wallow. Papa and Sanderson stomped dead branches from the log. White helped carry the broken pieces to a dried-up edge of the wallow where the grass didn't grow and they built up a campfire. Others brought their possible bags and from them produced a coffee pot, corn meal for making hoecakes, side meat, and a pan to fry in. The horses, with bridles hanging to their saddle horns, waded out into the dirty water to drink, then drifted away to graze.

I lay in the water and looked past a couple of green willows growing at the edge of the wallow, watching the sun go down. As it sank behind a cloud bank, it shot great banners of light high into the sky. The banners flamed red, pink, yellow, and green.

I lay back and fitted my head into a crotch between the

roots of the willow log. I caught my first smell of boiling coffee and frying meat and thought to myself that I'd get up in a minute and go eat.

When I woke up, fireflies were cutting the darkness with glowing streaks of light. Little frogs were piping. From the willows came the lonely quavering cries of screech owls. From out on the prairie rose the mournful howls of the wolves, gathering to feed on the dead buffalo once we'd stomped out the fire and gone. And, from beside the fire, came Uncle Pack's voice, harsh with a wild bitterness.

"Don't argue me the right or wrong of Injun killing!" he was shouting. "I see my cabin burning like a bresh pile. I see my woman and two childer kilt and sculped . . . Now, I kill Injuns!"

I'd heard Uncle Pack's story before, but it seemed to hit me harder this time.

After a long silence, Burn Sanderson spoke in a quiet voice.

"I wasn't trying to argue you out of Injun killing, Uncle Pack," he said. "I was just explaining how killing off the buffalo makes the Injun fight back all the worse. He's lived off the buffalo for too long. Since way back before the Spanish brung in the horse, he's lived off the buffalo. Afoot, he hung to the flanks of the big herds like the wolf packs, and went where they went. Horseback, he done the same.

"He et the buffalo's meat. He drunk his blood. He used his hide for clothes and shelter and bedding. He strung

[142]

bows with his hamstrings, made tomahawks and knives out of his bone. He even boiled the sap out of his horns and hoofs for glue."

"The siwash don't own the buffler," Wiley Crup said. "Don't nobody own the buffler."

"Maybe he don't earmark and brand, like we do cattle," Sanderson said. "But after hundreds of years—maybe thousands—the Injun *feels* that he owns him."

"Well, he can learn to feel different," Crup declared.

I saw Sanderson get to his feet. He said to Papa, "Jim, you better go wake the boy."

I got up then and was washing myself off when Papa came to get me.

"You feel better, son?" he asked.

I nodded.

He helped me into my clothes and we walked toward the fire. I wondered about Burn Sanderson. How come he could kill Indians—and I knew he'd kill them—and still argue that they had a better right to the country and the buffalo than the white man?

Before we reached the fire, Herb Haley asked, "Well, what about them sculped hide hunters me 'n' Ben found out yonder?"

"Leave 'em to the wolves," Sanderson said. "We're out to save a couple of children. Not to bury a bunch of fool buffalo hunters!"

I ate by the faint light of the dying campfire. Again, I ate the salty, greasy food like I couldn't get enough.

"Anybody feed Sam?" I asked.

Sanderson grinned. "Till his eyeballs bulged," he said. "He'll be ready when you are."

I wiped clean the greasy frying pan with a chunk of hoecake. I crammed it into my mouth and came to my feet.

"I'm ready now," I said.

Sanderson reached for the frying pan and shoved it into a sack. He turned and called out into the darkness, "Let's go!"

The men came, bringing the horses. Papa went to turn Sam loose and whistle him out. We mounted up, all but Ben Todd, whose turn for running came next.

We sat our saddles and waited while Sam ran swift, widening circles around the camp. In the dark, we couldn't see him; but we could hear him bounding through the grass, hear his loud hasseling as he searched eagerly for the scent he wanted.

Papa said anxiously, "He was crippling pretty bad when I turned him loose."

"Stands to reason," Sanderson said. "All the ground he's covered. But I greased his feet good. And I never yet seen sore feet keep a dog from running a trail."

Out of the darkness rose Sam's voice, stirring a strong feeling inside me.

Sanderson said, "He's got it!"

We moved out, riding fast at first, gradually slowing our pace to fit Sam's. We didn't want to overrun him or crowd him too close from behind.

We came to the wagon of the scalped buffalo hunters.

Here the rhythm of Sam's voice broke. We reined to a halt, giving him time to work the trail away from there.

Behind us, the top edge of a red moon lifted above the rim of the world, throwing a faint light on the wagon and on a drying rack standing close by.

The rack had been built of mesquite poles set upright into the ground. A few short strips of buffalo meat, out of reach of the wolves and other varmints, still hung from the high crossbars.

Uncle Pack rode under the rack and lifted down strips of meat. He bundled the strips and hung them to his saddle horn, like the Indians had done.

"Just in case we git lank where it ain't safe to shoot meat," he explained.

I stared at the dark shapes of the wagon and drying rack, thinking what a lonely, solitary thing a wagon camp could be, resting there under the pale stars, without men or mules to give it life.

I thought some about the murdered hide hunters who lay scattered about somewhere in the grass. I couldn't see them and didn't want to. Once they had been men. Now, they were no different from the buffalo they had slaughtered around the wallow—fit only for the wolves and the buzzards to feed on.

Somehow, the thought didn't bother me. Maybe it was because I'd never known them. Maybe it was because of what Sanderson had said about hide hunters. Mostly, I think, it was because somewhere along this trip, I had come to see a thing that had always been right under my nose, yet I'd never paid any mind to it before. That is, how close life is tied up with death, so that you can't have one without the other. Everything on earth kills to live, then turns around and gets killed, so that something else can live. That was the pattern. I could see it now; and I guessed there wasn't a thing, from a man to a tumblebug, could change it.

Sam opened, and my thinking switched to Lisbeth and Little Arliss; and as I followed after Sam, I came to know another thing.

Maybe me and Lisbeth and Little Arliss and Papa and Mama and friends of ours, like Burn Sanderson, didn't amount to any more in this world than any other living creature. But like all the other creatures—like the buffalo, the screwworm, the prairie wolf, the high-flying goose, or the hole-digging gopher—our lives were important to us, and each of us would fight to keep them just as long as we could—and try to help those we loved to do the same.

Papa

Eleven

I DON'T recollect much of the nightlong ride that followed.
The soaking in the buffalo wallow had taken most of the
bite out of my wounds and sunburned skin. That, topped
off with a full stomach of good food, was too much. My
bone-tired body relaxed. I slept in the saddle.

I'd heard old-timers tell about sleeping in the saddle
and always figured it for brag talk, but that night I learned
it could be done.

It was more dozing than real sleeping, I guess. For I do

remember pieces and snatches of things. Like the bitterness in old man Searcy's voice when Papa and Sanderson tried again to talk him out of taking his turn at running.

"She's my grandgirl," he argued. "I got as much right to run myself to death trying to save her as ary one of you young bloods!"

Most of what I remember, though, wasn't talk. It was the steady squeak of saddle leather, the muffled drumbeat of horses' hoofs pounding the turf, and, above all, the never-failing trail cry of Savage Sam, calling us on across the shimmering silver of the moonlit grass.

It wasn't till Sam's voice faltered, then hushed altogether, that I started awake. I looked around. In the pearl-gray light of dawn I saw Burn Sanderson, some fifty yards ahead, reining his mount to a halt on the bank of a small creek. In the bed of the creek a trickle of water flowed between crumbling banks of brown sandstone. The water puddled in places, and the still surfaces of the puddles shone bright silver between a scattering of live oaks, willows, and cottonwoods.

Beyond the creek, the ground lifted like a great shaggy dew-wet blanket, rumpled and creased, sweeping up to high, flat-topped hills, purple in the distance. The upper edges of the hills glowed pink with the light of a rising sun we couldn't yet see.

We rode jaded horses toward Sanderson, with Papa calling out, "What have you found, Burn?"

Sanderson was slow to answer. "Not for sure yet," he finally said. "I'm just watching that dog."

Ahead, I could see Sam racing up one side of the creek,

then down the other, darting this way and that between the trees, scrambling up the rock ledges, only to wheel and come splashing back through the water. He whimpered with eagerness, yet couldn't seem to straighten out the trail, and his hasseling was loud in the morning stillness.

Sanderson said at last, "Believe I'd call him in till we can scour around a little."

He touched spur to his horse and rode slowly down into the creek bed, searching the ground as he went. Papa whistled and called to Sam, who came racing toward him, looking excited. He must have thought Papa had located the scent he couldn't find; for when Papa stepped down and tied a rope around his neck, Sam tried to fight it for a minute, then gave up and stood, tail-tucked and droopy, whining like Papa had whipped him.

Ahead, Sanderson located something that caught his interest. He swung to the ground, squatted, and felt around over a bare patch of drift sand with his hands. As we rode up, he reached suddenly and lifted a buried bone out of the sand. It was a piece of rib bone, with shreds of gnawed meat still attached to one edge. A swarm of brown fire ants clung to the meat.

Sanderson rose from his squat and motioned with the bone.

"They buried their campfire here," he said. "Not more than an hour ago. And they left out in a hurry."

The men all peered down at the patch of clean sand.

"How you come by all that information?" Wiley Crup demanded.

Sanderson looked at Crup like he was tired of the sight

of him. "The sand is still warm," he explained patiently. "And since it was wiped clean, not one living varmint's had time to make a track in it."

An ant stung his hand. He flung the bone aside and wiped crawling ants from one hand with the other.

"And if they hadn't quit this camp in a hurry," he added, "they'd never have left a piece of meat sticking out where the ants could get to it."

"You reckon they heard Sam?" Papa asked.

"You can depend on it," Sanderson said.

I remembered how quickly the Indians had broken camp that first morning when they heard Sam.

Sanderson climbed back into the saddle. He looked around at the men and nodded to Papa.

"We'll take a little *pasear*, Jim," he said. To the rest of us, he added, "Y'all strip the gear off the horses and cook up a batch of grub. We'll be back in time to help eat it."

"Why ain't we pushing on?" demanded Uncle Pack. "Ever' minute we lose gives them hostiles that much bigger lead."

"Trouble is, Uncle Pack, we don't know which way to push," Sanderson explained. "From the way that dog acts, I'd say they've split on us. Been expecting that to happen."

"We take the dog?" Papa asked.

"Let him rest," Sanderson said. "We'll need him worse later on."

Papa handed me the rope that Sam was tied to. Sanderson led off across the creek and Papa followed. They rode north at a jog trot toward the high hills. Both leaned low

[150]

out of their saddles, combing the grass for sign. A mile or two out, they would separate and ride half-circles back into camp. That way, they could tell for sure if the Indians had split up.

I led Sam to a live oak and tied him to a drooping branch. I dismounted and, like the others, unsaddled my horse and removed the bridle. I stumbled down to the creek, where I drank and washed my face.

The horses drank, too, then hunted a sand bed to wallow in, which is a horse's way of washing up. They lay down on their sides and kicked and squirmed and raked their heads back and forth across the sand. They rolled over and did the same for the other side. They grunted with the pleasure of sanding off their sweat. Getting up, they spraddled themselves, shook the sand out of their hair, then moved on out to graze.

The men built a fire and started breakfast. Their movements were draggy. They fumbled at the simplest tasks. Most of what they had to say was soon said; after that, they kept the silence of men stupid with weariness and loss of sleep.

I guessed they were all worn to a frazzle. I know I was. I'd been on the go for so long, I couldn't hardly tell straight up from a good living. Now and then, I'd have a hard go of it just remembering where I was or what I was doing. I'd look at a tree or a rock or an old buffalo chip and have to study for a long time to lay the proper name to what I saw.

It wasn't the pain so much. That had eased off a good deal; and I'd pretty well gotten used to living with what was left. But the tiredness—it was a load nearly too heavy to pack around.

I caught myself standing and staring at Sam. After a spell, it came to me that he was whimpering and licking his feet. I guessed they were sore and something ought to be done about it. Let Sam wear out, and we'd be pretty well string-halted.

I went to where Herb Haley was squatted over the fire, dropping chunked-up pieces of fat-back into a frying pan. I picked up a couple of chunks and took them over and started greasing Sam's feet. The thick, tough pads were worn off till they were paper thin, with the pink showing through. One pad had a bad cut across it and the cut oozed blood.

Back at the fire, I heard Lester White say, "This looks like an excellent location for the horse ranch I have in mind."

"Some appearances," Uncle Pack said, "is deceiving."

"Possibly," White admitted. "But here is good water, fine grazing, a salubrious climate."

"Climate!" Uncle Pack snorted. "Man, this country's got no climate. All it's got is weather, and that comes whole-sale. Let a four-five year drouth hit, and it'd crowd a pack rat to find grass enough to line his nest."

"But the buffalo," White protested. "How can he exist under such conditions?"

"The buffler, he's smart," Uncle Pack said. "He drifts with the weather. Rain falls on the Rio Grande, he heads for it. Wet spell comes to Canady, he trails north."

I heard Bud Searcy call to me. I looked toward him. He

hadn't moved from where he'd stripped the gear from his horse. He'd just dropped his saddle right there and now lay, using it for a pillow.

I went to stand over the old man. He lifted his canteen.

"Travis, my boy," he said in a quavery voice, "my canteen's dry. Would you kindly fill it for a pore old man?"

I knew that tone of voice. I remembered all the times he'd used it to take advantage of Lisbeth. It was, "Honey, will you do this?" and "Honey, will you fetch me that?" Always in that quavery, pore-mouth voice. And always for "yore pore old grandpappy." Running her half to death to keep up with his wants, while he lazed around in the shade, brag-talking and spitting his nasty tobacco juice all over the place.

Yesterday and last night, when he'd argued to take his turn at running, I'd been about ready to look up to Searcy a little, thinking maybe there was some man in him, after all. Now, I decided that all had been just show-off; he was the same old work-dodging windbag he'd always been.

I came close to telling him to go fetch his own water, that there were others around could use some rest. Then I took a second look. I saw how his blubber belly had shrunk, how his hands trembled, how gray his face was— like all the blood had been drained out. I saw how blue his lips were and what a look of defeat his watery old eyes held.

It came to me then that—for this time, at least—he wasn't just trying to use me. This time, he was in real need of help.

I took his canteen and walked upstream, past where the horses had muddied the water. I filled it and started back, taking a little different route, and came across a thing so curious that for a moment I forgot all about Searcy.

It was a pile of some forty or fifty horseshoes. Every shoe was bright with recent wear. And over the heap of shoes, lying in the form of a cross, was spread a couple of long narrow strips of torn blanket.

I stood and stared at my find, but couldn't make anything of it. I heard Searcy call out and took him his water. He set out to build me up, telling me what a fine upstanding young man I was to help a pore old man; but I didn't stay to listen. I hurried off to tell the men about my discovery.

On the way, I caught sight of Ben Todd. He stood, still as a mouse, watching something he'd found in a couple of catclaw bushes.

I halted. I looked to where he was looking. I saw wild morning glories blooming in the tops of the catclaw bushes. Their vines were spindly thin, but the pale, powder-blue flowers were big as teacups.

Dipping and diving, darting from one flower to another, were two hummingbirds.

They were different from the hummingbirds that fed on Mama's flowers, back at home. Their nectar-sucking beaks were longer. Their black-green bodies were longer, too; or, at least, slimmer. And under their throats each wore a patch of pale yellow that somehow—when the light struck them at just the right angle—flashed red.

[154]

A stick popped under my boot, and the hummingbirds disappeared. Ben Todd turned, smiling shyly.

"Purty things, ain't they?" he said. "Ruby-throated hummingbirds, I think. Migrating south for the winter. Furtherest west I ever seen one."

I told Ben Todd about the pile of horseshoes. He called to the others. We all went to see. Nobody had any more idea of its meaning than I did.

We were all standing around, still trying to puzzle it out, when Sanderson came riding in from downstream. We pointed to the pile of shoes. He nodded, like it was a common sight.

"Nearly always," he said, "an Injun will pull the shoes off any horse he steals."

"But why?" Herb Haley asked. "A smooth horse, he just goes lame all the quicker."

Sanderson shook his head. "I asked an old Tonk scout about it once. Best I could learn, the Injun figures if the Almighty meant for a horse to wear shoes, He'd have put 'em on his feet."

"But the crossed strips of blanket?" Herb Haley asked. "What do they mean?"

"*Quién sabe?*" Sanderson said. "Makes no more sense than wiping out signs of their campfire, then leaving this pile of horseshoes right out in the open, where they're bound to be seen."

He rode toward the campfire. We followed afoot. When we got there, I noticed Sam licking his feet again. I went to finish my greasing job and found that he had eaten the chunks of fat-back. So I got some more, greased his feet

[155]

again, then watched him eat what was left of those chunks.

The men had started eating when I got back to the fire. I joined them and saw Papa come riding in from the west. Uncle Pack waved a hand toward the hills.

"What'd y'all find out yonder?"

"About what I expected," Sanderson said. "They've split up on us."

"How many ways?"

"I'll know in a minute."

We waited till Papa rode in, his face looking strained, his eyes sick with worry.

"How many trails did you locate?" Sanderson asked.

"Two," Papa said. "One heading west along this draw. The other'n leading back to the southwest."

"That makes three, then," Sanderson said.

Papa swung down from his saddle and squatted to eat.

Uncle Pack shook his head, frowning. "The question is, which trail do we foller?"

"We'll have to leave that to Sam," Sanderson said.

"But how is the dog to know?" Lester White inquired. He frowned, studying for a moment, then went on. "He trails by scent. When the boy is on the ground, the dog can smell him. But once the boy is mounted, where is the scent? It can't hang in the air for long in this wind. Which means that all the dog has left to follow is the scent of the horses. And now, with the horses separated into three groups, it seems inconceivable that the dog can know which group to follow."

My heart sank. I never had thought of it in that light before.

I looked to Sanderson for help, but found no real comfort in the thoughtful look on his face.

He shook his head. "You've got a real poser there, Mr. White," he said. "But the way I see it, you're overlooking one thing. When it comes to sifting scent, a dog with a good nose has got powers outside the reach of a man's understanding."

"It's like what tells a honker goose spring's broke at his nesting grounds in Canada," Ben Todd said. "Man can't explain it, but the goose knows. So he quits Texas and heads north."

"That's putting a lot of trust in a dog," White said.

"Right now," Sanderson said bleakly, "a dog's all we got left to put any trust in."

Apache

Twelve

WE had to catch and saddle Searcy's horse for him, then help him into the saddle. He made a show of trying to pass it off as nothing much.

"Jest a mite stiff in the j'ints," he said. "Old hoss don't travel like a colt no more. But it'll pass off."

He stiffened his back and lifted the slump out of his shoulders. But I couldn't help noticing that the skin of his face was still a pasty white and the hands holding his shotgun were mighty shaky.

When I went to untie Sam, I found him almost as far gone as Searcy. And Sam made no bones about his miseries. It took him a second try to get to his feet, and then he could hardly walk. Every time he set a foot down, it was like he expected to step in hot ashes.

Worry must have showed in my face, for Sanderson told me, "He'll loosen up, once he takes the trail again."

He touched spur to his horse and rode up close.

"But boost him up across my saddle for now," he added. "Won't hurt to save his old feet when we can."

I picked up Sam by his slack back hide and swung him up across Sanderson's lap. There he lay, belly down, with Sanderson holding him on, while we rode better than a mile to where Papa had found a trail of horse tracks leading to the southwest.

Sam would have nothing to do with this trail. We set him down in the middle of the tracks and whistled him out. He crippled around for a little while, smelling here and there, made one wide circle, then came back to sit on his tail and look up at Sanderson, whimpering and whining. He made it plain that all he was interested in here was another ride.

Papa got down and handed him up to Sanderson, then he rode north toward the second trail, the one following west up the creek.

It was the same thing there. The tracks of the horses were plain in a sand bar that the creek had thrown up in flood time; but Sam wouldn't trail them. He didn't spend more than a couple of minutes nosing around over the trail before he was back, looking up at Sanderson, begging for another ride.

When he got it, Wiley Crup, who was on foot now, snorted in disgust. "Now I've seen it all," he said. "Pothounds let to ride, while good men are made to run!"

Sanderson shook his head slowly. "Wiley," he said, "there's times when a good pot-hound can be worth more than a dozen men."

We rode eàst, with hatbrims pulled low against the light of the rising sun. We traveled spread out, with every man cutting for sign of the horse trail leading north toward the high, far-off hills that were now changing from purple to blue. We rode till Sanderson began to look bothered, evidently thinking we'd overridden the trail.

Then Sam, who'd been grunting his pleasure at getting to ride, cut loose with a shrill yelp. It came so sudden that it spooked Sanderson's horse. Then Sam let out a bawl and went to clawing for footholds against the polished saddle leather.

Quickly, Sanderson cupped a hand under Sam's rump and heaved him out of his lap. Sam hit the ground and went charging through the grass. A second later, without even bothering to wring his stump tail, he opened, whimpered a time or two, and opened again. Then he took off running, nose to the ground, lined out toward the hills, the rise and fall of his high-pitched trail cry coming back to us clear and regular.

Ben Todd slapped his leg. "He's got it!" he shouted. "The son-of-a-gun!"

Lester White was plainly impressed.

"He's a caution, all right!" Uncle Pack said. "Stacking the landscape behind him like a dog what's been laid up and rested for a week!"

I didn't say a word about Sam's finding the trail. Papa didn't either. But I could see the relief on his face, and I guessed he was as choked-up proud of Sam as I was.

So we took up the chase again, the man-killing, horse-killing, dog-killing grind that wore on and on.

It wasn't speed so much that beat us down; Sam wasn't that fast on trail. It was just the steady going, with never a letup for a real rest. It was the awful distances we had to cover. And, worst of all for me, it was the nagging dread that when we caught up with the Indians, we might be too late.

Who was to protect Lisbeth from Broken Nose? And Little Arliss. With that hair-trigger temper of his, he was bound to tangle with Gotch Ear again.

We kept driving toward the hills, and the hills kept moving away. The jaded horses jogtrotted with heads held low, snuffing and blowing. The men rode slumped in their saddles, silent for the most part, with the turnover of those who traveled afoot coming more often now.

I wondered how Sam could hold up for so long. His feet were worn clear down to the quick. If they weren't bleeding now, they would be before the day was over. Yet he still kept driving, as strong and steady as ever.

The grass thinned to scattered bunches, finally played out altogether. Now we moved across country that was all hummocky blow-sand. The sand was a grayish pink and lay there in the prairie like a huge lake, with the hummocks and drift mounds looking like waves on water.

The strip we crossed, maybe a mile wide, was nothing more than a narrow finger of this great lake of sand. Looking to the west, I could see it reaching on out, as far as the eye was good.

It was while riding across the sand that I took notice of how many creatures were on the move—all sorts of snakes, gray lizards, huge black tarantulas, and terrapins.

As we entered the grass again, I rode past the trash-littered mound of a red-ant bed and looked down on it. Narrow lanes led away from the hole in several directions, and along these lanes the ants raced frantically back and forth.

I knew then what was fixing to take place. Before I could mention it, Ben Todd, riding close by, spoke up in an anxious voice.

"It's coming on to rain," he said.

"Rain!" Herb Haley said, surprised. He looked up and all around. "Why, they ain't a cloud in sight."

"But yonder," said Ben Todd, "goes a bunch of doves heading for a roost—here in the middle of the morning."

I glanced up. The doves, dark against a milky white sky, went hurtling past, making little whistling noises.

"And down here," Sanderson added, pointing, "is an alligator turtle on the prowl. Catch one of them old boys this far off from water, and rain is a dead certainty."

The turtle was a big ugly rascal, with a shell ridged down the middle. His tail was nearly a foot long, and so was his thick neck. He had a head on him the size of your fist, and there was no fear in him. He rose on his short bowed legs, lifting his head and tail clear of the ground, and glared at us. He blew at us like a mad snake. He made it plain that he was ready to take on all comers.

As we slogged on, following the steady ring of Sam's voice, the air got heavy and hard to breathe. The grass stood dead still and silent. A thickening haze all but smothered the high hills that had stood out so bright and sharp-edged at daylight. More doves passed over, flying at top speed. Now and then, too far out for us to have disturbed them, great flocks of little gray birds would rise suddenly up out of the grass. They'd take off in a low, jittery flight, barely skimming the top of the grass, wheel, and maybe go right back to light down where they came from.

When the clouds came, they were big thunderheads, one beside the other, piling up back of the hills. Their ragged white edges lifted above the flat-topped ridges, giving them shape and color again.

We rode toward them, watching them stack up higher and higher, till finally we could see their dark centers, churning and tumbling with threat.

Little wind puffs began sneaking up from behind. For a cooling moment, one would tug hard at our sweaty clothes before racing on toward the storm; and you could mark its course by the grass bowing before it.

Gradually, the wind puffs came more often and cut wider swaths across the grass. They mounted in strength till they became great surges in a steady wind that pulled toward the storm. The increasing roar of the wind all but drowned out the sound of Sam's trail cry.

The trail led past a buffalo wallow. It was a big one, filling a swag that lay off to our right. In it, come to take comfort from the stifling heat, were some twenty buffalo —cows, calves, and a couple of bulls. Now, one by one, the buffalo lumbered to their feet. They stood in the wallow, with heads lifted, while muddy water streamed from their coarse black hair.

They had to have heard us, yet it wasn't us that had disturbed them and it wasn't us they were concerned with. If one ever looked our way, I never saw it. All stood with raised muzzles pointing toward the storm. When at last they began straggling out of the wallow, led by one old bull, it was toward the storm they moved.

The high-climbing front lifted higher. All the clouds became one. It reached out to spread over us and hide the sun. The underbelly of the cloud glowed yellow-green. Sight of that strange light touched some sense of warning far back in my mind. Great crooked fingers of lightning clawed suddenly across the face of the cloud and thunder shook the hills.

For a second, I felt the big lift of spirit that, for me, such storms always brought. Then, knowing how quickly a heavy rain could wipe out the trail scent that Sam followed, dread took over, and I rode toward the storm, hating the very sight of it.

We came to the foot of the hills, where the land slanted sharply up. Here, the smooth rolling plain gave way to rounded ridges snaking down from the hills like the brace

[164]

roots of great trees. Dividing the ridges were dry water-courses, ranging in size from small crooked gullies to great cut-bank draws with walls of bare earth standing twenty feet high.

The trail led Sam along the hump of a ridge. We followed him, watching the play of lightning deep inside the black cloud, listening to the boom and roll of thunder among the hills. Then, almost at once, the wild wind driving hard at our backs shut down, leaving us to ride in a dead calm. Nothing stirred, not even a blade of grass, and I got the feeling that every creature on the face of the earth, besides us, had found itself a hiding place, where it lay, hushed and waiting.

That's when we heard it—a sullen, mounting, hammering roar that smothered Sam's voice, that all but drowned out the thunderclaps themselves.

I knew then what the threat was I'd missed back there when I'd first noticed that strange glow of yellow-green light in the cloud.

My voice cracked with fear when I cried out, "That's *hail!*"

"Go catch the dog!" Sanderson yelled at me, then called sharply to the others. "The balance of you scatter and hunt for cover!"

Sam wasn't more than a hundred yards ahead; but I don't believe I'd have ever caught him in time. He seemed to be driving harder than ever, like maybe the trail was the hottest he'd ever smelled it. Also, my horse was too jaded.

Then Papa came spurring past on a horse that still had

some bottom left. Gradually, Papa gained on Sam, finally caught up with him.

"Hold it, Sam!" I heard him call. "That's enough, now. Hold it, boy!"

But Sam kept driving on, his voice faint against the roar of the oncoming hailstorm.

Papa spurred up and cut in front of Sam and yelled at him again. When Sam dodged around the horse, Papa downed his catch rope. He reached out and laid his loop on Sam like he would a wild hog, yanking it shut across Sam's shoulders and between his forelegs.

Sam yelped and struggled frantically, as Papa lifted him into the saddle. There, he tried to kick loose, then snarled and snapped at Papa. Papa boxed his jaws and scolded him, and after that, Sam gave up and lay still, whimpering and whining.

With Sam caught, I quit quirting my horse. Right away, he came to a full stop and I could feel the trembling weakness of him between my legs. As Papa rode back toward me, I looked past him toward the white wall of rain and hail beginning to fill a slot in the hills. It wasn't more than half a mile off, and coming fast, with a fearful roar.

Back of me, I heard somebody shout. Papa lifted a hand, pointing.

"Looks like Ben Todd's located something," he yelled.

I swung my horse around to ride beside Papa. Across a wide ravine, Ben Todd sat his horse on a high hump of ground, calling and motioning with his hat.

We rode toward him. From all around, I could see other

members of the party riding up out of the draws and across folded ridges, headed toward Ben.

"It ain't much of a place," Todd said when we reached him. "But it'll shelter us for a while."

"That'll beat anything I found," Burn Sanderson said. "Lead off. We ain't got much time."

Todd led off, and the rest of us straggled after him. We struck an old buffalo trail and followed it, riding single file toward a break in the rim of a wide canyon that led down out of the hills. The trampling hoofs of thousands of buffalo, following this same trail for thousands of years, had cut it deep into the soil. It was so deep and narrow that in places we had to lift our feet out of the stirrups and hold them high to give the horses room to squeeze through.

We nearly didn't make it in time. A shrieking wind, racing ahead of the storm, hit while we were still in the open. It struck with a jolt that staggered some of the horses and snatched the breath out of my mouth. Then we dropped down into the canyon, where the high walls broke the force of the wind but didn't hold off the first scatter of rain and hail.

The raindrops were icy cold against our backs. Some of the hailstones were big as taw marbles and bounced when they hit the ground. One caught me about the bur of one ear with all the jar and sting of a rifle ball.

Sam let out a startled yelp, and I knew that he'd been hit, too.

We hurried faster along the rock-littered bed of the dry watercourse. We whipped around a tight bend and pulled to a halt under the shelter that Ben Todd had located.

To me, holding a hand to my aching jaw and seeing more and bigger hailstones falling outside, Todd's shelter seemed perfect. It was a high clay bank, deeply undercut by flood water. It shelved out over us like a roof. No rain or hail could touch us here, and there was room to spare, for both horses and men.

"The only thing," Sanderson said as we swung to the ground, "is how long can we stay?"

"I said it wasn't much of a place," Todd said. "But it was all I could find."

Sanderson said quickly, "I didn't mean it as a complaint, Ben."

Todd nodded. "I didn't take it you did. But I'll allow it could turn into a trap."

"That sure ain't no lie," Wiley Crup said. "Me, I've seen floodwater with six- and eight-foot fronts come charging down draws like this, kicking up more dust than a runaway mule team."

He looked around like maybe he'd seen a lot of important sights nobody else had.

"Every man and horse in this outfit could git drownded here," he added. "Was enough water to fall fast enough."

Sanderson spoke with an edge to his voice. "You find a better place, Wiley?"

About then, the full force of the storm hit; and the hammering roar of it and the wreckage it brought on was enough to hold us all silent.

The first hailstones were piddling compared to what fell

now. Out of the roaring blackness above rained ice balls bigger than your fist. They'd hit the ground and bounce three feet high, then get busted wide open by the first chunk of ice that struck them.

Across the draw from us, the ground sloped up to prairie level. The slope was overgrown with tall grass. Huddled up under the protecting ground shelf, we watched in awe as the rain of ice chunks beat the grass to the ground, chopped it up, drove it into the earth, then overlaid the whole mess with a litter of shattered ice.

I thought of Lisbeth and Little Arliss, and a shiver shook me.

I looked around for Papa. He was squatted on his spurs. He had his elbows propped on his knees, his chin cupped in his hands. And he was crying.

It wasn't out-loud crying. But his face was all torn up, tears ran down his cheeks, and while I looked, his body jerked with a spasm that I knew came from a deep inside sob with the lid clamped on.

I felt again the great emptiness that I'd known back there before Sam caught up with me at the water hole. If Papa had lost all hope, I guessed we'd come to the end of our string.

Burn Sanderson moved quickly to lay an arm across Papa's shoulders. He gave Papa a rough shake.

"Here, now," he said. "Get a grip on yourself, Jim." He had to shout to be heard above the roar of the pounding hail. "We ain't near done yet."

Papa glanced at Sanderson, then away. He waved a hand toward the pounding hail and said hopelessly, "Nothing can take battering like that and come out of it alive. Not even a horse, if he gets hit on the head!"

"Now, hold on," Sanderson shouted. "Don't you never think for a minute them redskins didn't find shelter. We did, and they're a heap wilder and more knowing of the country than us."

Before Sanderson finished speaking, the hail quit like it had been chopped off. Rain still poured down in driving sheets, but after the awful racket of that falling hail, what noise the rain made seemed like a whisper.

"But the trail," Papa said. "It's been wiped out. We got nothing left to foller."

Sanderson studied on that for a minute, then said, "But we still got a direction, Jim. And we still got Sam. We foller the direction long enough, and Sam'll pick us up a trail."

Beside me, Wiley Crup raised a protest. "But that could take days!" he said. "With all the country we'd have to scour, trying to locate a trail."

Sanderson nodded. "It sure could," he said.

Crup stared at Sanderson like he thought he was out of his head. Then he stabbed a finger toward the tired horses that stood humped under their saddles.

"Just how much longer do you expect them dead-beat horses to hold out?" he demanded.

"Till they go down," Sanderson said.

"Then what?"

"Then we take it afoot."

Crup exploded. "You expect a man to ride his horse this far from home, then walk back?" he asked.

Sanderson said in a flat tone of voice, "You got any ideas about going back right away, you'll walk, anyhow. We're short of horses."

Crup stiffened. "You'd try to take my horse?"

"I mean we'll *take* it," Sanderson said.

Crup stared hard at Sanderson. With a casual movement, he shifted his heavy rifle to his left shoulder. Then, so quick it didn't seem like he'd moved, he had a six-shooter in his right hand, pointed straight at Sanderson. He bared his squirrel teeth and sneered, "What makes you think you can git away with that?"

Sanderson looked past Crup's gun like it wasn't there. He grinned and gave his head a sideways nod.

"One thing," he said, "is the direction Bud Searcy's got his scatter-gun pointed."

Crup started and looked around. I did the same. Old man Searcy sat with his back braced against the clay wall. He held his shotgun pointed at Wiley Crup.

"You turn one hair, Wiley Crup," he warned, "and I won't leave enough of you to scrape up with a hoe!"

The gun muzzle wobbled in his hands. Like always, there was too much brag and bluster in his voice. But the glassy shine in his eyes convinced me. If Wiley Crup was looking for a chance to get blown into scrapmeat, he'd looked far enough.

Evidently, Crup saw it the same way. He let his six-shooter sag. He took a couple of steps backward, saw other guns being drawn, and froze.

He didn't say anything, and nobody else did.

Back of him the rain began to slack off. Around the

bend of the draw swept a curling front of floodwater, pushing ahead of it a lot of trash and dirty brown foam. It lacked a good deal of being the horse-drowning flood Crup had predicted, maybe because too much water was locked up in ice. But it was enough to make Papa and Sanderson and Searcy get to their feet. Otherwise, nobody paid any attention to the water. They just stood waiting on Crup.

After a while, Crup swallowed and said grudgingly, "I reckon I was out of line."

"That's how we got it figured," Uncle Pack said.

Crup took a second look at the drawn guns and accusing stares. He sucked in a quick breath and terror showed in his face.

"But you ain't cutting me out of the bunch!" he cried. "Not way out here, clear to the backside of nowhere!"

"That's up to Sanderson," Uncle Pack said. "Don't make me no never-mind, one way or t'other."

Crup turned to face Sanderson. "Sanderson!" he begged. "You can't do it! Not *afoot*. Them siwashes—they'd lift my hair before sunset!"

Sanderson stood frowning down at a dead pack rat floating past on the muddy water swirling around his feet. The icy water was rising and beginning to fill my boots. I heard Sam whine, saw him wading stiffly toward higher ground. The cold water made some of the horses nervous. They snorted and stomped around.

I wished the men would hush arguing. I wished they'd set Wiley Crup afoot, shoot him, or do something. I couldn't stand much more of this. I was shaking all over.

[172]

Finally, Sanderson lifted his head. "Way I see it," he said. "Wiley's still another gun. Best shot in the bunch, too. And once we overhaul them Injuns, any extra gun won't be none too many."

He turned toward his horse. "Now," he said, "let's clear out of this draw before we get drowned out."

Travis

Thirteen

WE boosted Searcy back into the saddle. I waded out to where Sam stood shivering and handed him up to Papa. Papa held him in his saddle and looked toward Crup.

"Wiley," he said, "I'll give you a piece of advice. Don't pull a gun on Sanderson again. If he don't kill you, I will."

It gave me a lift to hear Papa talk like that. The tone of his voice told me that he had got hold of himself, that he was ready to push on again.

We rode out into the tail-end leavings of the storm that

[174]

boomed and roared as it rolled on toward the south. What rain fell now was thin and drizzly, but still enough to wet us.

We came to the break in the canyon wall. We found the buffalo trail a foot-deep millrace of yellow water, loaded heavy with trash and tumbling chunks of white ice. It didn't look like much of a way out, but it was the only one, so we took it.

The horses slipped and floundered, scrambling for footholds against the slippery trail bottom. They snorted and stomped at the icy water dragging against their legs. They grunted and strained and were badly winded by the time they'd brought us out on top.

There, we reined them to a halt, giving them a breather while we gazed out on a bleak and disheartening sight. In every direction, as far as the eye could reach, white balls and chunks of ice covered the ground. Where thirty minutes ago we'd ridden through grass that stood stirrup high, now a cow couldn't have picked a bellyful of graze off a thousand acres.

For all a body could tell, this might have been in the dead of winter. What little breeze trailed after the storm had all the feel of winter. Moving across miles of ice, it picked up the cold of it, and the cold reddened our hands and faces and drove through our wet clothes, chilling our whole bodies. We shivered and our horses shivered and our breaths fogged white in the air.

Cold like this, coming so soon after we'd all been so sweaty hot, was hard to bear.

Sanderson blew on his hands. He said he didn't guess

we'd get any warmer sitting there, so we moved out toward the gap in the hills that Sam had been headed for when we pulled him off the trail.

The ice crunched under the horses' feet. The cold drove deeper till I could feel the ache of it in my bones. My teeth went to chattering.

I glanced around at the others. They all looked as cold and miserable as I felt. Especially old man Searcy. He rode behind and a little off to the right of Wiley Crup, and the cold had him shaking till it looked like he might drop his shotgun any minute.

The shotgun, I noticed, was kept pointed in the general direction of Wiley's back.

After a while, that fact came to Crup's attention. I saw him cast a couple of wary glances back over one shoulder, then gradually sidle his horse toward the edge of the bunch.

Searcy sidled with him.

Crup, trying to act casual about it, shifted toward the other side. Just as casually, Searcy shifted with him.

There was no doubt left in Crup's mind now. He twisted in his saddle.

"Old man," he said angrily, "you got no call to keep pointing that scatter-gun at me."

Searcy pressed forked fingers against his lips and tried to spit through the fork, but he was so shaky with cold that most of the tobacco juice spattered down over his shirt front.

"Maybe not," he said to Crup. "But that's what I aim to keep doing."

Crup looked around at the others like he expected sympathy, but all he got was a couple of wry grins.

We rode on, past a dead coyote lying half buried in the ice; and after that, I saw all sorts of small creatures that had been beaten to death by the hail.

We passed a lone three-pronged live oak that grew beside a gully. The hail had stripped it. There wasn't a branch smaller than your arm left on it. The stub ends of the broken branches were split and shredded and had all the bark knocked off on the north side. It would take a long time for that tree to grow another top—if it lived.

I had to believe what Sanderson had said: that the Indians were bound to have located cover.

At last, we came to a high saddle between two hills. Here, Sanderson pulled up to make a study of the country that lay ahead.

I took a look at it, myself, but didn't see much. Just more flat-topped hills, separated by wide, sweeping valleys. The valleys were cut up some by deep ravines and old buffalo trails. These now ran full with flood water. The only hopeful thing I saw lay to the north, where the overcast of storm clouds was lifting, leaving a clear blue sky and the promise of warm sunshine.

The way my bones ached with cold, I could sure make good use of some sunshine.

Sanderson lifted a hand, pointing. He said, "See that main buffalo trail, leading to the northwest? I figure that's the route they took. Buffalo always pick the easy ground and the redskin knows it. Crowd him, and watch how quick he'll take to a buffalo trail for fast traveling."

Pack Underwood said, "You think we was crowding 'em? Back before the hail hit?"

"That's the way I read the sign," Sanderson said.

He paused, his keen eyes searching again the ice-littered hills and valleys.

"We'll foller that main buffalo trail," he said. "We'll spread out as far apart as we can see each other. That way, with everybody keeping his eyes skinned, somebody ought to cut their sign."

"What if we jump 'em?" Ben Todd wanted to know. "Sudden and accidental, I mean."

"However we jump 'em," Sanderson said, "we try first to cut 'em away from their main horse herd. We do that, we can handle 'em. We miss, and they'll blow out our lamps while we're still shooting horses from under 'em."

We spread out and rode forward in a mile-wide front. That is, all but Bud Searcy. He wouldn't spread out at all. He just dogged Wiley Crup's heels, with his shotgun held ready.

I heard Sam's eager yelp when he first caught the scent. I looked toward Papa and saw him boost Sam out of the saddle. Sam yelped again—this time in pain—when his sore feet hit the ice. Then he was circling, nose to the ground, and I heard the strain in Papa's voice as he urged Sam on.

"Git after it, boy," he said. "It's up to you, now!"

I reined to a halt and sat watching, listening, hoping.

Then Sam opened. He opened again; and if there'd been any doubt the first time, it was gone now. The ring of his voice was too sure-for-certain.

[178]

My heart swelled near to bursting.

Sam headed south, the regular rise and fall of his voice high-pitched and steady. I followed, hearing the excited shouts of the men and the pounding crunch of their horses' hoofs on the ice as they gathered in.

Uncle Pack called from a long way off. "You think he's got it?"

"I *know* he's got it," Sanderson shouted back.

I rode, wondering if it was pure accident that the Indians had cut square across the route Sanderson had expected them to follow; or was it a thought-up trick, calculated to throw us off track?

The trail led up a long slope, over a high hump, and down a steeper slant on the other side. Here, Sam swung right, trailing west, with loose ice clinking under his feet. I rode all alert and with a mounting sense of excitement, knowing that any trail on top of the ice had to be a fresh one, which meant we just might jump us some Indians any minute.

The overcast of clouds peeled back. A hot sun bore down, bringing comfort to our bone-chilled bodies.

It also set fire to the ice. Every chunk glinted and sparkled with such dazzling brightness that it all but blinded us. We rode now with tears blurring everything, following Sam more by ear than by sight.

I didn't like this, even a little bit. How could a body draw a bead on an Indian when he couldn't even see his gunsights? I worried with this for a couple of miles, then heard Uncle Pack grunt with relief.

"Be dog, if that ain't a sight for sore eyes," he said.

[179]

I wiped away my tears and looked ahead. Uncle Pack had sure told the truth. We'd come to the edge of the ice. Out front, not fifty yards away, stood tall grass again. The green of that grass was sure restful to the eye; and right then, looking out on the great sweep of it, I thought I'd never seen a prettier sight in my life. Even the smell of it was good.

Just before we rode into it, however, I glanced down and saw a thing that put a damper on my good feelings. It was a smear of blood in one of the tracks that Sam had left in the melting ice.

But if worn and bloody feet slowed Sam, I couldn't tell it. He set and held a pace that kept us jogging through the grass at a fast clip, forcing us to change often with whichever man ran on foot. The sun soon broke out the sweat on men and horses, but after that ride across the ice, nobody complained about sweating.

The trail led deeper and deeper into the rain-soaked hills. Some hills were big and some little, but each stood at the same flat-topped level, like they'd all been sliced off with one stroke of a big knife. A scattering of brush grew on some hills, and some didn't have any, but wind-rippled grass lay over them all.

Always, ahead of us, the hills seemed to lap and fold, one into the other, so that it never looked like there was an opening in between. Yet, before we ever got anywhere near a place that was solid, the hills seemed to move apart, leaving room for us to follow Sam through a valley that might be as much as a mile wide.

[180]

We crossed a buffalo trail and in the muddy bottom of it I saw blood in Sam's tracks again. Further along, we scared up a big band of antelope that swept across the trail in a blur of speed. Their scent muddled the trail for Sam and he had to circle several times before he could get lined out again. We rode up on him while he circled; and I saw him packing one forefoot and now and then lifting the offside hind one, so that part of the time, he ran on two feet only.

Then he opened, set all four feet to the ground, and was gone again.

It was along in the middle of the afternoon when the warning came.

There was nothing sudden about it, nothing the others could take note of. But it was strong enough to wake me out of the drooping, head-nodding doze I rode in. It put me on the alert again.

A slight but steady breeze blew out of the west, bringing Sam's voice straight back to us, loud and clear. But now there was a difference in the pitch of that voice. It was such a hair-thin difference that nobody who hadn't trailed varmints with Sam would have caught it, but I did—that little extra drive, a shade more urgency, a keener, wilder lift to the ring of it.

I knew what that meant, and the knowing of it tightened every nerve in my body. I crowded my horse up alongside Burn Sanderson, who rode with Papa and Lester White.

"Mr. Sanderson," I told him, "we're getting close!"

Sanderson stiffened. He gave me a quick look, then motioned for the others to pull in closer.

"You sure, boy?" he asked.

"Yes, sir," I said. "I'm *real* sure."

He reined to a halt. He made a quick search of the hill slopes on either side and of the long valley stretching out ahead of us. Papa and White did the same.

"But they ain't a thing in sight," Herb Haley said.

"The boy ought to could tell," Searcy said. "Was it my trail hound, I could tell in a minute."

Wiley Crup edged his horse away from Searcy. Searcy was quick to swing his shotgun around to cover him.

"Wiley, you hold still," he ordered. "I'm a feeble old man, but I ain't too feeble to press a shotgun trigger."

Wiley glared his hate at the old man, but he held still.

I felt desperate. Sam was closing in on the Indians. He might jump them any minute. And here we sat.

"Confound it!" I flared. "I tell you, Sam's moving in on them. Right now!"

"If we're that close," Sanderson said, "they're bound to've pulled off into some side valley. Maybe to get meat."

He sized up the bunch and nodded to Ben Todd. "Ben," he said, "you got a sharp eye. You and Mr. White, y'all take to the high ground on the right. Me 'n' Travis here, we'll go left. Jim, you and the others catch up with that dog. And stay caught up. Tromp on his heels if you have to, but be in gun range when he leads you to them Injuns."

He reined his horse to the left, then added, "And remember. The main thing is to cut 'em away from their loose horses."

He touched spur to his horse and rode, quartering left up a long slant toward a dip between two hills. I went with him. Out of the tail of my eye, I could see Ben Todd and Lester White riding at about the same angle toward the opposite hills. In the valley between, Papa and the others pushed their jaded horses to the limit, trying to overtake Sam.

I wondered if they ever could; for by now, anybody could tell that Sam was stepping up the pace. His voice was much keener, the beat of it much quicker. There was no longer any noticeable rise and fall to it. Now, it came to us in just one long quavering peal of sound, so wild and with so much drive that it stretched my nerve strings right up to the breaking point.

Maybe Sam's voice tore at Sanderson like it did at me; or maybe Sanderson sensed the strain I was under. Anyhow, he spoke up in time to keep me from going to pieces.

"Travis," he said, "when this show opens, it'll open fast. Them Injuns, they're not going to wait around for you to consider if it's best to do this or to do that. So the thing is, get your mind made up first, then keep it made up. You understand?"

I said, "Yes, sir," and waited to hear more.

"Good," he said. "Now, what we've come for is to kill Injuns. It's the only way we can save Lisbeth and Little Arliss. No matter what unexpected thing crops up during the fight, that's what you want to keep in mind. Kill Injuns."

"Yes, sir," I said.

He rode silent for a moment, then went on. "Heading into a fight," he said, "all you can depend on for sure is that you're going in scared."

I looked at him in surprise. I'd never thought of him as being scared of anything. As if he could read my thoughts, he grinned and licked lips as dry as mine.

"Man or boy," he said, "it's all the same."

The last hundred yards of ground we covered was plenty steep. Footing for the horses was bad here. Either their hoofs slipped on firm ground or sank hock deep into sloppy mud. They bowed their backs and grunted with the strain of the climb.

I glanced back for a last look at the others. Ben Todd and Lester White, they'd disappeared into some fold of the landscape. The hump of hill to our right hid all of Papa's party except for the drag end. I could still see old man Searcy dogging along after Wiley Crup.

I listened for Sam, but the wind direction was wrong now. I couldn't hear him any more.

Comanche

Fourteen

WE finally reached the gap between the hills. Just before
we got to where we could see over, Sanderson reined to
a halt. He dragged his Winchester from his scabbard and
stepped to the ground.

"We belly crawl from here," he told me. "We want a
good look-see at what's on the other side before we skyline ourselves."

I got down with my rifle. We dropped looped bridle

[185]

reins, to ground-stake our horses. We left them to catch
their wind while we went crawling through the grass.

I crawled close beside Sanderson. I watched how he
did things and tried my best to do the same. Any slip-up
made here, Sanderson would have to make first.

We crawled quiet and easy across the narrow ridge. We
came to where the ground dropped away on the far side.
We peered out through the grass—and both froze.

Just under us, less than a hundred yards away, grazed
some twenty head of horses. Among them was the big
stud that Gotch Ear had tried to ride. Beyond the herd,
holding the horses against the hillside, Bandy Legs sat on
his saddle of buffalo hide. He was staring straight at us.

It was probably a happen-so that he was looking our
way, for he didn't appear disturbed. But it sure proved
how smart we'd been to play it so cautious. If we had
come riding across that ridge, Bandy Legs would have
spotted us for sure.

A sudden outburst of yips and yells made Bandy Legs
swing around to look the other way. It caused us to inch
forward to where we could see better. And what we saw
set the blood to pounding my ears.

It was Lisbeth and Little Arliss.

They were down in the middle of a quarter-moon valley
that, half a mile away, opened into the bigger one we'd
just climbed out of. They sat their horses beside a shallow
wash now flooded with runoff water from the hills. Arliss
was still naked except for his buffalo headdress. Lisbeth's
garments were so tattered, they made her look like a scarecrow.

Near them, strung along the wash, were five Indians. Two I recognized: the Comanche and Broken Nose. The Comanche stood on the ground, holding to the bridle reins of my horse, Blue. The others were mounted. All, including Lisbeth and Little Arliss, sat staring toward the upper end of the valley, watching something I couldn't see.

I could hear it, though. It was a chase of some sort. The muffled drumming of heavy hoofs pounded the turf, and I could hear the familiar screeches of red savages closing in for a kill. From the sound of it, the chase was moving down our side of the valley and ought to cross our line of vision any second.

I wondered what the Indians were after.

Beside me, Sanderson whispered, "Not a bad setup. Knock off this close one, and we ought to could drive a wedge between the horse herd and them others before they can reach it."

I'd been packing my bottled-up rage for too long. It'd been lying like a hot rock inside my rib cage from the first time I saw Lisbeth and Little Arliss yanked around by the hair of their heads. Now, I stared down at the cruel, paint-streaked face of Bandy Legs and knew a big hunger to kill.

I eased my rifle forward. "Now?" I whispered.

"No. Hold it!" Sanderson said quickly. "Give Sam time to lead your papa and his bunch into the mouth of that draw. We'll have 'em in a trap then."

That wasn't actually true. Stopper both pinched ends of the valley, and the Indians could still get out on either side. Yet, to do so, they'd have to climb steep slopes, which would slow their getaway and give us good open shooting. The main trouble, as I saw it, was the width of the valley in the middle. I didn't much think a rifle ball would carry that far.

I lay listening and watching, trying to hold down the thumping of my heart. There was a brass-cartridge taste in my mouth. My lips stayed dry, no matter how often I licked them. I kept thinking: *We've come to kill Indians. We've got to kill them to save Lisbeth and Little Arliss!*

The noisy chase came into sight. It was a herd of some twenty or thirty buffalo. They came stampeding down the valley with a couple of Apaches riding hard after them.

One of the Apaches was Gotch Ear, still wearing his big black hat. He and his partner yelled at the tops of their voices.

The buffalo looked too big and clumsy for fast travel; yet their lumbering gait covered the ground at a pace that had the Indian ponies stretched out for all they were worth to gain on them.

Sanderson shook his head, as if finding it hard to believe what he saw.

"Now, that's young bucks for you," he said under his breath. "Stopping to pull off a frolic like this, when they're bound to know we're right on their heels."

I nodded. I remembered how they'd stopped their wild getaway run to watch a snake swallow a rabbit.

The chase came about even with Lisbeth and Arliss and the others watching. Gotch Ear's partner, riding on the far side of the herd, moved up beside a running cow. Plumed lance lifted high, he raced with her for a moment, edging in closer. Then he struck, driving the lance deep into the cow's side. The stricken cow bawled and made a quick sideways lunge with her head. The Apache wheeled his horse out of danger as the cow went down.

This was a daring kill, judging from the whoops of the Indians looking on. But laid up against the show Gotch Ear had in mind, it didn't amount to shucks.

I watched Gotch Ear now, as he edged his hard-running pony in beside a monster bull; and it came to me that he carried no lance or any other weapon I could see.

Then he made his leap. He quit his horse and landed astride the bull. I caught a glint of sunlight on polished steel and knew that Gotch Ear was making an even bigger bid for glory than when he'd tried to ride that killer stud.

He aimed to cut down this big bull buffalo with only a knife!

He caught up a fistful of hump hair to hold with; and the way he hung down off the side of that running bull and went to work with his knife was a sight to curl your hair.

"I'm going back for the horses," I heard Sanderson whisper. "This turkey shoot's fixing to open."

I was so taken with the daring of Gotch Ear's show that I hardly knew when Sanderson left. I watched Gotch Ear plunge the long blade of his knife, time and again, deep into the side of the running buffalo. He was reaching low, stabbing for the heart, but evidently missing it.

[189]

Blood spewed bright red from each new wound as Gotch Ear yanked his knife free for another lick. The bull bellowed with the pain of his wounds, but stayed on his feet and kept right on running with the others.

Then, riding in over the pain bawling of the bull, the pounding of hoofs, and the whooping and yelping of the Indians, came a sound that brought me up sharp. It was the quavering high-pitched voice of Savage Sam, driving full cry on a hot trail.

I glanced toward the lower end of the valley. I couldn't see Sam for the tall grass, but I could see Papa and the others rounding a shoulder of the hill, moving up to meet Gotch Ear and the stampeding buffalo.

I wasn't the only one to hear Sam. Already, the delighted yelps of the spectator Indians had changed to sharp, barking shouts of alarm.

I glanced toward them. I saw the Comanche leap astride my horse, Blue. I saw the others wheel their mounts around and lay the lash to them, and to the horses on which Lisbeth and Little Arliss were mounted.

Then here they came in a dead run, headed straight for the horse herd.

I couldn't wait to ask Sanderson when to shoot. The time was now, and I knew it!

I brought my rifle butt up to my shoulder. Bandy Legs caught the movement out of the tail of his eye. He swung around, holding still for an instant, trying to locate what he'd seen, and that instant was too long.

My ball lifted him out of the saddle like he'd been jerked loose with a rope.

Behind me came the pound of running hoofs and Sanderson's voice.

"That's laying 'em in the groove, boy!" he shouted. "Now, mount up and foller me!"

I leaped to my feet. Sanderson came spurring toward me, leading my horse. He dropped the bridle reins as he tore past. I grabbed them up and went into the saddle without touching a stirrup and took out after Sanderson.

Sanderson was spurring and quirting his horse, shouting at him, goading him into a frantic run down a slant of ground so steep it didn't look like a horse could keep on his feet.

My shot and the scent of fresh blood had spooked the Indian herd. Now, horses were whistling and snorting and scattering in all directions. Several headed straight across the valley where it would be as easy for the Indians to reach them as it would be for us to cut them off.

It took all Sanderson could get out of his tired horse to drive between these horses and the Indians racing toward them.

My horse never got that far. He stepped into a hole, stuck his nose into the ground, and turned tail-end-over-appetite.

I'd been looking for something like that, and when I felt him coming over, I quit the saddle, throwing myself as far away as I could.

I landed standing up, but my falling horse struck me from behind and slammed me to the ground. The way he lay, with his head doubled back under him, told me that he'd never get up again.

I crawled up behind him and used his body for protection. I reloaded and laid the barrel of my rifle across his rump. I looked along the length of it toward the screeching pack that raced uphill toward Sanderson and the stampeding horse herd. I heard two whiplash reports from Sanderson's repeater rifle. I saw one of the running horses go down. His flying hoofs slapped down a rider who'd tried to leap free of him. That Indian didn't get up.

I held off shooting for a second. I was searching for a certain target. I wanted Broken Nose, the Apache I hated the worst.

But I couldn't find him. Like every other fight I'd seen the savages take part in, there wasn't a whole Indian in sight. Each rode hanging to the off side of his mount, leaving nothing to shoot at except a leg hooked across a horse's back and a rawhide shield held against the animal's neck.

But yonder rode Lisbeth, sitting straight up, with her long blond hair streaming in the wind. Close behind raced a blaze-faced sorrel that Broken Nose sometimes rode. I figured that sorrel to be the one I wanted and lined my sights up on him, leading him a few inches, since it was a quartering shot. I squeezed the trigger and cut him down.

It was Broken Nose, all right. He landed running, and I worked fast reloading, hoping to get in a shot while he was still on the ground and in sight.

To my left, Sanderson's gun spoke again. At the same instant, I heard Little Arliss call out in a wild scream of joy. "Sam! Sam!"

My glance flicked toward him as he leaped free of a

running horse, and deep inside me I cried, *Wait, Arliss! Wait!*

I saw Arliss hit the ground and take off through the grass. I saw, too, the hard-driven arrow that barely missed him and how it went skipping across the grass tops like some live scared thing.

If Arliss saw the arrow, he paid it no mind. He went racing along a buffalo trail behind Gotch Ear and the stampeded buffalo. He was going to meet Sam. He kept calling as he ran, "Sam! Sam!"

Then there was no longer time to watch Arliss; for now I was reloaded, and yonder was Broken Nose, making a flying leap for the back of another horse that came running past him.

He landed astride; and as I swung my rifle around to cover him, I saw him lift a foot and stomp at the Apache clinging to the off side of the horse. He was trying to kick that one loose; but either he made a miscalculation, or the other Apache dragged him off, for they both tumbled to the ground before I could shoot.

They were out of sight for a second. Then, up out of the grass they came, running side by side, straight away from me; and now it *was* like a turkey shoot, and I pulled down on Broken Nose, drawing a close bead on the center of his bare back, knowing in my own mind that I had him dead to rights, with no chance for a miss.

Yet, at the very instant I squeezed off—like maybe he could tell my shot was meant for him—Broken Nose whipped his fire-hardened shield around to cover his back. My ball struck it, making it boom like a drum. But the bulge of the shield deflected the ball, and the high, keening wail of it spending itself harmlessly out across the valley filled me with bitter disappointment.

I worked frantically at jacking an empty shell from the firing chamber and thumbing a loaded one back into its bed. I slapped shut the breech lock. I brought my rifle up to my shoulder. Then, before I could shoot, Sanderson's repeater rifle cut loose again and sent Broken Nose and the other Apache plunging head first into the grass and out of sight.

Whether or not either had been hit, I had no way of knowing and no time to find out. For now, above all the yelling and shooting and trampling of hoofs, there lifted a long drawn-out, blood-chilling screech that was too close.

The hair prickled the nape of my neck as I swung my rifle around and brought it to bear on the Comanche. He'd split off from the others and now rode straight at me, not fifty yards away. He lay low along the back of my horse, Blue, and rode with a long arrow set in a short bow and had the bowstring pulled clear back to his ear.

The bowstring twanged. I ducked low and heard the whistle of the arrow cut short as it drove into the soft earth just behind me.

I raised to make a quick try at catching the Comanche in my sights. But I wasn't quick enough. Already, he was down off the side of Blue and swinging him away at an angle that used Blue's body as a protection.

Blue was my horse, the first I'd ever owned. I was proud of him; and it was a hurtful, sickening thing for me

[194]

to plant a ball in his heart and watch him roll dead—the same as you'd knock over a chicken-thieving coyote.

What drove the hurt deeper was the sight of the Comanche landing free and unharmed, to go racing off down the slant with his cowtail ropes of hair whipping the grass tops behind him. There went a perfect target. If only my rifle still held the bullet that had killed Blue!

Then I thought: *You've got a six-shooter, you fool!*

So I jerked out the side gun and snapped off a quick shot that struck the left side of the Comanche and set him spinning, with arms outflung, so that his shield slipped off his arm and flew in one direction and his bow in another.

I shot again and missed; and before I could get off a third shot, the Comanche had melted into the grass.

I held ready for a second, watching close, hoping he would show again, but he didn't, and shouts and shots beyond pulled my attention away. I looked out across a valley alive with scared and scattering horses and saw Sanderson shoot one of them, then kill the Apache who flung himself free as the horse went down.

I took a quick look around. Best I could tell, that was the last mounted Indian. Now, the only loose horse still packing a rider was the one Lisbeth rode. He'd shied away from the gunfire, veering off to chase after a stud and several mares that had cut in behind Sanderson.

The stud led them toward the far side of the valley at a dead run. I watched them taking Lisbeth with them and wished she'd jump off, but guessed she was too scared to think what to do.

I tucked away the six-shooter and began reloading the rifle. As I worked, I watched Sanderson rein his horse around to follow after Lisbeth. Then he leaped suddenly to the ground and stood in a half-crouch while he brought his rifle to bear on some target further down the valley.

He fired as I swung around to look, then fired again; but both shots missed and changed nothing about the picture laid out before my eyes.

It was a sight to choke off my breath.

Here came Little Arliss, headed back along the same trail he'd followed when he went to meet Sam. He was running like a scared jackrabbit. Close behind and gaining raced Gotch Ear, clutching his long, bloody knife. Moving up fast behind Gotch Ear came Savage Sam, running silent now, bent on catching Gotch Ear before the Apache could overhaul Arliss. And, straggled out far behind, riding past the dead bull buffalo, came Papa and the others, spurring and quirting horses too dead-beat ever to catch up.

All this I caught at a glance and understood at once.

Gotch Ear's show-off kill of the bull buffalo had led him head-on into a trap. When finally the huge beast went down under his knife, the Apache had leaped clear, expecting applause for his daring act. Instead, he'd heard Sam and caught sight of Papa and the others coming straight for him. He'd wheeled to head back toward his companions, only to see them racing away, leaving him afoot.

But yonder, coming to meet Sam, was Little Arliss, who

had helped to shame and disgrace him. So Gotch Ear had made for Arliss, bent on getting revenge. If a rifle ball didn't cut him down first, he aimed to sink his knife into the little scamp who'd eaten his ear.

It looked like he'd get to do it, too. Arliss had evidently been too close to Gotch Ear before he saw him and turned to flee. Sam was still too far behind the Indian. Sanderson had stopped shooting, and Papa and the others had never started. That's what rattled me so, I guess, watching the fast-running Gotch Ear drawing closer and closer to Arliss, knowing Sam could never catch him in time, and wondering why nobody would shoot.

Panic held such a strangle hold on me that I couldn't realize that the magazine of Sanderson's rifle might have run dry, forcing him to stop and reload, or that Papa and the others rode in such a direct line with the chase that they couldn't shoot at Gotch Ear without danger of killing Little Arliss.

Almost too late, I came to my senses and swung my own rifle around to line in on Gotch Ear.

It wasn't too long a shot, maybe a hundred and fifty yards, but time for making it was running short. The fleeing Arliss wasn't more than fifteen steps ahead of Gotch Ear when he hit the shallow water in the wash, stumbled and went down.

Now, though, I had my sights laid in on Gotch Ear, dead center, leading him by about a foot.

I squeezed off—and missed him completely.

But when Little Arliss came up out of that muddy

water, he was clutching a rock in each hand—and he didn't miss.

The first rock, bigger than my fist, caught Gotch Ear at about the belly button. It didn't stop him, but it must have sunk deep and been a real jolter, judging from the way he was bent nearly double as he came up.

Then Arliss cut down on him with the second rock. He bounced that one off the side of Gotch Ear's head with a force that sent the black hat flying. This straightened Gotch Ear up some and addled him worse. It sent him reeling and stumbling on past Arliss, holding his head with one hand and his belly with the other.

Arliss bent quick and came up with a couple more rocks, but he never got to use them.

This was on account of Sam.

Sam came in, driving full tilt and roaring like a mad bull He made a long leap, nailed Gotch Ear by the neck, and took him to the ground.

They landed in the water with a big splash. They rolled and wallowed and pitched and knocked muddy water all over Little Arliss. The black hat floated off down the draw. Arliss stood away from the fight, holding a rock drawn back and ready.

But Gotch Ear couldn't break Sam's hold on his throat. He'd lost his knife in the scramble, and he couldn't pull Sam loose with his bare hands. Sam had gotten the grip he wanted when he first tied into Gotch Ear; and from there on, all he had to do was just hold what he had.

He was still lying there in the water with his eyes squeezed shut, hanging grimly to his throat hold on a dead

Apache when Herb Haley finally got around to ramming the butt end of his quirt between the clamped jaws and prizing them apart.

This came later, though, and I never saw it. I didn't even get to see Sam finish off Gotch Ear, because a sudden wild whoop and Lisbeth's shrill scream reached out to me from across the valley, jolting my attention away from Sam's battle.

I saw an Apache springing up out of the tall grass to land astride the scare-running horse Lisbeth rode.

It was Broken Nose—you could bet on that. And you could bet it was a calculated thing, his picking Lisbeth's horse, when he could just as easily have mounted another and got away faster.

Lisbeth was his captive and he meant to keep her.

It didn't seem possible for Broken Nose to have crawled all that far since I'd glanced a ball off his shield and Sanderson's shots had sent him plunging for cover in the grass. But there he went, making off with Lisbeth, riding straight away from me, already so far up the opposite slope that it would stretch a gun barrel to reach him—and me with an empty rifle!

I was shaken, but I didn't panic this time. I reloaded fast, paying no attention to the shouts of the men with Papa or to the crashing reports of Sanderson's rifle.

Sanderson might be missing; but more likely, his lead was falling short. I kept this in mind when at last I drew a bead on the fleeing figures, now made so small by distance that the thin front sight of my rifle all but hid them.

What I wanted to do was kill the horse; but, shooting at that range, there was always a chance that I'd kill Lisbeth. Thought of this brought the ache of fear high in my throat. But I had no choice; I drew a coarse bead and held steady and squeezed off my shot, then watched my rifle ball clip grass stalks fifty yards behind the running horse.

I was too heartsick to reload. What was the use? My rifle wouldn't carry that far. I was closer than anybody, yet even I couldn't reach them.

From down in the wash, I heard Wiley Crup's voice, lifted high in desperate protest.

"But I might hit the girl!"

Searcy's blustery shout lifted even higher. "Tech a hair on that girl, and I'll blow a two-foot gap on yore backbone!"

I looked in that direction. I saw Wiley Crup, down off his horse, with the long barrel of his rifle laid across his saddle. He took aim. I heard the mighty blast of the Big Fifty and saw Wiley stagger back from its recoil in a cloud of gunsmoke.

I started up and looked ahead in time to see Broken Nose knocked ten feet sideways off that running horse.

He nearly took Lisbeth with him, but she managed to hang on a few seconds longer before she flung herself free and disappeared into the grass.

She was up almost instantly and running back down the slope toward us, scared out of her wits, I guess; but I was no longer scared for her. I'd seen the spread-eagled body of Broken Nose go flying through the air; and even at that distance, I could tell that it was limp as a wet dishrag before it ever hit the ground. Broken Nose wasn't going to molest Lisbeth again, or anybody else.

Herb Haley's voice rose high-pitched from down in the draw. "Man alive, what a shot!" he marveled. "A thousand yards, if it's a foot!"

But Wiley's shot wasn't enough to satisfy Uncle Pack. He shouted at the men, furious with impatience.

"All right!" he stormed. "Wiley's made a brag shot. But that ain't killin' them what's down in the grass. Spread out and git after 'em. Now! Before they git away!"

His anger lashed Haley and Crup into action. They mounted and rode out, combing the grass for hidden Indians.

But Papa and Searcy paid Uncle Pack no mind. Papa rode off to meet Lisbeth, while Searcy heaved himself out of the saddle and sprawled in the grass.

I reloaded, but didn't wait around to see if anybody flushed an Indian. All I wanted now was to get my hands on Little Arliss and Savage Sam, to hug them up close and feel the warm life in them, to be on hand and see the look in Lisbeth's eyes when Papa brought her in.

I didn't think that look would make me feel awkward and shy any more. I thought that, now, I could meet it head on and feel proud of what I saw there.

I struck a buffalo trail that skirted the foot of the hill. It didn't lead straight to where I was going; but it led pretty close and made for easier walking. I followed it, listening to, but not really hearing, the Indian hunters calling to each other across the valley.

I shuffled along in a daze. I'd suffered too much body

[201]

pain. I'd clung too long to the ragged edge of despair. And, now that it was all over, I felt too numb with relief to take any real notice of anything any more.

At least, that's the way I seemed to feel, up until I came even with Arliss and old man Searcy and left the trail to go to them.

I hadn't taken more than four or five steps out into the grass when I jerked up short, all my senses screaming danger.

It was the Comanche!

He'd played it smart. He'd crawled within fifty steps of Little Arliss and Bud Searcy, knowing that was the place we were least likely to look for him.

Now, he lay in the grass, staring straight up at me.

I guess it was surprise that held me at first. For a second, I couldn't seem to think what to do. Then it must have been the look in the Comanche's eyes that kept me stood off.

There was no fear in those black eyes, and no hate—just that same intense curiosity with which he'd studied me and Lisbeth and Little Arliss from the first. Best I could tell, he was just lying there with a bloody hole through his left side, waiting to see what I would do.

Wiley Crup's voice came to me from across the valley. "Here's a dead one!"

"Hang the dead ones, you fool!" Uncle Pack shouted back at him. "It's the live ones we're after! 'Fore they git away!"

Well, here lay a live one. Right at my feet. All I had to do to keep him from getting away was to shoot him.

Then why didn't I go ahead and do it?

To this day, I don't have a real satisfying answer.

During the thick of the fight, I'd wanted to kill him, I'd tried hard to kill him, and if I had, I'd have been proud of it afterward.

But now, with the fight all over and done, with Lisbeth and Little Arliss safe once more—well, somehow, things were different.

I could no longer look on him as a threat. All I could see was a badly wounded man, lying helpless, without one weapon left to defend himself. He lay there, looking death square in the face without flinching, without even appearing much concerned about it. In fact, the feeling I got was that what he wanted most of all was to bridge the wide gap that lay between his way of thinking and mine.

I left him there and went on down to where Little Arliss was squatted over Savage Sam, petting and praising him and talking up a storm with old man Searcy.

I went, fighting back the tears and hoping desperately that the Comanche got away.

But I still can't tell you why.

Sam

Fifteen

BEN TODD and Lester White rode in and helped to round up the scattered horses. Night was close on us; but tired and shaken up as we all were, Sanderson ordered fresh horses to be caught and saddled.

"The way I see it," he said, "we'll be smart to make wide-apart tracks away from here."

The only ones to argue with Sanderson about moving on were Uncle Pack and Bud Searcy.

"I can't go on," Searcy whimpered. "I'm a dyin' man, Sanderson. All's left for me now is the cold grave and the Misty Beyond."

He lay with his head in Lisbeth's lap, weeping with self-pity while Lisbeth bathed his face and cried and begged him not to die.

Sanderson looked down on the old man for a moment, studying, then spoke. "Well, to tell the truth, Mr. Searcy," he said, "we can't hardly spare the time to dig you that grave right now. Not with every redskin in hearing of our gunfire done drifting this way, hoping to lift some extra hair. You'd be doing us a big favor to hold off dying for a spell. Till we can get further away from this slaughter ground."

If Searcy suspected he was getting hoorawed, he didn't argue the point.

Uncle Pack, though, was harder to convince. He wept, too, with the rage and bitterness of defeat.

"But I tell you," he stormed, "we've let three of them hostiles git away."

"We got the children," Sanderson said. "That's what we came for."

"What I come for is to kill Injuns," Uncle Pack said fiercely. "Right down to their last louse and nit! We let ary one git away, I've broke a sworn promise to my dead woman and childer!"

Sanderson said bluntly, "Uncle Pack, your woman and children, they're gone. We're all sorry about it. But we don't aim to risk the lives of more children on account of it!"

[205]

He left Uncle Pack to study on that while he went out to where Wiley Crup was saddling a horse.

"Wiley," I heard him say, "there ain't another man in Texas could have made the shot you made, and I want you to know we all appreciate it."

As much as I hated feeling beholden to a man like Wiley Crup, I had to admit that Sanderson was right.

But Wiley didn't warm to Sanderson's praise. He glanced to where old man Searcy lay, grunting and groaning, enjoying his misery.

"That flannel-mouth old fool!" he sneered. "A hair-off miscalculation, and I'd a-kilt that little girl."

"The thing is," Sanderson said, "you didn't make that miscalculation."

We mounted and rode east up the long slope of the valley, driving the loose horses. Papa and Herb Haley rode on either side of Bud Searcy, keeping him propped up in the saddle. Lisbeth rode close by, silent and worried. I held the grunting Sam across my lap and listened to Little Arliss, talking like a house afire. Most of his talk was directed at Lester White.

"You see us?" he demanded of White. "Me 'n' old Sam? We done him under, didn't we? Cleaned that Injun's plows for him. Learnt him a lesson about killin' old Jumper. We'd a-wiped up plenty others, too, if they'd a-come around, messin' with us. Me 'n' old Sam, we ain't to be tampered with!"

All the excitement had Arliss wound up tighter than an eight-day clock. You never heard such brag talk and whopping big lies as he went on to tell. And White, he listened and kept a sober face and nodded his head every now and then, letting on that he believed every word of it.

We rode till long after moonrise, till Little Arliss ran out of wild talk, till I dozed in the saddle and old man Searcy had long since given up complaining.

Sometime past midnight, we came to a little creek where there was wood and water and shallow caves in the rock banks to hide the light of a campfire from any prowling Indians.

Here, we unsaddled and pitched camp. Sanderson put guards out. The rest of us cooked and ate and slept till around noontime the next day, then changed guards and ate and slept some more.

It seemed like I couldn't get enough of either one, sleep or food. Half the time, while I ate, I was more asleep than awake, so that my recollections of what happened there are pretty fuzzy.

I do remember that somebody shot a yearling buffalo and how good the hump ribs tasted after Ben Todd gave them a slow roasting over a mesquite-wood fire. I remember, too, what a bad case of the walking fidgets Papa had.

"She'll be near about crazy with worry," I heard him tell Sanderson, and knew that he was talking about Mama, and knew that he was right.

But Sanderson only shook his head. "I know, Jim," he said. "But we can't afford to travel by day. Injuns can spot us too easy. And we nearly got to feed and rest up these little old younguns and old man Searcy. They're all worn to a frazzle."

So we kept eating and sleeping till dark came on, then saddled and moved out.

We traveled with Sanderson riding nearly a mile in the lead and Uncle Pack about that far behind and with flankers out on either side. We rode all that night, ate and slept all the next day, then pulled out again about dark.

Like before, we were traveling too far and too fast. We never got enough rest or enough to eat, and hanging over us every minute was the threat of running into an Indian war party too big for us to handle. Twice, Sanderson spotted the glow of campfires far out on the dark prairie and rode back to lead us around them.

In spite of all this, I could still feel myself mending. Most of the pain was gone from my wounds, and my sunburned skin began healing and peeling till I looked as shaggy as a rusty tree lizard at shedding time. Every day, it seemed like I felt stronger.

What gave us the worst trouble was old man Searcy. Night and day, in and out of the saddle, he kept dying and dying. We sure got worn out with his eternal complaining.

The thing that riled me so was the way, at every camp, he kept calling on Lisbeth to fetch him water and food, to pull his boots off, to wash his feet, to grease his sunburn—keeping her in a trot every minute of our resting time, like maybe she hadn't suffered through everything he had, and plenty more. I finally got so fed up that I jumped Lisbeth out about it.

It was at a water hole somewhere in the Big Spring

country. I was cutting mesquite thorns for Lisbeth to use to pin together her torn dress. Old man Searcy started calling in that quavery, pore-mouth voice.

"Lisbeth, honey. Would you kindly fetch yore pore old grandpa a drink of water?"

Lisbeth started to go to him. It made me mad. I grabbed her arm and held her.

"Let him fetch his own water, for a change!" I said.

Lisbeth looked at me in surprise. "But, Travis," she said, "he's too old and worn out. He's nearly dead!"

"Nearly dead, my hind foot," I said. "That's just put-on, and always has been."

Lisbeth looked away, staring out across the grass. Finally, she said, "Even if you're right, it still wouldn't make any difference."

"How come?" I demanded. "You mean you like being run ragged by that old windbag?"

That cut deeper than I'd meant it to. It brought the start of tears to her eyes.

"Travis, you know I'm all Grandpa's got," she said. "He's been good to me. And menfolks—well, it seems like they're never real happy without they got some woman at their beck and call."

Back of me, I heard a short laugh. I wheeled around. It was Burn Sanderson and Ben Todd. I hadn't heard them come up, but there they stood, both wearing wide, knowing grins.

Sanderson pulled a sober look and spoke to Ben like me and Lisbeth weren't there.

"You know, Ben," he said, "that Travis Coates is a smart

[209]

boy. He's done found him a girl with more understanding of a man's needs than most women ever get around to learning."

I felt a blush spread both ways from my neck. I liked Sanderson; but right now, I could have clubbed him over the head.

In a way, Sam was as much trouble as old man Searcy. After his long chase, he was so sore-footed and stiff in the joints he couldn't hardly stand without whimpering. He suffered so much that every scrap of food and every drop of water had to be packed to him; and when it came time to leave, there was no question about his needing to ride.

The trouble was, he seemed to get worse instead of better. I got real worried about him.

But Papa didn't. "That old dog's just pulling the wool over your eyes," he told me one night. "He's sore-footed, all right, but he's not all that beat-up."

"Why would he want to do that?" I demanded.

"On account of he's got a taste of high living and don't aim to give it up," Papa said. "You keep pampering him, and you'll have him so rotten spoilt, he won't be worth knocking in the head."

That got my fur up. "What of it?" I demanded. "He's earned the right to some spoiling. Hadn't been for him, we'd never on earth have saved Lisbeth and Little Arliss, and you know it!"

But when I started to lift Sam into the saddle, Papa put his foot down.

"Leave him lay," he ordered. "He just as well learn now he's not going to ride horseback for the rest of his life!"

So, with me and Little Arliss both hurt and mad about it, we rode off and left Sam lying where he was.

The minute he saw that we weren't going to pack him, Sam rolled over and lay flat of his back, holding four limp feet in the air to show how crippled he was. And the farther off we rode, the louder and more pitiful his howling got.

Finally, Arliss couldn't stand it any longer. He burst into tears and wheeled his horse around.

"I ain't a-going off and leaving old Sam!" he stormed.

And back toward Sam he went at a gallop, paying no mind to Papa's threat of taking a quirt to him.

Well, the danger of Indians was too great. We couldn't let Arliss leave the bunch. All we could do was go back for him.

We found him down off his horse, hugging the whimpering Sam and telling him not to worry, that he wasn't going off and leave him, ever.

Papa was about ready to make good his threat with a quirt when Lester White stepped down and lifted Sam in his arms.

"Mr. Coates," he said, "I'd consider it an honor to share my saddle with this Genuine Amalgamated Pot-Hound for as long as he cares to ride."

He grinned at Papa, showing that he'd caught on to Papa's and Sanderson's spoofing.

So Papa gave up there, and Sam rode till the morning when we finally reached home.

It was just before daybreak when we arrived, but Mama already had a candle lit; and I don't guess I'll ever take more comfort from anything than I did from the sight of our little old two-room cabin, squatted there on the slope of the hill, with warm yellow candlelight streaming through the porthole windows.

We'd been gone less than ten days, but it seemed like a year, and there'd been plenty of times when I'd never expected to see that cabin again.

Papa hollered, "Hello, the house!" and the door opened a crack and a gun barrel was poked through.

Tom McDougal called out, "Who is it?"

But Mama had done recognized Papa's voice. She flung the door wide open and came flying out, calling, "Jim! Jim!" and all but dragged Papa out of the saddle before he could dismount.

McDougal and his woman, Sarah, they came out, too, and stood in the candlelight, smiling and looking pleased, while Mama laughed and cried at the same time and went from one to the other, hugging and kissing everybody, even to Wiley Crup, who was so startled that he dropped his Big Fifty and got sand in the barrel.

It was about then that from out near the corncrib, we heard a loud cackling, then the frantic squawkings of a caught hen.

"It's that confounded bobcat again!" Tom McDougal

complained. He started on a run toward the chicken roost, calling for somebody to bring him a light.

Before he had time to get halfway there, we heard the angry squawl of the cat, then the snarling roar of Savage Sam.

Sam and the cat mixed it hot and heavy for a minute, and we'd all started running toward the fight when Sam let out a shrill yelp that told us the cat had got in a mighty painful lick.

After that, everything but the cackling chickens was quiet for about half a minute while we ran on toward the roost. Then, a hundred yards off, we heard Sam open, his trail voice ringing out loud and urgent.

The way he was driving on the trail of the bobcat, you'd have thought he had never heard tell of a sore foot.

And sure enough, right close behind him, we heard Little Arliss yell.

"That's a-taking him yonder, Sam! Go git him, boy!"

Mama screamed at Arliss to come back and Papa threatened him with a whipping, but I knew better than to waste my breath. I wheeled and lit out for the saddled horses still standing at the front-yard gate. I mounted the big rawboned bay I'd ridden so far and quirted him into a run.

When finally I caught up with Arliss, I handled him just like the dead Gotch Ear would have done. I reached down and grabbed me a fistful of his tousled hair. I yanked him up across my saddle and held him there, kicking and yelling and threatening me with murder.

"You turn me a-loose, Travis Coates," he screamed. "You don't turn me a-loose, I'll bust you with a rock!"

He didn't have a rock, so I paid no mind to his threats. I headed back for the cabin, holding a tight grip on the back of his neck.

I aimed to make sure I got there without losing an ear.

About the Author

Fred Gipson was born in 1908 in Mason, Texas, where he now lives. He grew up on a dry-land farm and has worked at everything from cotton-picking to driving a caterpillar tractor. After attending the University of Texas, he worked as a reporter for various Texas newspapers and for a few months was a feature writer for the Denver *Post* Sunday magazine section. He took up free-lance writing in 1940, the same year he was married, and has published a great number of articles and short stories, which have appeared in *Collier's*, *Holiday*, *Reader's Digest*, and *Southwest Review*, to name a few.

Mr. Gipson's first book, FABULOUS EMPIRE, was published in 1946 by Houghton Mifflin. In 1949 he came to Harper's with his novel HOUND DOG MAN, which was a Book-of-the-Month Club selection. Since then Harper's has published most of Mr. Gipson's work, which has included books for both adults and for children. Among these are THE HOME PLACE, THE TRAIL DRIVING ROOSTER, and OLD YELLER. OLD YELLER won the 1959 William Allen White Award, First Sequoyah Book Award (Oklahoma) 1959, Pacific Northwest Library Association Award, 1959, and was a bestseller.

Mr. Gipson now lives with his wife and two sons on a part of the old Gipson homestead, where he devotes his time to writing and to managing a small stock farm. He raises cattle and hogs, and in season hunts deer, wild turkey and quail. He prefers fly fishing to all other outdoor sports, and is interested in the study of soil and plant growth. He has been conducting a number of experiments in the reseeding of rangeland to native and imported grasses.